TAKEN FOR HIS OWN

The Promise Me Series, Book 4

by

Tara Fox Hall

Published by
Melange Books, LLC
White Bear Lake, MN 55110
www.melange-books.com

Taken For His Own ~ Copyright © 2013 by Tara Fox Hall

ISBN: 978-1-61235-622-8 Print

Cover Art by Caroline Andrus

Taken For His Own
Tara Fox Hall

After learning Theo is alive, Sar immediately embarks on a mission to find him. Reunited, the lovers return to New York, Danial, Terian and Theo uneasily combining forces to protect Sar from Al's assassins who still seek her. But when Sar is taken prisoner in an all-out attack, only one man can save her—her old adversary, Devlin.

Dedication

To my new editor Jane, for all her help and suggestions.
To Caroline, for her excellent cover work.
To my Promise Me fans, for all your support of my work.
To Jessica and Cavity,
for lap-warming encouragement since the first typed word.
And lastly, to Tor, for typo-hunting, the many long emails, and being a true
friend.

About the Author

Tara Fox Hall's writing credits include nonfiction, horror, suspense, action-adventure, erotica, and contemporary and historical paranormal romance. She is the author of the paranormal action-adventure *Lash* series and the vampire romantic suspense *Promise Me* series. Tara divides her free time unequally between writing novels and short stories, chainsawing firewood, caring for stray animals, sewing cat and dog beds for donation to animal shelters, and target practice.

Chapter One

"What are you talking about?" I screamed at Terian. My heart was beating a mile a minute, the breath tearing out of me as I tried to get enough oxygen to my brain to process his words.

"Theo is alive," Terian said again.

I sobbed from sudden relief, my knees giving way. Terian grabbed me before I fell, then guided me over to a shady spot to sit down. A few minutes later when I got control of myself, I wiped my face with my sleeves and faced him. "Tell me everything you know."

"Theo came back here in February—"

"February! Why didn't you tell me?" I yelled at the top of my lungs.

Terian got to his feet, putting distance between us. "I'll tell you everything I know, but not if you keep screaming at me. Calm down."

I tried to breathe. I tried to be calm. I could do neither. Theo was alive. I ached for him already. The last two years seemed like a dream, and I wanted suddenly to go home to my house, where I crazily hoped he would be waiting for me.

"Where is he?" I demanded.

"Out west," Terian said. "In a little town in Wyoming called Casper."

I processed that, making plans at once. I could fly there in a day, most likely. Or I could drive there and take the dogs; I'd never travelled outside the state by myself. Ever. Maybe Elle would want to go. In any case, I was going, and I was going tomorrow. I wanted to leave tonight, but the day was already half gone, and I would need to pack and get maps and money … Hurriedly, I made a mental list.

"Walk back to the house with me," I said calmly, "And tell me all you know."

We began to move, I with a purposeful fast stride. Terian reluctantly matched my speed.

"I was out walking in the woods one night, doing guard duty. I came upon the tracks of a cougar and thought they had to be Elle's. But after studying the size and depth of them, I concluded that they were from an adult, not a child, and so deep that likely a male had made them. I followed them and found Theo. He was huddled in one of the sheds, trying to get out of the cold."

Theo had been so close to me and I'd not even known it. "Go on."

"I took him to my room and let him sleep in my bed. During the night he changed back to human." Terian took a deep breath and looked into my eyes. "He was hurt badly. He could get around okay, but he was covered with scars. He said it had been a lot worse, but most of the damage had healed."

I took a long shuddering breath, walked faster and motioned for Terian to continue.

"He asked me not to tell anyone he was here, especially you, Sar."

"Why?" I got out, too hurt to elaborate.

"He had seen that you lived here with Danial and that Elle thought of Danial as her father. He knew you were pregnant."

I closed my eyes then, trying to breathe. "Did he say where he had been?"

"He said he'd been captured and held by several different people. That he'd escaped each time, but the damage that initial sadist had done to him had crippled him, so he was unable to journey quickly. He said he'd been without a passport in more than a few countries. He had nothing to prove he was a US citizen and no money, no identification of any kind."

"There are such things as collect calls," I said deliberately.

"I only know what he told me."

"Why didn't he call us? Write us?" I said angrily. "He could have broken into an office and sent us an email! That's all it would have taken!"

"I don't know," Terian replied evenly. "The only other thing he said was to tell no one that I'd seen him, to let everyone think he was dead."

"What did you tell him about Danial and me?"

"He didn't ask," Terian said bluntly. "Theo wasn't the man he used to be. He was broken and bitter. He didn't want to hear what I had to say about you. He said he had seen all he needed to see with his own eyes."

My eyes flooded with guilty tears. I swiped at them angrily, then took a deep breath. "You're sure he said Casper?"

"Yes," Terian said confidently.

I turned to face him. "You are only telling me about Theo now to get me to leave Danial, you bastard. Would you have ever told me, if this hadn't have happened?"

"No," Terian answered. "I would have left things as they were, like he asked me to."

"Damn you, Terian," I yelled. "Damn you and damn your stupid moral code!"

Terian's eyes flashed red. "Sar, you spend all this time pining for Theo, but when you're with Danial you're happy to be with him. How long did you wait after Theo disappeared before going back to Danial? Were those three months you spent together really love or some kind of infatuation?" He stepped closer. "Or just good sex?"

I slapped Terian hard across his face. "I want you to know that I considered you my friend," I said hatefully. "I did. But that's over now, Terian. You have caused me more heartache with your potions and your keeping things from me than Danial has ever done. I'm sorry that you're part of my child." I paused for a moment, glaring at him. "I would rather it had been anyone else, even Devlin."

I walked away and left him there, too stunned to speak.

When I got back to the house, I used Danial's computer to check plane flights. There were no flights left to Casper that night or the next day within driving distance. Instead of that relaxing me, I just took it as a sign that traveling by car was the way to go.

As much as a flight would have cost, driving to Wyoming would be just as expensive, if not more, factoring in gas, food and hotels. Lucky for me, Danial had insisted on paying me for my help with his business for the past year and a half. I hadn't cared at the time, had just deposited the money in a savings account. That would give me the needed money to finance this trip with no trouble.

Strangely, doubts about what I was planning didn't faze me. I realized that most everyone would think I was crazy to be doing this. Sure, my life here with Danial was good, even with Dr. Camlyn's dire prognosis of me being on the threshold of becoming vampire. Yet all that was in the noise, really. I had only to think of seeing Theo again, of being with him and there was no hesitation, no thoughts of any other option but going to him.

I began printing out maps of Casper itself and the shortest route to get there. The drive would be a long one, four days of solid driving. That was a hell of a long drive. Yet flying somehow seemed too short. Too sudden. I needed time to think about what I was going to do. I couldn't just show up in town asking for him. He might have moved on like I had.

The thought floored me, but it was a good possibility. Theo thought I'd oathed to Danial, and he had been in Casper for four months now. He liked sex, loved it actually. It was unlikely I'd find him alone.

I sighed, reasoning that Elle shouldn't come on this trip, even if she wanted to. However, I had to go even if I found him with a live-in lover. I had to know what had happened to him.

I finished printing out the maps. Shit, it was already late afternoon.

I went downstairs and put the maps in Theo's truck. It hadn't been used in close to a year, but the engine started easily for me, and the inspection was still good. That was a relief. The problem was I had only two things left to do before leaving—pack my clothes and tell Danial I was leaving to find Theo.

I didn't want to wake him to tell him what I was planning. But there was no more putting off the inevitable. I went back into the great room, determined to face Danial.

Terian burst in the front door. "Sar!" he said raggedly. "You were right. I'm sorry—"

"Fuck you and your being sorry!" I screamed at him. "You knew what he meant to me. You of all people knew! How could you let it go so long? How could you not have come and gotten me when you knew he was here? I could have seen him, touched him, held him in my arms! I'd have been with him these last four months!"

"You were pregnant with Theoron, remember? You wouldn't have been going anywhere."

I sagged, defeated. Terian was right. I'd given Danial my word. My pregnancy with our half-vampire, half-human child had been anything but easy. "Maybe I would have had to wait to see him," I said quietly. "But Theo wouldn't have left if I'd told him how things really were." I turned from him.

Terian grabbed me. "Sar, please forgive me—"

Danial threw open his door, standing there in his robe. "What in the hell is going on out here?"

"Theo is alive!" I yelled, the echo resounding throughout the great room. "He is alive and somewhere out west, and Terian has known for months!"

Danial's face went white. He hissed at Terian, "Is this true?"

"It's true. He asked me not to tell anyone—"

"What kind of idiot actually does that?" Danial roared. "You are to tell me everything that goes on here, no matter who tells you otherwise. Is that understood?"

"Yes," Terian said, cowed.

"What happened?" he asked. "All of it!"

Terian relayed the message to Danial of Theo being badly wounded, that he had seen we were together and had left to go west alone.

Danial sighed deeply, then faced me. "You're leaving tonight to go to him, aren't you?"

"Yes," I said softly. "I'm sorry. I told you I'd stay and now—"

"Go," he said just as softly. "I love you, Sar. I don't want you to be what I am. And we both know that it would likely come to that, if you stayed with me now."

I gaped at him, not knowing what to say.

"Stephen said you were close to turning," Danial said tiredly. "I'm afraid

4

of losing control, like I did before—"

Terian gasped.

"—I haven't felt any urges," Danial said quickly. "But I trust Theo to watch over you—"

"You're telling me to go?" I said incredulously.

"I'm torn between protecting you, Elle and Theoron. I can't send Terian with you, not without risking them and myself. Theo will take care of you. Wyoming is far enough away you'll be safe—"

"Stop," I said softly, stepping closer and embracing him.

He hugged me tightly. "What I just said is the only reason I'm not making you stay here and going in your place. But where you'll go unnoticed, I'd almost certainly be attacked."

I drew breath sharply. "You said nothing about trouble."

"There is always trouble when you're a Lord," Danial said ruefully. "But that's not important. I want you to remember that if it doesn't work out with him, that you always are wanted here. If you return, I'll welcome you with open arms, be it in a few weeks or a few years." He kissed my cheek gently. "I understand that you have to do this. Don't worry about Theoron or Elle. I'll take good care of them."

"I love you," I said tearfully, kissing him. "You know that, right? That I wasn't with you all this time because you were good to me, or because you are amazing in bed, or because you are so desirable. I love that you were all those things, but they are part of you, not the reason."

"I know that, my darling," he said, embracing me tightly.

"Do you want the ring back?" I asked awkwardly.

We both looked down at it, sparkling on my finger.

"No. Wear it for me, Sar. To remember I love you and that I always will."

The front door slammed. "What is going on?" Elle said, taking in Terian, Danial and me.

Danial came and crouched before her. "Elle, your father, Theo, is alive."

She looked at him calmly with no intake of breath or gasp of surprise. "I know he is."

I gaped at her. Terian also was speechless.

"How do you know this when I have just discovered it?" Danial demanded.

"I smelled him … the night he came here. I saw Terian help him inside the were compound." Elle stared at me defiantly.

"Why didn't you tell me?" Danial asked her.

"You would have told Mom," she said finally. "Mom would have left us to be with him."

I wanted to scream at her. I wanted to call her a little bitch for daring to keep this kind of information from us. I longed to spank her. I did none of those things because she was right. I would have left, just as I was leaving now.

"Elle, Sar is leaving now to go to Theo. That is okay. If he is alive, officially she is still engaged to him."

I didn't think that applied to persons gone for two years, but maybe it did.

"You understand. Theo gave her a ring, and she promised to marry him. At the least, she has to give it back to him and tell him that she can no longer do that—"

"She should stay with you!" Elle cried out. "You're my dad! Not him!"

"Elle—" Danial tried to touch her, but she was having none of it.

"We're her family! You're her man, not him! He left us alone for two years. She cried every night!"

I'd hoped she'd forgotten, but by her words, her memory was all too clear.

"She only stopped crying when you came. That night we all slept in bed together."

The night I'd given in to Danial. The night we had had sex and he'd been there to help me with Elle. The night she'd first assumed human form. Would she have transformed that night if he hadn't been there? Would I have been able to handle her on my own if she had? Most likely not.

My resolve began to waver. I swiftly strengthened it. This was Theo. I had to go.

"Elle, I am leaving tonight," I said determinedly. "You can come if you want to. Even if Theo doesn't want to see me, he'll want to see you." I extended my hand to her.

"I never want to see him!" she snarled with disdain. "I wish he were dead!"

Her angry words enraged me in a heartbeat. I held myself still with effort. How she felt was not her fault. Some of it was mine for pushing her away in my grief. Some of it was Danial's for loving her so much and some was Theo's, for disappearing from her life in the months she had needed him most. Really, they just made this easier.

"That's okay," I said slowly. "You'll be better off here with Danial."

I turned from her.

"Mom! Mom!"

I went into Danial's room to pack my things. I put my toiletries in a bag, grabbed a few changes of clothes and extra sneakers. When I reemerged, the great room was empty.

Quickly I got the dogs in the truck and started the engine.

There was a sudden knock at my window. I started to see Terian there.

I opened the window.

"You were right about Danial," he said. "Do you want me to send someone with you?"

"No," I said, looking away. "I need to do this alone, as much as I'd appreciate help driving."

"I'm sorry for not telling you. Forgive me?"

I let out a sigh. "If you forgive me saying what I said to you earlier. I didn't mean it."

"I knew you didn't mean it, Sar. But it hurt all the same."

"I wanted it to hurt you," I said flatly. "I was in pain, and I wanted you to be in pain, too. I'm sorry for that. I'm happy you're part of Theoron, Terian. Without you, he wouldn't be here."

"Friends?" he said.

"Friends," I said, hugging him through the truck window.

"Do you have your gun?"

I knew which gun he meant—the one with explosive bullets. "It's at my house. I'll take it with me. Be sure of that."

"I'll be too far away to help you. Be careful," he said, giving me a worried look.

"I will. Keep them safe, Terian."

"Will do," he said, giving me a salute.

I saluted him back and drove off.

I arrived at my house about ten o'clock. After I turned on the water and checked everything over, I went to bed, exhausted, deciding to pack in the morning. The dogs settled down quickly, to my relief. But once I lay down, I couldn't relax.

I missed Danial. I'd slept beside him the last year and a half. I needed him to feel safe enough to sleep. He probably was having trouble sleeping, too …

I cried a little, then told myself to be strong. I'd likely have been sleeping here alone before much longer anyway if Danial's words had been truthful. I didn't want to be a vampire, and I knew how effortless it was to lose myself in him. It would have been easy to get caught up in the moment while making love and let him bite me. A few times of that and I'd have been vampire. It was better this way.

I told myself that until I believed it and then fell asleep.

* * * *

The next morning I packed a few last items and got on the road. There had been little enough to pack—just my exploding bullets gun, the diamond ring, my blue velvet robe and the vial of Terian's. I stopped at a local pet store for two dishes and a bag of dog food, having forgotten that important detail in my rush to leave Danial's.

I felt guilty about packing the personal items. Despite my rationalizing about how I needed to know where Theo had been, I couldn't hide anymore that

I was hoping for a big momentous reunion with him. Maybe that was unrealistic. But screw it, even if this trip ended badly, I was going to get closure one way or another.

We made it past Pittsburgh the first day and a little past Chicago the next. I tried to stay on the interstate as much as possible, yet still avoid the major cities. Each night I stopped a little before dark at public land to let the dogs stretch their legs before finding a motel that accepted pets. In snatches, I tried to formulate a plan.

As much as I'd dreamed of finding Theo on the front doorstep, I understood why he wouldn't want to just show up there. I didn't want to just show up on his doorstep, either, especially if he'd shacked up with someone. It was growing more and more likely that my going back to Danial had been the impetus Theo had needed to search for a female werecougar. Cia had told me once that the American West was where most werecougars lived. I needed to prepare myself that he might have found a female and mated to her.

I ran into trouble the third night when I couldn't find a hotel that accepted dogs. When even a bribe at a sleazy inn was refused, I gave up, found a rest stop and slept in the truck with them.

We left at dawn the next morning. I was exhausted, stinky, and hungry, but wanted to put a few more miles down before stopping for breakfast. Instead, we got caught in backed up traffic due to an accident. I ended up pulling over and feeding the dogs inside the truck—a huge messy endeavor—then taking them out one by one to do their business. By the time Ghost was done, the accident had been cleared to the point traffic was moving again. I put off grabbing some food, worried about getting caught in traffic again. Besides, we were only a few hundred miles from Casper now.

Through tiredness or some mental defect, I underestimated the distance badly. After stopping for breakfast and lunch, the dogs and I arrived in Casper about dinnertime.

To my relief, the town was pretty small, as Terian had said. There was only one motel, a little place on the outskirts of town. The manager didn't want to allow dogs, but for $100 extra a night, he said he'd make an exception, so long as I paid for any damage and gave him the rental money up front.

After giving him a week in advance—most of my money—I took a long hot shower, put the dogs to bed and passed out.

The next day, I got some groceries from a local market and breakfasted with the dogs on a nearby bench. The sun was shining, though the air was cold. Afterward, we walked down Main Street, then around the retail part of town. There were a lot of men and women in jeans, cowboy boots and hats, but no sign of any werecougars, much less Theo. Despite my not giving up until dusk, I ended the day with nothing more to go on than I had before.

The next morning, I showered again, fed the dogs and myself, and then settled down to brainstorm. It was raining anyway, thought it was not supposed to last, according to the Weather Channel.

I had to think like Theo to find him. First off: what had he come here to do?

Find a mate. Recover from his wounds. Get away from Danial and me.

Where would he go to find those things?

Wherever cougars might still exist in the wild, either the low hills or the mountains themselves.

If he were still injured, he wouldn't be in steep rocky places, but likely the surrounding hills. He would need an isolated spot, possibly adjacent to state land, so he could change form and hunt. Since no one was screaming about a killer cougar, Theo had to be keeping a low profile.

Visiting the lobby, I grabbed copies of every free brochure on tourist attractions and then bought some maps showing the closest public lands and state parks. I needed to visit all the parks in the area and walk as many trails as I could.

After a wet walk and an unsatisfying cheap dinner, I checked out the brochures and maps. Several trails were listed, especially those in the vicinity of Casper Mountain. They each stretched over ten miles. Worse, there was a lot of public wild land with no trails listed. My heart sank, realizing I might spend the whole week here and still miss Theo.

Sudden anger strengthened my resolve. If I had to, I would knock on every door in the town looking for him. He couldn't have lived here for months and no one notice him. He was too funny, too cute. Someone in this town knew him. How to find that person was the problem…

Sudden brilliance flared. Theo would need to have a ready supply of meat, especially if he was injured. The local butcher was another place to start.

I settled back in bed, able to relax now that I'd made some headway. Tomorrow at dawn, I'd begin.

Days passed. I walked the parks with the dogs. The land was different here, dry to my Northeastern standards. The earth crumbled under my feet, and there were few bugs. There were a lot of mountains, rock and scrub grass, but the huge towering trees I'd had around me my whole life were absent. The streams that were so prevalent back home were so scarce as to be practically nonexistent here. I felt strangely exposed and vulnerable, making sure to carry a large bottle of water each time I set out on foot. All my searching yielded no signs of Theo.

I gritted my teeth and kept looking. Despite visiting all the meat procurement places in town, no one remembered a man fitting his description. Strike two.

That night, I finally checked my cell voicemail and found a dozen messages from Danial, all wanting to know if I was okay. I called him back that night.

"I'm fine. In case you're wondering, I've found nothing."

"Maybe he isn't there?" he said hesitantly.

"He's here. I'd bet my life on it, Danial. He was okay leaving Elle, as long as he left Terian a way to get in touch with him if he needed it."

"If he's there, you'll find him," Danial said with a note of pride.

"How is Elle?"

"She's okay," he said with a sigh. "But she thinks you are mad at her, and she's trying hard to stay mad at you."

"Tell her I'm not mad, Danial. Tell her I love her."

"I will," he said. "The cats say hello, too. Cavity is here on my lap—"

He was going to tell me he missed me. "Pet him for me," I said hurriedly. "I'll call you if I find him. Bye."

* * * *

The next day, Ghost, Darkness and I began to walk the state lands. Day after day, we walked, with no success. Luckily, being mid-May, the parks and state lands weren't crowded with campers and children yet.

Finally, I went into town to withdraw more money from my savings. I'd need it for another week at the hotel if I decided to stay. After I made that decision, I visited the post office to mail a letter to my mother. As I slid the letter into the outgoing mail slot, I suddenly smelled Theo's scent.

I walked quickly to the back of the post office boxes and crouched against the wall, hiding behind a partition requesting used stamps for a children's stamp collecting program.

"Any mail?"

That was Theo's voice. I stopped breathing.

"Nothing today, Theo," the postal worker said in a friendly manner.

"At least there are no bills, right?" Theo said and laughed.

Damn it all to hell, why hadn't I checked here first? For the simple reason that Theo had never gotten any mail at my house in months. What had he gotten a post office box for?

"Was someone just in here?" Theo said urgently. I could hear the sudden tension in his voice.

He'd smelled me. I broke out in sweat.

"Nobody I saw," the post office man replied.

Theo paused a moment, then left, slamming the door. I waited where I was for five minutes, knowing he might be sitting in his truck waiting for me to show myself. Despite the fact I'd come all this way to find him, I was petrified suddenly of seeing him.

I breathed deeply, in and out, trying to relax. My heart refused to calm. All I kept imagining was Theo listening to my side of the story about Danial and having him say he didn't want me, because he'd found someone else like he was.

"Damn it, grow some backbone," I said aloud.

I got to my feet and walked to the counter. "Who was that man?" I tried to make my voice sound coy and bubbly, like a woman on the make.

"His name is Theo," the man said, giving me an appreciative look. "Where he lives I don't know. He rents out a PO box."

"I don't suppose that has an address?" I said, like it was an afterthought.

"I couldn't give you that kind of information," the man said, taken aback.

"Well, it was worth trying for," I said, giving him a wink.

I had my hand on the door when he said, "Ma'am, wait."

I turned and saw he was going for the information. Yes! Finally, something was going right! I put an expectant look on my face.

"Something's not right here," the man said in confusion.

"What is it?"

"Theo gave the address of the Redrocks Park as his home address—"

The one place nearby I hadn't been! Now I knew where to find him!

"Thank you for your help," I called over my shoulder, running out the door.

Chapter Two

I walked up the rocky hill, Ghost and Darkness running before me. The midday sun was hot, hot enough that I was sweating a little. At the crest of this hill, I opened up my sandwich and ate it, sharing bites with the two dogs. If nothing else, I relished spending time alone with them, something I hadn't done since Theo had moved in years ago.

"You enjoyed yourselves, too," I said fondly to them, petting one with each hand. "Give me a minute, and then we'll go look for some prairie mice."

I sat on a nearby piece of granite rock and looked at the wide blue sky above me, considering my options. I'd confirmed Theo was here in town, but I couldn't find where he was staying, despite two days of walking near the Redrocks. The only option left was to lie in wait at the post office until he came in for his mail.

Did I really want to do that? I'd initially come for closure, or so I'd said. Really, down deep, I'd come to see if there was anything left of us to revive. My emotions had led me here, not my rationale. Now that rationale was back from hiatus and taking a front seat, telling me to cut my losses and go home before I really embarrassed myself.

Tired now, I got up and dusted off my pants. After sharing water with the dogs, we walked to the bluff, then to a rock formation sitting at its pinnacle. As I climbed it, I saw Theo far below me, stalking up the trail in cougar form.

I didn't need to see his face to know it was him. I recognized his walk, even as a cougar. He hopped up on a rock ledge, lay down, then roared. Something in the sound made me tremble.

I got down from the rock and headed down the trail. To hell with my good intentions. Theo was here. I loved him and wanted to be with him. I couldn't see him there, within my reach, and turn away.

The dogs followed me. They'd heard the roar, but Elle roared now and then, and they weren't concerned about possible danger.

An answering roar sounded, echoing. I stopped, catching sight of another cougar coming up the trail. Theo's ears flattened back, and he charged it, running at full speed. The other cougar rose up, and they hit together, rolling over and over. I watched, transfixed, giving the dogs a command to be silent. We three watched, unmoving.

When the dust cleared, the cougars had stopped rolling, and one was on top of the other, moving rapidly. It was Theo; he was on top…

I shut my eyes, eased out of the line of sight and withdrew back up the trail toward the truck, trying not to make noise. But I couldn't shut out the familiar roaring noises, the same ones Theo and Tawny had made having sex together years ago. The dogs padded beside me, though they looked back often to see what was happening.

What I'd feared had happened. He'd found a real mate, one of his own kind. One who wouldn't be bruised in the morning after a night of his lovemaking. One who hadn't given herself to his one-time best friend and had a child with him.

Disillusioned and sad, I drove back to my hotel and arranged for early checkout in the morning. Now that I'd found out what I'd come here to find, it was time to go home. Theo was well enough to walk and copulate, so he had to be happy. He'd chosen a new life, one there was no point in me interrupting now.

I showered and got ready for bed, thoroughly depressed. There was no point in calling Danial to tell him the news. I could call him tomorrow on the drive home. Maybe by then, I'd have sufficient control over myself to talk about what I'd seen without breaking down in mid-sentence.

I cried a few tears, turned out the light and let my mind drift. Just as I was falling asleep, I remembered the potion. Terian had said the potion would recreate the dream with Theo, but that when it ended, the dream would fade from memory.

I needed to put my feelings for Theo to rest and let him get on with his life. It was time to be done with dreams and get back to reality.

I turned the light back on and got up, rummaging around in my duffel bag. I found it and spent a few minutes removing the vial from the bubble wrap I'd taped around it for safekeeping. I uncorked the top and drank. The taste was bitter. This was it, the end of him and me. I packed the empty potion vial for Terian for reuse, then lay down. I drifted in a sleep-sort of fog and finally began to dream.

It was my home, my farm. Again, I stood there, calling out to Theo to wait, not to leave.

Again, he stood motionless at the door for a second and then he turned to me, riding me to the floor. Kissing me roughly, as we tore off our clothes as fast as we could.

13

Every memory came back in full force, sweeping me away in a storm of emotion. It washed away the years with Danial, even everything I felt for Elle and Theoron. There was only Theo and me. We were one.

Theo made love to me again and again. I relished his body next to mine, his muscles holding me, moving me, pleasuring me. Soreness set in as night fell, but I renewed my efforts, knowing that the end was near. As Theo finished and reached for me, I pushed him away.

"Sar?" he said questioningly, his eyes worried, his hand outstretched.

In a few seconds, Danial's voice would sound. This was it—the end.

In desperation, I shouted, "Theo, I love you, I love you more than anything or anyone. I'll love you the rest of my life!"

As my words tore out of me, Theo's body flickered. Suddenly thin scars appeared on his shoulders from a whip, the edges raised and red, then similar scars on his chest. A mass of scar tissue bloomed whitely on his hip.

I lunged for his outstretched hand as he faded before me.

I fell out of the motel room bed, landing on the floor. The room reeked with the odor of lovemaking, the odor of sex.

"God damn it, no!" I screamed at the top of my lungs.

I'd fucked up badly. I'd forgotten Terian's words to me the night he'd given me the potion, telling me about the dream it would create for me one last time.

"And he's not here to renew it with you..."

Terian had said it, thinking as I did that Theo was dead. But Theo wasn't dead, he was alive. I'd reached out and touched him again with another dream. Moreover, this time, he'd know immediately that what had happened was no regular dream. He'd come looking for me, remembering the scent he'd caught wind of a week ago.

God, I had to get gone as fast as I could!

I threw on some clothes and frantically gathered up my things. There was no time for a shower or food. We had to get moving!

I grabbed up my duffel and ran for the door, my keys in my hand. A footstep sounded outside my door, and then the door was kicked open, flying back hard to slam the inner wall.

Theo stood there breathing hard, his eyes dark as a storm. He reeked of sex the way I did.

I hoped for his sake he'd woken up alone.

"Where do you think you're going?" he said, his voice deep and rough. He slammed the door behind him and locked it.

"Theo, I—"

"You are going nowhere, Sar." He strode over, anger pouring off him. He grabbed my keys and threw them. My duffel followed. He pushed me to the bed roughly, then covered my body with his own. "You want me so bad, Sar, here I am," he snarled, his eyes gone yellow. His fingers were claws, digging into my skin.

I closed my eyes, trembling.

He put his hand on the side of my face and gripped my jaw. "Open your eyes," he said roughly.

I opened them, my vision swimming with tears.

"Don't cry, Sar. You wanted this badly enough to send me another dream."

"I'm sorry—"

He bared his fangs at me in a snarl and roared deafeningly. I shrank back from him as much as possible.

"You're sorry? I loved you! You and Elle were all that kept me going, kept me breathing—"

"Why didn't you come back to us?" I yelled back. "We needed you!"

"You found someone to fill my place easily enough," he spat. "My best friend!"

"I did turn to Danial—" I said weakly.

"You are oathed to him!" Theo roared.

"No, I'm not!" I said loudly.

"The marks on your neck don't lie," Theo growled.

"One is Danial's, one is Devlin's. It was safer—"

"And the choker? Was that safety, too?"

I touched the choker as I had so many times before, and it fell off into my hands. Theo looked at me in shock.

"Yes, it was safety. It pleased Danial to see me wear it, like the ring on my hand. But I didn't give him an Oath—"

"You gave him a child," Theo said heavily. "I saw you pregnant."

"You were dead. I loved Elle, and I wanted one of my own. Danial wanted one, too."

"You love him," Theo said, his eyes tortured. "Don't bother denying it—"

"That hasn't ever changed," I retorted. "But I loved you more. Enough not to give him my oath, though I knew he wanted it."

"You aren't married? You aren't oathed?" Theo said frantically.

"No," I said defensively, beginning to cry.

Theo became enraged. "Tell me the truth, Sar! Don't lie to me!"

"No!" I screamed. "I couldn't do it, because I fucking couldn't let you go!"

His hand gripping my face loosened. I put my hand over his.

"I couldn't let us go," I said, sniffling. "Danial did everything for me, and all I wanted was you—"

15

With a groan, Theo kissed me, my tears wetting his cheeks.

I pushed him away. "You're a bastard! You left without even telling me you were alive—"

"I'm sorry," he said desperately, kissing me feverishly. "I love you. I love you so much, Sar—"

I grabbed his face and kissed him, cutting off his words. He reached down, pulled off my pants and his, then pushed my legs apart. Eagerly he pushed inside, thrusting fast and hard. With each movement of his hips, the climax built between us, spiraling quickly. Then we were there, crying out together, holding on to each other.

Theo was almost crushing me, panting hard. He loosened his arms and drew back to look down at me. His eyes were full of love and tenderness and that spark that was his and his alone.

"Marry me, Sar," he said softly. "Marry me today."

"Yes," I breathed, touching his face with my fingertips.

"I'm sorry, I don't have a ring to give you," he said, kissing my face, my eyes. "But we can get one today—"

"Yes, you do," I said, pushing him gently off me and going to my duffel. Removing the velvet box, I tossed it to him.

He opened it, and shock filled his face. "I thought it was lost! How did you—"

"The man who took you planted it on Will's body, to make us think it was you."

Theo hugged me fiercely, kissing me again passionately, then drew back. "Get dressed," he said, pulling on his jeans. "We are going now. Right now."

"Theo—"

"No stalling. I am not waiting one more minute to claim you as my own. Now get some clothes on."

After dressing quickly, my dogs and I dutifully followed him to his truck. Theo drove us to the town church. Luckily, when we entered the Methodist minister was right there.

"We want to get married," Theo stated. "Right now."

The minister raised his eyebrows at the dogs. "I usually charge—"

"Whatever your usual fee is will be fine."

"Are you sure this is what you want?" he cautioned. "Marriage is not to be entered into lightly or for carnal pleasures—"

I blushed. It was obvious he'd caught the scent of sex that permeated the both of us.

"We've got the money, and we're sure," Theo said forcefully. "Now please perform the ceremony."

"Yes," the minister said stiffly. "Let me just get my wife to be witness."

He walked through a door at the side of the podium.

"You're sure you've got enough?" I whispered. "It's likely to be a hundred or so, as we don't belong to the congregation. I've got about forty—"

"I'm paying for this," Theo growled. "All of it."

The minster returned with his wife. Then we were standing there, getting married.

"Do you, um…?"

"Sarelle McGarran."

"Do you, Sarelle McGarran, take this man to be your lawfully wedded husband, to have and to hold from this day forward, for richer or poorer, in sickness and in health, forsaking all others, until death do you part?"

I gazed at Theo standing beside me. There were no doubts. No reluctance. No fear. "Yes."

"Do you—"

"Theopolis."

"I need a last name, too."

"Theopolis O'Connor."

"Do you, Theopolis O'Connor, take this woman to be your lawfully wedded wife, to have and to hold from this day forward, for richer or poorer, in sickness and in health, forsaking all others, until death do you part?"

"I do."

"May I have the ring, please?"

Theo handed him the ring he'd gotten for me so long ago.

"Let this ring be a symbol of your love for one another—"

I flushed and discreetly moved Danial's ring from my ring finger to my other hand.

Theo noticed what I was doing and grinned. The minister's wife looked at me, appalled.

"Take her hand and the ring, and repeat after me," the minister said.

"This part … I have something of my own to say," Theo said and turned to me. "Sar, I promise to love you, to protect you and to never leave you or doubt you again."

I blinked back tears as Theo slid his ring onto my finger.

The minister spoke. "Sarelle, do you have something to say, or would you—?"

"Yes," I said, looking at Theo. "I, Sarelle, give myself to you, Theo. All that I am is yours and yours alone. I love you."

Theo brushed at his eyes quickly with his hand.

"Then by the authority vested in me by the state of Wyoming, I now pronounce you man and wife. You may kiss the bride." The minister beamed at us.

17

Theo wrapped his arms around me and kissed me for an entire minute until the minister cleared his throat. He led us into his office, then produced forms for us to sign.

"Ma'am, do you want to keep your last name or change it?" the minister asked as he signed his name.

I gave Theo a smile. "I'll take his."

"Sarelle O'Connor," he said happily, savoring it. "Sign here."

Theo and I signed the forms, and the minister handed them to us. "If you'd do me a favor and take these over to the courthouse? I've got a baptism to get ready for."

"Sure," Theo said, taking them. "It's only a few blocks."

We walked out of the church. It was an overcast day, but the sun was peeking through the clouds. Theo's arm was around my shoulders, and both of us were basking in the knowledge that it was done. I was his, and there was no going back.

Suddenly, a woman stepped in front of us. She stood there, glaring at Theo, and I knew immediately who she was: the other cougar I'd seen him doing yesterday. She was twenty-something, with medium brown hair and big brown eyes. As expected, she was clearly miffed to see her lover holding another woman.

"Theo, who is this?" she asked angrily.

I wanted to blurt out I was his wife, and I had prior claim, but that was Theo's job. I took Theo's arm off my shoulder and turned to him. "I'm going inside to file these. Take all the time you need." I walked off. As soon as I did, she began to scream at him.

I walked into the courthouse with the dogs. "I have some marriage papers to submit," I said to the desk clerk.

"We can't have any animals in the office."

"They're licensed rescue dogs," I said, lying through my teeth. "It will be okay." I handed her the papers before she could protest further.

"Congratulations, dear," she said, beaming.

"Thanks," I said, giving her a big smile.

The yelling outside became louder.

"What is going on out there?" she said, peering out the window to look.

"My new husband and his former girlfriend."

The clerk blanched, then quickly said, "Marriages usually take a while to record, but the marriage certificate will be ready in a week."

"We'll either stop by to get it or arrange for it to be sent to us if we leave town. Thanks again."

I walked back outside. Theo was still standing on the sidewalk, his Brown Eyed Girl still yelling at him. I walked up to them.

"—so you just screwed me because you were lonely?" she yelled at him.

"Well, yes," Theo said, shooting an uneasy glance at me. "I like you, Aspen, but I've loved Sar for years. I thought she was lost to me, so I came out here. You were the one who showed up at my door, asking me if I was lonely—"

I cringed and made a mental note to get tested for STDs.

"You fucking prick," she growled at him, the first tears sliding out of her eyes.

"I'm sorry," Theo said, putting a hand on her arm. "I didn't mean to hurt you."

"Fuck you," she said, her eyes a golden yellow. She walked away.

"Why is she so upset?" Theo said to himself, a sort of bewildered look on his face. "I thought she knew it was just sex."

"There is never any woman for whom it is just sex," I replied. "Even if she says that's all it is."

"I'm sorry you had to see that." He put his arm around me again. "Come on."

We walked back to the truck. The dogs followed us, whining from hunger.

"Theo, I've got to get back to the motel. I never fed the dogs," I said guiltily.

"We are going now," he said, grabbing my hand.

We got back to the motel just in time to gather up my things. The maid was cleaning my room and had my luggage in a pile near the door.

I had checked out after all. "Sorry." I gave her a ten for not throwing my stuff in the dumpster. Theo loaded the bags, and we drove off in Theo's truck, the dogs in the back.

"Where are we going?" I said.

"To my place," he said, putting his arm around me.

We drove for about twenty minutes, ending up at a small ranch house in the foothills of Casper Mountain, not far from the trail where I'd seen him yesterday. We got out of the truck, and he unlocked the door. I started to walk in, but he picked me up.

"I'm supposed to carry you over the threshold."

He carried me inside and set me on my feet. "Feed the dogs and explore," he said, giving me a kiss. "I'll be back in less than an hour."

"Where are you—?" I said, but he was already out the door.

I shrugged, then got out the bowls and food from my duffel. After feeding them, I let them out in the backyard. There was a view of the bluff and the trail snaking its way up the side of Casper Mountain.

After letting the dogs back in, I began to explore Theo's house. It was small but beautiful. The interior was all wood, with a small entryway, a kitchen to the left and a living room with a cathedral ceiling to the right. There was a door on the left of the living room that had to be the bedroom, and above it was a small loft. A closet was on the other side of the living room, on the right. There wasn't much furniture, but what was there was comfortable. Some of it had been carved of wood, likely made by Theo himself.

Curious, I climbed up to the loft. It was his studio, woodworking tools and a half carved piece of wood, a work in progress. It looked like a stool or perhaps an end table. Maybe this was how he'd been supporting himself out here.

I climbed back down and took my luggage into his bedroom. As I dropped my duffel on the floor and arranged my toiletries in the adjacent bathroom, I was again struck by how plain everything was. There was one small dresser and a bed with no headboard or footboard...wait, there was something on the dresser. A statue.

I went closer and picked it up. It was a carved statue of a woman, sitting, her knees drawn up to her chest. Her hair fell around her, covering her, but she was clearly naked. Her hands clutched her legs to her, but she seemed at ease, smiling. She had my face.

I sat down on the bed, musing. How often had he lain here, watching me, thinking of me?

* * * *

I was woken by the smell of Chinese food. It was about noon by my watch.

"Sar, lunch!"

Groggily, I walked out to the kitchen. Theo was there, unpacking Chinese food from a case-sized box.

"Did you get enough?" I teased.

"We've had a busy morning," he replied with a smile. "Let's eat."

We fell on the food like we hadn't eaten in days, eating almost all of it. Afterwards, he put the plates in the sink and led me to the couch.

"Sar, how did you make the dream happen for us again?" he said, his eyes searching mine. "I wasn't around to kiss you this time."

"Terian," I said, squeezing his hand. "He gave me a potion right after you disappeared. He said it would only play the dream for me again and that this time, the dream would fade like any other dream. I never used it, not wanting to lose my memories of you and me. Yesterday though, I decided it was finally time."

"Why yesterday?" he asked, forcing the words out.

"I saw you yesterday with Aspen on the trail."

Theo flushed and looked away from me, his eyes downcast.

"I didn't mean to make the dream happen again. I just wanted to be with you one last time, to remember how we were, before letting you go."

Theo spoke quickly. "As soon as the dream started, I knew it wasn't just a dream. You were the same, the way you were years ago. And I didn't have the scars I have now."

His last words were self-conscious. I squeezed his hand. "I didn't realize that we could change the dream," I said. "Terian said it would be the same, a replay of the first one."

"When you told me that you loved me at the end, I knew somehow that you had to be here, somewhere close by. Then I remembered catching your scent in town. There is only one motel around here, so I drove there first."

"With all speed. You must have nearly flipped your truck."

"Nearly," he admitted. "I was so angry. I wanted you so badly and I thought that you'd come here to have me and still hold onto Danial at the same time."

"Why didn't you tell us you were alive?"

"I saw you all together in the great room. You were happy," he said. "When I saw you were pregnant, I knew without Terian saying anything it had to be his." He paused. "I didn't think Danial would have done that unless you'd given him an Oath."

"Danial isn't the same man he was. Elle changed him, made him understand that he had to love without expectations to be loved in return. My having Theoron changed him further, made him even more secure—"

"Theoron?" Theo choked out.

"We call him Theo for short," I said, giving him a soft smile. "There isn't much of me in him, save for his eyes. He's the spitting image of Danial."

"You named him for me?" he said, the tears sliding down his face. "Danial agreed to that?"

"It was his idea," I said gently. "He searched for you for months. It ate at him inside that he couldn't find you."

Theo grabbed hold of me, sobbing in my arms. I held him, comforting him. We huddled there on the couch for the better part of an hour, clinging to one another. Finally, his tears stopped.

"We should shower," he said abruptly. "Come on."

Theo and I undressed as he got the water running. I saw then for the first time what they had done to him.

Chapter Three

There were the healed whip marks on his back and chest, as there had been in our shared dream. There was not only a mass of scar tissue on his hip, but also a similar one on his thigh and right arm. How many times had he been shot repeatedly to make scars like that on his body?

Tears flooded my eyes. I closed them quickly and moved into the shower's spray so he wouldn't see me crying for him. He was clearly self-conscious.

Theo climbed in beside me, soaping my body with his hands. I returned the favor, stroking him, unable to stop my fingers from discovering other scars running over his arms, legs and torso as I cleaned him. Most weren't long as the whip marks were. The edges were a little ragged, though healed. What had caused them, a knife with a serrated edge?

"I know you feel them," he whispered in my ear. "They'll keep healing slowly. I won't have them forever—"

"Hush," I replied, rinsing off soap. "I'd still be with you if they were permanent or the damage was worse."

"You'd still find me sexy, you mean?"

"I love you. You're always sexy to me," I said, reaching down and taking hold of him in my hand. He made a noise in his throat, half gasp, half groan. "And I'd still have married you. Now rinse off that soap like a good husband."

Theo quickly rinsed off, his storm cloud blue eyes dark. Then he shut off the water and kissed me hard, suddenly lifting me out of the shower and setting me down on the floor. He dried us off as I quickly put a handful of conditioner on my hair, then led me into the bedroom.

He pushed me back on his bed and climbed on top of me, his erection straining against my thighs. He kissed me softly, slowly, his hands cupping my breasts, rubbing the nipples so they hardened in his hands. I gasped, and he licked me, stroking me with his tongue, opening my mouth to his, as he rubbed himself against my thighs and then slid his body between them. I wrapped my legs around him and arched my back, trying to slide him inside. Oddly, he drew

22

back from me.

"What?" I moaned, writhing beneath him, wanting him to enter me.

Theo kissed my neck, then moved lower to my breasts. Again, I came off the bed, arching my back. He reached out with one hand, pressing me back to the bed, as he slid the other into me. He moved his hand gently, his mouth still busy at my breast. I writhed harder, trying to push his hand away, to draw him up against me.

Then I felt his hand spreading my thighs and the first thrust of his tongue inside me. I jerked slightly and shuddered as he held me there, licking me, touching me like he never had before. Too soon, I was meeting his thrusts with my own, and the orgasm broke over me, leaving me trembling in his arms.

Theo crawled his way back up my body, kissing me as he came. "Did you like that?"

"God, yes," I panted.

He kissed me again and suddenly slid himself into me as far as he could go. I cried out from the shock of it, so close to my orgasm. He lifted my hips up to slam himself into me again, moving fast, roaring out his pleasure as he came.

Satisfied, he rolled off and pulled me into his arms, kissing me tenderly. I rubbed against him suggestively, sliding my hair across his face. He let out a sigh of pleasure.

I pushed him back from me. "Lay down on your back."

Theo lay on the bed, a question in his eyes. I kissed his neck, biting down slightly, and his breath came out in a hiss. I kissed my way down his chest, paying special attention to the scars with my lips, running my fingers through his golden chest hair. Then I ran my hands down either side of him to the spot where his legs met his torso and gripped him hard. He began to sit up, reaching for me as I took the whole of him into my mouth.

His back arched instantly as I enveloped him, driving himself into me with a cry. I moved back instinctively to avoid choking, then began sucking him, sliding my tongue over and around his manhood. His body began jerking under me, almost frantic to get deeper. Ardently, I slid my lips down again to take him into me as far as he could go and began moving quickly in rhythm. He thrust into me, gasping with eagerness, clenching and unclenching his muscles. Theo made as if to pull me up, but I splayed my hands against him to hold him immobile and moved still faster. He screamed, arching his back, his fingers like claws tearing the sheets as he drove himself deeply into me, his body spasming, almost choking me. I tasted him on my tongue as he spurted into my throat, the warmth almost burning me. I swallowed, still moving on him, as he continued to shudder and spasm. He groaned and put his hands on my shoulders, still flexing weakly as he finished.

A second later, he slid out of me and rolled me over onto my stomach, still kissing my shoulders and back. He pushed into me again, pulling my head back to kiss me as he drove into me repeatedly from behind. I groaned, loving the feeling of his muscles bunching and lengthening against my body.

His movements became quicker as he kissed my neck. His mouth opened, then came the press of his fangs.

I jerked in sudden fear. His fangs sank into me slightly as he bit down, not breaking the skin, but holding me still. I relaxed slightly, and he moaned, moving faster. Within minutes, I was close again, and then I was there with him as we cried out together, the sudden heat blinding us as our bodies orgasmed simultaneously.

As our hearts slowed, we just laid there and breathed.

He kissed me delicately, rubbing my inner thigh possessively. "That was amazing, Sar. What you did to me … I've never done that before."

Tears came to my eyes then, that I had been the first to give him that feeling. "I'm glad you liked it," I said huskily.

He held me for a short time, while I listened to his heartbeat. Then he kissed my earlobe, tugging on it with his teeth.

"You know what I'm going to say," Theo teased.

I drew a sharp breath, then let it out slowly. "Say it."

Theo sat up, pulling me onto his lap. He kissed me lovingly, one hand running down my back and the other holding my face loosely, so that he was looking at me from only a foot away. He gave me a tender smile.

"Again, Sar. I want you again, my love, my wife, my Sar."

"Yes," I sighed, closing my eyes and moving in for another kiss.

He let out a laugh. Startled, I opened my eyes and frowned at him.

"That's not the right line," he said lightly.

"You're right," I replied with a smile. "I'm yours, Theo, as many times as you want."

* * * *

I was awakened by the dogs' hungry whining. As I got up to feed them, Theo stirred next to me, and it all came rushing back.

I'd found Theo. He still loved me. We'd been married yesterday. We'd made love so much that this morning my body was bruised and sore. And to my shame, I'd never called Danial to tell him any of it.

First things first: feed the dogs.

I got up slowly, my muscles aching. Being careful not to disturb Theo, I grabbed my robe from my bag and took care of the dogs. Then I looked out at the sunlit morning and debated what to do about the mess I'd just made of my orderly life.

I'd have to move out of Danial's place again and bring the cats with me. Elle most likely wouldn't want to come live with Theo and me, not with the way she felt about Danial. Theoron I'd promised to leave in Danial's care...

Guilt hit me like a fist. I was a terrible, selfish person to have disrupted everyone's life. Everyone had been happy with how things were or at least content. No matter what Danial had said to me before I left, he was going to be hurt. Elle and Theoron would be too, even though the latter was so young ...

Horribly, I didn't care. At least, not enough to want to undo the last twenty-four hours. I loved Theo, and I wanted to be with him. Everyone would just have to adjust.

Selfishness wasn't usual behavior for me, which led me to introspection. With a flicker of unease, I admitted that my love for Theo was so powerful, so strong, that it left almost no room for loving anyone else. I loved Elle, Danial and Theoron, but not like I loved Theo. Whether some of that had to do with the dream we'd shared twice now, or was due to the person he was, I wasn't sure.

Still, I owed Danial and Elle the truth now, this very morning. Danial been through enough with having a brother like Devlin; he didn't need trauma from me, too. Elle had been worried her whole life about me leaving her like her biological father Theo had. She'd never known her natural mother Tawny, who'd died just days after she was born. Theo had been taken from her, too, making her ultra-protective of me. While Theo would never replace her adopted father Danial, Elle needed to know I was coming back and bringing her natural father with me.

I checked my cell phone. There were three messages on it, one from Danial and two from Terian, asking if I was okay.

I dialed Terian first. He picked up on the first ring. "Sar, are you okay?"

"Yes." In that one word was everything I was feeling.

"You found him."

"I found him, Terian. Again, in no small way, thanks to you. I married him yesterday."

"I'm happy for you both, even though I'm going to miss you. But you'll be safer with him than with Danial."

"Is Danial up?" I asked, dreading the answer.

"He's asleep, but he said if you called I was to wake him up. Hold on."

I was sick with guilt and anxiety. "Put him on."

After a few moments, Danial came on the line. "Sar, are you okay?"

"Yes," I said sadly. "I found Theo."

There was no reply for almost a minute. "You're with him now, aren't you?" he finally said with a sigh. "He wants you back."

"Yes. I married him yesterday."

Danial's sharp intake of breath sounded loudly, and then the receiver was covered for a few minutes. Then came the soft sound of a door shutting.

"Sar?" Terian said cautiously. "You still there?"

"Yes," I said, upset. "I'm here."

"Danial said that he understood. That this is probably best, all things considered."

Knowing that was true didn't make it hurt any less. "Tell him I'm sorry. Tell him as soon as we can figure out a few things, we'll be heading back to New York."

"Aren't you staying out there?"

"I'm not staying out here states away from my children," I replied forcefully. "We'll work something out."

"Then I'll see you in a few days," Terian said. "Call and check in every day."

"Are you sure that's a good idea?"

"Yes. That request came from Danial, not from me."

I hung up, tears sliding down my face. I cried a little, feeling like a bitch for hurting Danial after all he'd done for me. Then I dried my eyes, rationalizing that I'd done the right thing by being honest.

I washed my face and got breakfast started. As I was finishing up, Theo came out of the bedroom and stood in the doorway for a while, watching me.

"Do you want three eggs or four?" I asked.

"Five," he said hungrily. "You wore me out, wife."

I laughed. "I'll put them in now. Grab some plates and start loading before it gets cold."

Theo began filling two plates with pancakes, toast, bacon, and sausage. When I finished making the eggs, I brought them to the table and divided them up between us, giving him the lion's share.

"This is great," Theo said between bites. "I missed your cooking."

"I'm glad you like it," I replied. "I missed cooking for you."

Theo pushed back his clean plate. "What do you want to do today?"

"Wrong question," I said quirkily.

Theo looked at me oddly. "What do you mean?"

"I mean reality took a vacation the moment we met up again, and this morning it's back in full force. I just called Danial to tell him I've found you, and we're back together. I also told him I was heading back shortly with you." I paused to let that sink in. "Despite we've had a good time, we've got a lot to decide and the longer we delay, the worse everything's going to be." I sighed. "What I want isn't this, but this is what we have to do."

"I get it," Theo replied, taking my hand in his. "I feel the same way. All I want to do is eat and make love with you, until you tell me that you can't take anymore. But you're right. I need to know what you want and to tell you what I want and see if we can't agree on what to do." He paused. "First off, do you want to live with me out here? Or do you want to go back to the Northeast? It sounds like you want to go back."

"We need to go back. Elle needs to see you, and so does Danial. I have my old house, though the cats are still at Danial's house. I'll have to get them and my stuff. But what about your house? Do you have a job you love here?"

"I don't own this place. I rent it. I have no job. I've just been carving to pass the time as I healed." He grimaced. "What you see on my body now is nothing compared to how bad it was."

I didn't want to ask for details. He could tell me if he wanted to, when he was ready.

"I'd like to live at your house again," he said. "We were happy there."

"Good."

"Will Elle want to live with us once she knows I'm alive?" Theo asked hopefully.

"No," I said sadly. "She may not forgive me for leaving Danial and coming to you, even though she knows what you mean to me. She thinks of Danial as her father and calls him Dad. She blames you for taking my love from Danial and likely, for he and I separating now."

"That is the truth, all of it," he said, sighing. "I haven't been much of a father to her."

"I should have gone with you that night," I said. "I—"

"Sar, you would have been killed or taken prisoner. Weres were not the only live goods that Gene dealt in."

That was chilling. I shivered slightly.

"I can handle Elle needing time to get to know me as a friend, if not her father. But what about Danial?" he said, his eyes boring into mine. "Are you going to continue to work with him? Terian say you'd quit your job at the metal fabrication plant."

"I'd like to, but that's up to him," I said slowly. "He's upset about you and me, though he said he understood. If it's just the money you're worried about, all of your savings are intact."

"That seems amazingly understanding of him," Theo said suspiciously. "Why isn't he fighting harder to keep you, especially as you're the mother of his child, Theoron? It's almost as if he wants you with me."

"From being with him so long, I was beginning to turn," I admitted. "But I'd promised him I'd stay in spite of that, though Camlyn told me to go. It was because of that Terian told me you were alive."

Theo stared at me for a moment with a worried expression. "How close are you?"

"Very close, according to Camlyn."

"Why are you calling your doctor by his last name?" Theo asked curiously.

"After all we went through during my pregnancy with Theoron, we got a little less formal," I replied. "I won't go into detail, but it was unusual, to say the least."

"Well, you won't be donating any more blood," Theo said, matter of fact. "That will help. That and time away from Danial."

His comment might have been the truth, but I didn't like the way he'd stated it, as if I had no say. "Speaking of health, I heard your words to Aspen. Should I get tested by Camlyn?"

Theo colored. "I'm sorry. We can both be tested, of course. I was never unprotected with Aspen except as a cougar. According to what Dr. Camlyn said to me in the past, STDs are hard to transmit in animal form, especially for you to get from me, as you aren't werecougar. But it's possible, so yes, we both should get checked out, just to be safe."

Prompted by his confession, I started to say I had only been with Danial. Theo cut me off. "Sar, I know you were only with Danial. But are you back on the pill?"

"No. Danial stopped taking the potion once I was pregnant with Theoron."

"Then you may be pregnant," Theo said, both scared and very excited.

I closed my eyes. How to say that there wouldn't be any children for him and me, not ever? "I'm not pregnant," I said finally, willing myself not to cry.

"You might be," he said, this time not trying to hide his excitement. "It's okay, Sar. I'd love that, especially now we're married and—"

Theo realized I was bawling, sobbing like my heart was breaking. He hugged me tightly.

"Don't cry," he said soothingly. "It's okay. You're scared, I know, but you don't have to be. What happened to Tawny won't happen to you—"

I couldn't stand it anymore. "I can't have any more children, Theo," I blurted forcefully. "I was hurt having Theoron. We can't have children."

Theo went rigid against me. "It doesn't matter," he said finally, holding me. "Not to me."

"You're lying," I said tearfully. "I can hear it in your voice."

Chapter Four

"I'm disappointed," Theo admitted after a moment. "But that's all. I love you, Sarelle. I'm not going anywhere because of this or anything else you might tell me."

"What if Aspen comes back to you in a few months and tells you she's pregnant?"

"Sarelle, she was on the pill," Theo said, irritated. "I made sure, after what happened with Tawny. And in human form, I always used protection myself, too."

"You trusted her?" I asked skeptically.

"I told her what happened to Tawny, making it as graphic as possible, then went with her to get a supply of pills. She didn't want to die or have a child. She just wanted to have sex."

That last statement made my stomach turn over, as I visualized again finding them together, Theo moving on her. Still, I'd had a child with another man, so who was I to bitch?

"We've settled enough for this morning," Theo said leading me to the bedroom. "Let's get some more sleep, then revisit this in the afternoon."

We lay down, wrapping our arms around one another. I buried my face in his chest and shortly fell asleep. We awoke after four in the afternoon.

"Do I seem any different to you?" I asked. "When I told you about my being close to becoming vampire, you acted as though it wasn't a complete surprise to you."

"I thought that you lasted longer with me than you had before," Theo said finally, studying me. "Your skin is a little colder, too, Sar. Only a few degrees or so. But otherwise no. You're just as wonderful as I remember you being."

"Thanks for the compliment," I said, giving him a kiss.

"Do you want any more Chinese?" he said, getting up.

"Go ahead," I said. "I'm not that hungry."

29

Theo nodded and left the room, the dogs at his heels. As the minutes passed, I began to feel oddly uneasy.

Theo came back in with a smile that faded when he saw the expression on my face. "What is it?" he said, sitting down and putting his arms around me. "You look scared."

"Part of me is afraid this is a dream. That I'm going to wake up back with Danial or back in my motel room alone."

He gave me one of his broad smiles. "After all this time, you know we can't just have a normal dream of one another. God knows I wanted to when I was alone and hurt. I don't know why, but it's something to do with the dream we shared twice now, I'll bet on it." He held up my hand, showing me his ring on my finger. "I gave you this as a symbol, so you'd know you'll never be without me again. Not on this earth."

That moving speech led to another round of lovemaking. When we'd finished, we lay in each other's arms, breathing hard.

Theo said, "Do you want to go out for dinner or stay in?"

"Depends," I said, tracing his jaw with my finger. "I guess I need to know when we're leaving."

"Do you want to leave tomorrow?" Theo asked.

"No," I said, kissing him. "I want a little time with you. Just us, together."

"Like a honeymoon?" he said, grinning at me.

"Exactly like that," I said, kissing him again.

* * * *

After seeing to the dogs the next morning, we drove into town. Theo closed out his bank account and his PO Box, asking his mail to be forwarded to my house.

"It was mostly just statements from my banks back East," Theo said as we left. "I had a little money stashed under a few aliases that I've been drawing on and depositing here in town. Do you want to get lunch? There's a good local diner near here."

"Sure."

We ate at the local diner, Pete's. Theo was greeted like a regular. I, however, drew looks of surprise and curiosity.

"The food's great. This cake is nice and gooey."

"Not as good as your pie," Theo murmured. "Your pie was always the best."

"I can make you one later. We should stop anyway and get groceries, as I'm nearly out of dog food. And we've got to go get my truck...our truck from the motel parking lot."

"The local store is just across the street. The truck can wait." He stood up and paid the bill. "Come on."

While we shopped, I kept expecting Aspen to show up and make a scene. But if she was around, I never saw her.

After putting away the food at his place, we took the dogs outside on the lawn and lay in the sun with them. It was a particularly nice day, the sun warm on our skin. We stayed outside until dark, dozing.

"I'm still tired," I said groggily, as he helped me to my feet.

"Go inside and go to bed," he answered. "I'll lock up everything and then be right it."

Before collapsing into bed, I called Terian as he'd asked to check in. Oddly, all I got was voice mail.

* * * *

The next morning Theo and I drove down to the motel to get my truck. Before he let me near it, he checked it over carefully, then started it up and listened to it run for a few minutes.

"It was here for days unattended," he said by way of explanation. "But everything looks okay." He patted the hood. "I'm glad you kept it, the newer model I've got is—"

"Why are you so worried?' I asked, not understanding. "Everyone thinks you're dead, including the other ranked bodyguards. There shouldn't be anyone here after you."

Theo's eyes looked very old suddenly. His eyes slid away from mine. "Sar, I've done a lot of things for Danial over the years. Most of them were justified, but some were proactive. A lot of them were simple and neat, but others were brutal. There is always going to be someone, somewhere, who would like to see me dead, who would pay to see it done. And if you, who have no formal training, could find me so easily, then so could they."

I shuddered. Theo was saying that he'd always be in danger. It followed that as his wife, I'd be in danger, too.

"Come on, let's go," he said. "The day is wasting."

I got in the truck and followed him back to his home.

"Come walk with me," Theo enticed, getting out of his truck.

"Let me grab the dogs," I replied as I shut the door. "We should walk them before it gets too hot."

After a three-mile hike, we returned to his front door around midday. The sun was hot now, and we were all tired. After a quick lunch, we left Ghost and Darkness snoozing and went out again.

"No long walks until tomorrow," I stated as I followed him. "I'm tired."

"It's not much further."

Theo led me to a patch of bluff overlooking a small depression in the earth. There was a small stream there, hardly more than a trickle, but it provided some green grass and a few pine trees. The sky was blue above us, free of clouds.

"I liked to come here and carve," he said, as he helped me sit. "The sun is always pleasant here and not too hot. It's hard to imagine the glaciers that created this depression and these valleys."

"Tell me about them."

We held hands as he told me about the glaciers that had once been over the whole west, carving various rock formations and shifting stones miles from their origin. Then he pointed out a few nearby rocks and told me their names.

"Impressive," I said respectfully.

"I wanted to know about my surroundings and I'd forgotten everything I'd learned when I was in school," he admitted. He gave me a sidelong glance. "Would you mind if I changed form?"

"No," I said curiously.

Theo took off his clothes and his gun and went to his knees. Abruptly, he shifted—faster than I'd ever seen him, his limbs contorting and stretching to become cougar. Within a minute, he lay before me, golden yellow eyes and buff colored fur.

He rolled to his feet and immediately began to stalk me. I backed away, laughing. Then he stood on his hind legs, reaching his paws up around my neck. He gently leaned on me, nuzzling my neck.

I eased down onto the grass. Theo backed away as I did, then returned to lick me, purring and rubbing me with his head. Carefully, I took his face in my hands and kissed him on the mouth. Theo opened his mouth on mine, his large tongue teasing my lips, then sat back on his haunches. He nudged me with his head, grabbing the bottom of my shirt in his teeth and tugging upward.

I knew what he wanted. Part of me was taken aback. The rest was excited.

"Be gentle," I cautioned, taking off my clothes.

Theo nodded earnestly, his tail twitching in excitement.

As soon as I was naked, Theo moved in close, jumping up on my back and growling softly. There was no force behind his paws, but raw energy coursed through his body, his movements clearly impatient.

We wouldn't be able to have sex the usual way. He couldn't really kiss me in this form or even touch me much. I shivered, going to my knees.

Theo immediately moved his body tight against mine, crouching on his hind legs. He put his front legs around my hips, then pulled back suddenly as he raised his hips. His penis penetrated me slightly, then began to slide deeper.

He trembled. His hot breath sounded loud in my ears. He pushed harder, growling slightly. He slipped in further, the thickness of him drawing a moan of pleasure from me. Suddenly he pushed hard, drawing a sharp gasp from me as his penis abruptly ran out of room.

I was afraid to move. He was too big. I was too full...

Theo licked my cheek gently. Then he pulled my hips backwards, tight against him, pushing the last inches of himself inside. I jerked and cried out at the sharp pain.

He licked the back of my neck, then his fangs softly bit me again, pressing, holding me still. I relaxed slightly. He tightened his paws again and quickly began to work his hips rhythmically. He didn't give any time between one stroke and the next. Though the feeling of being filled persisted, it quickly became one of pleasure, as his body stroked mine all over inside.

I no longer cared about the pain; I wanted to come too badly. I groaned with each thrust. Theo's growling intensifying. Then suddenly I was there, the rollicking movements of his body bringing me hard as I screamed loudly. Theo let out a snarl and kept going. A few seconds later he shuddered, then clutched me hard in his paws, letting out a long echoing roar as his body pulsated.

Dismounting, he collapsed onto his side, breathing hard, his mouth open. Carefully, I lay down on my side to face him, using his shirt and jeans to cushion the ground. A quick inspection revealed I'd gotten scraped knees, but that was all.

Theo shifted back to human. As soon as he finished he moved closer, taking me in his arms. "Did I hurt you?" he asked. "I'm sorry."

"I'll be okay," I said, hugging him. "I enjoyed it."

He smiled contentedly. "I had the fantasy of finding you here, then having you in my other form so many times."

I'd known it had to be something like that from the way he'd acted. "Was it like you thought it would be?"

"Better," he sighed happily. "I'd love a repeat performance, if you're up for it."

"Sorry," I said sheepishly. "I need a while to heal and recover. A day or so at least—"

He hugged me tightly. "Just tell me when you're ready. I can wait. I want it to be just as good for you as it is for me." He kissed me. "Sleep here with me, Sar."

He curled his body around mine, and we slept there naked in the weak sun. When the sun began to set, the cool air woke us.

Theo got to his feet. "Let me buy you dinner tonight."

After dressing and checking on the dogs, Theo drove us to a nearby bar. As we walked to a booth, some of the men we passed greeted him as they gave me appreciative glances.

"Large pizza," Theo said to the waitress. "Water for me, but she'd like a glass of red wine."

"You really want water, Theo?" I asked when she left. "Wouldn't you rather have wine?"

"Let's say I acquired a taste for it," he said, haunted. "In those months I spent away from you, wine was much easier to come by than water. Sometimes I think I can't ever drink enough." A shadow passed over his face.

I clasped his hand. "I'm here if you need someone to listen."

He looked up at me and the shadow disappeared. "Thanks."

My wine and his water came. Theo drank a few swallows, then set it aside.

I tasted mine. I'd known it was too much to expect a Shiraz here, but this Cabernet was quite nice.

"That's the local band, Redheart," Theo said, pointing to the live musicians in the corner playing Country and Western. "I like them."

To my relief, the music wasn't the twangy kind. This was the more modern rock played on most country stations with a younger audience. The band was playing covers, and some of the songs were familiar.

"Do you want to dance?" Theo asked, seeing me moving my foot.

"Do you know how?" I asked, then flushed.

He roared with laughter. A few people at the bar turned around to look. I flushed deeper.

"If I didn't know how, I wouldn't have asked you," he said finally, his eyes sparkling with mirth.

"Okay then, let's see what you've got," I said, offering him my hand.

He led me onto the dance floor and proceeded to show me that he did know how to swing dance. While Theo didn't have Danial's skill and grace, he had passion, which is half of dancing. He turned and swung me around until I was breathless and flushed.

As a slow song started, he put my arms around his neck and pulled me close. "How was that?" he said suggestively.

"Very good," I said huskily. "Except I want some more."

"After we eat," Theo said teasingly, leading me back toward the table. "Our pizza's here."

After two pieces and another half hour of dancing, I was hot, tired and ready for bed.

"I think it's time to take you home," Theo said softly, putting some money on the table. "You need some sleep, and I need more food."

"You had the rest of the pizza," I teased, following him outside. "Or was that a hint you wanted me to make you—"

"Shh," he hissed, stopping abruptly.

"What is it?" I whispered.

"There are men waiting for someone out here," he whispered back.

"How many?" I asked.

"Five or six," he said.

Great. I'd brought my gun, but it was in the truck. "Tell me what to do."

He took my hand. "We'll walk to the truck. If they approach us, get behind me."

As we reached the truck, a group of men materialized out of the shadows.

"Theo, we have business with you," one of them said.

"Get inside and lock the doors," Theo said, stepping in front of me.

I obeyed him. As the locks slid home, Theo turned back to the man who had spoken. "What is it, Doug?"

"We won't hurt your girl. But Aspen told us that you cheated on her, then roughed her up. We're here to let you know that isn't right—"

"And to beat the point into me, right?" Theo said mockingly.

"Smart man," Doug said.

"She lied to you," Theo said, looking him in the eye. "Not that my sex life is your business."

"I'm the deputy sheriff," Doug retorted. "We take a tearful woman's complaints seriously in this town, especially when they're against her fiancé."

"She and I were never more than lovers, and I never laid a hand on her."

I wondered if that was true. By her actions, Aspen had clearly thought she was more than a convenient lay. Maybe there was more to this story than Theo had admitted to.

"Doesn't matter. She's upset that you've taken up with this woman."

"This woman is my wife."

"Be that as it may, we told Aspen we'd teach you wrong from right, and we aim to do it, here and now."

"Then get on with it and stop talking."

Doug and his men moved in on Theo. One threw a punch, and he avoided it, putting his fist into the man's gut. The next jumped on him, while another tried to punch him. He threw the one on his back onto the other in front of him, and they both went down hard and didn't get up. Another tried to kick out his kneecap. Theo pushed him, but he didn't hold back as he had with the other men. The guy flew into the side of a truck, denting it and knocking the man out cold.

The last man standing pulled a knife. Theo pulled a knife of his own, and they circled one another.

"Let it go, Doug," Theo said angrily.

"No," Doug said coldly. He darted in, yelling, trying to slash Theo with his knife.

Theo silently knocked the knife out of Doug's hand and pushed him into the side of the building, dazing him. He picked up the knife, then held Doug firm as he brought the blade down in an arc. Doug let out a scream as it sunk in a few millimeters above his left collarbone, trapping him there by his shirt collar.

"How did you do that?" Doug whispered, quaking. "Who are you?"

"No one," Theo said tiredly. "I'll be leaving town tomorrow for good. Don't follow and you'll never see me again. You do, and you'll regret it."

Theo turned and walked back toward the truck. I opened the door for him, then heard the click of a safety.

Theo wheeled, blocking me as he turned to face a man holding a gun.

"Gary, let it go," Theo said reluctantly. "I'm only going to tell you once—"

"No!" Gary yelled furiously. "I loved Aspen. She and I were starting to date. Then you came along, and she dropped me."

"Shouldn't you be angry at her then?" Theo said sarcastically.

"It's your fault!" Gary shouted. "If you're dead, she'll want me again."

A shot rang out, and Gary yelped, dropping his gun. Theo turned in surprise.

I kept my gun trained on Gary. "That's my husband you're threatening," I said coldly. "Get going before I put a hole in your heart for real."

Gary slowly backed away, then took off running. Theo grabbed Gary's dropped gun, then got behind the wheel. I kept my gun ready to fire until we'd left the bar parking lot.

"That was some shooting, Sar," he said, reaching over with one hand to pull me close. He kissed me hard, then jerked away as the tire went up over the curb. Theo spun the wheel, and the truck righted itself back on the road.

"Nice handling," I laughed and shook my head.

Theo shot me a grin.

"You were right to insist I practice all those years ago," I continued more somberly. "Do you think it's safe to stay at your place tonight?"

"I'll hear anyone who comes around," Theo said with a reassuring smile. "But likely they'll leave us alone. They're a bunch of cowards."

* * * *

I awoke the next morning and began packing everything that I knew was going with us. While emptying the kitchen, I found the supplies for pie that Theo had bought.

Well, there was no use dragging them all the way home. After putting the bags and boxes in the trucks, I made Theo the pie and set it to baking. As it baked, I snapped a few photos of the house from outside and inside and then ate a late breakfast.

Theo was still in bed. I undressed and took a long shower, washing my hair and then packed the rest of the toiletries up. Slipping into my robe, I put them in the truck.

36

When Theo still didn't emerge, I headed back inside. As I sat down beside him on the bed, he opened his eyes.

"Is it *later* yet?" he whispered, grabbing me in his arms.

"No," I said, pushing him away. "'Later' is after we leave tonight. When we're safe."

"I think I can tell we're married now," he said, frowning at me.

Ouch. "Hey," I said, giving him dagger eyes. "If that's the way you feel, I'll just go and toss out the pie I slaved over this morning." I got up and started for the door.

"There's pie?" Theo said, immediately alert. "You baked?"

"Not for long," I said in my best bitchy tone.

As I opened the door, Theo pulled me back, then pushed me up against the wall to trap me between his arms like he had that first night we kissed. He kissed me eagerly, then licked my lips in a teasing motion until I opened my mouth, allowing him entry. He ground his pelvis into mine, his erection sheathed in the velvet of my robe rubbing between my thighs. I let out a moan of longing.

Theo stripped off his shirt, revealing himself completely. He opened my robe, then pushed it off my shoulders. It fell to the base of the wall, and he kicked it aside. He pulled me against him, then rubbed the tip of his penis against my clitoris.

"Is it *later* now?" he asked in a guttural voice.

"Yes," I moaned. "Now is *later*."

"Good," he said, lowering me onto the robe.

He devoured me, wringing cries of climax from me easily as I writhed beneath him. As many times as I came, Theo did also, his body only surrendering after the third time. After we were spent, he brought me to the bed, laying me down with a few tender kisses.

"You rest," he said, covering me up carefully. "I've got to see about a pie."

I lay there, blissful. Would it always be like this? We'd had so short a time together years ago, I couldn't remember if Theo had been this adventuresome in bed. Yet I did remember how he'd made me feel. It was the same way I felt now—cherished, loved and utterly protected.

* * * *

Theo nudged me. "Wake up. It's about two. We should leave."

I sat up groggily. "Do we have time to walk the dogs?"

"We should probably get going," he said, running his hand in my hair reluctantly. "Sorry."

"No big deal," I yawned. After putting on some clothes, I let out the dogs, then settled them in my truck.

"I've got everything else already packed," Theo said, handing me my purse and keys. "There's water in a small cooler on the floor."

"I'm going to drive one truck and you the other?" I asked.

"Yes. I'd rather ride with you, but we need to get both vehicles home. Let me make a last quick check, and we'll go."

He emerged a minute later. "I have to drop off the keys to the landlord. Follow me."

I nodded. "Lead on."

As I pulled out of the driveway, I looked back just once at the house. It sat there in the sun, the mountain rising behind it. Some part of me wanted to stay here with him and never go back. The few days we'd spent here had been perfect and simple, the way real day-to-day life was not.

So much turmoil was waiting for us at home and little was certain. Would Terian welcome his role model? Would Danial want Theo to work for him again? Would Theo want to? We'd talked about him getting out of the business, about him being a carpenter. But if his life was in danger, it would be better if he had Danial or Terian around to watch his back.

Would Danial want me to work with him as I had this past year? I'd liked the work, but seeing him every day would be hard on both of us. Maybe I could telecommute? He wasn't up days, though Elle would be...

She was going to be another concern. I didn't know what Theo expected. Or how to tell him Elle had known he was alive and hadn't said anything to us, that she said she hated him.

I pulled onto the highway, watching Theo driving ahead of me and was reassured. We had each other. We'd make it work.

* * * *

Theo and I made it to just outside Kansas City the first night and to Indianapolis on the second. The following morning, I told Theo I needed a break from the driving.

"We need to do only a half-day's worth today, so I can move around some. The dogs need a break, too. Walking around the block twice a day and keeping them cooped up in the truck the rest is making them spastic and me edgy."

"I'm sorry, Sar. I shouldn't have pushed you. We should be far enough away now from anyone who'd be after us. We can stay here for most of this morning and head out this afternoon."

After a quick breakfast, Theo and I took the dogs for a long walk. It was nice, seeing a place I'd never been before. After what had happened to Theo and me in Orleans, Danial had never taken me with him again on his trips, and he hadn't taken many of those either, compared to how he had in the past. I hadn't missed traveling exactly, but this brought back the feeling of being on vacation and seeing the sights, even if that only comprised a different park that looked similar to the ones I'd been to at home.

The scenery had changed as we left the west for the Midwest. We had left the prairie foliage and pine trees behind and were now back to where green was a common color and the trees mostly large deciduous. The scent of spring was on the wind, along with tree blossoms and the sweet smell of fresh cut grass.

After our walk, we had lunch at a drive-in, our meals delivered by roller-skate. Within minutes of ordering, Theo became increasingly anxious.

"What is it?" I asked him nervously.

"When the food gets here, pack it up. We need to leave right away."

Alarmed, I did as he asked, handing the surprised carhop a huge tip. Theo drove back to the motel, ushering the dogs and I inside.

"Wait here. I'll be right back." He left.

A few moments later, he was back, his expression grim. "We've got someone coming after us."

Chapter Five

My breathing immediately sped up. I took a deep breath, then asked, "Who? How do you know?"

"I saw the same car behind us three times today, Sarelle. I've just seen it again in the parking lot, checking discreetly to see if our vehicles were here."

I pushed down my rising fear. "Do we wait for dark and try to leave then?"

"We'll stay here tonight. I don't want them to catch us at night in separate vehicles on a deserted road. We'll leave right before dawn tomorrow. I'll plan out an alternate route home, one that wavers enough so they won't know our exact destination. They may already know it, but we can't help that. If this has to do with Danial, I don't want to lead them straight to him. If it has to do with me, I don't want them knowing where we live."

Danial's home was a closely guarded secret. The entrance was disguised, and he had guards. My house was wide open by comparison.

"It must be someone from Casper that is following us, right? Someone from the Northeast wouldn't have needed to keep tabs on us so closely. They'd have known our destination."

"Maybe. They're either very good or amateurs. I'm guessing the latter because no one checks out a car in daylight that carefully if they're any good. Still, they may have sent the person who did that as a decoy and be hanging back themselves, waiting for us to foil the decoy so we think we're safe and relax. It's an old trick."

"That sounds way too complicated for real life," I said skeptically.

"Not really," Theo countered. "They most likely already know where we're going. Your license plate is from New York, so they know we're liable to be headed there. If they checked either the post office or the courthouse, they'd even have your address."

A shiver of fear ran down my spine. "What if they're lying in wait at home?"

Theo held me tighter. "You're safe with me," he said, giving me a kiss.

"Don't worry. Everything points to amateurs. That means they won't wait for us to get home before they act. They'll try something at the first opportunity. Tonight we're going to draw them out if we can."

He sat me on the bed. "Get some sleep, Sar. I'm going to check over the maps and figure out a few alternate routes."

I curled up on the bed with both dogs, too nervous to sleep or even read. As Theo plotted, I stroked Ghost and Darkness, listening to them breath and filling my mind with memories of the last few days, letting the happiness I'd felt then comfort me now.

"We should go out tonight," Theo said finally, setting down the maps. "Somewhere where there are a lot of people."

"What about the dogs? I don't want to just leave them here."

"Whoever is looking for us isn't going to be interested in them. They'll be safe enough in the hotel room. We won't be gone long. This is just an exercise to see if I can spot one of the men following us."

"What if they shoot at us or attack in a group?"

"If they wanted to do that, they'd have done it already. That car's been following us all day, and there were moments in that park today we were in spots isolated enough for a sniper. But we weren't isolated enough for them to grab us. For whatever reason, we're wanted alive."

Apprehensive, I went over and hugged him. "Just tell me what to do, and I'll do it, Theo. I trust you. I'll follow where you lead."

He crushed me to him with a possessive growl. "Saying I love you doesn't cover it. It's not close to what I feel having you in my arms, knowing you're finally mine, or that the life I wanted for us is possible now. We're going to make it through this."

"I'm scared," I murmured

"Stay close. We can do this. Come on."

We left the dogs in the motel room with some Cheweez, hanging the Do Not Disturb sign on the door. Taking Theo's newer truck, we drove to the nearest strip mall and splurged on a large dinner of cheese fries with bacon, steaks, and vegetables thrown in to soak up some of the heart-stopping cholesterol. Both of us were ravenous, our appetites spiked by the danger we were in. Theo kept watch circumspectly but saw no sign of our stalkers.

"We'll give them one more opportunity," he said, after paying the bill. "Somewhere away from crowds. Feel like a drink?"

"Not really," I shrugged. "But I can playact."

We walked to the bar across from the restaurant, got a booth and ordered two glasses of red wine. The place was almost deserted.

"Tell me about Elle," Theo said, sipping his wine. "Start at the beginning when you got her back to America."

I told him everything. Theo was fine until I got to where Elle began to see Danial as her dad. It was obviously painful to him that Danial had the place that should have been his. But he didn't say anything until I mentioned my mother's disapproval.

"Did your parents ever come around to you being with him?" Theo asked.

"My mom always liked you best," I told him, clasping his hand. "They'll be happy we're married."

"Do they know about your baby with Danial?"

"No," I replied, my eyes downcast. "He was only born a little while ago, Theo. He showed his human side only a few days after he was born."

"So they haven't seen him? Ever?"

"Theoron's only a month old now. There wasn't time—"

"You left your baby at a week old?" Theo said harshly. His eyes were disbelieving and appalled. "You just got in the truck and drove away?"

Hurt, I took a deep breath. "I can't nurse him, Theo. I can't even touch him. Every time I do, he attacks me." I wiped away tears. "It's not his fault that he wants my blood. He doesn't know he'd hurt me."

"I'm sorry," Theo said, taking my hand. "I didn't think."

"No, it's good to talk about it," I said, wiping at my teary eyes with the napkin. "I feel oddly detached from him. Theoron came from me, but Elle feels more like my child than he does. That makes me feel so guilty." I took a gasping breath. "I love Theoron. That's a given. But I don't know how long it's going to be until I can act like he's my son. And I wonder down deep if I'd have been so quick to leave if part of me wasn't running away from that. I worry that he might think one day that I left Danial because of him, because it was too hard to care for a half-vampire child."

"Danial's taking good care of him," Theo soothed. "I'd stake my life on it."

"But I'm not," I said guiltily, putting my face in my hands. "I abandoned him."

Theo got up, came over to my side of the booth we were sitting in and hugged me. "I'm sorry, Sar. I didn't mean to hurt you by what I said. I didn't know he'd attacked you. Don't cry." He handed me another handful of napkins. "You didn't abandon him. You left him in the care of his doting father who is much better able to handle his nature than you are. Camlyn himself told you to go—" Theo cut off, finally noticing that I was sobbing too hard to hear him.

My tears poured out of me. I made no attempt to stop them. It felt good to finally cry out all of my frustrations, to not pretend I was fine.

Theo handed me more napkins and hugged me.

After a few moments, I wiped at my eyes, then stood up. "I'll be right back."

"Take your time," Theo said, motioning to the waitress. "I'll pay the bill."

I headed across the room to the bathroom near the far wall. Opening the door, I stepped inside. The first stall was occupied, so I used the second. When I came out, the mirror over the sink showed I was still a mess, my face red and my eyes very green.

I washed my face with cold water, then checked again.

The stall opened, and I cast my eyes down, embarrassed.

"You look stunning," a familiar voice said from behind me.

I turned toward it, saw a blur of brown hair, and then everything went black.

* * * *

I opened blurry eyes. My jaw hurt. I tried to reach my hands up to my face and couldn't move them. I looked down. I was tied to the chair.

"Sit there and keep quiet."

Aspen stood there watching me. Her beautiful eyes looked through me. I'd expected to see hate there, but instead there was only disinterest.

"What do you want?" I said, trying to talk normally.

"Is this the one?"

A man came in behind her. He laid a hand on her shoulder and looked at me.

"Yes, that's her," Aspen said. Again, there was none of the anger I expected.

"Who are you?" I said to the man.

He came closer and crouched down in front of me. "I'm Aspen's father," he said gruffly.

This was getting weirder and weirder. "What do you want with me?" I asked.

"Is it true that you're married to Theo?" Aspen's father asked.

"Yes," I replied. "I'm his wife."

"Not for long," Aspen growled.

"Aspen, be quiet," her father growled back at her. "Look," he said in a conversational tone, turning back to me, "Aspen thinks she's in love with Theo. She wants to be with him, to see if it will work—"

"It was working fine until this blond showed up," Aspen growled.

"Aspen, I said for you to shut up." Her father sighed and rubbed his eyes. "Your name is Sarelle, right?" he said to me after a while.

"That's right," I said.

"I want you to go back to wherever you came from, Sarelle. Tell Theo you need some time, that this Vegas-type wedding was a mistake. Tell him to come to you in a few months, but you need that time apart to make sure it's right. Will you do that?"

"No way in Hell," I said flatly.

"I told you she wouldn't do it," Aspen said, beginning to pace back and forth.

"Sarelle, what if I sweetened the deal. How would a 100K sound?"

I looked at him in disbelief. He wanted to pay me off to leave Theo, so his daughter could try to make it work with my husband? Unbelievable!

He saw my expression. "200K?" he said, his tone still conversational. "Tell me, what does it take?"

"You have no idea what I've done and gone through to be with him," I said angrily. "Suggesting a bribe is ridiculous."

He looked back at me, resolute. His expression told me he was a man who was used to getting his way, used to telling other people what to do and having them run to do it. "Everyone has their price. Just tell me what it will take, and then you get yourself gone with the money."

"I should have known," I said acidly. "With a name like Aspen, your daughter was either the daughter of a small town mother with pretensions or the daughter of a rich daddy who likes to ski."

Aspen and her father looked at me angrily but didn't correct me.

It made sense. Aspen was in Colorado, just south of Wyoming. Likely that was close to where Daddy was based or had his vacation home. Aspen had come up here to have a little fun and wow the local boys. Then she'd found Theo. After discovering he was a werecougar like she was, the romance probably had seemed fated. When it suddenly stopped being fun, she'd called Daddy to come and sort it out for her.

Aspen's father leaned in, as if to tell me a private thought. "Sarelle, if Theo loves you, giving it some time won't matter. What are you out? A few months? If you agree to let Aspen have another chance—"

"Save your breath," I said. "Nothing is coming between him and me this time."

Aspen exploded. "Did he tell you that he had me every night?" she shouted, desperate and angry. "That sometimes that wasn't enough for him? That he would seek me out wherever I was to make love to me?"

It hurt to know she was probably telling the truth. But that didn't matter in the least. "That was before me," I said disdainfully.

Tears formed in her eyes. "Did he tell you he'd asked me to move in with him?" she said roughly. "He said he wanted me around in the morning, to wake up to."

That hurt, too. I rationalized that Theo had been alone, that he'd known I was back with Danial and having his baby. He'd had every right to try to start over with someone else.

"He doesn't now," I said flatly. "He told you it was over."

Aspen strode to me and kicked the chair over. I fell over with it, crashing to the floor, crying out from the jarring pain.

She stood over me. "Why did you have to come here?" she screamed. "We were happy!"

"Not like I am with her," Theo said, appearing in the doorway. "Now back away."

Tears of relief flooded my eyes. He had some blood on him, but it was sprayed across him, so likely not his. He held my explosive bullets gun in an unwavering hand.

Aspen's father slid Aspen behind him. "Where are my guards?" he whispered.

"Dead," Theo retorted, his eyes cold.

Aspen's father backed away further, pushing his daughter behind him. Theo crossed to me and pulled his knife. He cut the ropes holding me and helped me to my feet, all the while holding the gun on Aspen and her father.

"Why do this when I told you it was over?" Theo said coldly. "Why couldn't you just accept it? And how could you think I'd want a woman who'd kill someone I loved?"

Aspen was crying too hard to reply. Her father answered for her. "You hurt her," he spat at Theo. "She loved you."

"I never hurt her," Theo said, his tone cool, but no longer like ice. "I never did anything to her she didn't want me to do."

"You broke her heart," Aspen's father said. "And you're going to pay for that, pay through your nose. You have no idea who I am—"

Theo abruptly dropped his gun to his side and stepped closer to Aspen's father. "You're Derek VanMerill."

"Yes," Derek answered, surprised.

"Do you know who I am?" Theo said, his tone implying he was enjoying this, savoring it.

"Aspen said your name was Theo, that you did woodworking—"

"I go by Theo. But my full name is Theopolis O'Connor," Theo said, his eyes staring into Derek's.

Derek's face went white, and he backed up several steps. "You used to work for Danial Racklan. You're—"

"That's right," Theo said, stepping forward, his gun still held at his side.

Derek backed up fast, Aspen behind him looking confused.

"Am I the kind of man you want your daughter with?" Theo said softly, holding his gaze.

"No," Derek said in a whisper, his abhorrence tangible.

"Get going," Theo said, ice cold again. "We were never here. Someone attacked you and killed your men. You and your daughter were unharmed by some miracle."

"You'll let us go?" Derek said hopefully.

Theo turned fast and stepped right up into Derek's face. "Only because Sar is unharmed. If you had done anything to her at all, you wouldn't be leaving this building. Not in one piece." He looked over at Aspen. "Neither of you."

Aspen choked out a sob and held onto her father.

Derek looked at Theo angrily, then dropped his gaze and led Aspen to the door. "Come on, sweetheart. We've got to go home now." They went out, their footsteps quickly fading.

Theo grabbed my hand and led me out the door, his gun at the ready. On the way out, we passed the bodies of at least five guards. All were dead, one with his throat cut and the others with single bullets to the head or the heart.

"They were human," Theo said. "I used your pistol. There was no point making a bigger mess than necessary."

We drove back to the motel in silence. Theo's movements were still tense and angry.

When we got back to the room, he paused at the door. "Have you had any contact from Danial?"

I gaped at him, confused. "Not since Wyoming. I left a message for—"

"Wait here. I'll be back." Theo slammed the door.

I curled up on the bed. It had cost Theo something to act that way to Aspen. He was angry now because he'd cared about her, and it had bothered him to upset her.

Although I was sympathetic, I was also irritated. I hadn't stolen him away from her or set out to seduce him back to me. I hadn't asked to be attacked in the women's bathroom. In fact, my head was beginning to pound. Where was his concern for me?

I got some aspirin from my travel case and swallowed them. Then I lay down in bed, too tired and sore to take a shower.

Sometime later, Theo slid into bed next to me. But he said nothing, and neither did I.

Chapter Six

When I awoke, it was morning. Theo and I had slept the night in our clothes, his still bloodstained.

"Sar?" Theo said sleepily.

"Hi," I said softly, touching his face.

"Shower?"

"Yes."

We left our clothes in a pile and cleaned off the grime of last night, taking turns in the warm spray. I was washing out the conditioner in mine when I noticed something was wrong.

I pushed my hair out of my eyes and moved closer. "Are you okay?"

Theo got out of the shower. "I'm fine."

He'd been crying. It hadn't been just the water. But I let it go.

As I finished showering, I debated for the first time if I'd been wrong to come after him.

Theo might have had a good life with Aspen out here in the West. Maybe he could have been the carpenter he'd wanted to try being. No one had been looking for him. Everyone thought he was dead. Now he was back in the spotlight and back to killing, as if he'd never left. And it was all because of me.

I turned off the shower, dried off and went out to find Theo lying silently in bed. I got in beside him and held him, saying nothing. Minutes passed.

Finally, Theo said, "I was starting to fall in love with her, Sar."

I didn't reply.

"I'm sorry that I said it was just sex. It wasn't. We went hiking together. We ate together sometimes."

"Do you want to talk about it?" I asked, hoping he wouldn't.

"Aspen came to Casper back in January. She was taking a semester off from school. She dated a few of the local boys, and then I came into town. I never saw her until she came to my house one night. She asked me if I wanted her, and I said—"

"I know what you said," I snapped. "I don't need to hear the graphic details."

"She and I…it wasn't like it is with you and me. Tell me that you know that."

"She said you asked her to move in with you. Is that true?"

To his credit, he didn't look away or deny it. "It's true. She was going to move in next week."

I closed my eyes, upset. After my going back to Danial, it wasn't fair to act like Theo was wrong for getting on with his life. But down deep, I'd wanted him to have been out here waiting for me to come back to him. It wasn't fair or right, but there it was.

"Sar, say something."

"Look, you didn't owe me anything. You thought I'd moved on without you. You found someone to take my place. It's okay."

"She never could have taken your place, Sar," Theo said, pulling me tight against him. "Not any more than Danial could take mine with you. I would have lived with her, but I wouldn't have married her."

I didn't believe him. He couldn't know that, not really. He and Aspen didn't have the aging problem that Danial and I had. They didn't even have the problem of being were versus being human…

"Sar?"

"Theo, it doesn't matter," I said tiredly. "You married me. You're with me. I'd say I forgive you, but there isn't anything to forgive—"

My cell phone rang. I reached over and answered it. "Hello?"

"Sar," Terian said. "Are you almost home?"

"Terian, we're just leaving the motel, but we got a late start—"

"I need to know right now when you'll get here," Terian said angrily.

My hackles went up. I wanted to shout that we'd have been a day closer without the persistent Aspen but stifled it. "What's the rush?"

"Danial's upset, nimwit," Terian said. "He's going crazy here waiting for you to get back. It's trickling down to all of us."

"I'm sorry," I said, then covered the receiver. "When should we make it home?" I asked Theo.

Theo groaned and looked at the ceiling. "Maybe two days? If we drive all day and some of the night and then crash and do it again the next day—"

I wasn't going to be able to do that with the pets, much less my aching head. Time for Plan B.

I uncovered the receiver. "Terian, it's going to be at least two more—"

"What is the problem?" Terian said bluntly. "You made it there in less time."

"What do you want from me?" I said angrily.

"I want you to come and get your cats and your cooking stuff and your clothes and get them out of here so Danial can start coming to terms with you leaving. He's sitting here thinking about you and Theo screwing your way home—"

I hung up on him. The phone rang again promptly, and I let it ring.

Theo answered it finally. "No, it's Theo. Listen, Terian, someone was following us. Sar was taken last night by them, from the ladies bathroom of the place where we were eating—"

Theo stopped abruptly, then resumed talking. "She's fine, but I had to kill a few of them as a point to make sure that it wouldn't happen again. It's resolved, but that delayed us for over a day. We'll leave shortly, but part of the problem is we have two vehicles, and we can't share the driving—"

Theo cut off again, anger clouding his words. "Terian, don't think I don't care about Danial. I do. It wasn't just for Sar that I left things as they were back in February."

Theo paused, then resumed again much more calmly. "Go and pack up Sar's things from Danial's room while he's working tonight. Get the cats and anything you know is hers and have the werefoxes take them to her house. Station one of them there to wait for us. Danial will be able to handle her loss if he's not confronted by it every time he goes to sleep. Call if there's a problem."

Theo hung up and tossed the phone back to me. "We should go," he said, giving me a lingering look of longing. "Not that I wouldn't prefer—"

I got up, still too preoccupied with his talk of Aspen to be very romantic. "Let me take care of the dogs first. About ten minutes."

* * * *

Theo and I drove the rest of that day and into the night, stopping only to pick up food and to let the dogs out to do their business. Finally, at about eleven p.m., we pulled into a motel that had a lounge attached. Happily, they accepted pets.

The dogs lay down in the room, relieved to stretch out after the confines of the truck. I was tired, too, but also hungry.

"The lounge serves until midnight," Theo said, heading for the door. "Let's get some hot food."

I followed him to the lounge. Within a few moments, we were seated and had put in our dinner order.

"We're lucky they serve anything this late," Theo said, placating. "Much less salad and steak."

"I'm not irritated about the food," I said grumpily. "It was a long and stressful day. Skirting Chicago with all that rush hour traffic was awful."

"At least we didn't get stuck. The lines were moving along." Theo clasped my hand. "Is it really that, or are you upset over what I said about Aspen?"

"I'm just tired," I lied. "Give me a couple days of sleep and no driving, and I'll be the same old Sar."

"Good," Theo said, relieved, letting go of my hand. "I'll be right back." He headed toward the men's room.

I watched him go, wondering why I was still so irritated over him caring about Aspen. I'd had a baby with someone else, and Theo wasn't bent out of shape over that. Yet, just the memory of him doing her…

I put it out of my mind. Aspen and Theo were history. He was my husband. And we would have enough to deal with when we arrived home.

A burst of music broke into my thoughts. A man had put some money in the jukebox across the room and the strains of "Bad Moon Rising" came pounding out. He returned to his seat at the bar.

Belatedly, I noticed that besides a few men at the bar—likely truckers—the lounge was empty. Maybe on Saturday nights things livened up…

The food came, and I dug in. Theo came back a few moments later and wolfed down his steak and fries.

The music ended, and silence descended. I dug in my purse for change.

"What is it?" Theo asked.

"I'm going to play something. Feel like dancing?"

"Not tonight," Theo said tiredly. "I'm whipped. I'm ready for bed."

Anger sparked. I was about to tell him that was fine, that I'd dance with the man at the bar who liked music, then noticed the man was gone. The words died on my lips.

"But go ahead and play something," Theo said, "I'm happy to listen."

"I don't want to listen," I said, enunciating every word clearly. "I want to dance."

"Then go ahead and dance," he said easily, giving me some money. "No one's stopping you."

I bit my lip, then formed a small smile. "You're sure you don't mind?"

"Not at all," Theo said, making a shooing motion. "Go."

If he wanted to watch, then I'd make sure he got a good show. "All right."

I walked over and scanned the jukebox songs to find the one I was looking for. Locating it, I slid in the quarter and took off my sweatshirt, smoothing down my tank top that had ridden up.

As the first strains of George Michael's "I Want Your Sex" came rolling out of the jukebox, I went into motion. I worked my hips, gyrating and then my shoulders, rolling my head backward, my hair undulating down my back.

Parting my lips, I closed my eyes and slid my hands up into my hair, letting some of it fall while I tangled my hands in the rest on top of my head. Then I titled my head down and opened my eyes.

I had Theo's full attention. In fact, his jaw had dropped, and his mouth was open.

Still moving to the beat, I crossed my hands and put them on my shoulders, sliding them down over my breasts, down my waist to my legs. Then I turned to lean on the jukebox, looking over my shoulder at him, still moving my hips to the beat and slid first one, then the other of the straps of my tank top and bra down to bare my shoulders.

As I turned away, there was a loud whistle. I grinned widely, then turned back to Theo. With eyes partly closed, I beckoned to him with one hand, the other undoing the top button of my jeans as I sauntered to him.

I'd only gotten a step when Theo grabbed me by one arm and tossed me over his shoulder. He strode to the room and keyed open the door, growling softly for the second it took for the key card to work.

He dropped onto the bed, moving me beneath him. He pulled off my jeans and his and then pushed inside me, thrusting as far as he could, as fast as he could, groaning loudly. I kissed his neck, licking him, running my hands over his shoulders, feeling the muscles contract with each thrust. He bit me gently on the neck and then harder, pressing down with his teeth.

"I take it you liked my dancing?" I whispered.

He growled and began kissing me hard. A moment later he came, his moans muffled against my neck.

"Yes," he said, rolling over on his back. "I did. But don't do it again, at least, not out in public."

"Why not?" I teased.

"Because that wasn't me whistling at you," Theo said jealously. "You're my wife. I don't want anyone else ogling you."

"Give me enough attention and I won't," I teased.

"You're going to get my full attention tonight. Come here."

* * * *

I opened my eyes to see bright sunlight streaming into the room. Shit. We'd overslept. My fault, for instigating another night of marathon lovemaking. Selfishly, I told myself that a few hours wouldn't make much difference anyway.

"Good morning, Wife," Theo said softly.

"Good morning to you, Husband," I said, smiling at him.

Theo pulled me into his arms and let out a groan, putting his head back on to the pillow. "We're never going to make it home tonight," he said, looking at the ceiling.

"Tomorrow then," I said, kissing him. "A few hours won't matter. We've just found each other after a year and a half of being apart. I'm not going to feel bad for—"

"Sar, when we get back home, I'm going to have to find a job. I'll take at least a few weeks off before applying anywhere," Theo replied. "I'll make up to you what we're missing now."

He had a point. Terian had taken his place working for Danial. He'd have to work for someone else.

"It's a deal," I said. "Give me about ten minutes."

After feeding the dogs and giving them a quick walk, we got on the road. The day passed quickly again, as we stopped only for gas and lunch. Nightfall found us a little east of Pittsburgh.

Determined not to oversleep again, we picked up takeout, got a room, and went to bed early, the dogs stretched out on the floor.

The next morning, I woke up to find Theo was missing.

Chapter Seven

First, I checked the bathroom. Then I threw on some clothes and went out in the parking lot. Both trucks were still there.

Sudden panic hit me like a wave. It was all happening again. Theo was gone, and he wasn't coming back…!

With effort, I calmed myself. Theo likely had just gone out to get us some breakfast so we could get on the road faster. And I'd better do what I could to be ready when he came back.

I showered quickly, then fed the dogs and took them outside. Initially, I walked them around the block, sure that Theo would appear momentarily. When he didn't, I made subsequent laps, until the dogs and I had walked for almost an hour.

It began to rain. I took Ghost and Darkness back inside the room. The clock said it was after ten a.m.

Theo had been gone at the minimum over two hours. Something was very wrong. Time to call the cavalry.

Terian answered on the first ring. "Sar?"

"Terian, have you heard from Theo?" I said, worried.

"Are you telling me he's not with you?" Terian replied, stressed.

Terian's worry broke my calm resolve like a snapped twig. "Terian, he's not here! I woke up, and he was gone!"

"Are both trucks there?"

"Yes," I said.

"Are all the guns you had with you there?" he asked.

"I don't know," I replied. "I'm not sure how many he had." I went to our bags and rummaged inside. "The two I brought are here. There are several others he brought, but I don't know how many he had to start—"

"Where are you?" Terian interrupted.

"A motel just east of Pittsburgh. A Comfort Inn."

"Stay there in your room," Terian said. "We had an attack here last night."

I sat down heavily on the bed. "Is everyone okay?" I said hesitantly, not wanting to know if they weren't.

"No," he said sadly. "Demetri was killed, Ivan was injured. Suri is missing, presumed dead. Janice heard her screaming—"

"Who attacked?"

"Bears."

One name came immediately to mind. "Why would Devlin attack?" I sputtered with anger. "Danial's his brother. They—"

"These weren't grizzlies, they were black bears. It wasn't Devlin."

"Who was it then, and what did they want?" I demanded.

"It was a vampire by the name of Manir. He's nowhere near the power Devlin is, or was, but he's built up a formidable force. At least ten bears attacked with at least that many men."

"What did they want?" I said, my words clipped.

Terian was silent. Then he said, "Danial thinks they were after Theoron."

I made a sound halfway between a squeak and a cry. "Is he okay?"

"Danial, Elle and Theoron are fine, Sar. They didn't even see any fighting," Terian said with a note of pride.

I was glad he hadn't hesitated this time. "Did you kill them? All of them?"

"I left one alive. That's the one Danial questioned to get the name of Manir. Danial drained him this morning. He is waiting until you returned before he launched a reprisal."

"Should I start back by myself and leave one truck here? I've got the explosive bullets gun."

"No. Stay there. I'll speak to Danial and call you right back."

I clicked off the phone, anxious. A few minutes passed, then it rang.

"Hello?"

"Danial said to sit tight, Sar. He will send someone tonight to guard you."

There was a shuffling of the handset being transferred, then Danial's familiar voice.

"Sar, are you okay?"

The concern and love in his soft tones suddenly made me long to be with him again. Embarrassed by my feelings, I cleared my throat. "I'm fine, Danial. But something's happened to Theo."

"Tell me everything you remember since you woke up this morning."

I relayed to him 'everything'.

"It's possible he might be out doing reconnaissance," Danial said finally. "But that's unlikely. I'll make some calls. I have an idea where he is, but let me check on it first."

I wanted to demand he tell me, but I didn't feel I had the right to demand anything from him. "Thank you. I'm glad you're okay. Terian told me about Manir's attack."

There was silence, and then Danial said, "Sarelle, I need to know something."

"Anything," I said, hoping it wasn't going to be something too painful.

"Are you still going to work with me? Help me with the business?"

I almost laughed that this was his question. Yet knowing him, I probably should have guessed it. "If you want me to, I will. I like the work, though I might have to do some of it from my home via computer or phone sometimes. I didn't know if you'd be okay with that though."

"It will be hard at first, it's true," Danial said slowly. "But I've grown to depend on you now for it, and it would be easier if you kept doing it. You always did an excellent job." He paused. "You should know, too, that I'm going to offer Theo his position back as well."

I didn't reply, though I was very surprised.

"This attack made me aware of how thin my guards are spread now. I need someone to watch my back if I'm away and someone here all the time to guard Theoron and Elle. There are too many targets now and not enough of Terian to cover them all." He sighed. "Worst of all, I should have seen this coming."

"How could you have seen this coming?" I said flatly. "I've never heard of Manir. Ever. He wasn't even one of the vampires who attended your parties, was he?"

"What I mean is that the attack last night is probably the first of many. Dhamphirs were legend: a myth. Now that you and I created a real one, everyone wants to know how it was done, or just to possess Theoron for themselves as a source of power or status."

"He's just a baby," I whispered.

"A baby who is already much stronger than a human child. He's growing fast, too. He's already toddler sized. He'll need blood, probably for the rest of his life, but he's eating regular food as well. We found out yesterday when he ate some of Elle's ice cream cone."

I laughed, picturing that. Danial laughed as well for a second, then resumed his serious tone. "The main thing is he can walk in the sunlight. He has been playing with Elle outside for the past few days, Terian watching like a hawk all the time, of course. He loves feeling the sun on his face. I watch from the house in the late afternoon..." Danial trailed off.

His love was like a physical force, it was so strong. It hit me hard like a slap in the face: I was missing some important firsts of my child growing up.

"Can I hold him yet, you think?" I whispered hopefully.

"Most likely not," he said reluctantly. "He bit Mary, caught her alone one night when she was tidying up. She's fine. I was there when it happened and got him away from her fast. But she said she was only coming to work days from now on. He's not like that with the any of the weres, Elle included, or Terian, Devlin or myself. He prefers human blood to all others, and his appetite is sometimes…insatiable."

I took a deep breath and let it out. "I understand."

"Sar, I know how you feel. I can't be out there in the sun playing with him, no matter how much I want to."

"It's not the same," I said sadly. "I feel like…like…"

"Like what?" Danial prompted.

I sighed. "Just tell me the moment you think I can hold him, Danial. Please?"

"I will, darling," he said tenderly.

"Terian said you're sending someone to guard me?" I asked, changing the subject.

Danial's tone changed, becoming hard. "Stay close to your room and carry your gun. Don't hesitate to use it. Theoron isn't widely known about yet, but the news is traveling fast. Those who would take him are going to be after you too, for giving birth to him."

"Danial," I said skeptically. "Why would they be after me? The potion is what made it possible for you and me to have a child. There is nothing special about me—"

"Sar, that potion has been around for centuries. It was tried by many with no success. Devlin tried it at least three separate times this century that I know of. With three separate women. With no success. He has tried for more than two hundred years and nothing—"

"They didn't have Terian's blood," I said quickly. "Maybe Devlin didn't stop taking blood from the woman or keep them warm enough—"

"The potion was the same. Devlin was tested, and the tests said he was fertile. Yet the women couldn't get pregnant. He managed only once and that was almost two hundred years ago. When that woman lost his child, she also lost her life."

Jesus. Glad I hadn't known THAT when I'd agreed to try. "Did she…was she in the first month?"

"Like you the first time, yes," Danial said softly.

Devlin hadn't wanted to refrain from sex any more than Danial had. Both he and his woman had paid dearly for his impatience…and Danial had known he was risking my life by trying to have a child with me.

"You knew I might die like she did?" I said incredulously.

"Sar, you'd already survived one miscarriage, horrible as that ordeal was. You had the advantage of decades of medical advancement." He paused. "Many women died in childbirth and miscarriage in the early 1800's. Regrettably, it was a common death then."

Mollified, I said, "Then I don't see where you get that I'm special—"

"You got pregnant right away. Even the second time, it only took a few months. That is the peculiarity." His awe-filled words inspired both fear and pride.

"Do you know why?"

"Remember how I couldn't feed from you metaphysically?" Danial said, an electrical charge running through each word. "I think you're naturally resistant to my blood, to the virus that makes me vampire. I've talked it over with Stephen, and he agrees. That is why you could carry my child without turning vampire." He paused. "Do you have your choker with you?"

"Yes."

"Put it on. Don't take it off, not for any reason."

I got the choker out of my bag and put it on. It slid together easily.

"Is it on?"

"Yes," I said, relieved. "But if they're willing to kidnap Theoron, why would a choker be any detriment to them grabbing me?"

"There are laws to protect Oathed Ones," Danial said. "There are no laws to protect dhamphirs. I'm working on changing that, but the process for new laws is slow—"

I half listened, preoccupied with thoughts of Theo missing, Theoron's imminent danger and now my own new status as hunted creature.

"—don't drive the trucks. There may be people watching, or the trucks may be wired—"

With a jolt, I came fully back. "With explosives?"

"Yes."

"Eek!"

"Sar, just stay put. I'll have someone to you by dawn."

"Okay."

"I love you, Sar. I won't let anything happen to you."

"I know you won't," I said softly. "Take care of—"

"Tell me you love me," Danial asked.

"You know I do," I said softly. "I—"

"Say it for me anyway. I need to hear it."

"I love you, Danial," I said tenderly. "You're the father of my child, our child. I love you."

Danial gave a satisfied sigh. "Take care. Call if there's any problem, okay?"

"Yes."

I hung up and then called down to the hotel office. It was close to eleven now: checkout time.

"Excuse me. I'd registered last night for one night, and now I'll need to stay another day. Do I just tell you that, or do I need to arrange payment?"

There was a shuffling of papers. "We definitely have a room available, ma'am. But we might have to move you to another room."

"Why?" I asked, suspicious.

"We have a gentleman who stays here regularly, and he always requests the same room." The man laughed. "He's superstitious, I guess. It happens to be the one you're in, and he reserved a room for tonight an hour ago."

Weird, but not supernaturally weird. "That's okay. What room are you moving me to?"

"The one just across the hall. As for payment, we have your credit card on file, so an additional night is no problem. If you're ready to move, I'll send a maid down with the new keycard in ten minutes. Give her your old keycard."

"That'll be fine, except I'll pay with cash. Thanks."

I gathered up all of our stuff and packed our bags. While I waited for the maid, I looked out the window. Across the road was a strip mall, in one of the first stores a Laundromat.

At least I could get our dirty clothes washed. I was in my last pair of clean clothes.

The maid knocked. I handed her the keycard, and she handed me the new one, giving Ghost and Darkness a wary look. I took everything into the new room, gave the dogs some water and the last of the Cheweez and headed over to the mall with an armful of dirty clothes.

I set the clothes to washing, then ran next door to a chain restaurant and grabbed a takeout salad. Returning to the Laundromat, I settled down to watch the clothes. Trying to read was hopeless. I was too nervous.

"Nice necklace," an old man sitting nearby said. "That looks almost like real gold."

I gave him a fake smile. "Thanks. My boyfriend gave it to me."

He nodded, then went back to reading his newspaper.

Two hours later, the clothes were all done. I folded and packed them into the duffel bags. The old man gave me a smile as I walked out.

I went back to the hotel room. Both dogs were glad to see me and anxious to be walked. Anxious myself, I took them for a long walk around the strip mall's exterior, looking at the shops within. To my relief, there was a pet superstore at the farthest corner.

Taking the dogs inside, I bought them some extra food, some Cheweez and a toy for each of them. They'd tried hard to be good, despite all the time cooped up in the truck and the hotel room.

"You get a free recyclable bag with purchase," the cashier said. "Pick one out."

"Thanks." That solved having to walk back alone later for the cans of food. I handed her one, and she packed it full, its sturdy cloth just holding the contents.

Shouldering the heavy bag, the dogs and I headed back to the motel, continuing our perimeter circuit. Before long, we came up upon the large glassed windows of a jewelry store.

Despite the dogs' impatience, I dallied, looking at the wedding bands. What kind would Theo want? Plain gold? One with a diamond chip? One with a pattern? I was betting plain…

Ghost whined, then barked. I looked up, but no one was around. Uneasy, I stood still for a moment watching, but nothing stirred. Darkness didn't bark, but her hackles were raised. She was intently facing the rows of cars, her head scanning back and forth, her ears straight ahead.

"You're right," I told them. "We're sitting ducks out here. Come on."

When we reached the hotel, it was close to six p.m. I dropped the bags off at the room, then decided to walk Ghost and Darkness around the parking lot of the hotel. If I was going to be stuck in the room all night, I should make sure the dogs were as tired as possible. They didn't cooperate, bored after the fifth repetitive loop, having smelled everything already. But whatever had unnerved them near the mall was gone.

Strangely, I was the one growing more and more uneasy. I felt almost as if I was being watched, yet I never saw anybody.

Near dark, I gave into my nervous tension and brought the dogs with me to the mall again to get takeout for dinner. This time they were relaxed, if watchful, of the people around us. The mall was much more crowded now, vans letting off teenagers and many adults in pairs and groups.

We returned to the hotel without incident. I gave the dogs Cheweez, then wolfed down my salad so fast I felt sick. Afterwards I sat on the bed, wondering if I should call Danial. He hadn't called all day…

There was a knock at the door. When I checked through the peephole, my eyes narrowed. I opened the door to my least favorite person. "What are you doing here, Devlin?" I said, surprised and angry.

He was leaning nonchalantly against the door, smiling at me with a smile that didn't reach his eyes. "Why, I'm here to guard you, Sar," he said, grinning to bare his fangs.

I remembered those fangs well. "How did you get here so fast?"

"There are more efficient ways of travel than car," he said, moving past me into the room. Oddly, the dogs didn't growl, but instead walked up to him and licked his hands, their tails wagging. Heartened by their positive reaction, I shut the door. "Like what?"

Devlin didn't answer, moving to look out the window into the dark night. Unease filled me, and I quickly dialed Terian.

"Hi, Sar."

"Terian, is Devlin supposed to be here?"

"Danial sent him to guard you," Terian replied. "I know he's not who you'd pick, but we're stretched thin."

"Thanks. Just checking," I said and hung up before he could say anything else. I turned to face Devlin, who was smiling in triumph.

"Always accusing me of ill will—"

"Why did you come?" I said, folding my hands across my chest. "Really?"

"To guard you, as I said," Devlin replied. "And to bring you home safe to Danial, as he asked me to. I know you don't like me, Sar, but—"

"Don't call me Sar."

"Everyone else calls you that," he said, offended.

"Everyone else can. But not you."

He rolled his eyes, annoyed. "Sarelle, what I told you before is true. What you did for Danial means something to me. You are always going to mean a lot to him. So when he asked me for help, I was glad to oblige."

"Why?" I asked. "Why does it matter so much to you?"

Devlin considered me. "I love my nephew, as I told you. I've been honored with a great many wondrous gifts in my long years. He is by far the most precious to me."

It was somehow hard to imagine him loving anyone, even though his voice held deep emotion. Perhaps it was his handsomeness. I sat on the edge of the bed. "Danial told me tonight about how you tried before to have a child of your own."

Devlin sat down in the chair near the far side of the room. "It's true," he said heavily. "I've tried for years now and gotten nowhere."

"Danial was attacked. They were after Theoron. He said they'd be after me, too."

"They will be," Devlin assured me. "But you're as safe as I can make you, my dear."

His surety made me feel better, if only slightly. "Danial said you'd known a woman back when you were king—"

"Ruler," Devlin corrected sharply.

"Ruler," I repeated. "He said that she'd died in miscarriage—"

"That was long ago," he said abruptly, glaring at me. "You weren't even born—"

"I'm sorry," I said quickly. "I felt terrible after losing my baby. I'm sorry you went through that. That's all I was saying."

Devlin was silent a few minutes, studying me, then he looked away. "I have to go feed," he said abruptly. "Give me the key and don't leave this room. I'll be back in an hour, tops."

I handed him the key to the room. He left, shutting the door quietly.

Suddenly exhausted, I showered, then dressed in my pajamas and got into bed. Devlin would wake me up coming in, but at least I'd already be in bed. There would be no awkward moments with me walking around in my pajamas...

Wait. There was only one bed. *No. Way.*

I got up, moved the table and chairs over and then laid down the extra blanket and the one from the bed plus two of the pillows. Hopefully, he'd take the hint.

I lay down and went to sleep. The ringing phone woke me.

"Hello?"

"Sar, Theo is safe," Danial said.

I let out the breath I've been holding for hours. "Where is he?"

"He's in jail."

"In jail? Why?"

"Because he paid for the hotel room with his own credit card. When they ran his name, the local sheriff was alerted. Theo should have paid cash or used one of your cards. He knew better."

"Explain."

Danial paused, obviously trying to choose his words very carefully. "Theo did a job for me once in that town, and the sheriff remembers him. Theo left no evidence, but the man knew he was guilty all the same and arrested him. Theo spent a week in jail, while the sheriff tried everything he could to make the charges stick. It was only the threat of legal force that got him out finally."

"Should I go post bail?"

"He hasn't been charged with anything," Danial said patiently. "I got my lawyer involved, and he's backed the sheriff down. Theo will be let out tomorrow, and he'll call you when it's time to pick him up. Then you, he, and Devlin can wait for nightfall and come home."

"Sounds good," I said, finally relaxing a bit.

"Get some sleep, sweetheart. Things will be better tomorrow evening."

I hung up the phone and went back to sleep. Bright light woke me. I looked at the clock and read four in the morning.

"My apologies," Devlin said, turning off the light. "I wanted you to know I was back. Shaking you awake was my only other option."

I'd expected him to be covered in blood from having ripped someone's throat out. Yet there was no blood on him that I could see. His longer hair and stubble were back, making him look pretty rough.

"Thanks for letting me know."

"So I'm sleeping on the floor?" he said, raising his eyebrows.

"Yes," I said, turning my back to him. "I'm a married woman."

"Yes, I heard," he said patiently. "But I'm not asking for intercourse, merely for a softer bed than the floor. Can I not implore you to change your mind?"

"Next you'll be telling me you're harmless," I snorted.

"I am not harmless nor was I ever," Devlin said, laughing easily. "But I've no cause to be hurtful. You can surely see that." He moved the bedclothes back onto the bed, slid off his boots and then crawled beneath the covers beside me.

"Hey," I said, turning toward him. "I didn't say you could get in here with me."

Devlin held my gaze. "Do you really see me as a threat even now?"

I shifted uneasily beneath the covers. Yes, he was a threat. Not only was he dangerous to my health, his good looks were dangerous to my virtue, especially those eyes of his...

"Will you not answer?" Devlin prompted curiously. "You have the look of a woman lost in thought, but they do not seem to be ill ones."

"Were your eyes always that color? Before you were a vampire?"

He leaned closer. I leaned back involuntarily.

"You like my eyes?" he said softly, intrigued.

I mentally tried several responses on for size and then said finally, "They're unusual."

Devlin held my stare. His eyes were a gold color that was lighter than a werefox's eyes, yet darker than Theo or Elle's cougar eyes. The color was somehow richer, like actual gold was, though not so brassy or shiny. There was a liquid aspect to them, something alive that was missing in everyday metal that enhanced their singular beauty. As I stared into his eyes, I decided that they were almost certainly the most beautiful eyes I had ever seen.

"You do like them," he said happily, with a tone of sinful pleasure.

I flushed and didn't reply.

He laughed. "Yes," he said. "They were always this color."

Devlin moved forward suddenly. I recoiled back hard, letting out a gasp. He laughed and kissed me on the forehead.

"Get some sleep," he said. "I'll be a while in the bath." He got up and went into the bathroom. The shower began to run.

I rolled over and went to sleep. When I woke up, Devlin was beside me under the covers, though not touching me. I deliberately turned my back on him, telling myself he'd had an opportunity while I'd been asleep to kill me, and he hadn't. There was nothing to fear.

* * * *

When I awoke, it was early morning. Devlin was beside me, either asleep or faking it pretty well. I turned over and went back to sleep.

Sometime later, I woke up. The dogs were lying beside the bed watching me, taking turns whining and yawning in intervals, trying to rouse me. I went to move and couldn't. Devlin's arms were wrapped around me, his body tight against my back.

Immediately I was wide-awake. I slowly tentatively looked over my shoulder. One golden eye peered back at me sleepily.

"I suppose you want to move?" Devlin said, stifling a yawn with one hand.

"I need to get up and feed the dogs."

"Fine, just let me wrap up." Devlin released me and pulled the covers up over his head.

"I lived with Danial over a year, and we stayed in hotels sometimes," I retorted, getting up and grabbing some clean clothes. "I'm not going to open the drapes."

"You never know with women," Devlin said from under the blankets. "Sometimes they wake up in moods far different than the ones they ended the night with."

"You're jovial for it being so early," I said, going into the bathroom.

Devlin didn't reply.

I hurriedly showered, then dressed. When I emerged, Devlin was finishing knotting the drape ties together. He turned to me, then went back to the bed and lay down, getting under the covers again.

I fed the dogs, then went to the door to let them out, grabbing my gun on the way.

"Walk around the hotel," Devlin commanded. "Don't leave the parking lot or go near the trucks."

"I won't," I lied and shut the door.

As the dogs did their business, I debated how long I was going to be able to stay in one room with Devlin. Spending the whole day together was right out. And what was the point, anyway? Theo had been in this kind of situation before obviously, and he didn't need me to bail him out. So why stay here waiting? I should get in one of the trucks and leave now for home...

Darkness let out a growl, then Ghost did, too. Both of them were looking over at the edge of the parking lot at a car. Someone was sitting there, in the driver's seat.

"It's nothing," I said reproachfully, moving toward Theo's truck. "Just someone texting or talking on their cell phone."

The car's engine suddenly started. But the car didn't move.

I watched for a split second, then bolted with the dogs for the strip mall. We made it across the street, narrowly missing being hit by a speeding Toyota, then across the parking lot to the chain restaurant. Reaching the bench outside, I sat down and tried to catch my breath. As soon as I had, I ordered some takeout from the window, complete with a big slice of cake. This was no time to be dieting.

As I waited, I petted the dogs and tried to decide what to do. I didn't want to call Terian or Danial; I was irritated they'd trusted Devlin enough to send him to guard me. Yet I didn't want to risk leaving by myself, not when I had the dogs to worry about. There seemed to be no option but going back to the room and waiting for nightfall. Resigned, I paid for my food and went back to the hotel.

The car and man were still there, yet now the engine was off.

I hurried inside and went up to the counter. "Hi. I'm the one who needed to stay an extra night yesterday? It turns out I need to stay tonight, too."

"Room number?"

I gave it to him.

"Your husband called down and already booked another night, ma'am."

Saying the man in my room now wasn't the husband I'd come here with last night was too much. "Thanks," I said quickly. "Do you have some more towels?"

"He asked for them as well and for fresh sheets and an additional set of blankets," the man replied, his tone carefully neutral. "They'll be delivered in a few minutes."

I flushed, quickly thanked him and walked hurriedly back to the room with the dogs. Devlin was waiting there for me, irate.

"I told you not to leave the parking lot."

"I needed some breakfast."

"They have breakfast in the hotel lobby every morning until eleven," Devlin replied, taking my food from me. "You were brainless to risk your life for some chocolate cake."

Livid and trembling with frustration, I slammed out of the room and stalked back down to the hotel lobby, entering the small kitchen/cafeteria. Eyeing the clock, I speedily got some cereal and made some toast from the remains of bread on the counter. The breakfast crowd had all descended like locusts and left. There was only one other man there on the other side of the room, dressed all in black, reading the latest Peter Straub novel as he ate. I thought about asking him if it was any good, but his back was toward me, and I was still too angry over Devlin calling me brainless.

The enraging part was that he was right; I had been stupid to go out by myself and ditch my guard. That carelessness stemmed from my anger at Theo for not being here when I needed him, for having to rely on Devlin for help. After this, I'd be indebted to him. I didn't want to be indebted to someone I hated...who cared even if his eyes were spectacular...

"Ma'am?" the hotel desk clerk called. "Your husband asks if you're done that you come back to the room. He says he misses you."

Son of a bitch. I gave a fake smile to the clerk, tossed my garbage and then started for the room. Walking down the hallway, I noticed fearfully that the man in black was coming after me.

I darted into the room and locked it fast behind me. Through the door came the dim sound of a key sliding into a lock, then a door opening and shutting.

Duh, Sar. He was following you because he was staying in the room across from you. That must be the superstitious salesman. I snorted. He must sell funeral plots, with that black attire...

"How was breakfast?" Devlin asked from the bed. "I put your salad and cake in the small fridge near the closet to save for lunch."

I didn't reply.

"Come back to bed. I have been missing you."

I gave him a shocked look.

"I'm cold," he said easily. "You're warm. I loved snuggling next to you last night."

"I'm a heater for the undead. What a compliment."

"I'm not undead or dead," Devlin said angrily, turning his back to me. "Yet you somehow think you should be regaled as a vampire expert or given compliments?"

He really sounded offended. I didn't care.

There was a knock at the door. Devlin was beside me in an instant, moving me behind him.

"Yes?"

"Towels and sheets, sir."

Devlin gave me a shove toward the bathroom and then opened the door. He took the linens, handed the maid some cash, then shut and locked the door. To my surprise, he then stripped the bed and began to make it.

I went to help him, taking hold of the other side of the sheet. Together we finished the bed, and then he handed the used bed linens to me. "Put these outside the door, please, then go into the bathroom."

I took the linens. "Should I take the dogs with me?"

"They won't mind me undressing. I thought you might."

I flushed, then went into the bathroom. Devlin let out an amused sound as I shut the door. I sat on the toilet for several minutes, until the sounds of him moving around outside stopped. But I didn't move, lost in thought.

I'd been tempted to tell him I wasn't leaving. The odds were good that wouldn't have fazed him a bit, and he would have undressed anyway. I was curious to know what would have happened next. Would he have tried to seduce me? Would he have gotten dressed? Intriguingly, I thought maybe something else would have happened, though I wasn't sure what.

"You are needed, Sarelle," Devlin called.

I went outside to find him in bed again. A heavy cotton shirt was his only visible clothes.

"What?"

"Take my clothes and put them outside the door. I've asked for my clothes to be cleaned today and be ready later tonight."

That seemed excessive since we were leaving tonight, but I did as he asked. "Are you going back to sleep?"

Devlin gave me a considering look. "I don't really need to sleep more than I have already, if you want someone to talk to."

I didn't want to talk to him, but I didn't want to say that. He seemed to be trying to be an actual person instead of the bastard I'd known him to be in the past. I didn't want to ruin it.

"I'm not sure," I said, sitting down on the bed. "I'm sick of being stuck in this room. Even a pay-per-view movie sounds uninspiring."

"Come sleep with me," Devlin said, patting the bed next to him.

"Do you have on pants?" I asked skeptically.

Devlin snorted. "Of course. If I wanted to have sex, I'd have asked you to have sex."

"You wouldn't have gotten far if you had," I said, irritated at his lack of interest.

"I know," Devlin said, a smile curving his lips. "Which is why I didn't ask."

I didn't reply.

"Any man would welcome you in his bed," Devlin said pleasantly. "First you charge me with being a sex fiend, and now you're offended I'm not hitting on you. Why don't you tell me what you want me to say? It will make our conversations much less tense."

"I'm sorry," I said, glancing over my shoulder. "I'm just upset. It seems like ever since I found out Theo was alive I've been on a rollercoaster. I just want the ride to end."

"Life is a rollercoaster," Devlin said musingly. "It only ends when you die."

"I'm not the only temperamental one here. Your happy mood's turned black."

"Touché," Devlin said with a smile. "I'll try to be less morose, if you'll agree to come back to bed."

I got the dogs some fresh water, used the bathroom, kicked off my shoes and then crawled back in to bed with him. I waited for him to cuddle close, but he kept his distance.

Well, I wasn't inviting him to snuggle up to me. "Are you warm enough?"

"For now. But why don't you tell me why you're so upset?"

"Theo's in jail. Elle hates me. I can't touch my son at all. Vampires are hunting me, and I've broken Danial's heart, for starters."

"Theo will likely be out by nightfall. Elle will adjust, and your son will gain more control as he ages. He is already much bigger than he was at birth."

"I'm jealous of you," I whispered. "That you can hold him and I can't."

"You'll hold him soon," Devlin assured. "As for being hunted, you are well-protected here. As soon as you return to Danial's, he'll likely make sure you're guarded night and day." He paused. "As for Danial's heart, it isn't broken, just slashed a bit. The only way to break his heart now would be for something to happen to Theoron." He took my hand in his. "I'm glad you have kept your word to leave him in Danial's care."

"I'm not brainless," I said scathingly. "I know I can't take care of him as Danial can."

Devlin drew me closer, settling his arms around me. "I'm sorry for my insult earlier. It came from worry over you leaving by yourself in daylight where I couldn't protect you. This is my least favorite time of year, when the solstice looms, and the days are at their longest."

"I always loved it," I chuckled. "But then, that was before I spent so much time with people who lived exclusively in the dark."

"Well put," Devlin said, also chuckling.

"Danial plans to go after Manir, but he thinks more attacks will take place even if he does," I whispered, scared. "He's gearing up for war."

"It's already begun," Devlin said darkly. "Danial is doing the right thing. There are several vampires and weres I can think of off the top of my head who might try for Theoron. I'll have my people give him the list. He can send Theo or Terian to stop them before they act."

"That's murder," I said, sickened.

"That's being proactive," Devlin corrected.

"Danial wouldn't compromise himself like that," I retorted. "He's got a strict sense of justice."

"Maybe he won't," Devlin said after a moment. "But he should." He moved back from me.

"Why do you say that?"

"I've been a king, a good one. It's better that a few die to ensure peace."

"The problem there is that you choose who lives and dies on a whim."

Devlin sat up, visibly angry. "It is never on a whim. Sometimes killing one can avert disaster. How many people have to die before you think it's enough? There are many who speak about turning the other cheek. I know from experience it is a rare being that is willing to die for another person's moral stance."

"What about what you did to me?" I whispered, gazing at him and biting my lip.

"That wasn't a whim," Devlin said, dropping his eyes. "That was my bad judgment. Sadly, it wasn't the worst mistake I've made in my life."

"What was?"

Devlin didn't answer. I reached out and took his cool hand in mine.

"When you lead others you must do whatever you have to in order to save your people," he said with a sigh. "Compromising values should matter less than saving lives."

"I agree with you," I said. "If you rule others, you have a responsibility to them above the responsibility to yourself. But even then, I think your family should come first."

"They should," Devlin said in a cracked voice. He swallowed hard. "But the past can't be undone."

I squeezed his hand. "What happened to Danial wasn't your fault."

"Yes, it was," he said softly.

"How is it your fault?" I said curiously, easing closer to him.

"Because I should have known what the thing was when it attacked. I didn't know anything back then, except strategy and tactics. I was too concerned about rising through the ranks as fast as possible, so I could leave my family behind and become someone important."

"What did you want to be?"

"A commander of men, either soldiers or police."

I was surprised that Devlin would want to uphold the law or spend his life guarding others. Yet it made sense. When he'd taken me from my house years ago, he'd insisted on taking me to Danial, because I wore the choker. He was here putting himself in danger now to keep me safe.

"I knew something had attacked a few people on that road in that last month," he continued. "I knew that there was a chance we might be attacked transporting the prisoner. But the road was the quickest way to our destination.

I'd been assured that if I made the journey in good time, I'd get the promotion I wanted, and Danial would get my old position."

"You aren't at fault for what you did. It wasn't for an evil reason."

"Yes, I am," he said despondently. "It was my greed and pride that doomed us."

Carefully, I reached for Devlin and put my arms around him. He tensed at my touch, then relaxed.

"You did the best you could. You aren't damned."

"Yes, I am. You have no idea what I've done."

I shifted uneasily.

"And I wouldn't want you to," Devlin added, his arms snaking around me loosely. "My ends have always justified the means, no matter what they were. I've done great evil in the hope of averting worse evil. Sometimes it worked and sometimes not. Still, it's likely that given the chance to do my life over, I'd do the same things, make the same choices. I'd find myself here, at this same point in time, a fallen king."

"In case you're wondering," I said deliberately. "I'm waiting for you to add into your speech somewhere that you regret everything you did to me while you were king…um, ruler."

"I regret hurting you," Devlin said quickly. "Yet I don't regret coming for you that night or taking you to Danial." He looked up at me. "You might not have gone back to Danial after Theo went missing, if I hadn't. Theoron might not be here. I can't regret any action of mine that led to him being born."

I didn't reply, considering his words.

Devlin laid his head against my chest, and his arms tightened on me slightly. We lay there like that for a few moments, not speaking, then I slipped into sleep.

I woke sometime later when Devlin stirred. According to the bedside clock, it was almost dusk.

"I have only one regret," Devlin said finally, propping himself up on his elbow, his expression intent.

"What's that?" I said, covering my yawn with my hand.

"That it wasn't me you found in your quarry that night," Devlin said, kissing the back of my hand with cool lips. His golden eyes locked on mine, transfixing me, as he drew my hand away from my face.

He was going to kiss me. My lips parted as my breath caught in my throat.

Devlin leaned in close, then froze.

There was a soft click. Both dogs leapt to their feet, growling. The door burst open, and the dogs fled behind the far side of the bed, still growling as Devlin dropped his weight onto me, clutching me tightly.

A brown haired man dressed in a suit and tie ran into the room. He turned quickly toward the bed and fired, the semiautomatic in his hand flashing. Before I could scream, bullets hit Devlin, thudding into his back in rapid succession, the impact twisting him around on the bed. He grunted in pain, gritting his teeth. The dogs began barking loudly, but hung back, afraid of the loud noise and the smell of gunpowder.

The man turned and dashed out. The dogs scrambled out from under the table and ran after him, barking. I let out a scream for them to stop. The door slammed hard, and both dogs pulled up short, growling at the closed door.

"This is why I told you not to go out," Devlin groaned with effort.

Chapter Eight

I eased myself out from under him. "Hold still. I've got to get your shirt off."

I removed it, tearing the bloody cloth. His back was a mass of bloodied flesh. I wadded up the shirt pieces and tried to soak up some of the blood oozing from his many wounds.

"I'm healing," Devlin grunted painfully. "The bullets were normal hollow points, thank God. You don't have to do that."

If he hadn't been here to shield me, I'd be dead. He'd saved my life. I grabbed him in my arms and held him, shaking.

"You're bleeding," Devlin said suddenly. He sat up with effort, then grabbed my arm, extending it in front of me. Sudden pain made me gasp, and tears came to my eyes.

"The bullet went through me and into you," he said. "Hold still."

I bit my lip hard. "What are you going to do?"

"I'm going to pull it out," he said. "It's not very deep."

"No, I—"

"You can't go to the hospital with a gunshot wound," he said, forcibly laying me back down. "Now hold still."

I opened my mouth to protest and let out a scream as he squeezed the wound. Quickly, he put his mouth over it, then came the pressure of intense suction. I whimpered in pain, struggling.

Devlin removed his mouth and spat out the bullet. Then he brought his mouth to the wound again. The pain lessened. I relaxed in relief.

Devlin took his mouth away, then grabbed a large piece of his shirt and wrapped it around my arm. "It won't look like a bullet wound now. Keep pressure on it." He grabbed one of Theo's shirts from his duffel, my keys and my purse and then picked me up in his arms.

71

"My dogs—"

"We have to get you to the hospital. You're going to need stitches."

I didn't argue. I was in too much pain. He carried me outside, then leaned me against Theo's truck.

"Hold onto the mirror. I'll be as fast as I can." Devlin proceeded to check underneath my older truck quickly. Then he got to his feet and started it.

"All set," he said, coming toward me.

"I'm surprised you know to do that," I said weakly.

"Who do you think Danial learned from, Sar?" he said sarcastically, opening the side door for me.

"Don't call me Sar," I said weakly, then began sliding down the side of Theo's truck.

Devlin caught me in his arms before I hit the pavement and sat me in the front seat, moving from under me into the driver's seat. I sagged to lie partly on him and partly on the seat, my movements feeble.

"Stay down there," Devlin ordered, pulling out with a squeal of tires. "There may be someone watching. I want them to think that you're badly injured."

His phone rang. He answered it with one hand, using the other to drive

"Yeah, we're fine, because I was there—" Devlin paused. "Good. Take off. I'll be—"

I blacked out for a second. When I woke up, Devlin was still on the phone.

"Listen, Theo, she got grazed. I'm taking her to the hospital—" Pause. "Suit and tie, 9 mm, black finish. Mid-thirties, brown hair, brown eyes probably. I didn't see. About five-eight or nine."

He hung up and looked down at me. "Theo is out finally. He's going to see if he can track down the man who shot us. He'll meet us at the hospital."

"That's good," I mumbled. "He should fucking kill him—"

I blacked out again. Devlin shook me awake with one hand.

"This is taking forever," I moaned. "How far is the hospital?"

"Another block. Lay still."

"You're just enjoying having my head in your lap," I murmured.

"You'd know if I was enjoying it," he said, grinning down at me. "Your mouth—"

He hit a pothole, jarring me. I cried out, my arm agonizing.

"Hang on!" he said, holding me with one arm. "We're here."

Devlin parked and helped me out. Picking me up again, he hurried into the hospital's Emergency Room, slamming through the waiting room doors with his shoulder.

Devlin went straight to the desk, with me in his arms.

"Can I help you?" the woman behind the counter said. She was late forties, with wire-rimmed glasses and very short frosted blonde hair. The set of her mouth was grim

"She needs emergency help," Devlin said quickly.

"Is she pregnant?" she asked.

Devlin looked down at me in consideration. "Possibly."

"I'm not pregnant!" I said irritably. "I'm bleeding. I was—"

Devlin squeezed me hard.

I paused. Hospitals had to report gunshot wounds. That nice sheriff who had held Theo would be coming to see me, if I didn't watch my words.

"I was burned," I said more carefully. "I was careless with the grill. We were having a cookout on vacation." I rummaged in my purse with my good arm and produced my insurance card and driver's license. "Here."

The woman looked at me skeptically as she took them. "Have a seat, please," she said. "I'll go tell the attending physician you're here."

We waited patiently for a few minutes, though there was no one else in the waiting room. As the time stretched, Devlin grew more and more angry.

"Why is this taking so long?" he said in fury after a half hour. "We have an emergency, and we're being made to wait. What is that bitch woman's problem?"

"This is nothing," I said weakly. "If more people were here, we might have to wait for hours—"

Bitch Woman came striding toward us. "Follow me." She led us into one of the cubicle type emergency rooms, and Devlin helped me lay down on the bed.

"Your name is Sarelle McGarran?" she said, looking at a clipboard.

I opened my mouth to tell her it was O'Connor now, but she cut me off. "This is your husband, Brennan McGarran? The insurance is through him, right?"

Devlin cut me off. "That's right," he said, sliding his hand onto my thigh. "She's mine. Now get a doctor in here to see her."

The woman raised her eyebrows, annoyed. "I'll be right back," she said, glaring at both of us.

"What were you thinking?" I said irritably when she'd left. "If the marriage certificate was filed, they'll know I'm married to Theo."

"Then they might delay in treating you," Devlin retorted. "Theo likely doesn't have any insurance."

"They have to treat emergencies, insured or not. Anyway, they are going to know you aren't Brennan. He died years ago, Devlin. Not to mention you look nothing like him—"

"I wanted her to help you. I don't care what I have to say to get it done—"

73

A female doctor came into the room. She gave Devlin an appreciative glance, then quickly came to my side. "Hi, I'm Dr. Brenda Hanyr. You have a burn? Let's see."

I gingerly unwrapped my arm for her. Devlin stood up and looked over her shoulder.

"This isn't too bad," Brenda said, turning my arm this way and that as I grimaced. "You shouldn't need stitches. I'll give you some ointment for it, though. You'll need to put it on for a week. You should also follow up with your doctor."

I nodded assent.

Bitch Woman yanked back the curtain. "We need to deny services to them," she said haughtily. "This is a fraud case."

"What is the problem?" Dr. Brenda said, concerned but not unduly worried.

"He," she said, pointing at Devlin, "said that he was her husband, Brennan McGarran. Sarelle was once insured under him as his spouse. According to this, though, her husband Brennan is dead, and her current husband is a man named Theo O'Connor—"

"That would be me!" a voice said loudly.

Suddenly Theo was there, pushing his way past Bitch Woman. I reached out for him gratefully. He hugged me eagerly, letting out a deep breath of relief.

"You're her husband?" Bitch Woman said snottily.

"Yes," he said coldly, turning to face her. "The one and only."

She opened her mouth to say something else, and he extended his hand to her, holding a credit card in two fingers. "Put whatever charges there are on this," Theo said smoothly. "My brother here was just being a prankster."

Clearly angry, Bitch Woman took his card and left as Brenda repeated to Theo what she'd said about my arm, spreading ointment on it as she talked.

"I'll make sure it's was taken care of. Thank you." Theo put his arm around me. "Let's go."

We walked to the parking lot. After some discussion, Devlin agreed to drive my truck back to the hotel and then home, and Theo would drive his truck. I was uncomfortable letting Devlin drive my dogs home, but in my condition, there wasn't another option. We got into our vehicles and pulled out of the parking lot, Devlin in the lead in my truck.

"Sar, tell me what happened," Theo said. "Someone attacked the room?"

"You first," I said angrily, crossing my arms.

"I was in jail, like Danial told you. The sheriff here knows me, back from a job I did for Danial—"

"Someone you killed for him?" I said, glancing at him.

He looked squarely at me, then back at the road. "Yes," he said coolly.

I didn't reply.

"He was waiting in the parking lot when I came out in the morning. He wanted to know why I was there, if I was going to rack up the bodies again. So I told him to go and fuck himself, it's a free country, I can go where I like—"

I shut my eyes. In my pining over Theo, I'd edited out some of his flaws, like this arrogance and ardent dislike of human authority figures. Belatedly, I remembered Terian had also been on Theo's Do Not Get Along With List. Hopefully that would change if they had to work together.

"—then he put his hands on me and said he was going to escort me to the county line. I lightly shoved him off me, and he pulled his gun and arrested me for disturbing the peace."

Lightly was likely a relative term. "He threw you in jail for shoving him?"

"He took me to jail, threw me in a cell and refused to give me a phone call. Danial's lawyer called shortly afterwards, and although feet were dragged, they finally released me. They couldn't hold me over twenty-four hours anyway, not without charging me."

"You sound like you have some experience with jail."

"Sar, if you're trying to say something, why don't you just say it?"

I didn't reply. When we got back to the hotel, I got out without a word, Devlin and Theo following me inside.

Devlin paused in the doorway. "Theo, Sarelle, I've got to go feed. Now."

"Take your time," Theo said irritably. "We won't leave until you get back."

As Devlin turned to leave, I went to him, grabbing his arm. He turned back in surprise.

"Thank you," I said, squeezing his hand.

He smiled faintly. "Don't forget your lunch is still in the fridge." Then he left, the door shutting quietly behind him.

"What was that all about, Sar?" Theo said, jealously coating his words like syrup.

"Check the bed and see for yourself," I said angrily, sitting down on one of the chairs and stroking the dogs.

"There are two bullet holes in the mattress. Devlin's blood is here, and so is your blood," Theo said, his voice shaking. He opened his hand, letting a handful of mushroomed bullets fall glittering back on the bed.

"Come and walk with me," I said, grabbing his hand and the dog's leashes.

"Sar, I'm so sorry," Theo said suddenly, trying to hug me. "I thought we were safe. I thought that—"

"No," I said accusingly, pulling away from him and heading out the door. "You didn't think. You got angry, and you shot your mouth off, and you didn't care that what you said might have consequences, both for you and me. If

Devlin hadn't taken those bullets for me, I'd be dead, Theo." I snapped on the leashes, both dogs already whining to get going.

"I understand that," he said, his shoulders slumping. He shut the motel door and took my hand, walking outside with me and the dogs. "I'm grateful to him. If I'd known what he did for you, I'd have offered to feed him myself. I won't fail you again."

"Theo, you didn't fail—"

"Yes, I did. I wasn't there that night they bit you together. You almost died—"

"That isn't like this—"

"Isn't it? You needed me, and I wasn't there. I'm zero for two. I can't let that happen again."

"Then don't."

"I have to admit that you were safer with Danial," Theo said reluctantly. "He protected you for the two years I was away. He never left you in a situation where your life was in danger—"

"Who says I'd leave you even if you told me to?" I interrupted, giving him a kiss.

Theo kissed me back with a groan, his tongue sliding between my parted lips. Quickly, he began to back me against a tree, grinding into me with his hips.

I broke away. "Stop," I said, softening my word with a smile. "We've got to get going."

"You're right. It's not safe here in the open," he said reluctantly. "Come on."

When we got back to the room, Devlin was there.

"Are you guys ready to leave?" he said, looking at his watch. His skin was shining with that luster that meant he'd fed well. "We need to go. The night is wasting."

How had he gotten blood so quickly? Did Devlin seduce women as Danial sometimes had for blood and leave them with nothing but a few kisses? Even if he had regular donors, being what he had been, with his looks, he likely had many admirers … I dropped my eyes, not wanting him to catch me staring.

Theo had already given his assent to Devlin and was cleaning up the evidence that there'd been gunplay in the room, as Devlin carried the bags to the car and checked us out. Before long, we were back on the road.

The trip back was interminable. Happily I slept through a good portion of it, waking finally just outside Binghamton, New York.

"We're almost home," Theo said, glancing at me when I awoke. "Danial called."

"I didn't hear a call," I said groggily. "What did he say?"

"He said that he wants us to come there first, tonight, because he can't wait to see you," Theo said, grimacing.

"Don't you want to see Elle?" I asked pointedly. "Danial is right. Waiting will only make things worse."

"I do," Theo said carefully. "But is this really best, to wake her up to tell her I'm home?"

"At least the hotel didn't call, asking about bullet holes in the sheets."

"Because there weren't any, they all went into Devlin," he grumbled. "Those sheets will be stained, but with luck they'll attribute it to menstrual blood."

I grimaced at him, but didn't reply.

* * * *

We reached Danial's after midnight. Devlin promptly got out of my truck and handed Theo my keys.

"I'm taking off."

"Devlin, I know what you did for Sar," Theo began. "If you need a hand sometime, let me know. I know you have—"

"It's a deal," Devlin said, giving Theo a smile that didn't reach his eyes. "Catch you later." He got into a shiny black Hummer. With a roar of tires, he was gone.

"You really want to work for him?" I asked Theo.

"I pay my debts," Theo said, taking my hand. "Let's go inside."

Ivan met us on the front steps. The dogs ran to him eagerly. "Mind if I walk them?" he said. "I'm sure they could use a run in the forest."

I wished I were going for a run in the forest instead of inside. "Sure," I said, giving him a smile. "Go ahead."

They walked off together toward the fox compound, Ghost and Darkness jumping in eagerness.

I turned to Theo. "Are you ready?"

"No," he said. "I'm not ready at all. I'm terrified."

"You'll be fine," I said, giving him a smile. "Come on."

"What if she hates me?" he said. "What am I supposed to say when she asks why I didn't come back?"

"She's your daughter, Theo," I said, hugging him. "Even if she says otherwise, deep down, she loves you. Just realize that she thinks of Danial as her dad and be prepared for that."

He took a deep breath, then together we ascended the stairs.

Chapter Nine

The front door was locked, so I used my keys. No one came to greet us. There was no one in the great room either.

Danial's door was shut. I couldn't bring myself to knock on the door. As much as I didn't want to face her first, I walked further on to Elle's room, finding her door standing open, the room empty. Danial must have brought her with him somewhere to make sure that when we arrived, Elle wouldn't run into us without him there. I walked in into the nursery, worried it would be empty, too.

It wasn't. Theoron watched me come stand in the doorway with those green eyes so like my own. He was much bigger; he looked almost two already. He was growing faster than Elle had as a cougar.

Never mind what Dr. Camlyn and Danial had said. It was past time I held him. What was I afraid of; I'd been bitten before with much larger fangs. If I waited much longer, my son would become a stranger to me.

I crossed quickly to the crib and reached out to him. Quickly, he bared fangs and bit my finger, sucking hard. Carefully, I picked him up and held him to me, letting him drink. He curled his hands around my hand, holding onto it tightly as he fed.

"Will he stop?" Theo was at my side, watching apprehensively.

I didn't answer.

Like magic, Theoron stopped drinking after just a few swallows. He stared at me, then recognition flooded his eyes. He smiled and opened his arms, reaching eagerly for me.

"Yes," I said, tears in my eyes. "I'm your mom."

I hugged Theoron, and he put his arms around my neck. Sinking into the nearby rocking chair, I stroked his dark hair. He had a full head of it now, not just a few wisps.

Theo went to his knees beside the chair, watching Theoron. Theoron turned and looked back at him calmly. He seemed so reserved, so much like Danial.

"He's beautiful." Theo looked at Theoron as if he was the most precious thing he had ever seen. He'd once looked at Elle that way, after she had just been born. It was enough to melt any woman's heart.

"Do you want to hold him?" I offered.

"Can I? Won't he bite me?"

"No, Danial said he only bites humans." I looked down at Theoron. "Theoron, this is Theo. You were named for him. He's going to hold you now."

Theoron looked at Theo. Theo put out his hand for Theoron to smell. As he had before with Cia, Theoron smelled Theo, noted he wasn't human and didn't bite him. Carefully, I handed off Theoron to Theo, who took him gingerly, as if he might break.

Emotions assaulted me, watching Theo cradle my son. There was a horrible sense of loss, knowing that because of Theoron, Theo would never hold a baby of his own...I shut down the mean thought angrily, chastising myself.

"He's asleep," Theo whispered. "What do I do?"

"Give him to me. I'll put him back."

Theo handed Theoron to me. I hugged him once more before I put him in his crib on his back. He slept on, a peaceful expression on his face.

"He's so beautiful, Sar," Theo said longingly. "He's the best of you and of Danial."

"We should go," I said reluctantly. "We still have two more people to see."

"We've got to find them first."

Theo and I left the nursery and went back to the great room. Steeling myself, I knocked on Danial's door. There was no reply.

Opening it revealed that all of my things were missing. Even the dresser I'd used was gone. Saddened, my eyes fell on the sheets. To my surprise, they were the same ones I'd had on the bed when I'd left over two weeks ago.

When I'd come to stay with Danial, I'd started doing our laundry, mostly from the embarrassment of knowing Mary would otherwise see some of the sexy lingerie I wore for Danial in the wash. By the overflowing hamper visible through the open bathroom door, no one had told Mary her laundry services were again needed. Immediately it became clear just how wrecked Danial had been by my leaving that he hadn't already talked to Mary about this.

Guiltily, I began stripping Danial's bed myself, oddly thinking that I'd just done this very thing with his brother a day ago.

"What are you doing?" Theo asked gruffly.

The comforter didn't need washing. If it still smelled at all like us, I wasn't about to take that away from Danial. "Stripping the bed. It needs it."

"Mary can do that," Theo said curtly. "You don't have to."

"I don't mind," I retorted. I carried everything to the basement and set the sheets to washing.

"I'm heading over to the fox compound," Theo said, still gruff. "Someone's got to be there. I don't like finding no one here this time of night."

"Go ahead," I said, settling into the couch. "I'm crashing right here."

Theo left. I lay down on the couch and closed my eyes, glad finally to feel safe again. Sometime later, the light touch of cool hands woke me.

"You looked so at peace I didn't want to wake you." Danial smiled down at me.

"Thank you for sending Devlin," I said gratefully. "He saved my life. I wouldn't have expected it from him."

"He's reprehensible, both morally and otherwise," Danial said matter of fact. "But usually when I've needed him the most, he's come through."

"He took a lot of bullets meant for me. One went through—"

"I know," Danial soothed softly, stroking my hair. "Devlin called me from the road. He told me everything that had happened." He turned angry. "Theo hasn't given me his official version yet."

"Where is Elle?"

"On her way here," Danial said, sitting beside me. "I thought it better to get this over with, especially as she's expressed concern about Theo making her go live with you both."

"I want you to know, I'm sorry for putting you through this—"

"I appreciate that," he interrupted. "But tonight isn't about you and me. It's about Elle and setting parameters for her immediate future." He hugged me tightly, then whispered in my ear. "I have only one thing to say, as a gentle reminder—if there comes a time you want to come back to me, I'll welcome you with open arms. No conditions, no expectations." He drew back to look me in the eyes. "No time limit."

"Danial, don't wait for me—"

"Sar, I'm in love with you. I'm not going to fall out of love with you easily. You are married to Theo now, and I respect that. But that doesn't change how I feel. If enough time passes, I might take a lover," he said, then paused dramatically. "But I'll love you, just you. And while you live, I will love no other."

"Been watching *Excalibur* much?" I said with a smile.

"Devlin quoted that to me on the phone," Danial said, annoyed. "I thought it was some poetry he'd been reading. I thought it was appropriate. I didn't know it was from a movie—"

"Danial, I'm teasing. I've always loved that line and I'm moved you said it to me. The only thing peculiar is to put Devlin and poetry in the same sentence."

"He's a great lover of poetry," Danial said curtly. "But we have much more important matters to discuss, wouldn't you say, Theo?"

"Yes," Theo answered, coming to my side, "Where is my daughter?"

"Safe with Cia," Terian said. He had somehow come in silently, unnoticed, and was leaning against the wall behind Theo. "She's explaining that Sar's going to live with you, that you've married. When Cia's confident Elle's ready, she'll bring her here."

"It will be some minutes," Danial said. "Which is good."

"What do you want?" Theo said, folding his arms across his chest, his expression severe.

"Your help," Danial said. "I need you. Elle and Theoron need you."

"Same position?" Theo said, looking at Terian pointedly.

"Terian is aware and has agreed," Danial said, glancing at me. "Sar's safety is a key priority. There are people after her—"

"She told me there was a man named Alphonse that sent his men to kill her and laced the trap with bait she was not likely to refuse. Probably he was behind the attempt today, too."

"You're most likely right," Danial said. "The problem is we don't know who this Alphonse is. Sar doesn't remember him or the insult she supposedly gave him."

"Like I told her, I don't know an Alphonse either," Theo said.

"Then we are back to square one," Danial said with irritation.

"Maybe not," Theo said. "I have the spent shells and bullets from the hotel. We still have that contact in ballistics to see if the gun was used in another shooting. According to Devlin, the guy was a professional."

I hadn't known Danial had contacts within the police department.

"I'll call him tonight," Danial said. "Terian, there's a man listed as Bill/Ballistics in my rolodex on my desk. Get the bullets and shells to him tomorrow." He cut his eyes to Terian who nodded.

Danial looked back at Theo. "You didn't answer me, Theo. Yes or no?"

"You didn't answer me, Danial. I need to be here for Sar, so what happened at the hotel doesn't happen again."

"Terian will come with me on all my trips. You will stay here and guard the children and Sar when we aren't here. She will have to come here for those times, no exceptions, until we have Alphonse removed as a threat. Since she still wants to help with Solutions, Inc., there shouldn't be a problem keeping her safe while letting her retain most of her old routine—"

Now the reasoning behind Danial's odd question on the phone became clear. "It will also give me some extra time with the kids," I interjected. "I'm for it."

Theo didn't look pleased I was siding with Danial. "That's all fine if Terian and I are here together. But I can't guard both of the kids and Sar when you're gone, Danial. I'm going to need more backup," he said finally.

"What do you suggest?" Danial said.

"We need brute force, physical or magical, in case we get attacked the way Terian reported you were a few days ago. Terian was able to take them out, but if I'd been here alone, I'd most likely have been hit once at least. And I wouldn't have been able to fight the werebears, not ten at a time, without a lot of help. That means at least two more weres—probably more like four or five—either as strong as me, or we need another sorcerer."

Danial sighed and looked at Theo. "I don't suppose more guns would help?"

"You know how it is," Theo said, a cheerless smile on his face. "The drawback of new technology is that the advantage is always a temporary one. No one in our world expected the explosive bullets gun, and it gave us a needed edge. But anyone with money can get their hands on one now. Speaking of which, Danial, we need to get you a vest to wear on all your trips. Anyone after little Theo is going to know you have to die before he could be successfully taken."

"Agreed," Danial said after a moment. "I'll look into it and also armor for you. Do you have any recommendations for possible new guards?"

"I don't," Theo replied. "Do either of you know anyone we could trust who doesn't already work here?"

"I have a friend," Terian said slowly. "She might be convinced to help."

"I have a few names," Danial said.

"Give me the names tonight, and I'll set up at least one interview tomorrow," Theo said to Danial. He turned to Terian. "Ask your friend if she'd interested, and if she's for real, give me her name and number."

Terian nodded.

"Make the call now please, Terian," Danial said, staring at Theo. "Use the kitchen phone."

Terian cast his eyes to meet mine briefly, then went into the kitchen. Danial turned to Theo, his eyes red tinged, full of restrained fury.

"Theo, I want an explanation of what happened yesterday morning that led to you being arrested."

"I messed up," Theo said guiltily. "It won't happen again. I've apologized to Sar—"

"Do you think that covers it?" Danial said, seething. "Your apology?"

"Look, you and I both know Noah. He was going to arrest me no matter what I did—"

"Don't make excuses for yourself!" Danial hissed. "Sar and you would have been home yesterday night if you could control your temper. She wouldn't have needed a guard if you'd have been there for her. But you had to smart mouth the police when they came asking questions. If you'd gone along with them, you'd have been back at her side in a few hours and not spent the night in jail."

Theo was angry, but his words were calm. "You're right. All of it," he said finally. "What else do you want from me besides an apology?"

"Did you know that Samuel intended to kill you?" Danial asked.

"For what?" Theo retorted. "I didn't say anything, despite his I'm-a-vampire-and-you're-a-piece-of-shit-were-attitude." He looked at me for support.

"He's right," I said as gently as I could. "Samuel heard your possessiveness of me in your voice, that night he confronted us in Europe. It didn't matter what you said. He thought we'd been having an affair behind Danial's back. He made a scene at Danial's party later that year—"

"It was more than a scene," Danial growled. "Samuel knew you and Sar were lovers, Theo. He has been Europe's Ruler for centuries, and he would have killed you that night if he had found you. You're standing here, married to Sar, only because he thought you were already dead."

Theo glared at Danial. "What the fuck do you want from me?"

"I want you to start thinking with your head and not your heart," Danial, replied. "None of us can afford that, least of all your wife." He paused. "Or our son."

I wanted to leave suddenly. This was too awkward. But leaving would only draw attention to myself.

"I know he's the first dhamphir," Theo said slowly. "What's the word?"

"Nothing so far," Danial replied, worried. "Not officially. I think that most vampires think it's a hoax, something I made up to give me time to solidify my position as Lord—"

"Ruler," I corrected, then blushed as Danial and Theo both turned to look at me.

"In any case," Danial continued, turning back to Theo, "I need you focused. I'm not saying I expect you to protect Theoron over Sar. But I expect you to protect them equally."

"Of course," Theo said angrily. "How could you even—?"

"Because I'm his father," Danial stated. "And because of the history the three of us have. We have a rocky road ahead to make this work. I need to know I can count on you, that there isn't anything you feel for him but acceptance."

"I accept what happened when I was gone," Theo said. "All of it. I wouldn't be working for you again if I didn't." He moved to stand before Danial. "But there's something besides acceptance—there's love." He took a breath. "He's beautiful, Danial."

"He is," Danial said proudly. "We can—"

Terian came back in. "She said she's interested, though she's not sure if you would think she's qualified."

"Give us some background," Danial said, all business.

Everyone sat down.

"Her name is Monica Remmin. She is human, but she is a sorceress. She can do most minor spells and is working on learning larger ones. She has talent. She's just young and not too experienced. I met her while she was on vacation. We spent some time together."

Was Monica an old lover of Terian's? He'd never mentioned a woman friend, at least to me.

"How is she qualified?" Theo asked. "We need power, not simple illusions."

"Monica does healing, for one," Terian replied. "Something I can't do at all. And her illusions are just like reality."

Danial and Theo looked skeptical. Terian understood immediately that they were not impressed and began to elaborate.

"Say we had another bear attack like last time. Monica could make them believe they were in a fog. They wouldn't be able to see anything and would have to move slowly. The foxes could take them out then by themselves, with the tactical advantages of knowing the lay of the land and being able to see normally."

"Have her come here," Danial said, after a moment. "We will meet with her and decide then."

"Sounds good to me," Theo said. "What names do you have, Danial?"

"There were several weres who wanted your job after you went missing. I ended up hiring Terian and so never contacted them. Even though it has been a year and a half, the pay we'll offer should garner interest. I'll get you the resumes."

"What are they?" Theo asked pointedly.

I gave him an odd look, curious.

"All are worthwhile candidates: a golden eagle, a vulture and a grizzly bear."

"Male or female?' Theo asked.

"Female for the eagle and vulture. Male for the bear," Danial replied.

"Is the bear one of Devlin's?" Theo asked.

"Yes, he was," Danial replied. "He said Devlin was scaling back his operations."

"Did he say why he was being let go?" Theo said, his eyes narrowing in suspicion.

"No, but Dev's done this before, on and off," Danial said, as if it wasn't important. "He decides someone isn't ruthless enough and gets rid of them."

"Is the bear one of the ones present that night Sar was attacked?" Theo growled.

There had been only two bears left standing that night, when all was said and done, the ones that had held down Devlin, that he'd later fed on. The rest had been killed.

"No," Danial said. "He's young, just out of high school. He's got brute force, but not much skill, not yet anyway. I can't remember his name."

"What about the eagle?" Theo asked.

"Erin is older, and she's held a similar position to this one for an ally out West. You remember David?" Danial said.

"David Helm, Ruler of the state of Colorado?" Theo asked.

"The same," Danial said in reply. "David speaks highly of her. She wanted to move back here because she just split up with her mate, and it was messy. But her work attitude, he says, is all professional."

"I think we should forget the vulture," Theo said to Danial. "Their character, as a rule, is down there with reptiles, not to mention it might be some relation to Garrett's dearly departed flock. Let's interview the three others. If they interview well, we'll hire all of them. We need that much strength until Theoron gets bigger."

"Hopefully by then he won't need anyone to protect him," I murmured.

"Hopefully." Theo turned to Terian. "Do you have any thoughts?"

Theo's question was really a peace offering. In a few moments, he'd retaken his place at Danial's side completely, effectively cutting Terian out of the decision-making process.

Oddly enough, Terian looked relieved instead of annoyed. "I'm good with everything you both said. I'll be back shortly with Elle. Cia just texted me that Elle's ready."

"Good," Danial said, "I should have just enough time to send out some emails requesting interviews." He ascended the stairs and went into his study.

Theo came close, slipping his arm around me. "I'm glad this is going so well."

"Danial seems to have been busy plotting everything out."

"It's a sound plan," Theo said. "Do you want something to eat? I'm going to have a snack before she gets here."

"You go ahead. I'm not hungry."

Theo went into the kitchen. A few moments later Ivan walked in with the dogs. Ghost and Darkness came in and lay down, stretching out on the floor, breathing hard. I gave them each a pat, thanking them for being good on our trip and promising Cheweez when we finally got home. As I was getting to my feet, there came the loud beep of the washer cycle finishing. Descending the stairs, I put the sheets in the dryer and then put the load of laundry in to wash.

The front door suddenly slammed with a crack.

Elle yelled "Mom?"

"I'm down here," I yelled. "I'll be right up."

I was at the top of the stairs when Elle threw herself into my arms.

"Mom! I've missed you! Are you back to stay?" she said, hugging me.

"We both are," Theo said from behind her.

Elle froze. "What's he doing here?" she said to me coldly.

This didn't sound like Cia had done her job. "Elle, this is your father, Theo. Theo, this is your daughter, Elle."

"He's not my father!" Elle said with scorn. "Danial is."

"Danial will always be your adoptive father. No one wants to change that," I said. "But like it or not, Theo is your father, and you will respect him."

"Then where was he all this time?" she cried in solid accusation.

"Elle, come here please," Theo said, coming closer to her.

She ran away from him, but Theo was faster. She got only a few steps, and he caught her, falling to his knees to grab her around the waist.

"No!" she screamed. "Don't touch me! I hate you! You left us alone, and Mom cried every night. She was never happy! Even her smiles had tears in them!"

"Come here!" Theo yelled, struggling with her.

"No! I wish you had stayed wherever you went! I want you to leave!"

"I don't care what you want!" Theo growled, grabbing hold of her. "I want to hold you. I haven't held you since you were a few days old."

Though she fought, he was stronger than she was. She screamed and cried, but he just held her to his chest, stroking her hair. She tried to bite him, and he growled something to her, the tone stern, but loving. Elle went utterly still and promptly burst into tears. Theo held her tightly, again making more soft growls, tears running down his face. She hugged him back, burying her face in his neck.

I wiped my filling eyes, then felt cool arms embrace me.

"I'm glad I didn't miss this," Danial whispered. "But I must ask, how is your arm?"

"Much better," I said, giving him a smile. "It hardly hurts at all."

Danial reached down and lifted my arm, removing the bandage. "That's because it's almost completely healed," he said anxiously.

I examined my arm, my eyes widening in shock. As he'd said, the wound had scabbed over. Now it looked like a shallow scratch that was at least a few days old.

"It's a sign of being partly turned, isn't it?" I said, raising my eyes to his.

"Yes. Devlin may have added to that when he sucked out the bullet, but most of it's my doing. You'll heal faster than normal until you return completely to human." He held me tightly to him, stroking my back. "I'm very glad you're all right."

"Mom, Dad, is it okay if Theo and I go for a walk?" Elle asked.

Theo closed his eyes and swallowed hard.

Danial and I turned to Theo and Elle, moving apart. "Of course. Go ahead," I answered.

They quickly left by the front door, growls and loud purrs barely audible over the sound of four legged feet running fast.

Danial turned to me. "It will be dawn soon, Sar. I—"

"Hold on!" I said in panic, running downstairs to get the laundry. After I started the clean wet laundry drying, I brought the clean sheets upstairs and made the bed. Danial watched me, leaning against the doorframe, as he had so many times in the past. When I was done, I turned down his side as I always had and then turned to face him.

"There you go."

He looked away. "Go, before I say things better left unsaid."

I put my hand on his shoulder and squeezed it. Then I left, shutting the door behind me.

Wiping away a tear, I went out to look for one of the foxes to escort me home. I was happy for Theo and Elle, but I wanted more than anything to gather the dogs and just go home. Sleeping for the next few days sounded like the best idea in the world. Theo could join me at our house when he was ready.

Beside the front door, I found a small box marked with my name. Curious, I opened it. Inside were the silk shifts Danial had gotten me so long ago. The colors were faded now, having been worn so many times. I took them out of the box and put them in the garbage. Part of me wanted to keep them, but I had other things to remind me of Danial. Underneath was the black velvet robe. I considered for a moment if it was safe to take, then decided yes, I'd take it. Most of the rest of the box was older worn clothes and I tossed them out. On the bottom of the box was the red dress, the one Danial loved so much. Wrapped in it were my gold fox earrings with the ruby eyes.

I folded the dress carefully and then rubbed it on my skin, so it would have my scent, at least for a while. Then I walked downstairs to a corner of the basement, where Danial had moved his memory boxes after I'd come to live with him. Opening the topmost gray plastic box and without looking in, I placed the dress inside. It was Danial's as surely as if he owned it. I'd never wear it for anyone else.

I took the earrings into Elle's room. We'd had her ears pierced last month. I left them on her vanity with a note:

Elle,
I want you to have these. Danial gave them to me our first Christmas together. As my daughter, they would have come to you anyway someday. But I think it's more fitting you have them now. Wear them with pride and always remember you are loved.
Your Mother, Sarelle

I walked back into the great room, exhausted. I'd driven all day, been up all night, and now it was probably close to seven a.m. I stretched out on the couch, draped the velvet robe over me as a blanket and fell asleep.

Terian shook me awake, though he was careful not to touch my arm. "Sar?"

"I'm here," I said with a yawn. "Are Theo and Elle back? What time is it?"

"Early afternoon. No, they aren't back yet." He sat beside me. "I just wanted to make sure you knew before you left that the funeral for Demetri is tomorrow at noon."

"Is Suri still missing?" I said, concerned.

"Yes," he said, depressed. "We've heard nothing."

"So they took her?"

"Yes," Terian said darkly. "And we don't know why."

Chapter Ten

"Terian" I asked tentatively, "Could Suri have been in on the attack?"

Terian gaped at me, aghast.

"I'm sorry to make it seem like she wasn't trustworthy. She was. But why take her, if there wasn't some reason? Manir's men killed Demetri. They didn't take him."

"I assume that they wanted her for intel of this place. After their attack failed, they grabbed her to make sure the next attack wouldn't fail." Terian paused. "As a woman, statistically, she'll crack more easily than a man would under pressure. I'm not saying that's what I think," he added hurriedly. "Suri is pretty tough. The toughest female we have. She won't tell them what they want to know."

I flushed, embarrassed. "I feel like a jerk now. I shouldn't have suspected her."

"No, you're right. There may be more going on here. If Suri just shows up, we need to keep a close watch on her. She may be planning to turn on us in exchange for her life."

I'd considered Suri a good friend, but he was right. "Okay."

"You're troubled," Terian said, studying me. "So am I. This never stops."

"What never stops?" I said, looking up in confusion.

"The killing," he said in repugnance. "The attacks. The violence."

"This is how things are—"

"I don't want to become like Theo," Terian interrupted. "There is something in him that likes this—the constant tension and the sudden violence. He has a taste for it, Sar," Terian said, holding my eyes. "And so does Danial."

"That's not true of Danial," I said. "And as for Theo, he is what he is, and I've been grateful for that more often than not." I looked at him searchingly. "But why are you so riled up? You protected Elle, Theoron and Danial during the attack. You did your job. That isn't a bad thing."

"This isn't me, Sar," he said, starting to pace.

"Maybe it is," I replied. "We need you, Terian. If you don't want to use guns—"

"I'd rather use a gun than magic to kill any day," he said, disgusted. "It perverts the magic to use it for evil means."

"Even killing to protect loved ones?"

"Even then. Killing by magic is evil, according to everything but the black arts."

There was no point arguing if he was drawing the line to include self-defense. "What are you saying? Are you going to leave?"

"Not until Danial has hired someone we can trust," Terian said, resigned. "I won't leave you or the children unguarded, even if I have to kill hundreds of attackers."

That made me feel better, though his unhappiness worried me. I tried one last thing. "Terian, what if you talked to Theo about this? Danial said that he didn't like killing any more than you do when he started this job. Maybe he could help you come to terms with—"

"I don't want to come to terms with it, Sar. It's not who I want to be," Terian said forcefully, blackness oozing from him. He stalked out, the front door slamming behind him.

Terian was way off base about Danial, but Theo…about Theo, he was right on target. My new husband had been happy carving out west. I'd brought him back to this violent life, and he was taking to it like he'd never left. He wasn't going to be a carpenter now; he was going to work for Danial, and I'd be washing blood out of his clothes again soon. He'd killed over five people just on the way here.

But what he was wasn't his fault. And if Theo was just a carpenter, he would never be able to protect me as he had…

Danial opened his bedroom door, the noise breaking my thoughts.

"Did you hear all that?" I asked.

"Yes," Danial said heavily. "This is all we need, a demon with a moral crisis."

He was still dressed. "I thought you were sleeping?" I said, looking him up and down.

"I was waiting to talk to Theo. He and Elle still aren't back?"

"No, but they may be gone hours. This is the first time he's seen his daughter."

"I'm glad they've made peace," he said, sitting down beside me. "Children should have good relations with their parents."

I leaned over and kissed his cheek. "Elle isn't the only one who made peace today. I held him, Danial."

Danial turned to me instantly, gripping my arms frantically. "You held him? He didn't bite you?"

"He bit me," I admitted. "But then he recognized my blood or something and stopped. He knew who I was. He held his arms out to me and smiled."

"I'd have given anything to see that, Sar," Danial said enviously.

I got up and held out my hand. "Come with me."

Danial took it and followed me in to Theoron's room. Theoron was asleep, but when I entered, he awoke. I crossed to his crib and reached down to him. Danial was at my side, apprehensive.

"Theoron."

Theoron bared his fangs at me when I picked him up, grabbing my hand with his fingers. After he scented me, his fangs receded. As before, he smiled at me and held his arms out, putting them around my neck.

I cradled him against me. "You're the quietest baby I'd ever heard of and the most serious. It must be from Danial. You sure didn't get it from my side of the family."

Danial hugged us both. "He's just happy, darling. There isn't anything that needs to be said. This moment is utterly perfect in its silence."

I leaned into him, blissful. Danial was right; we were complete now in a way I'd never felt before; him, our child and me. A sudden longing to tell Danial I'd stay—that I'd made a mistake marrying Theo—slammed into me. This was where I belonged. I was half turned at least, close to becoming vampire. Danial had the power to take me the rest of the way. With a word from me, he would do it, and then the three of us could be together forever…

"I love you," Danial whispered. "Both of you."

I took a deep breath and held my words inside, praying the feelings would pass. Danial didn't need any mixed messages from me after what I'd already put him through.

"It's dawn," Danial continued. "It's time for sleep, my son." He took Theoron from me, kissed him and then put him back in his crib. He extended a hand to me. "And time for us, too."

We walked back out to the great room, hand in hand. Danial sank down on the couch then and pulled me onto his lap. "Want to wait with me?"

I nodded. He lay down on the couch, and I lay down beside him. I was asleep in moments, the familiar cool presence of his body next to mine comforting me, telling me I was safe and loved.

* * * *

Hours later, the front door slammed. My eyes snapped open, and I sat up as Elle bounded in. "Mom! I had so much fun! Theo is teaching me all kinds of things! We climbed a tree, and he showed me how to drop onto a deer—"

I swung my gaze to Theo, who was smiling widely, and breathed an inner sigh of relief.

"— then we ate some, and it was so good! Nineva never showed me I could climb a tree!"

"Elle, remember, that was because he was still healing. He probably wasn't strong enough to climb a tree—"

"Theo is! He's super fast and super strong and—"

I was happy, but her loudness was too much for me with only a few hours' sleep. Danial, ever the more patient parent, pulled Elle onto his lap. "You, Miss, have lessons to attend, or have you forgotten? Your tutor is waiting for you at the fox compound. You have enough energy clearly."

"Shit! Sorry, I forgot!" Elle said.

I let out a gasp. Danial raised his eyebrows at Theo, who was looking out the window very hard at something.

"Elle, that's not a word you should use," I said, trying desperately to think of words to use that would discourage and not encourage.

"Why not? Theo said it."

Theo kept looking out the window, only now he looked very guilty. Well, he was her father. It was time to start being one.

"Theo will tell you why it's not appropriate, Elle," I said pointedly.

"Why can't I say it if you said it?" Elle asked him.

"Because, um..." he said, grasping at straws. He looked at me desperately.

I returned his gaze, waiting. I wasn't helping him. I'd been after everyone to watch their language around her, and now he'd taught her to swear the first time he spent any time with her.

Danial was amused, but managed to keep a straight face.

"Why?" Elle repeated, folding her arms across her chest and pinning him with her eyes.

"Because," Theo said finally "it isn't a good word. Crap is a better word to use, Elle."

With that analogy, I was glad he hadn't taught her to say the F-word instead.

"Will you use the word crap instead?" Theo said, looking down at her. "For me?"

"Do I use it the same?" Elle asked him.

"Yes," he said.

"I'd better go," Elle said. Then to make her point, she looked at her watch, said "Crap!" and ran out the door.

Danial immediately roared with laughter, and I chuckled.

"It wasn't funny!" Theo said, irritated. "It slipped out, and then she wanted to know what it meant, and when I told her what it meant she wanted to know why I was using that word to express frustration. I was trying to explain—"

Danial and I had tears coming out of our eyes, we were laughing so hard. With difficulty, I reined it in.

"It's okay, Theo," I said, wiping my eyes. "It's not any worse than the time Elle caught Danial coming out of the shower and wanted to know why his body looked different than mine."

"Not my finest moment," Danial admitted, a smile on his face. "But with children come embarrassing moments." He cast his eyes to Theo, his smile fading. "You haven't asked, so I assume that you know Elle prefers to stay here and live with me."

"Sar indicated that she would," Theo said reluctantly, sitting down beside us. "But I expect her to come and stay with us on occasion. I'm hoping there will come a time when she might want to live with us."

"That time might come," Danial said slowly. "But you must accept that it also might not." He got up and crossed the room, then turned to face us. "As for her staying with you and Sar, I advise you to leave that until she's more comfortable with you. It goes without saying you are both welcome to visit her anytime she isn't sleeping, eating, or being schooled. At Elle's agreement, of course."

I'd dreaded this moment, knowing Danial's protectiveness. "That's all fine," I said quickly, not looking at Theo. "We all want what's best for Elle. I'm happy she's accepted Theo. After her reactions to most other strange men, it's like a miracle."

"I agree," Theo said stiffly. "Were you able to set up any interviews?"

"The interviews are set up for next week," Danial replied. "We've got one coming on Wednesday and the other two on Thursday."

"I'll be here," Theo said. "I assume that if you're not traveling I'll be working days?"

"For now," Danial said, glancing at me. "Terian is thinking about leaving."

"That's just great!" Theo exploded. "We'll have to hire them all, regardless of whether they're a good fit—"

"It's okay," I said calmly, putting my hand on Theo's shoulder. "Terian said he wouldn't leave us unprotected. You have time to make a good choice."

"Or so he said," Danial added. "That probably depends on how many more people he has to kill himself."

Theo gave Danial a dark look. "I need today and tonight to sleep. I'll be back here early tomorrow to work on tightening defenses."

"Good. Sar, what days are you coming in?" Danial asked.

"What days do you need me most? I need to straighten out my house and get some planting done, but I'm flexible."

"Come in with Theo tomorrow and Friday," Danial said. "Then maybe every other day? So long as the work gets done, it doesn't matter to me. But I want you either here with Theo or else with at least two of the foxes at your house."

"That sounds fine," I said, giving him a smile.

"You aren't the only ones needing sleep," Danial said, coming to hug me goodbye. "I'll see you tomorrow night." He drew back a little, then paused. Quickly, he darted in and kissed my cheek. "Be safe."

My first impulse had been to kiss him, too. Old habits die hard. "I will. Goodbye."

Danial went into his bedroom and closed the door.

Theo moved for the door. "I'll meet you out there."

"Ghost! Darkness!" I called. Both dogs came running.

Theo was already in the truck waiting by the time I came out with the dogs.

"Sar, are you okay to drive?"

Shit. I'd forgotten we had two vehicles. "I'm okay. Give me a minute."

I got into my truck with the dogs, started the truck and then followed Theo home.

* * * *

I woke up when Theo's hands slipped up from behind me to cup my breasts, squeezing gently.

"How are you this fine morning?"

"Much better. You?"

"Rested. And I took care of the pets already." He pulled me close for a passionate kiss.

* * * *

At seven, Theo said grudgingly, "We need to get going. I should be there by eight."

Making a Herculean effort, we managed to make it to Danial's by eight a.m. Theo headed to the fox compound, and I went up to Danial's office.

I'd been gone only a few weeks, but the work had piled up. By noon, I'd prepared a list for Danial of all the calls he needed to return, filed the stack of paperwork needing filing, called back the people who needed information I could provide and straightened out his desktop. Handling email would have to wait until afternoon.

Terian's desk was neat. Knowing all the time he spent in his lab, I was curious if he'd ever really used it, other than to return calls. Danial had always treated him with respect, but Terian had been more of a guard and less of a friend and partner in business. Maybe if Theo hadn't returned, their friendship would have progressed...

The office phone rang, startling me.

"Solutions, Inc." I answered. "This is Sarelle. How can I help you?"

"That depends on your enthusiasm," a velvety voice said.

"Good Morning, Devlin," I said pleasantly, recognizing his tone.

He didn't reply, and the silence stretched.

"What is it?" I said, trying to be nice.

"I need to speak to Danial obviously," Devlin said, drawing out the words slowly.

Could he be any more annoying? "He's sleeping. Do you want me to wake him?"

"Sar, you must have returned to brainlessness in the two days since I saw you. I know Danial's sleeping. I should be sleeping, too, but instead I'm having a tiresome conversation. Now go wake him up."

"I'll get him," I said pleasantly, restraining my urge to kill him. I punched the hold button before he could say anything else and then brought the phone downstairs to Danial's door.

"What is it?" he said in a sleep-filled voice, as I put my hand up to knock.

"Devlin, for you," I said.

"Tell him I'll call him back," Danial said, muffled.

"He said it was an emergency," I said hesitantly.

Danial swore, then came to the door in his robe a few seconds later. "Wait here, please," he asked, taking the phone. He shut the door.

He must want me to take the phone upstairs when he was done. I settled into a nearby chair and waited. As the minutes passed, I tried hard not to ease back into the softness of the cushions that were calling me.

The next thing I knew, Danial was nudging me awake.

"Sar," he said softly, sitting down beside me. "You should have stayed home if you were that tired."

"I'm okay," I said, shaking myself. I stood. "Do you want me to take the phone back upstairs?"

"Yes," he said, "And then come back down here to me."

I did as he asked. When I was again sitting beside him, he spoke.

"I apologize for Devlin. He's in a foul mood."

"Don't worry about it," I said, standing. "I'm used to taxing clients—"

"Are you so eager to escape my presence?" Danial said softly.

"I'm uneasy," I admitted, sitting down in a chair across from him. "It's hard for me not to touch you casually. Things are going so well I don't want to cause problems."

"No touch you could give me would be unwelcome," Danial said with a smile. "But my intent was not to seduce you, just to ease your mind about that werebear who's going to interview with us."

"Go on."

"I mentioned to Devlin last night via voicemail that I was thinking of hiring Brian, requesting any feedback Devlin had on his performance. Dev called back this morning to say Brian was green, but he should be a good fit here. The general idea was that Brian wasn't bloodthirsty enough, so Devlin was encouraging him to find other work."

"Why is it always about violence with him?" I said with a grimace. "Does he really want everyone who works for him to be like he is?"

"Simply put, yes," Danial said. "Some of that is from having so many enemies, which I understand much better as a Vampire Ruler. The rest is just control—Devlin likes controlling people. He wants to know that no matter what he asks his people to do, that they'll do it, without question or hesitation. Knowing Dev, Brian's lucky he's managed to retain his job this long."

The night Devlin had attacked my home, his bears hadn't cared that I was being taken against my will, or that they were smashing up my house. I shivered, thinking of the worse damage they would had done if Devlin had ordered it.

"In the course of the conversation I asked Devlin if he knew an Alphonse," Danial continued. "He said he only knew one, Sar, a notorious gang lord based in Washington, DC. This guy has a lot of money from his dealings and acts respectable, but underneath the veneer of civility, it's all corruption, fraud and racketeering."

Not a surprise he was based in Washington then.

"Devlin asked where you could possibly have run into him. I said we didn't know."

"Danial, I've racked my brain over this. I can't remember meeting him at all. I was never introduced to an Alphonse—"

Then it suddenly hit me. It was true I had never been introduced to an Alphonse or even to an Al. But not all the men who'd shown an interest in me had told me their names.

Danial was instantly crouching before me. "Sar, what is it?"

"What color eyes does this man have?" I said slowly. "Are they hazel?"

"Devlin didn't say. Why?"

"That night in Switzerland, Samuel rescued me from a man with hazel eyes who didn't want to take no for an answer. I always assumed he followed me and Tawny to the hotel from the café down the street. But maybe he was staying there himself. He never said his name—"

"That was Al?" Danial said, furious. "Your insult to him was being faithful to me?"

"It must have been him," I said, shivering. "Samuel embarrassed him, sent him running. For a man used to power, that probably infuriated him. Al couldn't punish Samuel; he's too powerful and well protected. But I'm not."

"You are ... protected by me, Sar. I'm powerful, and this hunting of you is going to stop."

Danial had been going to say I was his and had caught himself at the last moment. I managed a small smile.

"Go get the phone again if you would, please," Danial said. "I'll call Devlin back and tell him what you've said. He can help arrange a meeting between Al and me to get this settled."

"That would be a relief," I said, standing up and heading for the stairs. "We have enough to worry about."

"Sar, don't forget the funeral is tonight for Demetri," Danial called after me. "Sunset."

"Terian told me it was at noon," I said, stopping and turning toward him.

"Yes, but I wanted to attend," Danial said. "They pushed it to tonight so I could."

"I'll have to go and let the dogs out," I said, trying not to sound put out about it. I wasn't irritated, as it was only right that Danial be able to attend. The change of time just meant an extra trip home and back.

"Make sure then that Terian or Theo goes with you. Or maybe I should send one of the foxes to walk them. It would be easier."

"No," I said, returning and handing him the phone. "They're all grieving. I'll get Theo or Terian to go with me."

"As you will." He took it into his bedroom.

Feeling hungry, I went into the kitchen and made myself some soup and toast. After eating, I headed back upstairs to work on the email. After three hours, I was close to done.

Danial's business was mostly done over the Internet—despite him not having a website for Solutions, Inc.—which made for a lot of emails. I printed the most lucrative looking jobs and left them in a neat pile for Danial to review. The others I made a quick written list of, stressing the main information given for each, to see if they were of interest to him.

As always, there were a few pleas for revenge and justice, which I'd starred and left for last. They weren't subtle: one woman came right out and wrote in her email that she wanted a mercenary to find her daughter's killer. All these I responded to, saying we did just corporate work, and we were sorry we couldn't help them. But when I finished the replies, I forwarded all the starred emails onto Devlin's e-mail address, marked a question mark in the subject field. If he wanted the jobs, he would contact them directly.

Regrettably, as always, there was some hate mail, too. Most of it was simplistic, like the vengeful man who'd lost his job after Danial caught him using company money to take his mistress—i.e., secretary—on trips and buy her expensive presents. Now he was jobless, his wife had left him, and he was probably going to lose custody of his children. His long email was full of self-pity and anger. Instead of replying to tell him he'd brought it on himself, I just printed the email out and put it in the hate mail file. Danial kept an ongoing record of anyone who threatened to harm him, his reasoning being in case an attempt was made on his life, it was better to have a ready list of possible suspects.

I checked the clock and saw it was nearly four. Time to grab Theo and head for home.

I walked to the fox compound, enjoying the beautiful day. The sun was shining, the birds were singing, and everything was wonderfully green and alive. The dogwood trees that poked out here and there on the forest's edge were beginning to bloom. The first trilliums were out, their white and purple heads peeking out of the forest floor.

When I arrived at the fox compound, there was no one in their common room, a large open room with a fireplace at one end. A few groups of couches and chairs were scattered here and there, with decorative plants. Most of them were likely below resting after coming off the night shift. Most bedrooms were in the basement, with a few—like Theo's once had been—on the main floor.

Elle suddenly ran into the room, chased by a shrieking Aran Jr. She evaded him, narrowly missing a houseplant and darted right into my arms.

"Mom!"

"There you are," I said, hugging here. "I figured you were sleeping in this morning."

"I got done with classes early. Bill says I'm making great progress."

"Good," I said. "We—"

Aran grabbed hold of Elle. "You're it!" He shrieked with joy and then ran. Elle chased him out of the room, where they almost knocked over Cia.

"Hey you!" Cia said, grabbing him up. Aran Jr. shrieked again, laughing and wiggling.

"Hi, Cia," I said.

Her face broke into a smile. "Hi," she said, then turned to Elle. "Why don't you take Aran Jr. and put him down for his nap now?"

"Okay," Elle said happily, and she led him away.

"She had lunch with me and Jr.," Cia said haltingly. "Danial said to get her used to that, so she wouldn't miss you as much."

"I'm sorry," I said guiltily. "I never meant—"

"Whatever you meant, you're not going to be living here now," Cia finished gently. "I'm going to miss you, but I'm not going to condemn you. Theo being alive was a shock to us all."

"I needed to see him," I said. "I couldn't *not* go to him once I found out he was alive."

"I'm just glad he's back. The attack earlier this week scared me. Now," she said, a gleam in her eye, "Tell me all the sordid details."

I laughed and told her about going to Wyoming and finding Theo, mentioning Aspen.

"Sar, you had to know he was going to find someone," Cia said, looking at me like I was naive. "Even if it was just physical."

"It wasn't," I said. "They were going to move in together."

"But he chose you," Cia said firmly. "Why are you even upset?"

"He was happy, Cia. Was I right to drag him back to all this?"

"It doesn't matter if it was right. It matters that he wanted to come. He married you almost immediately, and it was his idea. How romantic," she said, sighing.

"It was," I said proudly. "It was almost magical."

"Has Danial spoken to you privately?" Cia asked.

"About what?"

"About you and him. It's obvious he's come to terms with you leaving, but all of us foxes are worried—both about him and about how this threesome is going to work."

"He seems to be taking things well. But even if Theo hadn't been found, I would have most likely had to go away for the summer on Dr. Stephen Camlyn's orders. I was turning vampire, Cia."

"I know," she said softly, her words sending shivers down my spine. "You started to smell differently. Not a lot, but enough that I knew something was up. We all noticed, Sar."

"Why didn't you say something?" I said shrilly. "Danial and I didn't notice it until Stephen read us the riot act."

"What could we say, don't heal her?" Cia said quietly. "Danial didn't do it on purpose. Those first months you were pregnant he had to give you his blood for healing."

"I know that. That pain in the ass Lust made sure of that."

"You probably couldn't have had Theoron without being half turned," Cia said. "Most women who get pregnant with a vampire's child die, or so I heard."

"I know. Danial told me."

"Then why are you upset?" Cia upbraided me.

"Because I didn't notice it happening. I didn't even consider the possibility," I said finally, closing my eyes. "And because I don't know how long it will take me to go back to normal."

"Does it matter?" Cia said. "The problem's solved. You're with Theo now, not Danial. You won't be giving him any blood, or taking any of his, or bedding him."

I blushed, and she laughed.

"Has he made any vampires?" I asked suddenly. "He never talked about it with me. And he was so adamant about wanting that power."

"Yes," Cia said, looking uncomfortable. "Just one though."

"Who?"

"It was an accident," Cia said. "A few days after the night Terian and Theo rescued you and Danial became Ruler."

"What happened?"

"He was feeding from a woman, one of his regulars. He'd fed from her a few days before and taken a lot. He needed a lot of blood in those first few days, either from missing you, or the blood exchange with Devlin. The woman came back a few nights later, again to give him her blood. She'd been able to do that before with no problem. She was very strong and healthy. Again, he took too much, and this time she lost consciousness. Without thinking about it, he gave her some of his blood to heal the wound. She woke up and kissed him, and in the kiss he felt her fangs."

"What happened?"

"It was terrible." Cia paused, sorrowful. "She was so happy, Sar. She said she had always hoped for it, and now he'd finally turned her. She said she wanted to be with him. That now she was like him, they could be together forever. Danial apologized to her. He said that he hadn't meant to do this to her, but that he'd help her to embrace her new life. Then she saw that he didn't want her the way she wanted him."

"What did she do?" I said breathlessly.

"She attacked him, and in his anger, he threw her away from him into the nightstand downstairs, breaking off all the legs. She attacked him again with one of the table legs. When he stopped her from putting it through him, her momentum put it through her instead. She died in his arms, choking on blood."

"God, that's awful." The women who gave Danial blood were more to him than food. He didn't love them, but they weren't disposable.

"He hasn't made another vampire since then, at least that I know of," Cia said quietly.

Trying to think of a new topic, I suddenly remembered why I'd come. "Is Theo here? I have to run home with him for the dogs and then get back here for the funeral."

"He's in the inside shooting range downstairs," Cia said. "With Terian."

Great, I would be lucky if they weren't shooting each other. "Thanks," I said, rising. "We need to get moving, so we can be back in time."

"Tell me what days you'll be here next week. I'd like some kitchen time, if you have a few hours to spare. It's been a while since we spent time together like that."

"It's a deal," I said warmly, giving her a hug. "I missed you, too."

I left the common room, went down the stairway and turned, going past the walk-in freezer that housed the emergency meat rations. Danial built it in case of siege, or so he'd told me. Disturbed by its possible impending use, I walked down a few doors to the basement shooting range. The light was on above the door, indicating that the range was in use.

I pushed the intercom button and said "Hello, Theo?"

"What is it, Sar?" he said back through the intercom. A shot rang out behind his voice.

"I need to run home, to let out the dogs. The funeral is in a few hours, and I need to change, too. I need either you or Terian."

"Okay, wait for me there," Theo said.

I waited, and a few seconds later, he appeared.

"Ready to go?" he said, irritated.

"If you are."

He gave the door a dark look. We walked outside, heading across the grounds toward the truck.

"What's the matter?"

"I was trying to talk some sense into Terian," he said gruffly. "He said that he didn't like how he felt after killing. I told him it would get easier over time."

That was a little chilling. But I'd said the same words to Terian, hadn't I? They'd sounded like truth when I'd said them, but I understood now why Terian had recoiled from me as he had.

"And?"

"And he said he didn't want it to get easier, Sar. That he didn't want to be cold like me."

Asshole. "He hasn't seen what you have."

He stopped still and faced me. "What are you saying, Sarelle?"

"He hasn't lost anyone because he failed to kill."

"Danial told you about Rebecca?"

I hadn't known her name, but that didn't matter. "Yes," I said, reaching out for his hand.

Theo rubbed his forehead, then clasped my hand in his. "Let's go."

The trip back to our house went quickly, my mind moving from problem to problem. Theo also was quiet, lost in thought. Ghost and Darkness picked up our mood, and were anxious on their walk, needing reassurance half the time and discipline the other half. After giving them their Cheweez, Theo and I changed into black clothes. I had just let Cavity in and was taking a breath to call for Theo when something moved in the bushes behind the house. Something big.

"Saaarrrr," the wind whispered.

"Hello?" I said hesitantly. "Is someone there?"

A gangly figure stumbled from the trees, shambling toward the house.

"Theo!" I screamed. "Come quick!"

Theo was at my side in three seconds, his gun drawn. "Suri," he said quickly, then took off at a run. I followed him.

Suri lay on the back lawn, badly hurt. Her front half was human, but her bottom half was only partially transformed. We made it to her side, and Theo grasped her torso, turning her over.

She was moving feebly.

"Saaarrr," she rasped, looking up at me weakly.

"We're here," Theo said to her, his eyes scanning the nearby trees. "You're safe."

"Not...safe," she rasped at him, then looked at me. "Saarr..."

"Stay with her," Theo said, leaping to his feet. "I'll check to make sure no one is around." He moved into the trees.

"Saarr," Suri said again and choked. Some blood ran out of her mouth.

"Shh," I said, grabbing her hands in mine. "Don't try to talk. We'll get you to Danial's."

"Too laate," she said, managing a painful smile.

I grabbed her close to me and hugged her, tears of frustration and panic leaking from my eyes.

"Don't trust," she gasped urgently, her eyes suddenly wild. "Don't trust..."

"Suri, save your strength," I urged. "Hold on!"

Her eyes looked into mine with desperation and then, suddenly, they went blank. Her body abruptly relaxed in my grip.

"Suri!" I screamed. "Suri!"

"Sar!"

Theo loped across the lawn to me, kneeling down beside us. He put his fingertips on Suri's chest and then her neck. "She's gone," he said softly.

Chapter Eleven

Theo gently moved me back from her, then picked up Suri's body and carried it into the garage. "Get a tarp. We've got to get her to Danial's unseen."

I got a tarp from the paint supply cabinet and helped him wrap her in it. Together, we lifted her into his truck and secured the tarp with cargo netting. I brushed back tears at tying my dead friend down like a load of wood, but Theo was right, we had to get her to Danial's. If someone saw her in her half-changed state, there'd be a media frenzy.

After hurriedly locking the house up tight and setting the alarm system, Theo and I drove to Danial's, my hand tight in his the whole way. By the time we arrived, it was dusk.

Theo went directly to Danial's bedroom and knocked on the door hard. "Danial, Suri's dead. She showed up at Sar's badly wounded—"

Danial came out at once, dressed in a black silk suit. "What happened?"

"I heard her," I said, wiping my eyes. "She was in the backyard, hurt badly."

"She'd been shot multiple times, likely tortured," Theo said. "She'd probably been there most of the night, too weak to move. When she heard Sar calling the cat, Suri used the last of her strength to try to make it to her."

I broke down crying. Danial grabbed me quickly, holding me in his arms. "Shh, sweetheart."

"Suri was shot close to Sar's home," Theo growled. "The wounds were from an explosive bullets gun."

"She went for Sar's house because whoever took her probably had the routes back here watched," Danial said to Theo as he patted my back. "Did she say anything?"

"She was hurt too badly to transform fully," Theo said gruffly. "It was hard to understand her words. Sar might have heard more than I did."

The growling wasn't just grief; Theo was upset I'd embraced Danial and not him. "She said we weren't safe," I said, wiping my eyes and stepping away from Danial. "She said not to trust."

"Not to trust who?" Theo and Danial said together. They glanced at one another and then back at me.

"She didn't say," I said raggedly, grabbing the nearest box of tissues. "She died."

Danial called Terian from his cell phone. "Terian, it's Danial. Can you move earth quickly?" He paused. "Then we need another grave, as fast as you can make it."

Danial shut his phone and put it in his pocket. "Theo, will you help me with her? We'll have a double funeral," he said heavily.

"You're going to ruin your suit," Theo said, glancing at Danial. "I can carry her."

"She died trying to warn us. My suit can be cleaned or tossed out," Danial said flatly and headed outside. Theo and I followed him.

Together, they carefully lifted her out still wrapped in the tarp, then Theo helped Danial heft her. He carried her to the graveyard, Theo and I following.

There were a few graves scattered here and there, marked with carved wood or rock, but not many. In the center of them was a massive maple tree, easily a hundred and fifty feet high, its branches spread in a canopy over them. The graveyard wasn't a churchyard; it was just a secluded spot in Danial's forest about a half-mile or so from his house. He had taken me there once, when I'd asked about Lander and then later on for Theo's funeral. Some of Danial's fallen guards had families. In those circumstances, the body was sent home, and a simple memorial service conducted here. But for others, like Lander and Theo, Danial and the other werefoxes were the only family they had, and his was the only home they knew. He had once told me that they belonged here where someone who knew them would remember them.

Discreetly, I looked over at Theo's headstone and saw it had been removed. Unbidden, my eyes lingered on the other graves, looking for the grave of the woman Danial had accidentally turned. Then my eyes found Terian. He was standing with his back to us beside a freshly filled grave with a headstone on one side, his left hand outstretched. On his other side lay a deepening hole, a tornado whirling the dirt up and out to deposit it in a neat pile nearby. As I watched in wonder, the last of the earth fell in clumps and the whirling air dissipated into nothingness.

Terian put his hand down at his side and turned to us. "I've told the others she's dead."

Danial nodded to him. "Thank you. Let me put her in, then we'll cover her. She would not have wanted to be remembered as she looks now."

Theo jumped lightly into the hole. "Hand her down to me."

Danial lowered her in carefully until Theo had hold of her. He laid her down in the hole and then Terian grasped his hand and helped him out. Together, the four of us pushed in enough dirt over her to cover her. Once we had, Terian used magic again to redeposit the earth, filling the grave. As the last dust sprinkled down, the foxes began to appear.

Terian turned to Danial. "I'll be at the house guarding the children with Cia."

Danial nodded, and Terian walked off quickly toward the house. As he did, the last of the foxes assembled.

Ivan stood up before all of us, fighting tears before he even spoke. "Demetri was my pack brother," he managed finally. "Suri was my friend and lover. I loved them both. Seeing them together tore me apart, but I wanted them to be happy. I know that in the brief time they had together that they were. It is fitting that they rest here, side by side."

He knelt by Demetri's grave. "Farewell, brother. The world is a colder place for me now that you are gone. But I take comfort that you are at peace and that Suri is with you. I will see you again."

He did not go to Suri's grave. I surmised that was not because he cared for her less, but that her loss was so new.

After a minute, he got to his feet, to stand in front of us again. "I have fallen," he said.

"Our sister and brother have fallen," everyone said back. I bit my lip awkwardly. They hadn't done this at Theo's funeral. Theo put his arm around me, whispering it was okay that I didn't know the right words.

"I have left you," Ivan said.

"They have left us here in this life to go on before us," everyone said, Danial and Theo included.

"Yet I am still with you," Ivan said.

"They are still with us in our hearts and our memories."

"Until we meet again, remember me," Ivan intoned, tears running down his face.

"We will remember you, Suri. We will remember you, Demetri. We will see you again when the path of our life ends at The Forest's Edge. Dwell forever there in spring until we rejoin you. Be at peace."

Tears were streaming down my face, and I wiped them with a tissue. Everyone was crying, the sound of sniffling and blowing noses frequent. I handed a tissue to Theo to wipe his eyes and then turned to Danial. He was already using his own handkerchief. Taking my hand, Theo led me back toward the house, leaving the others behind.

"Shouldn't we stay?" I asked.

"No," Danial answered, coming behind us. "Now the foxes will shift and run in the forest, all of them together. It's tradition." He paused. "Theo, did you want to go? Sar can stay with Terian and me, if you'd like to."

"No," Theo said. "I'm not a fox, and this run is really their tradition. They would welcome me if I came, but they won't be sorry I'm not there. Besides, we need to get home. I won't feel calm until I'd checked over the house and grounds."

His tone was stiff, but whether from jealously or grief I couldn't determine. I kept silent.

* * * *

The ride home was hushed. Worry and fear hung over everything, even my grief.

Theo checked the house over carefully inside before he let me go in. "Go ahead in," he said finally. "Lock the doors, all of them. It may be an hour or two before I come back. I want to find her trail, if possible. It may point us to what direction she came from."

"Do you want me to fill the tub?" I ask tiredly. "Maybe it will help us relax."

"I want you," Theo said possessively. "I feel like death has been hanging over us since we got back. I need you, Wife. Do whatever you like, but please don't go to sleep."

"I understand that completely," I said, giving him a smoky look. "If I'm asleep, you had better wake me."

Theo shot me a quick smile, then headed off into the brush. I let the dogs out, got them ready for bed, locked up and then hurriedly ran the water and lit some candles.

Theo was right; we'd been under a dark cloud since we'd made our way back from out West. We needed something to make us feel hopeful, something special... An idea dawned suddenly. Yes, I'd wanted to change the sheets anyway!

I hurried to the cellar, pulling out a plastic storage box. I'd ordered a complete bed set of green satin back when Theo and I were together. It had come too late that horrible summer he'd been taken to use, and I'd left them in storage ever since, unwilling to use them with Danial. They would be perfect.

The set was still in the original packaging. I hauled the bag upstairs, made the bed up and then dumped the dirty sheets in the laundry room. Returning to the bedroom just in time to shut off the water, I stood back and admired my effort. The satin glowed, almost shimmering in the candlelight. There was only one more thing needed for perfection: an outfit. I went to the closet and hastily dug out the matching satin nightie, stripping off my clothes and slipping it over my head. It fit well, to my relief. I stripped it off and left it on the bed, grabbed

106

my discarded clothes and put them in the hamper and then eased into the hot tub, letting out a sigh of pleasure.

Theo came in a minute later. Without preamble, he stripped off his clothes and sank into the water. "Ahh," he groaned. "This is great."

I turned the jets on for us, and we sat back in the water, relaxing. Soon, my tight muscles gave up their tension to the pounding water. As soon as they had, I got out carefully, lifting myself with my arms. Grabbing a towel, I dried myself off, unbinding my hair.

"Why are you leaving?" Theo asked grumpily.

"I'm not going far," I said, smirking. "I'll be right over here, when you're ready."

Theo was already rising up from the water as I turned from him. I had time to slip on the nightie and then he was kissing me, his body still wet from the bathwater. He pushed me down forcefully, kissing me hard, his tongue exploring my mouth. His erection pressed against me, trapped between our bodies. Then he moved suddenly, trying to thrust into me and the silky satin comforter slipped off the bed, carrying us with it to the floor to land in a tangle of arms and legs.

Theo grunted something.

"Are you okay?" I asked, moving off him.

He rolled his eyes at me. I laughed and got to my feet.

"What the hell kind of sheets are these?" he growled, picking himself up off the floor.

"Satin," I said sheepishly. "I thought you'd like them."

"Not if we can't have sex on them," he said, frowning. He reached toward the bed and, with one movement, ripped the top sheet off and threw it aside. Most of the pillows fell off too, landing on the comforter.

I had one moment to feel disappointed, and then Theo pushed me back onto the bed, moving his body atop mine, his kisses feverish. His hands roamed my body, stroking, squeezing, caressing. I let out a moan as he bit me gently, then raised my pelvis, to make it easier for him. With one plunge, he was inside, moving fast, groaning with each thrust. I groaned in pleasure and sought his lips, the taste of him suddenly irresistible.

He rolled me on top of him. "Tell me you're mine," he growled up at me.

"I'm yours," I moaned to him softly, moving fast.

"Yes, you are," he growled again, wrapping his arms around me.

Our panting was loud, our movements possessed, frantic. Too slowly, the climax built. I strained harder to gain it, not caring that my pleasure was marred by slight pain. Suddenly I was there, the orgasm breaching my mind, overpowering it. I screamed Theo's name, and he shuddered under me. Before I stopped moving, he rolled me over and thrust so hard and fast there was pain. I jerked in discomfort, whimpering, but he seemed to like that, kissing me harder. Then he roared out my name, digging his fingers into me as he emptied himself.

Theo pulled back from me immediately. "Did I hurt you?" he asked, worry in his eyes.

He had, but not badly. "I'm okay," I said automatically.

He rolled off me. "Go check, Sar. Please."

I went into the bathroom, closing the door and grabbing a washcloth. Wetting it, I examined my pelvic area. There was soreness and mild bruising, but that was usual with Theo. Unusual and more disturbing, I was bleeding. As I washed, I wondered if this was my period returning. Dr. Camlyn had said my period might take a few months to return after having Theoron to get back to its normal cycle. If it was my period, then it was a good month early.

Shaking off my trepidation, I went back out to Theo. "I'm okay. There was some blood, but I was expecting my period to start any day. What we did may just have started it."

Theo held me tightly. "I'm sorry," he said with reluctance and a trace of fear. "I usually hold back with you. I'm strong enough to hurt you easily, if I don't."

I almost told him that Danial had also torn me a few times when he'd lost control, and I'd been under The Lust but held back, knowing the comparison would not be soothing to him. "Did you not hold back this time?"

"My control slipped a little," Theo said.

My uneasiness became real fear. Danial had been enraged; the damage he'd done had been provoked and——disgustingly—wanted. Theo had just gotten carried away in the moment.

Suddenly it came to me this wasn't the first time; I'd bled after he'd had me in cougar form, too.

"You're afraid," Theo said hesitantly. "I'm sorry. I didn't mean to hurt you."

"I know that," I replied. "But I need to know how much of your strength you hold back."

"Why?"

"Because how can you enjoy sex if you don't lose control?"

"I'd rather be careful than hurt you."

"Are you going to break my bones? How much holding back are you doing exactly?"

"Are you jealous of Aspen?" Theo said suddenly. "Because she could take anything I'd do to her? Don't be."

I hadn't been, but him saying her name brought it back in an all-consuming wave. I shut images of them out of my mind. "No, but I need you to make love to me and this time to not hold back."

"No," Theo said, biting his lip, his eyes yellowing.

"I'm partly turned, remember? I healed a gunshot wound in record time. Besides, lots of bodybuilders and very muscular men have sex with women and don't damage them."

"You sure you want this?" Theo asked, his eyes searching mine.

"Yes." I kissed him fiercely. "I want you right now."

Theo kissed me back very hard, then growled softly. He bit me hard, unexpectedly, on the front of my neck, his teeth closing around my jugular and a mouthful of skin. I cried out, going motionless. He didn't break the skin, only held me with his teeth as he got into position over me. Shaking in anticipation, he thrust inside and began to move, pumping like a jackhammer.

Initial discomfort quickly became pain. I squirmed under him, his growling loud in my ears, his breathing ragged. I tried to draw breath and couldn't, his weight pressing me into the mattress. I made a choking sound, and Theo released my throat, still moving frenetically. He kissed me hard and then bit me again, on my right breast. Aggressively he pumped harder, my breast in his mouth. Abruptly Theo let out a roar. I relaxed suddenly, thinking him done, but instead he strained harder, his body pounding mine recklessly, his recurring roaring almost deafening.

Pain became burning agony. I let out a scream, thrashing, and then he screamed, letting loose a long wavering primitive cry. He convulsed on me, still screaming, and I felt him come, his penis contracting rapidly over and over as his hot semen spurted free. He collapsed down onto me, then fell over onto his side, still uttering soft cries, his body twitching.

I was afraid to move. I was afraid to look. But I had to.

My eyes roamed Theo and my lower body. We both had blood on us, but it wasn't all over, just in the expected places, coating our sexual organs. There was a lot of it, though.

As I got up to get a washcloth, a sharp pain hit me, making me gasp. Carefully, I shuffled slowly to the bathroom and got a washcloth. Wetting it with warm water, I cleaned myself off. Under the blood, there were some new bruises. They didn't look serious. I was more worried about whatever was hurt inside.

I put on a pad and underwear and went back to Theo carrying a fresh wet washcloth. He was still lying on his side, twitching. I cleaned the blood off him, making him gasp and convulse again in pleasure. I put aside the cloth and stroked his side, amused he was so reactive. He jerked under my hands, moaning softly. Pleased I'd made him near comatose with pleasure, I cautiously slipped into bed beside him.

* * * *

Theo was gently shaking me. "Sar, wake up."

"What is it? God, it's two in the morning—"

"Tell me you're okay."

"I'm okay," I said sleepily, then reached for him. Aching pain hit me, startling me awake.

"You're hurt," he said guiltily. "I found the bloody washcloths."

"I'm fine," I said, trying not to move at all. "I checked myself out afterwards, and everything was okay. I expected to be sore." I gave him a triumphant grin. "What's important is I rocked your world."

Theo closed his eyes, and a tremor went through him. "You did. It was so good to finally have you without worrying about how hard or deep I was thrusting." He opened his eyes. "But I should have worried. You're a mass of bruises. I'm sorry—"

"I will need a while to recover," I interrupted. "But you don't need to apologize to me. I asked for you to do what you did."

Theo carefully covered me up and lay down beside me. "Get some sleep. I'll be right here if you need me."

* * * *

When the alarm went off, I opened bleary eyes and reached for it. Letting out a gasp, I stayed where I was. Everything hurt except my arms.

Theo got up, shut off the alarm and dressed. Then he turned to me. "Do you need me to help you up?" he asked, offering me his hand.

I reached for him, wincing. "Yes, just so I can get up."

"No," he said, gently lowering my hand. "You need to stay here today. Rest, maybe stay in bed. I'll arrange to be home early, to take care of you," he said, again guilty.

"I'll be fine—"

"You can barely move."

Anger flooded me. Pushing aside the pain, I got my feet on the floor and stood. "I'm fine, like I said. Yes, you were rougher than I liked. But I can take a lot more than you thought."

Theo studied me. "You aren't as hurt as I was worried you would be," he said finally.

"I might not be able to take everything you are," I said carefully. "But I can do probably eighty percent."

"What are you saying?"

"I'm saying let's work up to my limit when I'm healed."

"You don't have to—"

"I want to," I said firmly, kissing him with my bruised lips and trying not to wince. "I loved hearing you come so hard, knowing how good it had to feel. I want to see you like that again."

He sat down beside me and hugged me gently. "I don't deserve you."

"We deserve to be happy together," I said firmly. "We are going to be happy. I never want to be apart from you again."

"I feel the same way," he said, kissing me. "So I guess you're stuck with me."

After Theo took care of the pets, he left, admonishing me to stay in bed and rest. About ten minutes after he was gone, I carefully got out of bed and went in to take a shower. I'd be damned if I stayed in here all day. At the least, I'd take the dogs and go sit outside in the sun.

My pad was full of blood, but again, that was normal. I tossed it in the garbage, then took a long shower, winding my hair out of the way so it wouldn't get wet. If I really felt bad and needed to lie down later, I didn't want it wet and cold on my back, making me feel worse. The warm water helped my aching body, relaxing my sore muscles. When I was done, I dried off and surveyed the damage.

Not too bad. I had a bruise near my mouth and another two on my neck, the one over my throat darker. There were fingerprint-sized bruises here and there on my body and a hickey of sorts on my breast. Whatever the pain inside me had been, it was gone.

The phone rang. I answered it.

"I knew you wouldn't stay in bed," Theo grumbled. "Are you feeling better?"

"Much better," I answered. "The hot shower worked wonders."

"Well, relax today. Also, please make an appointment to see Dr. Camlyn as soon as you can."

"For what?"

"We both still need to be checked for STDs, just in case. But really, I want to know what he says about you." He took a breath. "I want him to check you inside."

"Theo, I'm sure you didn't damage me and anyway—"

"I want him to tell me that you might be able to still have my child," Theo blurted. "Or else tell me it's impossible."

I was floored. "I most likely can't," I said slowly. "He already said so."

"But you're healing on your own now. Like you said, being partly turned accelerated your healing abilities."

"Theo, you said it didn't matter—" I said hesitantly, my voice breaking.

"It doesn't. But we've been having unprotected sex since the moment we got back together again. What if you are healed and I get you pregnant? I don't want a surprise pregnancy."

Shock flooded me. He was right. Again, being stupid, I hadn't even though about that possibility.

"If we have a child, I want it not to be an accident," he continued tenderly. "I want you to know if it's possible and to only have one if you want it."

Hearing his eagerness, there was a sense of foreboding: if I got pregnant, he'd want me to have the baby. After all I'd gone through with Theoron, I wasn't sure I wanted that. I'd better find out sooner than later if that were possible. "I'll call today. Is there a better day for you?"

"Whenever he can fit us in, Sar. As soon as possible."

"Okay," I said. "I'll call you back shortly."

"Talk to you then."

I hung up and called Dr. Camlyn's office. By luck, he'd had a cancellation and would be able to see us on Friday at eight. I thanked his secretary and then called Theo. He picked up after the first ring.

"Sar, did you get an appointment?"

"This Friday," I said. "Eight p.m."

"That'll be fine. I'll tell Danial that you'll be in Monday. He said yesterday that you didn't have to come in Friday anyway."

"Drive safe."

"I will."

After hanging up, I sat for a little while, trying to sort out my feelings about Theo, Danial and babies in general.

Theoron had given me some feelings I'd been unprepared for. It had deepened my love for Danial and his for me. We were less possessive of each other than we had been, more sure in our love for one another. It boiled down to knowing there was a part of him that was completely mine in Theoron and that no matter what happened, that was never going to change.

Part of me wanted to have Theo's child, to make him happy as I'd made Danial happy.

However, as last night had just proven, I was mortal. There was bound to be some problems with a were pregnancy, just as there had been with a vampire pregnancy.

No. I had two children. I didn't want to die having another, not even for Theo. If I was healing, I'd either have an operation to ensure sterility or go on birth control.

When I got up, I forgot to be careful and again, a sharp pain within bent me over. I straightened carefully and took a deep breath. Bitterly, I told myself that I only needed to remember this moment to know I was making the right decision.

* * * *

After spending the first half of the day resting and thinking, I made some chicken soup from scratch and then pumpkin pie with canned pumpkin. After that was done, I began sewing a new bed for Darkness. Despite that both turned out well, my mood was sour. The initial feeling of happiness and triumph I'd had this morning had oddly turned to bitter resentment and frustration during the day. When Theo returned after his shift, I didn't greet him with the welcoming smile he was used to.

"It smells wonderful in here," he said, taking off his shoes.

I didn't reply, working hard to ladle the soup into bowls.

Theo grabbed me gently around the waist. My back was to him, yet I smelled his scent, that smell of forests and earth and sunshine. I began to smile and then stopped.

"What is this?" he said, looking tentatively at the soup.

"Chicken soup with rice," I said.

"You didn't have to," he said gently.

"Why don't you take a shower?" I said bitchily. "By the time you're done, I'll have the table set."

"I'll shower and be right back," he said, then kissed my cheek and left.

By the time I had dinner on the table, he was back, his hair still damp. He tried the soup before I even sat down. "This is good," he said with a smile, appreciative.

His earnestness mollified me somewhat, and I managed a smile. "Thanks."

Theo had a few helpings to my one and then asked for a piece of pie. He had smelled it, even cooling out of sight in the fridge. I brought him a piece, which he ate in a few bites. He got up, then came back to the table with another large piece. I wished silently that I had his metabolism. Then again, I didn't work out for an hour every other day with three hundred pound weights.

I got up to take his plates, but Theo deftly held them away. "I'll clear. You are to go sit down and rest."

After he'd put everything away and the dishwasher was murmuring, he sat down on the couch with me. "How are you feeling?" he said, concerned.

"I'm okay. The bleeding stopped."

His eyes widened. "You said it was your period."

"There's no point in getting upset," I said, exasperated. "Dr. Camlyn can tell us both Friday what's safe and what isn't. We can't be the only were/human couple he knows of."

"Okay," he said uncomfortably, checking the TiVo. "There's nothing recorded. Do you want to watch a DVD?"

"No," I said, taking the control from his hand. "I want to talk to you."

"Are you going to tell me what's wrong? You're angry."

"I'm not," I said wearily. "I've just had a busy day, and nothing seemed to get done fast enough. I don't like not feeling a hundred percent." I paused. "But I do need to ask you something."

"About what?" he said warily.

"Nothing bad," I assured him. "I just have a question to ask you, a kind of moral puzzle."

Theo gave me an odd look. "Is this some kind of game?"

"No game. I just want to know what you think."

"Okay. Ask away."

"Say you're a leader or a prince. You have a bunch of people you oversee. You have plenty of food and money, but there's a great evil coming. If you fight the evil, it will either destroy you utterly or at best, kill a lot of your people. You can choose not to fight and save your people, at least most of them, but that means you have to kill someone or several someones in cold blood. What do you do?"

"Are the ones I have to kill to save the rest innocent?" he asked.

"For the sake of argument, yes."

"Children?"

"No," I said uneasily. "They're adults."

"You kill them," Theo said easily. "The quicker the better."

I looked at him, aghast.

"I don't see the fun in this, if you're going to be upset," Theo said, studying me.

"I'm not upset," I said. "Just unnerved a little that you could make that decision so easily."

"Like you said before, I've seen what happens when you delay in acting," Theo said coolly. "I wouldn't put any of the foxes in danger because I was afraid to kill, no matter who it was."

"What if it wasn't a stranger? What if it was someone you knew?"

"If it was someone I knew to be good, yes, I might hesitate. If it was someone who was an asshole, that might speed my hand."

"What if it wasn't one person?" I asked softly. "What if you had to kill a hundred, or a thousand to save ten times that number?"

"The more people involved, the more the line begins to grey," Theo said thoughtfully. "I can't say I condone murder on that magnitude. I couldn't be responsible for making that kind of decision." He bit his lip, then suddenly smiled. "But a couple, sure."

"Why?"

"You have to have priorities," Theo said after a moment. "Take mine in guarding Danial. I have to be ready to shoot anyone who comes after him, male or female, young or old. Without keeping that directive first, I could lose my resolve and not act in time. The same thing when it comes to defending myself—it's them or me. The choice is easy."

"What if it wasn't just business? What if it was personal, a vendetta, or—"

"Are you worried about Danial and me fighting again?" Theo interrupted. "You don't have to be. That's settled."

I gave him a curious look.

"When I was with you, after Danial found out, he could've sent someone to kill me and bring you back to him. But he knew it was between us. When he didn't come after us himself, I knew he was going to let us be together." His eyes locked on mine. "That is why we had to go to him that night. I knew it would come to a fight sooner or later, so it was better to have it out."

"That was your plan?" I said with exasperation. "What if you had lost?"

"There was no way in hell I was losing," Theo said with a grin. "I'd waited too long to be with you. I fought as hard as I could as fast as I could to end it quickly. Now why are you asking about all this?"

"I was curious," I said distractedly. "It doesn't matter."

"Good," he said, satisfied. "I'm going to put on *V for Vendetta*. Your question got me in the mood. Is that okay?"

I mentally shook myself. I wanted to be here with him and not thinking of someone else, no matter how nice his eyes might be. "That's fine."

* * * *

"Why is he taking so long?" Theo asked for the fourth or fifth time, pacing.

"I don't know," I said impatiently. "Just be happy you aren't the one on this table."

I was lying partly naked in Exam Room 1 of Dr. Camlyn's office, as we awaited new information on the state of my reproductive system. We were both nervous and irritable.

Dr. Camlyn opened the door, his expression calm. "Theo, sit down," he said.

Theo sat, his arms crossed over his chest.

"Sarelle, I have good news for you. The damage to your womb doesn't seem to be permanent. Your scars are healing themselves. They were extensive, as you already know, so there is no way of knowing how long it will take for the scar tissue to regenerate, or if it will heal to the point you'll regain your ability to have children."

"Danial and I haven't exchanged blood in a month, and I'm still vampire enough to regenerate like that?"

"The virus that was present in your blood is not as prevalent as it was, but it's still there. You should go back to your normal human self with time. Can you still take the choker off?"

"Yes." I demonstrated that it still slid together and unclasped easily for me.

"Then you're still partly turned, Sarelle," he continued gently, putting his hand on my shoulder. "I'm sorry, but I have no way of knowing if you'll ever heal to the point you can have another baby. All I can tell you is that you can't get pregnant now, not and keep it to term. A year from now, maybe. By then you should be completely human again."

"It's going to take me a whole year to revert?"

"Yes and for the whole of it, you need to be very careful, Sarelle," Stephen cautioned.

"Why?" Theo said instantly, getting out of the chair to stand beside me.

"Because if she gets a mortal wound now, she'll finish turning," Stephen said. "Even just a bad wound might do it."

Shit, that was enough to make me start shaking. If Devlin hadn't taken those bullets, I'd have turned right there in that hotel room with him. Then I'd have had to feed, which meant he would have had to help me. There were worse possible things to have happen probably, but none came to mind.

Theo came and put his arms around me. "How long until she's out of the woods?"

"Maybe a month, maybe two, I'm not sure. I've never seen a person be partly turned for so long," Stephen said curiously. "But I've never heard of a woman carrying a vampire's child to term either, until you, Sar."

"Don't mention this to anyone," I said defensively. "I know Danial and I gave permission for you to document and write about Theoron's birth and my unusual pregnancy, but I don't want this known. Even with you not using our real names, it's too dangerous."

"That's regrettable," Stephen said with a nod, "But I understand your concerns completely. I won't mention this in my papers."

"Do you know how much blood she'd have to lose to succumb?" Theo asked hesitantly. "I'm getting from you that it's only a small amount. Would a bad cut do it?"

"That I can't answer. When Sar was pregnant and Danial gave her blood repeatedly, sometimes day after day, again, she should have turned. I still don't know why she didn't. According to my knowledge of vampires she should be a vampire now, from the amount of virus in her blood right at this minute."

If I lost just a little blood, I might turn … I trembled in Theo's arms.

"When will we know she's completely free from turning?" Theo said, phrasing carefully to leave out the part about me dying.

"Say six months?" Stephen answered. "I'd need to check her blood to be sure. Closing and opening the collar may not work as a great indicator. It hasn't in the past. You two also need to face that the possibility that Sarelle will stop healing her scars before she completely heals. Once she's human again, whatever scarring is left will stay there permanently."

"Danial could—" Theo began.

"I don't recommend trying to keep her in this state to finish healing her, not for any reason," Stephen interrupted. "Danial's blood is potent. A tiny bit might be enough to cause her to turn."

That didn't seem right to me, not with how well I'd handled all the blood Danial had exchanged with me since he'd become more powerful. How much was Dr. Camlyn guessing at, and how much did he really know? Still, I couldn't take a chance with my life…

"What about the STD test?" Theo asked gruffly. "Are we okay?"

"I'll know in a few days for certain. With what you've told me, I'm fairly sure you're both fine. The werecougar virus—like most other were viruses—resists if not cures most all human diseases. Both you and Aspen were tested only a few months ago, and you told me those tests were negative. That you saw the paperwork for them. Also, you say you only had unprotected sex as cougar—"

"We really don't need to get into that again," I interrupted stiffly. "We'll just call for the results. Now can we get to the actual exam?"

Dr. Camlyn checked me over. "You have bruises, Sar, inside and out. That is normal between were and human lovers, as it is with most human and non-human sexual relationships."

"Is she hurt from what I did to her?" Theo asked.

"Sarelle, Theo, you are both adults. What you do in your own bedroom is your choice. Rough sex causes bruising and tearing sometimes, even between human partners. No, I don't see anything on Sar's body that makes me think you were too rough, Theo. It really depends on what she is comfortable with."

Theo was relieved. "Good."

"Can you write me a pill prescription?" I asked. "Until we find out how much I'm going to heal, I want to be protected."

"That would be best," Stephen agreed, taking out his prescription pad. "It will prevent a miscarriage. I'd advise staying on birth control until I can determine you're completely human again and can give you a clear answer about your child-bearing status."

Whew. I'd dodged the whole baby issue, maybe for good. "Thank you."

"Yes, thank you." Theo shook Stephen's hand.

After I dressed and the bill was paid, Theo drove me home, stopping on the way to pick up my prescription for birth control and some takeout for us both.

"Sar, you should really come with me tonight."

What I wanted was to forget the name Aspen forever. Second to that was to take a long bath by myself and forget the conversation about cougar sex that had run through my mind all the way home. "I'll be fine. The dogs will be with me, and I'll set the security system, too."

"But you'll be alone until midnight," Theo fretted. "Terian's got to leave for a meeting with Danial at dusk, and I've got to be there to watch over Theoron and Elle until they get back at midnight."

"That's only about five hours," I said, exasperated. "I'm a big girl, Theo."

"Al's threats are real," Theo replied. "Danial's on it, but—"

"But nothing. Don't forget the alarm will be on. You'll have to disarm it when you come in. I'll be in bed sleeping," I said, kissing him quickly. "Wake me up when you get home, so I know you're safe."

"You be safe," he said seriously. "Remember if you walk the dogs to bring your gun."

"I will."

He sped off, the dust floating away on the wind, obscuring our waves goodbye to each other.

I went inside and to my first order of business: showing Darkness her finished bed.

I replaced the old one with the new one and showed it to her, patting the middle. She promptly came and laid down on it, settling into it with a large exhalation of breath. That meant it was okay, she could maybe get used to it. I laughed and then quickly cut up the old bed into rags, saving the zippers to reuse. Then I took the dogs outside for a long walk.

It was near dusk, but I had my gun and wasn't afraid. The dogs were relaxed and happy, chasing a large flock of geese off the manure-spread fields. They rose in the air with disgruntled honking, speeding their way north. The dogs watched them wistfully as they disappeared over the trees.

"Come on," I yelled, laughing. "It's time to go in."

A half hour later, the dogs were eating their Cheweez, the doors were locked, and I was settling into my long anticipated bath. Since Theo wasn't home and the TV was off, I put on some music: the *Phantom of the Opera* CD my stepfather had burned for me. With no one to hear me garble the high notes, I sang loudly and unabashedly, belting out the various songs from memory.

Abruptly, I realized it was dark, and I'd forgotten to call in the cats. The coyotes were still around in summer, and a cat Cavity's size was a good meal. I dressed quickly, putting on some leggings and a tank top in case I needed to go outside to grab a reluctant feline, and grabbed my gun.

Jessica was already in, sleeping in the chair and Asher was somewhere in the basement. That left only Cavity.

A nice breeze hit me when I opened the front door, caressing my face. "Cavity!"

A black furry form sprang up the deck steps quickly, then looked behind watchfully, pausing. Then Cavity ran inside.

I shut the door quickly, locked it, then bent down to pet him. "Hi. Do you need a treat?"

Cavity gave eager assent, causing Jessica to come running, followed by the dogs.

I went into the kitchen, doled out treats to everyone and went to load the dishwasher. It was full of dirty dishes, the soap dispenser full. Grumbling at Theo for forgetting to turn it on, I turned it on and then began to wash the breakfast dishes. The kitchen was soon stuffy with heat from the hot water being used, and I opened the window. The cool night was alive with crickets and singing frogs. It made me happy to hear them and to feel the cool breeze again on my face.

I had a very good life here with Theo. There was a lot to get used to now that he was back. We'd both gone through a lot in our time apart, and it had changed us. But that didn't mean we couldn't be as happy as we'd been once, if we both worked hard.

Cavity hopped up on the counter, purring.

"Want me to sing to you?" I asked him with a smile, then launched into "Think of Me", one of the songs I'd been listening to earlier. I finished it in the time it took to do the dishes and then went to the back door to let the dogs out before going to bed. As I grasped the door handle, there was a knock from the other side.

I drew back my hand. This door opened up on my fenced yard. The gate was locked, and the only other entrance was through the garage, which was also locked.

The knock sounded again.

The dogs weren't growling, but they weren't wagging their tails either. I grabbed my gun from the kitchen counter and went to the door. "Theo?"

"Not even close," an amused voice answered.

I opened the door, gun in my hand. "Why are you here?"

Devlin gazed back at me, dressed in a blood red silk shirt, white khakis and a faint smile. "I didn't know you could sing, Sar."

He had heard me. Of all the people I wouldn't want to hear me sing, he would be the topmost one on the list. A flush crept up my neck.

"Your voice is good, though it needs polishing," he continued, not seeming to notice I was mortified. "Some of your notes are flat. Others are completely wrong."

"How would you know?" I said snidely. "And don't call me Sar."

He looked at me and then began to sing. "Floating, falling, sweet intoxication—"

I was rapt, standing there in the doorway listening to him sing "The Music of the Night", gun forgotten in my hand. His voice was amazing: rich and smooth, like Godiva chocolate. He sang just a few lines and lapsed into silence, looking at me patronizingly.

I flushed again and said grudgingly "Okay, I see you know what you're talking about. I only had a few years of choir—"

"I can polish your voice, Sar," Devlin said. "If you want to work with me, that is."

"Would it take a long time?" I asked hesitantly.

"No," Devlin replied. "You have a good voice—surprisingly good, for not having any training that counts. Understand that I'm not making you stage ready. I would just work on a couple things, for example so you don't waver so much and your voice doesn't go flat. Even with my help, you'll never be able to hit the truly high notes. You're not a soprano, as the Broadway actress who sings in that play is. But I can improve your natural gifts."

"I would like to hit the right notes," I said slowly. "I never really learned to read music. I just memorized the songs for choir."

"I can teach you that," Devlin assured me. "But don't feel badly. I also learned many songs by memorization and not actual written music."

"But you're so good—"

"May I come in?" Devlin interrupted. "It's not wise to stand here in the light. Anyone within rifle range has a clear shot at you."

I stepped backward instantly, and Devlin entered, locking the door behind him.

He turned back to me. "Thank you for the compliment. I was a professional singer, as in people paid me to sing for them. But that was hundreds of years ago." He gave a wry smile, a mirror of Danial's. "Sheet music was a staple of the rich. I was lucky to sometimes get paper with the correct lyrics."

"I don't mean to be rude," I said. "But why are you here?"

"You're alone, aren't you?" he answered, pushing past me into the living room. "I don't hear anyone else here."

I was instantly afraid, though I knew I shouldn't be. Devlin had saved my life. Yet I was still leery of him, especially remembering the last time he'd visited. "You know I am."

"You shouldn't be here alone. Alphonse rejected Danial's deal. He still wants you dead. I'll stay with you."

Devlin's words were chilling. I gripped the gun in both hands, leaning back against the wall. He looked at me to say something else, stopped and then handed me something quickly.

"For you, my dear."

It was flowers, more fire and ice roses. God, they smelled wonderful. I inhaled deeply and sighed. "Thank you. I like that the ones you get for me always have a scent."

"A flower without fragrance is like food without taste," he said. "May I sit?"

"Make yourself comfortable," I said. "Did Danial send you to guard me?"

"I was on my way to see you anyway. But yes, he called to tell me Al rebuffed him and to ask that I stay with you until Theo got back."

I reminded myself that Devlin had to be telling the truth, that there was no reason to be so leery of him. "Did Danial meet with him tonight?"

"Theo did," Devlin said impatiently. "Apparently he said he wanted to be the one to go, Danial said. To take note of who worked for Alphonse and what his defenses were."

That was my Theo. I felt immediately better. "Good. He'll take care of this."

"The choker won't protect you from Al," Devlin said, irritated. "But it will from Manir. He is still a threat to you, even if not to your life. You had best be careful."

"I'll be careful." I whispered.

"Put those in some water before they wilt," Devlin instructed, petting Ghost. Oddly, my dog was wagging his tail now, and Darkness was also moving closer to Devlin, her tail beginning to wave.

I ran water into a vase and stuck the flowers in. "I guess they know you mean no harm this time."

Devlin didn't reply.

I set the gun on the counter and got a small glass of wine. Between Devlin being here and what he'd just told me, my nerves were jangling.

As I went to sit down, Devlin purred "Aren't you going to offer me anything to drink?"

My grip on the glass slipped, but I managed not to spill the wine. "No," I said tiredly, knocking back the glass. "You said you were headed here before Danial called. Why?"

"To return Theo's shirt, of course," Devlin said. "I laid it on the washer as I came in."

"And how in the hell did you get in the backyard?"

"I told you before. There are more ways of traveling than by car," Devlin answered. "But that's unimportant. Why are you so bruised?"

"Overzealousness," I said bitterly, then promptly regretted it. "Do you think Al is going to keep trying? It wasn't my fault that Samuel kicked him out of the Jacuzzi room."

"Al's a man with a lot of pride. It would gall him just that he wanted you, and you didn't want him. He's killed women for less." Devlin looked me intently in the eyes. "He'll try again until he gets you."

His words were like a crushing blow. Hopelessness swept through me.

"I'm tired of being hunted," I said wearily, rubbing my brow. "I had Theoron because I knew how much Danial wanted a child. I never knew it would cause all these problems. I can't remember a time when someone wasn't trying to hurt me, when I wasn't afraid…" I broke down sobbing, my long hair falling forward to cover my face.

There was a light touch of fingertips pushing my hair aside, and then they touched my cheek gently.

"No more talk of darkness. Forget these wide-eyed fears. I'm here. No one will harm you, my words will warm and calm you—"

I looked up and met Devlin's golden eyes. They were solemn and yet also intense with some inner fire, shimmering as he sang to me. My lips parted as my breath caught in my throat.

His fingertips gently wiped my tears away, then cupped my face. "Let me be your shelter—" He leaned in, his cool lips deftly meeting mine.

For a second I lost myself in him, then I pushed him back. "Stop it."

Devlin shot me an amused look. "No need to get incensed. I was just helping."

"Oh, really? How?"

"Your bruise on your mouth," Devlin said, more amused. "It's healed. A thank you would be in order, though more than I'd expect from you really."

"Don't give me that—"

"I'm not giving you anything more, so you can calm down anytime," Devlin said dismissively, turning the television on. "I've done my good deed for the day."

I was relieved, crestfallen and offended all at once. I sat there watching him, frantically trying to think of a good comeback and failing.

"Why don't you go to bed?" Devlin said, all his attention on surfing channels. "We seem to have run out of things to say to one another. I'd rather not get into any more of your dramatic scenes just now."

"You won't need to," I said, standing. "Get out."

"No," Devlin said, unmoving. "You need a guard. I told my brother I'd watch over you, tedious as that duty is."

"I hate you!" I yelled, losing all composure in a split second. "Get out of my house!"

Devlin turned to me so fast I stepped back in fear. "And what are you going to do if I don't?" he said, baring his fangs at me. "Have some respect—"

"For what?" I said sarcastically. "A has-been?"

Devlin's eyes widened, then he lunged for me. I let out a shriek as his hands closed over my arms.

"That's enough," he said irritably. He picked me up and carried me into the bedroom where he dropped me on the bed in a heap of arms and legs. "Goodnight," he said and left, shutting Ghost and Darkness in with me.

I got up, gathered my pride and composure, and then went back out to the living room. Devlin got up and came toward me, annoyed.

"Do I have to tie you in place, or are you coming to see if I'll join you in bed?" he said, fixing me with his golden eyes. "You were pretty straightforward about your feelings for me. But perhaps your hatred hides secret desire."

"I'm sorry I said that," I said coolly. "I appreciate you're watching over me. But you're right. We don't have anything to say to one another. I just came to get my flowers before the cats use them as playthings."

"Cats tend to do that," Devlin said indifferently, handing me the vase. "Here."

"Thank you. Goodnight." I turned quickly and left him standing there.

After I closed my door, I set the vase on my vanity counter and inhaled another deep breath. The smell was exceptional. A quick look in the mirror showed he'd told the truth; the bruise that had been by my mouth was gone.

Part of me wanted to go back out to Devlin and ask him what his problem was. The other part of me already knew it was sexual tension and that to go back out there would lead to another kiss, if not more. There was some chemistry between us, likely from his eye-catching looks and his recent heroics on my behalf, at least for my part. Why he desired me was a mystery, but that didn't matter. What mattered was staying in here and not making a bad mistake.

I lay down and was asleep in moments, breathing in the heavenly scent of his roses.

Chapter Twelve

The first thing I saw the next morning were my roses. The whole bedroom smelled of them. The clock said six a.m. Today was Saturday, and Theo was beside me, sleeping.

"You didn't wake me up when you came in," I whispered in his ear.

"Sar," he said sleepily, hugging me. "How are you feeling?"

"Good." I gave him a kiss. "But you didn't wake me to tell me you were home."

"You needed your rest. What do you want to do today?" he asked yawning. "I know you mentioned we had outside work to do."

"We need to plant the garden. There is outside work to do. Plus, we have to visit my parents. My mom's been calling every day. Pretty soon she's going to show up here. They really want to see you."

Theo groaned.

"I know," I said, giving him an apologetic look. "My parents are protective. My house is old. Not living here for a while took its toll."

"We'll enjoy ourselves today," Theo said, eyeing me happily. "I need to get some more new clothes. We also need groceries and plants to plant. Afterwards we'll see a movie and then your parents. Tomorrow we'll work. I know you have to mow, and I can till up the soil. We'll plant it together, like we did last time." He tilted my face up to him, and his blue gray eyes looked into mine. "I'll be here this time to see it grow," he said softly. "And to help you in the winter."

I kissed him madly, wrapping my arms around him. He abruptly went still.

"Sar," he said in an odd voice, pulling back from me "You smell of Devlin."

"I'm sure," I stated, flushing. "He and I had words, which ended with him carrying me in here and dropping me on the bed. I stayed in here after giving him a piece of my mind."

Theo laughed. "He was watching TV when I came to the door. Some movie with subtitles. He didn't say much, just that he'd catch me later."

"What was he watching, Mr. Too-Good-For-Action-Movies?"

"Some Italian movie called 'The Seduction of Mimi'?" he said, raising his eyebrows. "It sounded pretentious. But he's always been like that, at least in my view."

"So much for my voice lessons," I said with a yawn. "Now that I told him I hated him, he's not likely to want to help me."

"He mentioned that," Theo said, stretching. "Sorry I forgot. He said to let him know when you'll be at Danial's nights and that he'd meet you there for an hour at a time every week."

"I don't understand," I said, incredulous. "He said he wanted to go through with them?"

"I guess. That's what he said."

My conscience told me it was a bad idea, but my curiosity won. "Is it okay with you?"

"Sure, if it's something you want to do," Theo said. "You can probably go in late those days. Danial won't mind, and I can arrange with Terian to stay later. Pick up some overtime."

"I don't want to mess up your schedule. Maybe I could come to work later and drive home with Devlin tailing me. He must live somewhere nearby. He was here not long after dark."

"Yes, he does," Theo replied "He lives in a large fortress type home near the village of Hayden. That's the name of his house as well."

Hayden. That had a nice ring and wasn't fancy as I expected.

"So is there any breakfast?" Theo asked jokingly. "I could carry you to the kitchen."

Despite his joking tone, his words brought back how injured I'd been a day ago. "No," I said quickly, getting up. "I'll make it. Come on, we've got a lot to do."

* * * *

With luck and a lot of planning, we managed to get everything done. We reached my parent's home close to dinnertime.

My mom hugged Theo tightly as soon as she opened the door. I hadn't been able to resist telling her we were married.

"Call me Mom," she told him. He nodded to her, but was obviously very affected. "Where is your wedding band?" she said, eyeing my hand. "And yours?" she asked Theo two seconds later.

"I'm having them made," Theo said politely. "It's taking longer than I expected it to, ma'am."

"Mom," she corrected him.

"Mom," he said, sounding a little unsure but very happy.

I turned and looked at him. I hadn't known he was having bands made. "When?"

"A few more weeks," he said, grinning widely.

I gave him a smile. "Good."

After a firm handshake and a welcome to the family, my stepfather dragged him off for the required scotch tasting session.

"Did you warn Theo he had to go fishing soon, or there would be dire consequences?" my mom asked.

"Yes, I told him it was part of being married to me. He said it was a small price to pay."

"Sar," my mother said. "All kidding aside, is Theo still working for Danial?"

"Yes."

"And you're still working for Danial, too?" she said, incredulous.

"Yes," I said uneasily, knowing I couldn't tell her about Theoron.

"Isn't that awkward?" she asked. "And what about Elle? How is she?"

"We're making it work actually," I said. "As for Elle, she thinks of Danial as her father. She likes Theo, but she said she doesn't want to live with us."

"That's too bad," my mother said, sorrowful. "But you never know. She may come around."

I nodded like I was sad, too, but in my mind I was glad of Elle's devotion to Danial. She was safer with him than with Theo and I. Even if Alphonse backed off and Manir was killed, there would always be someone else.

"When will you be bringing Elle to see us?"

I hugged my mother. "Next week or the one after. We can maybe go shopping."

"That would be wonderful. We've missed you. Christmas last year wasn't the same without you here."

I felt awful, despite I'd had to stay away or risk her finding out I'd gotten pregnant. "I'll be here for next Christmas," I assured her. "Theo, me and Elle."

She hugged me tightly. "I'm glad you are back with him," she said. "Danial was good to you, I know. But Theo loves you, too, and he does things with you that Danial never did."

I opened my mouth to defend Danial. It wasn't his fault he couldn't eat, go out in the sun or do the things with me that Theo could. I knew how much he wanted to play with Elle in the sunlight or join Theoron in eating ice cream. He'd never asked to be what he was. But defending him would only cause problems, so I let it slide. "We need to be going, Mom."

"You're going to have to pry him out of your stepfather's clutches."

I hugged her once more and then went to collect Theo. My stepfather Chris had already given Theo a few scotches and had a few more ready to sample. Nicely I said that was enough and got him to the car.

"Thanks, Sar. That was close," Theo said, blinking his eyes rapidly.

"I had to do it," I said with a smirk. "I need your help unpacking the car."

We unpacked, and I made a quick dinner of box macaroni and cheese. After Theo and I ate and took the dogs for a walk, we sat outside on the deck, sipping some wine.

"Theo, tell me what Alphonse said when you went to see him."

Theo sighed, but didn't hesitate. "Good old Al said that it didn't matter who Danial was or what he threatened. He said that you were a woman, and since there was no ring on your finger the night he approached you, he didn't see the problem. I let him know that there was a ring on your finger now and that for all purposes, there had been one that night as well. He said it didn't matter. I wanted to shoot him then, but I was under orders from Danial not to start anything. So I told him Danial hoped he would reconsider because he would take any action against you as action against him and retaliate. That gave Al pause, and he said he would get back to us."

"Isn't that good though?" I said hopefully. "Maybe he will reconsider."

"No," Theo said, coming to put his arms around me. "He likely just wants to get to you before he has to deal with Danial. He'll attack soon."

"Why are we out here unprotected at night then?" I squeaked. "He could have people out there—"

"Sar, he knows who I am, too. He knows it's my ring on your finger now. He is not going to attack you with me here and lose a bunch of men. His one thought now is how can he get you alone, unguarded, so he doesn't lose men taking you." Theo let out a frustrated grunt. "Our ballistics guy got nothing on that gun, so we're back to square one. From now on we're sticking to Danial's plan, that you never be without myself, him or Terian with you. No exceptions."

I burrowed back into Theo's chest.

"You're safe," he whispered. "I'm here. We'll plant that garden tomorrow like you want—"

"I want to go inside," I said softly. The night suddenly seemed vast, with too many people within it waiting to harm me.

* * * *

That next week on Friday, Danial came out of his bedroom at dusk, dressed. "Is Devlin here yet for your first lesson?"

I was uneasy, remembering Devlin teaching me my first "lesson" years ago in this very room. Annoyed, I shoved that line of thought aside. "He should be here anytime."

"If the door rings, will you answer it? The first interview is tonight at ten."

"Which one is it?"

"Brian the werebear is first. Terian's friend Monica will be by about midnight. Erin the eagle is coming by tomorrow evening. As for Brian, just tell him to wait in the great room. I'll be on a conference call until a little after ten."

"Sure," I said, nodding once. "Elle's in her bedroom. You should see her now if you're going to be busy."

"I'm going there now," Danial said, coming over to me. "How was your day?"

At Theo and Danial's insistence, I'd begun coming everyday to Danial's. In actuality, it worked out better for everyone. "Good. Theoron didn't speak. Don't worry."

"Good," Danial said in relief. "I'm so worried I'm going to miss his first word."

"Terian went with us to a park for an hour with a couple of the foxes. Elle played with a couple kids she met there." I made a face. "They were scared of me, I think."

"Why would you say that?" Danial said, concerned. "Did Theoron show his fangs?"

"No, they weren't near him at all," I assured him. "But daylight accentuates the faint luster to my skin that I have now. I think the kids thought I was sick and that the foxes were nursemaids."

"An unflattering but reasonable conclusion," Danial said, coming over to me. "I'm sorry."

"Don't be," I said, managing a smile. "I was just happy Terian hasn't said anything more about leaving."

"I think it's because of Theoron," Danial replied slowly. "I sometimes walk in on Terian holding him. Our son reaches for Terian the way he reaches for you and me."

"Does that bother you?" I asked.

"It makes me jealous a little," Danial admitted. "But I'm content to share my son's love with another man that has the power to protect him that Terian does."

"You're very understanding," I said, patting his hand.

"No, I'm old enough to be very practical," Danial retorted with a smile. "Devlin's at the door, if you want to answer it." He walked toward Elle's room.

Before I got to the door, Devlin had come in and was walking toward me with a clipboard. "Shall we begin?"

"Yes," I said respectfully. "What do you want me to do?"

"For the first lesson, I want you to copy the notes I'll sing as best you can. I need to know which you have mastery of and which need work."

"Okay." I envisioned that there were only what, nine notes on a scale? How many scales could there be? Two or three?

An hour later, I was bored to tears. I'd somehow thought we would be singing songs, and this was plain tedious. We had gone through the entire range of notes I was able to hit with my voice as Devlin made extensive notes on his clipboard.

"Okay, Sarelle," he said finally, putting down the clipboard. "There are about ten notes we need to work on. The rest you can hit with no problem and hold long enough for most any popular song."

"That's good," I said carefully.

"That's better than good," he said, giving me a dazzling smile. "I should only need about five weeks, give or take a week."

"That sounds great," I said, relieved he was pleased. "But I still think I should pay you."

"Non," Devlin said.

I didn't know if he had misspoken, or was attempting to impress me with a little French. I didn't reply.

There was a knock, and then a man came into the great room hesitantly and nodded to Devlin. Devlin nodded back once, then glanced to me. "This is Brian," he said.

Brian was burly, with wide shoulders and a head of thick dark brown hair. He had a five o'clock shadow and brown eyes that were surprisingly friendly. I'd expected him to be fearsome or to try to intimidate me, but he did neither.

"Danial is expecting you," I said. "Have a seat. I'll let him know you're here."

Leaving Brian and Devlin in the great room, I climbed the stairs to the study and notified Danial.

"Good," he whispered, covering the receiver on his speakerphone. "Let Theo and Terian know."

I passed on the news to Theo and Terian via the other office phone, then went back to the great room. Brian was waiting, but Devlin was nowhere in evidence.

"He left," Brian said. "He said next week, same time."

"Thanks," I said and took a seat in a nearby chair. "Danial will be right down."

A few minutes later, Danial, Theo and Terian arrived. After introductions, they settled in chairs and on the couch to do the interview. I excused myself and went into the kitchen, wanting to make a list of what I needed to pick up at the store tomorrow. My baking with Cia was later this week, and we were preparing several desserts, all of which had uncommon ingredients. I'd just completed my list when a loud animal bellow shook the room.

I trembled. I'd heard that same roar echoing in the air long ago when Theo and Terian had fought Devlin's guards. Quickly, I splashed cold water on my face, angry at my ill-placed fear. This bear was going to protect me, not hurt me. Wiping my face, I followed the sound of the roaring outside to the front lawn.

Terian, Danial and Theo stood there, looking at the largest bear I'd ever seen. Brian stood on his hind legs and roared at them, standing easily twelve feet tall. His teeth were huge.

"Impressive," Danial said.

"Climb a tree," Theo said casually. "I need to check your speed."

Brian turned fast and loped to the nearest tree that would hold him, a huge beech tree at the edge of the driveway. He climbed it so fast he seemed to run up it. Then he slowly backed down and loped back.

I had never seen a bear in the wild. He was fast, faster than I was by far. He was big, too. Really big.

Danial noticed me and beckoned. I came to his side, to stand between him and Theo.

"You should go over to him," he said to me softly. "I can sense you're afraid. If he's going to successfully protect you, you need to trust him."

Suri's last words had been not to trust. Fear ran through me. "Why don't we wait—?"

"Danial is right," Theo interrupted. "Go and pet him, Sar. You're in no danger," he said, drawing his explosive bullets gun and slipping off the safety.

Emboldened, I walked up to Brian. He stood there waiting until I was almost to him, then lay down on his side and rolled onto his back. I smiled, despite myself and then reached down to pet him. His fur was thick and not very soft, more wiry. He licked my hand, then he rolled back onto his feet. He was so tall he could look into my eyes from all fours. Abruptly he stood up again on his hind legs, towering over me. His claws were huge, as long as my fingers were. He took a step and wrapped his paws around me gently. I was enveloped by him; he blocked my view of everything, even the sky, his scent oily and musky, yet not unpleasant.

Then he suddenly let me go, backed off a few steps and sat down.

"Thanks for the hug," I said with a smile and returned to Danial.

"Go inside," he said softly. "Brian is going to change back and needs some privacy."

That meant the interview was over. "Will you meet Monica out here when she comes?"

"No, she called to say she'll have to come in a few weeks, she has a few last contractual obligations to fulfill to her current employer. We're done interviewing for tonight."

"Her suddenly canceling sounds suspicious," I said quickly.

"Not really," Danial said, steering me toward the door. "It means she's a responsible employee. That's a good thing."

Already not fond of Monica, I went back inside and grabbed my list and purse. As I was putting on my coat, Theo came in. "We hired him," he said, hugging me. "He'll start tomorrow on days."

"Good," I said. "He seems nice. I expected him to be more, I don't know, terrifying."

"It is probably his lack of that trait that caused Devlin to let him go," Theo said. "But don't worry. He won't hug Manir or Al. Let's go home."

* * * *

Erin came the next day for her interview. She was beautiful, with long dark red hair and a shy smile. Again, I'd expected her to be cold and have a severe personality. But she was gregarious and very friendly. I didn't see her transform into an eagle, but heard her screaming out her cry as she flew in the night sky for Danial, Terian and Theo.

My final private opinion was that Erin was too nice to kill to protect us. However, Theo said they had hired her when he came in to collect me that night. She started the day shift soon after. With the addition of her and Brian on days, my access to traveling to stores, parks and other places increased to what it had been before Al and Manir, something that made me very happy.

After the delay of a few weeks, Monica the sorceress arrived for her interview on a night I was visiting the foxes with the children. When Theo came to collect me, he announced with a strange note in his voice that Danial had hired her, too.

"Don't you like her?" I asked him later in bed that night. "You sound as if you think she might not be an asset."

"She seems more than capable," he said slowly. "Her illusions had us all believing we were at a beach—that it was daytime."

"Danial must have liked that," I said, laughing.

"He was worried," Theo said, cracking a smile. "But once he relaxed, he enjoyed seeing the sun without having to worry about burning."

"That's good," I said, pleased. "I take it she's working nights?"

"Yes, and it's a good thing. Terian told me tonight that he wants to leave at the end of the year."

"I'm surprised he's waiting so long," I replied, my eyebrows raised.

"Only because of Suri's message," Theo said, pulling me close for a hug. "He's worried about you and Theoron. But I'm beginning to think his leaving will be a good thing."

"Why?"

"He doesn't care as much about Danial or Elle as he does about you and Theoron. They're secondary. He values the baby most of all. You can't have favorites when you're a guard. You make mistakes and take risks. That jeopardizes everyone."

That was true, and I didn't correct him. "Our marriage certificate finally came in the mail today. I left it on the counter for you."

"I saw that. I'll take it into Danial tomorrow. He'll put in a request to add you onto my insurance and take you off of his."

"Good," I murmured distractedly. Switching insurance would break the last paperwork between Danial and me. Even though I wanted that, I felt a momentary pang of sadness and loss.

"Oh, here, before I forget." Theo handed me a ring made of plain gold. Noticeable on his hand was one almost identical to it. "I picked them up today."

"I never asked you," I said, slipping the band on. "How did you know my ring size?"

Theo looked pointedly at the diamond on my other hand, the one Danial had given to me.

"Who do you think had to sneak into your room and check your other wedding rings for the size years ago? It sure wasn't Danial."

"No," I said tenderly. "It would have had to be you." I gave him a kiss.

* * * *

That summer was one of the best of my life. I had so much: a flourishing garden, plenty of sunny days and huge, fragrant flowers. I even enjoyed mowing the lawn.

Elle and I had mended our relationship. She was slowly accepting Theo into her life as a second father, much of that due to weekly hunting trips in cougar form on Danial's land. My pets were all happy and healthy. All the foxes were good, even Ivan finally ending his grieving for Suri and Demetri with the help of an attentive and loving Janice.

Elle turned two—in human years; her physical and mental development was still accelerated with all the time she'd spent during those years in cougar form—and I turned thirty-three that summer. We had a joint party at Danial's house, with cake and ice cream and balloons in late July. All the foxes were invited. It was at that party when my perfect summer began to crack in places.

"Sar," Danial said, drawing me aside into his bedroom. "I need to ask you something."

"What?" I asked. "You're upset, I can tell."

"Are you able to remove the choker still?"

I slipped it off easily. "Yes. Why?"

"You're still healing," Danial said, both worried and relieved.

"I know," I said quietly, casting a look at the door. "I've got to go back to Dr. Camlyn this fall. He's probably going to tell me I'm completely healed."

"Don't you want that?" Danial asked neutrally.

"I don't know," I said evasively. "Why are you upset?"

"Your scar from me is healing," Danial said sadly, his hand brushing my neck. "It's noticeably lighter than Devlin's."

The one mark I'd wanted to keep was fading, while the other I would kill to get rid of was still as deep as the day it was made. "I'm sorry. I noticed it, too."

"Do you miss us?" Danial asked softly, his dark eyes looking into mine.

"Yes," I said honestly. "But why are you asking me when you already know?"

"Because I needed to hear you say it," Danial said, turning from me. "Come, before we're missed."

That night, Theo awakened me, thrashing hard in the grip of a nightmare. I shook him awake.

"Thanks," he gasped, his chest heaving.

"Do you want to talk about it?"

"No," he answered, as he always did.

"Theo, you have to tell someone what you went through. Most of the scars you had when we reunited are gone—"

"Not the scar tissue," he growled. "Those exploding bullets left their mark."

"My point is that your physical wounds have healed, yet your psychological ones seem to be getting worse. Your nightmares are getting more frequent. You're beginning to lose sleep."

"My nightmares would become yours, Sar. I can't have that."

"I can handle what you tell me. It's in the past."

"I can't tell you," he said painfully. "Not now. I will someday, Sar, but not now."

"Tell Danial if you can't tell me," I said softly, putting my hand on his. "Please?"

He nodded. "All right. I'll do that this week."

That next week, Theo stayed one night at Danial's while Terian watched over Elle, Theoron and me at my home. After that, Theo's nightmares seemed to stop. At least he slept better and no longer woke me up.

* * * *

The days grew hotter as August matured. Oddly, I found myself bonding with Erin more and more. I liked her a lot, despite her being almost a decade younger than I was. She was usually in a good mood and always willing to help me with whatever I was doing. It was with shock I discovered one afternoon that she had an ulterior motive to all her friendliness: Terian.

"He never treats me as anything but a coworker," she admitted wistfully, mixing a batch of sugar cookie dough for me. "I have to admit that all his signs point to him not being interested."

"Erin, ask him out. He's single, and he's been that way for a while. You're young and good-looking. Do the math."

She flushed slightly. "I'm wereeagle though. Are you sure he won't care?"

"Not if you don't care he's part demon," I replied. "What's the worse he can say—no?"

"He can say it's unprofessional," she murmured.

No way he was going to say anything but yes, not when he'd bedded all those strippers so voraciously. I held that thought in. "Ask him."

"Okay."

Brian walked in. "Sar, are you going to be here for another few hours?"

I looked at him in exasperation. "Brian, really, you don't have to check on me every hour. I'm safe here. You only need to worry about someone getting into the grounds."

"I have my orders," he said, pausing to look at me for a moment. "Danial and Theo don't want anything to happen to you."

"You don't do this with Elle or Theoron," I complained, hands on my hips.

"Theoron is with me or Terian all the time," Brian replied, courteous yet firm. "I don't need to check on his whereabouts. Elle is either with her tutor, you or me." He gave me a resigned look. "You are the only one who wanders alone. Even when you are on the grounds, I need to know where you are at all times to do my job. Please cooperate, Sarelle."

Brian had been like this from the first: not too friendly, polite yet dogged. He was often solemn, or maybe the better word was committed. In any case, it was hard to fault him for it.

"I've told you I'd call you if I left," I reminded him. "You can trust me, Brian. You'll know my every move from the moment I step onto Danial's grounds to the moment I leave with Theo or Terian."

"Good," he said, satisfied. "Erin, Monica told me to let you know she'll be late coming on duty tonight."

"She's been doing that recently," Erin grumbled to me as Brian left. "I'm not sure why Danial doesn't reprimand her for it."

"I'll mention it to him tonight," I said with secret glee. "I plan on staying late for my last voice lesson. Is the dough mixed?"

Erin nodded.

"Good. Hand it over. It's almost two already."

* * * *

I'd worked hard for five weeks as Devlin worked his magic on my vocal cords. I'd hoped for a grand finale; a big duet with him, or maybe for him to ask me to sing something to him now we were done. Instead, he simply shook my hand and told me I'd done a very good job. My letdown was palpable, though I tried to conceal it.

"Can't we continue?" I asked hesitantly. "There is much more I could learn from you about music. You were obviously taught by a professional. Were you on stage?"

"When you have eternity, you find things to keep your mind occupied, or you go crazy," Devlin replied tiredly. "But no, I've taught you all you need to sing passably, Sar. Go forth and burst into song with aplomb."

Try to be graceful, damn it. "Thank you again," I said, walking him to the door.

"You're welcome," he said, turning away.

Impulsively, I hugged him. "I'm sorry for what I said. I don't hate you."

Devlin turned in my arms and then hugged me back. "I know you don't, not anymore at least." His lips grazed my ear, and I froze. "Be careful, Sar," he whispered. "One of these new people is a spy."

"Are you telling me not to trust Brian?" I said, trying to pull back from him.

His arms tightened around me. "You can trust him," he whispered. "But not the other two. Remember that." He let me go and left, shutting the door behind him.

Not to be thwarted, I followed him out the door and down the steps, calling for him to wait. Devlin kept walking, ignoring me. I caught up with him finally at the door to his Hummer.

"Explain yourself," I said, grabbing his arm with my hand.

Devlin turned to me, held my eyes for a moment, and then said:

"I find no peace, Sar and all my war is done
I fear and I hope; I burn and I freeze like ice;
I fly above the wind and yet I cannot arise;
And naught I have, but all the world I seize on."

He gave me one long look and then got in his truck and drove off, ignoring my yells at him to stop.

"What's that even supposed to mean?" I grumbled, watching his taillights fade.

"That he is unhappy," a feminine voice said from behind me. "He was quoting Wyatt."

I turned quickly at the unfamiliar voice. Behind me stood one of the most seductive women I had ever seen. She had perfect features, long black hair and green eyes, like mine though with more blue. She was a bit taller than me, close to Danial's height.

"You must be Sar," she said. "I'm Monica. Good to meet you."

I almost told her not to call me Sar, but stopped myself. "Nice to meet you, too."

We walked in together, and she hung up her coat. I didn't like her instantly, envying her beauty which was so much more than mine. Yet I couldn't help but look at her in admiration.

"It's good to finally meet you," I said once more, making myself smile at her.

She smiled back at me. "I was beginning to wonder if we ever would meet. But you prefer the days and I the nights."

I gave her an odd look, then heard Danial behind me say, "I was wondering when you'd get here."

His words weren't a reprimand; they were teasing.

"Thanks for letting me come in late," she said lightly. "I caught up on my sleep."

"Good," Danial replied. "Please wait for me upstairs. We need to go over some of the perimeter loopholes you discovered. But I must see Sar out first."

"I'm fine," I made myself say hastily. "Go ahead. I'll see myself out. Goodnight." I walked quickly to the door and outside to Theo in the truck.

There was no giggling or murmuring, no soft sighs of passion from behind me. But Danial did not come after me and that somehow hurt more than seeing them embrace.

"I saw you meet her," Theo said gently as we drove down the driveway. "I couldn't tell you. I'm sorry."

"It's fine," I sighed. "I'm with you, and he has no one. I'll get used to it. I want him to be happy."

"You're practically enraged. Is some of it because she resembles Angel?"

"Don't say her name," I replied harshly. I didn't want to hear about my old hated rival for Danial's affection when a new one had just caused me fresh pain.

Theo raised his eyebrows, but only said, "Is it?"

"Some, yes," I admitted. "But it doesn't matter. My lessons with Devlin are done, and I'll just avoid her. Brian can come and stay at our house the nights you need to work, and I'll just come over days." Angrily, I remembered her comment about preferring nights. *Bitch.*

"Do you want me to—?"

"I don't want you to do anything but drive. Let's not talk about it, okay?"

"Okay."

* * * *

With planning, I was able to avoid seeing Monica as I had before. Days passed, then a week. Danial treated me exactly as he always had, which made me think I'd imagined his affection and interest in her. That lasted until the following Friday morning, when I went in early with Theo to work on emails and found Monica coming out of Danial's bedroom. She was clearly heading to her rooms for the day, her hair mussed from bed, her clothing somewhat wrinkled.

I took pleasure in the fact he wouldn't let her stay the day with him. "Good morning. I see you're still in need of sleep."

She stopped still, then relaxed. "Hi," she said uneasily. "I expected to be gone before you arrived."

That implied she'd been fucking him right along, maybe from when she'd first been hired. Likely he'd let her come in late to work, because he'd been keeping her up all night. "He's the boss," I said, daggers in my eyes. "If he doesn't care, I don't." I went past her and headed upstairs to work.

"Sar," she called after me, "I won't apologize to you for this. We wanted to—"

"Don't apologize to me, you whore," I said icily, turning to glare at her. "I've got no problem with him moving on or using you to do it. But you have no self-respect to be fucking your boss." I raised my voice. "And I just lost a good deal of respect for him, too."

"I'd happily leave his employ if you and his children didn't need me so much," Monica replied sweetly. "Be assured the time will come when I will." She gave me a triumphant smile. "But I'll never be leaving his bed, Sar. You can count on that." She stalked away, then slammed the front door.

I resisted the urge to go after her or yell. What was the point? She had every right to be in Danial's bed if he wanted her there. I was just jealous, and that was that. I went upstairs and sat down at the desk, looking at my hands, studying my diamond ring from Danial on my right. I resisted the spiteful urge to leave it on his computer keyboard and got to work.

Doing email for hours mellowed my mood slightly, enough so I joined Elle outside after lunch. We were in the backyard, just a little ways beyond the house. Theoron was sitting in the afternoon sun on a blanket, playing with some flowers, as Elle sketched him. Brian was sitting to the side of the blanket, dozing in bear form.

I'd no sooner gotten settled when my cell rang. It was Danial.

"Hi, Danial," I said. "Shouldn't you be catching up on your sleep, too?"

"Sar, come inside."

"I'm good here, Danial," I said, my voice cracking a little.

"Come inside. I want to talk to you," Danial said and then hung up.

I sighed. I might as well face him. It wasn't going to get any easier.

I got to my feet. Everyone looked up. "I'll be back," I said. "Danial needs to talk to me."

Brian nodded, then gestured with his head to go.

Feeling like I was walking to a scaffold, I went inside to the great room, where Danial waited for me on the couch, fully dressed.

"Come and sit with me, Sar," he said softly.

I sat down across from him and gave him an expectant look.

"I heard what you said to Monica this morning."

"I taught you a bad habit," I said sarcastically, glancing at him quickly. "Now you are listening at doors."

"You said it loudly, hoping I'd hear it," he said, ignoring the barb. "I'm sorry you don't respect me as you did. I want to know if you'd rather not work for me anymore."

I cast him an astonished look, absolutely crushed.

"I don't want to upset you," Danial continued. "But I'm not going to fire her or stop seeing her, which is what you want me to do. Can you work with her or not?"

He was saying I had to go unless I was willing to accept them. I got to my feet hastily, blinking back tears. "No, I won't. Go ahead and fire me if you want. You can have your clone."

I took a step toward the door, and Danial grabbed hold of me.

"Let me go!" I shouted furiously, trying to yank my arm from his iron grasp.

"No," he hissed fiercely. "I won't. You don't want me, but you don't want anyone else to have me, either."

"That's fucking right!" I yelled. "You're mine, and we have a child, and that should mean you don't want to fuck bimbos anymore! You should want me!"

"I do want you," Danial snarled and brought his lips down on mine forcefully. I responded to him, kissing him back hard, my tongue slipping between his parted lips. He pushed me back onto the sofa, then crushed me to him, kissing me thoroughly as his hands roamed my body, touching and caressing me. Danial's kisses moved to my throat. He sucked gently at my skin, his hips grinding into mine, pressing his steel-like erection between my legs. I arched my back and pressed close to him, letting out an eager cry.

My heart was racing. This was so wrong. I knew it, and I was doing it anyway!

Danial pulled back from me, panting. "Tell me yes," he murmured, moving in to lick my throat. "Tell me yes, and I'll tell her she's fired." He kissed up my neck. "I'll be yours again if you'll be mine."

That was enough to shock me back into reality. I pushed him off me with one fast movement, scrambling to my feet. Breathing hard, I put some distance between us. "I love you," I gasped, lust and love mixed together in my words. "I'm sorry for this, all of it. I'm so sorry." I turned and fled, Danial's lunge just missing me.

"Sar!" he shouted.

I ran from him and everything I was feeling into the woods. I walked quickly out of sight, stopping to gather myself together.

I'd wanted Danial so bad I could taste it. What had happened to me? Was it just jealousy?

My cell phone began to ring. It was Danial. I ignored it. Knowing he'd call Brian next to hunt me down, I walked to Terian's lab, hoping by the time I got there my eyes wouldn't look upset or lustful.

Terian was there mixing some potion studiously. "Hey, Sar," he said, glancing up at me. Then he did a double take. "What's wrong?"

Quick, think of something, anything. "Terian, I need a charm or something to ward off Monica's illusions. Do you have anything like that?"

I expected him to say no, but he went to a drawer and wordlessly pulled out a charm on a leather thong. He handed it to me. "Wear it against your skin."

I put it around my ankle, under my sock, figuring that was the last place anyone would look for it. "Thanks." Standing, I added, "You had these ready. Who else has one?"

"Danial asked for one a month ago and I made extras, because they're a pain in the ass to make. Theo asked for one this morning. I get why they want one, but why do you?"

"They must be some kind of truth spell, right? So you can only see what's real?"

"I don't need one to see you're pissed at Monica. I can guess why."

"You know why, so stop with the questions," I said, irritated. "Where is Theo?"

"Working out," Terian said. "And if you are done with me, I'd like to get back to work."

Always the moralist. It must come from his mother's side of the family. "Don't work too hard. You need to save some energy for Erin."

Terian blushed red, confirming my hopes. "Well, at least something is going right today," I said, giving him a smile. "Good luck. I hope she makes you happy."

I headed to the exercise room and found Theo exercising with close to three hundred pounds. He finished a set rapidly, then put the weights aside.

"I didn't expect you," he said happily. Then he sniffed the air, and his face registered anger and jealousy. "Did you come here for a confession?"

"Yes, of sorts. I confronted Danial about Monica, and the next thing I knew we were kissing. I stopped it going further, and I want you to know I'm sorry. The bottom line, though, is I think it might be best if I looked for another job."

"No," Theo said flatly. "Things are working well just as they are. I don't want you leaving."

I stared at him in surprise. He'd never before just told me what to do. My hackles rose instantly, but then oddly, they relaxed. Theo was my husband. He had a right to give me his opinion, and I was supposed to listen, not just brush it off as meaningless. "I thought you'd insist on it after what I just said. What do you think I should do?"

"I think you should work here like you have been. Not only do you do a good job, but also I'm nearby, the way I wouldn't be if you went to work somewhere else. I'll talk to Danial. Monica can work nights as she has been doing, but I'll ask her to avoid you."

"We're going to run into each other sometimes if we both work here."

"Monica can teleport," Theo stated. "That means she can travel without her feet, and she can do that if you're around, so you never have to see her. Don't worry. She'll do it, or I'll fire her. I don't care who Danial fucks, but I expect any employee here to listen when I tell them something." He gave me a hug, then added teasingly, "That goes for you, too."

"If he cares about her, he's not going to like you giving her orders," I said, dubious.

"That's my job here—to give orders," Theo said confidently. "Let me talk to Danial. We'll sort it out."

* * * *

Days passed, then a week. Theo's plan worked, at least to the point I never saw Monica in the flesh. Even so, hearing her open Danial's door some mornings when I was above in the study was enough to infuriate me.

Danial himself also avoided me as much as possible, except when we chanced on one another. When that happened, we were polite but distant as we speedily parted. He took to leaving any questions or instructions he had for me on his desk to find when I came in the next morning. As much as the arrangement was odd, I got used to it.

When the first of September came, I began harvesting the garden. Despite that everything had grown well, my passion for it was nonexistent, something Theo quickly picked up on.

"You don't have to harvest more if you don't want to," he said, hugging me from behind one night as I steamed and froze vegetables.

"You want me to leave it for the rabbits?" I joked.

"Yes, actually," Theo said eagerly. "I like rabbit a lot. If you open the gate, they'll be drawn to the food, and I'll bag us a few."

I reminded myself he was part animal, and a rabbit wasn't something cute to look at for him. It was food. "You'll have enough meat. I bought a cow's worth from the farmer down the road. He's bringing it by in a few days along with a dozen chickens."

"Good. I've also purchased some meat through Danial. We have a reliable source for the werefox larder, a farm in the Midwest that is organic and free of antibiotics."

"How is he?" I asked tentatively.

"Danial's fine," Theo said flatly. "He's adapting to you being gone and using Monica to do it. For what it's worth, I think he's happy with her. But don't worry, there aren't going to be any Oaths spoken anytime soon. Danial said he was done with that."

"He told you that?"

"No, he told you that," Theo said, releasing me and going into the other room. "He said it, knowing I'd tell you if you asked, knowing you would ask. He knows I don't care if he takes vows, so long as they aren't to you. He knows you do care, despite you're married to me."

I didn't reply. What was there to say? Theo was right.

Chapter Thirteen

The phone rang at three a.m. Groggily, I grabbed it. "Hello?"

"I'm sorry for waking you, Sar," Danial said politely. "Please put Theo on. It's urgent I speak with him."

I nudged Theo awake. "Danial."

Theo took the phone, mumbled a few assents, then hung up. "Shit."

"What's wrong?"

"I need to go to L.A for a meeting tonight with Danial. Terian was supposed to go, but he can't now."

"Why?"

"Danial didn't say. Anyway, this means you'll have to come in with me to work and stay overnight there."

"Not with Monica there, I won't."

"She'll be on guard with Terian, but she can guard from outside the house and pull night shift. Brian and Erin will be there all day. Has she given you any trouble?"

"No," I admitted reluctantly. "You think Ivan and Janice can come and watch things here? It's almost the weekend."

"Sure," Theo said, dialing. "I'll arrange it. Go back to sleep. We won't leave until close to dark. I need to be rested enough to be up all night."

* * * *

An hour after our arrival at dusk, Theo and Danial were airborne for L.A., Erin had gone to rest up for her next shift at dawn, and Terian, Elle, Brian and myself were in the great room playing Pollyanna, an older version of Parcheesi.

"So why didn't you go?" I asked Terian. "You've never bailed on a trip before."

"I need to be somewhere else later tonight," Terian answered, rolling dice and moving his pieces. "But Monica should be here by then to take over. I won't be gone long."

I gave him a fake smile. "Thanks. I'm so relieved."

"I'll be here, too," Brian said, yawning.

"Your shift ended an hour ago," Terian said. "I know your stamina's good for another day, but you don't have to stay if you're tired."

"I do," Brian said, straightening up visibly. "I'll put in for the overtime. Don't worry. Your turn, Elle."

"I caught you," Elle exclaimed in glee. She sent one of Terian's pieces back again to start. "Now I get twenty extra spaces." She began to count them off aloud in a smug voice.

"Whatever. It's Sar's turn," Terian said irritably.

"Why didn't Monica go?" I asked Terian suddenly. "It's going to be an overnight, so—"

"I hear something," Brian said, his voice edgy as he stood up. "There's a small group moving toward the door."

"We were playing," Elle said, scowling. "It's probably the foxes coming back."

"No," Terian said, leaping to his feet. "There's too many of them."

"Elle, get your gun," I said, moving fast for the nursery. "I'll get Theoron."

Elle got to her feet without a word and ran after me. I grabbed Theoron from his crib, then my explosive bullets gun from my holster on the chair and raced back to Terian and Brian. Elle joined us a moment later, her explosive bullets gun in her hands.

"Should we go to the basement?" I said anxiously.

Terian closed his cell phone. "I can't get anybody at the fox compound. Wait here."

Terian abruptly vanished. I gaped in shock. Elle gasped. Brian's mouth hung open.

Terian reappeared. "Manir is here," he said. "The foxes are shut inside, a force of twenty werebears pinning them down with gunfire. They can't help us."

"We need more guns—" I said quickly.

"No, more ammo," Brian interrupted. "Go quickly, Terian. Manir may have a sorcerer of his own."

Terian disappeared. A few moments later, he reappeared with additional explosive bullet guns for Brian and me and a case of ammunition. He handed them out quickly. "Sorry, this was all I could get. The armory's been looted."

"We can't hold them off, not with all these windows," Brian said, scanning the room. "Upstairs is exposed, too. They'll burn us out—"

"Terian, can you teleport us out?" I asked.

"Not everybody," Terian said worriedly. "And if he does have a sorcerer, I'll get one trip out before I'm blocked. I won't be able to return."

"How many can you take?" Brian asked.

"I've never taken anyone," Terian admitted, peering outside. "Monica just started teaching me a week ago—"

"Help!" someone called from the porch. "Let me in!"

Brian went for the door.

"Don't open it," I said flatly, pointing my gun at him.

"It's Erin," he said in disbelief. "She probably was attacked on the way to the compound. She might be hurt—"

"You heard her," Terian said, aiming his gun at Brian. "It's got to be a trick. Don't go another step, or I'll shoot you."

That was his lover pleading for help out there. But he knew as well as I did that the coincidence was too great that Erin had escaped the werefox compound and made it to us when no one else had.

Brian stood there looking at us, aghast. "What if it isn't? She's eagle. She might have flown out—"

Erin began to scream outside, and I wondered for a half second if we had made the right choice. Then the door burst open, and it didn't matter. Men poured into the entryway, and we fell back behind the couches in the great room.

"Live captures only," a snot-nosed voice said. "Don't risk hurting the dhamphir. We have no idea what might be lethal at his age. He's no use to me dead."

Guards moved into the room, fanning out.

"Fire!" Terian yelled.

The room filled with noise and smoke as our bullets exploded flesh and bone. Five guards went down fast, but the rest fell back to the entryway.

"How many are there?" I whispered to Terian, who had a clear view.

"About forty or so at least."

"We can't kill them all," Brian said. "They're going to rush us any minute."

"Shoot until we're empty," Terian said coldly. "I'll kill whomever is left."

"Terian, kill them now with your magic," I demanded. "We need to save the ammo for the twenty more bears guarding the foxes. Manir might even have more in reserve!"

Terian held my gaze, then reluctantly dropped his gun to the floor. He began to call out words loudly. Sudden gasps, then screams rang out.

"Attack!" Manir yelled.

The men rushed out at us to be stopped by Brian's bullets. When he clicked on empty, the other men behind them rushed in. Terian crushed their hearts with magic as they came. One by one, they fell convulsing on the floor, their mouths covered in blood.

"So much for your intel."

Manir. He was furious by the sound of him.

"You should have waited," Erin said bitterly. "I told you Terian was here—"

"Too late to be of any use," Manir hissed.

"No!" Erin yelled. "You said—"

A shot sounded, and her voice was suddenly cut off. Manir walked out in front of us, his explosive bullets gun smoking. He looked about eighteen, maybe nineteen. Short, black clothes and platinum hair to his shoulders, cut in a punk style. He wasn't handsome, but he did look kind of pretty.

"He's from the early eighties," Brian whispered. "Rich vampire trash."

I smirked. "No wonder he's pissed, stuck with eighties hair for eternity."

"Terian," Manir called in a high voice. "You may have killed my men, but I have reserves. There are another twenty bears outside right now. Give me the child and the woman, and you and anyone else can walk out of here."

"Never," Terian said resolutely, blackness oozing out of him.

"Then I'll take them by force. You don't have enough magic to stop us all," Manir cackled eagerly. "Attack!"

Terian threw a bolt of lightning at Manir. It caught Manir full on the chest and knocked him backwards, his chest smoking, just as all the great room glass windows shattered. Bears came through, their hulking forms darting and weaving to evade our bullets. We managed to hit only half, and of the ones we hit, some were only wounded.

Terian grabbed Theoron out of my arms. "Fall back to Danial's room!"

We managed to make it inside and lock the door. In the next moment, it began to shudder under fierce blows, the growling of bears deafening.

There was only one way this could end if we stayed together: capture. "Terian, teleport Elle and Theoron out of here! Brian can get me out."

"You trust him?" Terian shot me a worried look. "Erin betrayed us."

I remembered Devlin's words. "Yes. Go! Get them to safety."

"I'll come back if I can." Terian grabbed Elle's hand, and the three of them vanished.

"What's the plan?" Brian asked.

"There are studs here," I said, going to the outside wall of the back room and spreading my hands. "Between is just drywall at most and insulation. Break us a way out."

Brian changed to bear so fast his clothes exploded outward in shreds. He smashed into the wall with his shoulders. I crouched as plaster chips flew in all directions, shielding my face with my arms. The wall held; the sturdy two by fours only cracked. Brian smashed into it again, and the central stud broke cleanly in two. Brian squirmed through, me at his heels, just as Danial's bedroom door was broken down.

"Go after them!" Manir shouted. "No shooting! Get the baby!"

Brian ran into the forest, and I did my best to follow him. It was dark, no moon, even the starlight obscured by cloud cover. Though my night vision was phenomenal now due to Danial's blood, I still tripped, falling more than once. Brian's eyesight as bear was also poor, but he smashed a trail that was easy enough to follow.

We finally stopped in the heart of Danial's woods, near the graveyard. I sat on the ground, exhausted. There were no sounds of pursuit. Brian stood over me in bear form, panting shallowly. I clutched my gun in my hands. There was some comfort in its cold weight. There was most of one clip left and an extra full one in my hip pocket.

"Can you hear anyone?" I whispered finally, standing.

He shook his massive head.

"Can you get me to the road? Maybe I could flag down a car—"

Brian shook his head again.

"We can't just wait here to be taken prisoner—"

Brian put his paw on my chest and gently pushed me back down. He gave his paw a little extra pressure and then lifted it off.

"I get you want me to stay here. But I need to know what happened to Elle and Theoron."

Brian didn't move.

"Do you think Monica finally showed up and routed them?"

He nodded, then shrugged.

I handed my shirt to him. "Change back so I can talk to you."

Brian's fur quickly became hands and skin. He wrapped the shirt around his waist. "Sarelle, you need to stay here until we can determine it's safe to return."

"We should try to get to the road or even a neighboring house. Terian might not have made it. We have to contact Theo and Danial—"

"I don't answer to them, Sarelle," Brian answered. "Contacting them isn't a priority."

I stood quickly, then backed away from him. "Who?"

"Devlin," he said almost sadly, then moved to block me. "Please, don't be afraid. I won't hurt you." He held up his hands.

"Danial said you'd wanted Theo's job years ago," I hissed at him. "Devlin put you up to it, didn't he? For revenge?"

"Yes, that was the plan then, but—"

"And you agreed? What kind of a prick are you?" I shouted.

"I refused when his motive was revenge," he said, his eyes willing me to believe him. "He doesn't want revenge now. He wants you safe at all costs—"

"You lied to us!"

"He has my wife!" Brian yelled back. "He said if anything happened to you, the same would happen to her."

This was why Devlin was sure Brian could be trusted: he held all the cards. No wonder Brian had wanted to know where I was all the time. "I suppose you had better call him and report in," I said sardonically, throwing him my cell from my back pocket.

"I'm sorry," he replied, dialing rapidly. "I had no choice."

I sat down near the tree, wrapping my arms around my knees to ease my shaking. Brian reached Devlin and briefed him on the night's events.

"We're near the cemetery. Home in on the cell phone signal. We'll leave it on. We may have to move."

Brian hung up and moved to toss the cell phone back. I put down the gun to catch it, but he didn't throw it.

"Why is it so misty all of a sudden?" he asked, putting out his arms. "Where did—?"

"Get down!" I yelled, dropping flat.

There was a gunshot. Brian let out a cry of pain and dropped down face first, his back a smoking crater.

"Sar," a voice called hesitantly. "Where are you? I can't see you—"

"You know I'm here, Monica. Just come out," I replied scornfully.

"Impressive," she said, stepping out of the woods. "I'm surprised you can see me."

"I can see the explosive bullets gun in your hand."

"You are safe now," she continued comfortingly. "Come with me back to the house—"

"Bullshit," I spat at her. "Do you think I'm stupid?"

She laughed. "Yes, I do. There's someone at the house who wants a word with you."

"Manir can come here if he wants me," I said much more bravely then I felt. "You've betrayed us."

She gave me an evil smile. "Not him, Sar. Alphonse is the one waiting for you. Get going," she said, gesturing with the gun at me.

Fear slipped like ice down my back. I went on my hands and knees to Brian's side, rolling him over to see how badly he was hurt. The gaping hole near his shoulder was healing, his eyes filled with pain. Weakly, he pressed his gun into my hand hidden behind his body.

"He'll heal," Monica said. "I purposely missed his heart. You want him to keep healing, come with me. His life is in your hands."

She was good at being hard, I gave her that. "Why are you doing this?" I asked angrily.

"Because I'll get what's left of you when he's done—"

I shot her with the gun, pulling it out in a smooth movement. She screamed as the exploding bullet blew her arm off and fell backward into the dirt. I got to my feet and kicked her gun away, her arm still attached. She was screaming hysterically as blood rapidly pumped out of her.

Ick. "Brian, put pressure on her wound," I ordered.

He obeyed, using my shirt.

Double ick. I wouldn't be wearing that again. "Don't try a spell. Tell me what you meant, or next time my aim won't be off," I said, leveling the gun between her eyes.

Her eyes were wide, full of fear and agony. "You'll kill me anyway," she gasped.

"I'll let you heal yourself, if you tell me the truth," I offered. "How long do you think you have before you bleed to death?"

"I did it for Danial," she moaned softly.

Of all the things I expected—money, power, maybe even prestige—this was a surprise. "Explain," I said, pressing the gun muzzle hard against her temple.

"I'm in love with him, but he loves you. He called me by your name once."

Not hard to imagine how that had felt, especially in the probable context. "Go on."

"If you're dead, he'll grieve, and then he'll go on. You won't be around as a constant reminder of his epic love. He can start to forget you, start to really love someone else." She swallowed. "I might try to have a child with him. I think I can alter my blood to make it resistant as yours is. I need your blood and DNA to study. Besides, with you still hanging around, he would never settle for a life with me—"

"So you decided to give me to Al?" I said sarcastically.

"I knew Manir would attack again. When he did, you could disappear in the confusion. I knew Erin was one of Manir's agents. She's been waiting for Theo and Danial to go out of town together. She stupidly puts credence in that bullshit ranking. Too many non-humans do these days."

"What are you saying?" Brian interjected.

"That Theo would have been much easier to kill."

"Monica," I said flatly. "We'll let you heal. But I want your help fighting whomever's still attacking, Manir or Al. Swear to your Goddess right now that you will help me."

"I swear to my God and Goddess," she gasped out. "If I don't help you as you've asked, or if I raise hands against you in any way, let Them strike me down."

I moved the gun away from her head. "Brian, take her gun and put her arm near her."

He did as I asked. Quickly, she began to heal herself, saying words in a chant.

"Sar, this is unwise," Brian warned me, his eyes scared. "She's a witch—"

"She answered my questions," I said composedly. "I keep my promises."

Monica healed herself slowly, flexing her reattached hand in relief when the healing was complete. She got to her feet, dusting herself off with her hands. "What's your plan?"

I looked at her for a split second and then emptied the rest of the clip into her. She was dead when the first bullet exploded her heart. The rest of them shredded her chest and torso, smoke rising from her charred flesh.

"Good," Brian said in relief. "I'd thought you'd gone crazy, trusting her at her word."

"I've wondered for some time what explosive bullets would do to a human."

"I could've told you they make a mess," he replied, picking up my cell phone and handing it to me. "Devlin's on his way. We need to head for the road."

I remained standing, staring down at Monica's ruined form. "She had it coming."

"If you believed that, you wouldn't sound so guilty," Brian said. "She was your enemy and mine. Let it go. If I'd had another clip to waste, I'd have shot her a few more times myself for her treachery. Now follow me. I'll lead you to the road."

He changed at once, and we began walking again. We finally reached the road about a half hour later. No Hummers were there, as we'd hoped.

"Where's Devlin?"

Brian nosed my pocket with the cell phone. I took it out and pressed redial. It rang only once. "What is it, Sar?" Devlin said calmly.

"How close are you?"

"About a half hour, give or take. Hummers aren't built for speed."

"They are going to find us and take me," I said emphatically. "Al is here—
"

"Stay alive. I'll find you," Devlin said commandingly. "Which side of the driveway are you on?"

"The right. I can't see the driveway. But I'm close to that big maple that's about a mile away from it."

"I know where that is. Wait back from the road at least twenty feet. Don't come to the road until you see me personally."

"Got it. Now that we're synchronized, why did you take Brian's wife?"

"Hang up," Devlin said coolly. "You know why already."

"Let her go."

"She is free to go," Devlin said, a thread of malice twining into his flat tone. "As soon as you are safe. I want his best effort and so should you."

"That's not fair. He's one against—"

"I'm bringing my best people, Sar. That will more than even the odds."

A man's voice grumbled something in the background. Devlin irritably told whomever it was to shut up and drive.

"Even with them, you can't hurt an innocent woman—"

"I am not Danial or Theo, that you can plead with me and get somewhere," Devlin said, coldly. "Now sit tight and wait." Click.

That said it all, right there. I shut the phone. "He said to wait here until we see him."

We sat down to wait. I was tired, cold and hungry. "Damn it, I should've thought to grab that shirt. It was bloody, but I'd have been warmer."

Brian motioned me to come into his arms. Shivering with cold, I went to him, and he enveloped me in a bear hug. Within moments, insulated by his thick fur, I was warm.

Suddenly, Brian went rigid, then fell to land hard on his side, blood pouring out of his craterlike chest wound. He gasped, but couldn't breathe.

I rose up, raised my gun and fired, hitting the first attacker in the neck and blowing his head off. Then I was grabbed from behind, the gun knocked from my hand. Despite my struggling, the man held me easily. More men came out of the trees, holstering their guns.

"He's out for a while, and we've got what we came for," said the man holding me. "Call it in."

Another man called in his position and that they'd captured me. They moved in a group toward the road. When we reached it, a van picked us up. I was thrown into the back seat and told to lay there. We drove northwest, according to the vehicle's compass.

I worried about Brian, wondering if he was too hurt to heal. I worried about my children, if they'd gotten out. But most of all I worried about what was going to happen when these men got me wherever we were headed. My one comfort was that the cell phone in my pocket was still on, and the signal was being broadcast. The question was would Devlin find me in time.

* * * *

Some hours later, we arrived at a huge mansion so large it looked like a resort. The men got me out of the van and led me struggling up the stairs and in the front doors.

Al was waiting there for us. He looked the same as he had those years ago. He was even dressed in a robe.

"Sarelle," he said softly. "You look as lovely as ever."

I didn't reply, averting my eyes.

"Are you sorry you insulted me?" he said angrily.

Maybe I could soothe his ego. "I was married when you met me years ago," I said contritely. "I meant no disrespect—"

"You enjoyed seeing me thrown out of that room like a naughty child caught with his hand in the cookie jar."

That was true, but admitting it would be bad. I didn't reply.

"Part of me wants to finish what I started with you that night," Al said evocatively, coming to stand beside me. "There's no vampire here tonight to ruin things."

Not yet, anyway. "Look," I said persuasively. "I'm nobody special, really. You've clearly got the world by the ass. You could have supermodels or Nobel Laureates. Why waste your time with me?"

"I said part of me wanted you, a small part. But this isn't about sex. This is about revenge." He grabbed a handful of my hair, enough to make me grimace. "I'm going to have my men work you over." He grinned at me evilly.

Screw him. The worst he could do was rape and kill me and then, according to Stephen, I'd turn vampire. And when that happened I was going to drain his ass dry. Better to be killed as soon as possible, then.

I gave him a blank look. "This is so B movie-ish. Can't you get an original idea? Or better yet, skip the rape scene and just kill me? Or are you just impotent?"

Al snarled and backhanded me hard enough I tasted blood on my way to the floor. With a sneer, he grabbed me up, then pushed me in front of him out the door, down a half flight of stairs and then down another hall. Finally, we went through a door and into a bedroom.

It was beautiful, with a large canopy bed of carved wood, made up with pure white sheets of fine cotton that shimmered as Danial's sheets always had. The rest of the room was ornate, overly so. A showplace for a rich man who had pretensions.

He threw me on the bed. "Strip her and tie her down spread-eagled."

His men did as he asked, one with mean eyes licking his lips suggestively. Al sat in a velvet-covered chair and smirked at me, watching as I struggled.

"We should use the whips first," one man said.

"She might faint," another countered. "Besides, I want her before there's blood all over her."

"Yeah, we want her to move a little, not just lay there," another said.

They weren't just going to rape me, they were going to beat me to death in front of Al. I closed my eyes, suddenly scared.

"No more comments?" Al asked, his pleasure in his words. "Feel free to say anything on your mind, girl. I welcome your full participation."

The man with mean eyes uncoiled the cat of nine tails, then snapped it in the air a hair's breadth from my face. I flinched, my eyes wide, even though the lashes hadn't landed on me.

My response brought nods and exclamations of admiration for the sadistic bastard with the whip. I began to shake and whimper, though I tried hard to be strong.

"Just give her a taste," Al said lecherously. "Soften her up, Vanni, but watch the lashes. I want her to be able to scream when Henry puts it to her."

Vanni nodded, then snapped the tails again. This time they landed on my hips and thighs. I let out a loud scream, yanking at my bonds.

"Again," Al said eagerly.

Ten times more Vanni hit me, and ten times more I screamed, the welts becoming bloody cuts that burned and dribbled blood unto the sheet beneath me. By that time, I was sobbing, begging them to stop, my voice a cracked whisper of helplessness.

"Go to it, Henry," Al said. "She's yours first."

Henry began to unbutton his shirt. "Good, I was hoping you'd stop him before she was ruined for—"

The window in the room exploded inward suddenly, glass flying everywhere. I closed my eyes and ducked my head as glass rained down over me in an arc. Screams filled the room, then wetness touched my bound hand. I opened my eyes. Henry was convulsing, his eye oozing blood, a large glass shard sticking out of the socket. He'd dropped his gun on the bed and was using both hands in an effort to get it out, his efforts working it deeper. He gave a sudden sigh and relaxed onto the bed, then slipped off the side.

The room was plunged into darkness. There were sounds of fighting, then the bright flashes and noise of gunfire. More screams sounded, then came a wet ripping sound and greedy gulping.

Three shots fired quickly. The frantic gulping becoming a short yell that quickly died.

"Why are you here, Dev?" Al said in the blackness. "We are friends! My family had always been your ally. You knew my father and grandfather!"

"I offered you money to leave Sar alone," Devlin said heavily. "I offered you free kills. You refused both. So I knew you had found some way to get to her."

"You want her for yourself? Why? You've never lacked for women—"

"That isn't your concern," Devlin said nonchalantly. "She is valuable, and you would waste her with this pointless and common torture scenario. I can't let that happen."

"Don't think I won't use this," Al replied, his voice now coming from the far side of the room. "Take her and leave if she's so important. But you come for me, you're dead."

"Your men are already dead around you," Devlin said mockingly. "And it's too late for bargaining, Al."

There was sudden fumbling as Al tried for the door.

"You are common evil. The worst kind," Devlin said, his voice dark with bloodlust. "Your grandfather would be ashamed to call you family."

"We have been allies for a decade!" Al pleaded. "You're throwing that away for a woman? After all we have gone through together? All the times I helped you?"

"You never helped me for any other reason than that it suited your purposes. The same as my reasons for helping you. Here is where we part ways."

Another shot rang out. There was a grunt of pain, then frantic struggling. That died until the only noise in the gloom was unrelenting sucking.

I lay still tied in shock, everything around me surreal. For a minute or so, I was still, my entire thought on breathing so I might reach the next moment. Then a draft of chill air gusted through the shattered windows, bathing my naked body in gooseflesh and shocking me out of my stupor.

"Devlin?" I called hesitantly.

There was no reply. But the silver moon suddenly appeared from behind clouds, lighting the gloom with faint cool light.

"Shouldn't we go?" I said, my voice quavering.

Devlin got up and came toward me slowly, his skin shining faintly in the gloom. He had healed his bullet wounds, pale skin shining through the ragged bloody holes of his shirt. Wisps of smoke still curled up from him in places. His hair was also longer. It reached his shoulders now, and the stubble I had seen before on his face was now thicker, almost a beard. Blood covered his face and hands.

He sat beside me on the bed. "I'm sorry," he said gently. He wiped the blood off his face and hands on the edge of the sheets, then untied my hands.

"For what?" I asked.

He touched my shoulder lightly. "For not being in time."

"You were in time," I said, dissolving into tears. "You were in time."

"Shh," he said, hugging me.

"They were going to—"

"Shh," he said, holding me tighter. "They did not get to do it. And now they are dead. Hold still, I must untie your feet."

I held still as he untied them. Instead of shaking less, I began shaking harder, suddenly feeling Henry's dropped gun lying beneath my back. With a cry of terror, I lunged for it.

Devlin grasped my arm, stopping me. "Leave it. You don't need it." He led me to the nearby closet. "What we need are clothes."

He grabbed two black shirts and handed one to me. We put them on. They hid the holes in his shirt, my cuts and most of the blood.

"Hold still," he whispered, then went to his knees. I felt his hands grasp my waist, then the touch of his mouth on my thighs. With a few light kisses, the burning of the worst of the whip marks went away.

"Dev," a voice hissed in the gloom. "Stop screwing around with her, and come on."

"Are all of Al's men dead?" Devlin asked, tangibly relieved.

"Pretty much," the voice replied. "Get moving. I'll meet you by the car. And if you're looking for her clothes, they're here in a pile by the door." The door opened, a dark figure slipping quickly through it.

"We must go and fast," Devlin said, standing and taking me by the hand. "We need to be far from here when daylight comes." He guided me outside to an idling Hummer and helped me into the backseat, handing me my clothes. I hurriedly slipped them on, just finishing as he returned.

"Where to, Boss?" the driver said.

"Get on the highway and find the nearest decent hotel that we can reach before sunrise. And stay under the speed limit. There's too much blood on me to get pulled over."

As we began moving, Devlin gathered me into his arms and then settled back. I lay there still in shock, trying to get my mind around what had happened to me and what had almost happened. I vacillated between sobbing and staring into nothingness.

"Penny for your thoughts, Sar," Devlin said, grinning down at me.

"Ass," I said crossly, snapping back to myself. "Can't you try to be less creepy? I was getting to like you."

"Don't you mean you *are* getting to like me?" he said, laughing.

"Sometimes," I said, before I thought. "Then I usually remember the night we met."

Devlin looked down at me, eerily. "Blake said it best, Sar.

I went to the Garden of Love
And saw what I never had seen.
A chapel was built in the midst,
Where I used to play on the green.
And the Gates of this Chapel were shut
With "Thou Shalt Not" writ over the door.
So I turned to the garden of Love
That so many sweet flowers bore.
And I saw it was filled with graves,
And tombstones where flowers should be
And Priests in black gowns were making their rounds
And binding with briars my joys and desires."

He lapsed into silence.

I turned toward him. He looked normal, despite the awful words he'd just uttered.

"Tell me what's wrong? Why are you so angry? So bitter? You saved me, and you were strong and fearless and brave. You shouldn't be feeling like you are nothing. Like you have nothing. That's what that meant, right?"

He looked at me, his expression unreadable and didn't answer.

I tried again. "Devlin, answer me, please. Why are you so gloomy?"

"I'm sometimes morose," he replied, a faint smile on his lips. "Don't concern yourself."

I gave up questioning him, put my arms around him and laid my head against his chest, listening to his heart beat. It was slow, as Danial's was. After few moments, he tightened his arms around me, hugging me back.

It was almost dawn when we finally stopped at a Courtyard Inn in some small city. Devlin got out, cast a quick look at the lightening sky, then grabbed a bag from the back of the SUV.

"Hurry, Sar."

Eager to rest, I went with him quickly inside, the guard following. To my surprise, renting a room wasn't easy.

"We have nothing but the honeymoon suite," the clerk told him apologetically. "All our rooms are booked."

"You're joking," Devlin said flatly, giving him eyes that said he'd better be.

"No," the clerk replied. "It's Labor Day weekend next week. We've got an end of summer celebration starting tomorrow for families in town, and it lasts most of the week."

"A fair?" I said blankly.

"Rides, games, fireworks, arts and crafts, wine tastings, live music, parades. You name it," the clerk said proudly. "I'm glad of it. We haven't been so full all year."

"This is like a bad episode of a sitcom," I said, rolling my eyes.

"You said it," Devlin said in disgust, handing him a credit card. "We'll take it."

He led me to the room, instructing his guard to stand in the hallway outside and watch the door. Only the one had left with us. I wondered where the others were now but didn't ask.

"Well, let's see how bad this is," he said portentously, opening the door and gesturing me inside.

I walked into the suite, Devlin following me. The room had a king sized bed, but no atrocious decorations. There was a Jacuzzi tub for two that wasn't pink. Other than the bed, the room contents were the usual—a small table and two chairs, a love seat, a TV, a dresser and a nightstand.

"Not too bad," Devlin said as he sat down on the bed. He let out a groan as he peeled off the shirts, revealing an odd device.

I sat down beside him, peering interestedly. He had on some kind of armored plates over his heart, covering both his front and back, almost like a metal bulletproof vest. Six separate straps held the plates in place, but only two intact straps were left. The others were ragged pieces, where the straps had been shredded by explosive rounds, and some of the metal itself was missing. All of it was stained in blood, most of it his.

"So that's why you aren't dead," I said.

Devlin nodded, attempting to undo the twisted straps. "Yes. I wear it wherever I go now. Those exploding bullets are far too common anymore, and I have too many enemies."

I pushed his hands away and quickly unbuckled it. "You're smart to do it. Danial thinks he's invulnerable."

"I know," he smiled ruefully, as he slipped the plates off. "I've been talking to him, trying to get him to wear one, and he keeps saying it isn't necessary."

"I'll tell him about what happened tonight," I said staunchly. "I'll get him to wear one."

"I'd be grateful if you did," Devlin said, taking the plates into the bathroom. Water began to run.

"Can I borrow some clothes of yours?" I called hesitantly. "I don't have any to change into. I don't want to wear Al's if I don't have to, and mine are torn and bloody—"

"When you shower, put yours into the bag in the bathroom, and I'll have them cleaned today. My bag only has a change of clothes for me. I keep it in my SUV in case of emergencies."

Devlin returned, his armor plates cleaned of blood. He wrapped them in a cloth from his bag, stowing them inside.

"Like rescuing women?" I teased.

"I don't usually rescue women," he replied mordantly. "It's women that usually need rescuing from me."

"For someone proud of that fact, you don't sound very happy about it."

"Who said I'm unhappy?"

"Monica heard what you said to me that night in the driveway. She recognized the poet. She said you were unhappy. And so was the poetry you quoted tonight—"

"Drop it, Sar," Devlin said, his back to me. "Isn't it enough that I saved you when no one else did?"

"Yes, but—"

"No 'buts', Sar. Don't try to get inside my head. I don't want you there. It's going to have to be enough for you that that I took bullets for you yet again."

I almost blurted out that he'd owed me those bullets from way back, but thought better of it. He had rescued me. I was in a strange city miles from home with no money, no ID, no phone, no car and blood on my clothes. Who knew what had happened at home or where everyone was? Trying to contact anyone who'd been at Danial's might lead to disaster. I couldn't bring my human friends and family into this. But maybe Theo had tried to contact Devlin...

"Can you check your cell? I don't have mine. I want to know everyone's okay."

Devlin pulled it out and checked the log. "Theo's called five times."

"May I use your phone?"

He hit a button on the phone and handed it to me. "Push call when you are ready," he said, walking past me. "I'll be in the shower. There is a guard outside. Call him if you need something." The bathroom door clicked shut.

"Thanks," I called after him and pushed the call button.

Theo answered immediately, before a ring even sounded. "Devlin?"

"It's me," I said softly. "I'm okay."

"Sar," Theo said, very relieved, "I am never leaving you alone again—"

"This wasn't your fault," I said quickly. "Erin and Monica planned this."

"Monica was in on this? We thought she was the one who saved you from Manir."

That bitch wasn't going to be thought the hero for long, even if she was dead. "She wanted Danial," I said tiredly. "She was going to give me to Al to get me out of her way."

"Sar, are you sure?" Theo said skeptically. "The foxes were able to break through Manir's guards at the compound because of the mist she made. Hans and Warren made it to the house to find you gone."

"Who're Hans and Warren?"

"Two of the newer foxes Danial hired. Sorry, I forgot you hadn't met them yet. They found dead bears inside the house, but no Manir."

Not a surprise. Monica had needed to let him escape so she had a scapegoat for my death. Danial would never believe he hadn't taken me after the attack ended, if I had been missing.

"Where are you, Theo?"

"Still in California," he said grumpily. "It will be a few more hours until we leave."

I was angry suddenly that he wasn't on his way, that he hadn't dropped everything to try to rescue me. But that was stupid really. He'd been much too far away to be of any help.

"Everyone but you is accounted for," Theo continued. "Terian called us from your house hours ago. He, Elle and Theoron are there now with Janice and Ivan. They're safe."

"Tell them to stay there," I said wearily. "Danial's house is trashed. In fact, he needs to call someone to fix his home, or he's going to have to sleep downstairs when you both get home tomorrow night. There's a wall missing in his bedroom now, and all the windows are broken—"

"What the hell did Manir attack with? Heavy artillery?"

"Brian knocked through the wall so we could escape," I said. "He is the one who saved me from Manir, the one who called Devlin. He can tell you all of this."

"The foxes say they can't find him, Sar. He wasn't there with the others in the house. The foxes looked for him first, knowing how closely he always watched you. We thought he helped to kidnap you, or he was dead."

"Then he's most likely still lying by the road, in the trees," I said angrily. "He got shot many times and couldn't breathe well or talk. I thought you said everyone was accounted for?"

"He either healed enough to go into a sort of coma, or he's dead, Sar," Theo said sadly. "I'll call Aran. He'll get down there fast and find Brian. If Brian's alive, he can heal whatever wound is there, given enough meat and rest."

"Please hurry," I said worriedly. "I'll talk to you later."

"And by 'everyone,' I meant you and the kids, the people being protected. Several guards are still missing. In fact, one of them is Monica. Danial is worried she's not answering her cell."

Fury filled me in an instant "She's out in the cemetery, Theo," I said irately. "She tracked Brian and I there, trying to lead Al to us. She shot Brian, and then I shot her."

Theo didn't reply. But it came through loud and clear that he doubted my story. That he thought I'd used this chance to rid myself of my rival for Danial's affection. That made me angrier.

"She's hamburger, Theo," I said flatly. "And I'm happy she's dead."

"I need to tell him," Theo said distantly. "Get some rest, Sar."

Immediately, I felt guilty. "Theo, I—"

"I'll see you soon," he said, something missing in his voice. "Bye."

I pushed End and lay back on the bed, trying to sort out my feelings of guilt and anger.

Devlin came out of the shower then, wrapped in a towel.

"Thanks," I said, handing him his phone.

"Sure," he replied, putting it on the nightstand. "What do you want to do about sleeping arrangements?"

"What we did before should be fine," I answered. "The bed's big enough."

Devlin didn't answer, getting his clothes from his bag, his back to me. I watched him in the wall mirror, as he rummaged through it, letting my eyes roam over him.

Devlin's build was much like Danial's, save him being a little shorter, but there was definite resemblance. Yet where Danial was dark, Devlin was light. His chest had that same gold hair shimmering on it as his head and face, water droplets still caught here and there, glistening. He was nowhere near as buff as Theo was, but his arms and torso were well defined, like Danial's. His skin was pale, but it didn't detract from his beauty. He had shaved and like his brother, he was very handsome, though Danial was more beautiful, where Devlin was more striking. His gold hair was soaking wet, steadily dripping on the carpet. My eyes traveled up as I opened my mouth to tell him he was making a mess, then froze, staring. Like his brother, Devlin had a thin line of hair running down his body from his lower chest and abs down to his navel and below...

"Admiring the view?" Devlin said, his back to me.

I quickly looked up. He was watching me in the mirror, his golden eyes pleased. I blushed furiously, looked at the far wall and didn't reply.

"Go shower, Sar," Devlin said, amused. "Unless you'd like to watch me dress."

I blushed harder, shot a glare at his back and then went into the bathroom.

He'd wanted me to look at him that way, so he could embarrass me. Jerk.

I took a long hot shower, washing off the blood and dirt. When I got out, I reached for the towel and noticed there were some forest green silk pajamas on the vanity counter in my size.

Maybe Devlin wasn't so bad. I put the clothes I'd been wearing into the hotel bag, dressed in the pajamas and took a good long look at myself in the mirror. Except for my frizzing hair, I looked normal.

I mixed a little hair conditioner with a small amount of water, then put it on my hands, running them through my hair. That would have to do until I got home tomorrow night.

I came out hesitantly, self-conscious in my pajamas. Devlin was there, dressed in a new pair of jeans and a black shirt, perusing the room service menu.

"Are you hungry, Lady in Green?" he asked.

"Are you?" I said, folding my arms across my chest.

Chapter Fourteen

Devlin gave me a calculating look. "Are you offering?" he said calmly. There was the hint of surprise beneath his well-crafted cool exterior

"Yes," I said, sitting down on the love seat and facing him expectantly.

"I'll bite you if you want me to," he replied, smiling faintly. His eyes shone with some emotion, possibly mirth or malice.

"Look," I said, sitting down on the bed. "I'm not playing games. I know you took five explosive rounds to your chest, at least. That's a lot to heal."

"You're worried I'm weak," Devlin said scathingly. "Don't be. As you saw earlier, my wounds have closed—"

I cut him off. "The night Theo disappeared, Danial got shot. He was able to heal his wounds, yet he still collapsed not long after. He'd had blood from at least two men, which is more than you had tonight. He needed mine that night, too. I don't want you to suddenly pass out, as he did."

"If I drink from you, there is going to be pain." Devlin said frankly.

"I know. Helping Danial hurt," I replied. "But what alternative is there?"

"I can take some from the guard if I have to."

We had one guard and with daylight coming, we might need him to protect us. We needed him strong. "Won't he be undermined, if you do?"

"Of course," Devlin said with a shrug. "Blood loss weakens any creature."

"Take my blood instead. I'd rather suffer a little pain and blood loss than be dead."

"You have a way with words," Devlin said, nonplussed. "But I agree with your logic."

"Just don't take more than you need," I cautioned. "I'm still half turned."

"I know," Devlin replied. "Danial told me months ago when you first found out. He thinks it was part of the reason you left him for Theo. Was it?"

161

Was there anything Danial hadn't told him? I mentally rolled my eyes. "It was, partly. I don't want to be a vampire. I can't live in darkness, never seeing the sun."

"You get used to it," Devlin said sadly.

I was ashamed immediately that I'd said that aloud. "I'm sorry—"

"Don't be. It's honest." Devlin lay back on the bed and put his hand through his still wet hair, pushing it out of his face. "When I was first turned, I used to miss the sunlight, Sar. But now words are all I have, with no real memories to go with them. I've forgotten what it felt like on my skin. All I remember is that it was somehow warm and that I thought it was wonderful."

His words were difficult to hear, not from the sadness in them, but from the uncertainty.

"You should eat now, Sar, so I can," Devlin said, handing me the room service menu.

I took it from his outstretched hand, looked it over quickly, then picked up the phone. I ordered a glass of wine, two hamburgers, a large order of fries and chocolate cake. Screw my diet, I'd been kidnapped and almost tortured. I wanted fat and calories and food that made me feel alive. If they'd had cheese fries with bacon on the menu, I'd have gotten some of them, too.

I flipped on the TV while waiting for my food to arrive. I expected to hear nothing about Al, for the night's events to be hushed up. Nothing to do with the supernatural world had ever been reported in the news, not in all the years I'd known Danial and Theo. Yet this time, I was wrong.

"We are reporting live from the scene of notorious gangster Alphonse "Al" Carrera's vacation home tonight. A fire with fatalities broke out tonight in the pre-dawn hours. All that is known is that a chance spark from a propane heater ignited some flammable items in the basement, which quickly spread to the house and the propane tanks. The resulting explosion leveled the home, and as you can see behind me, there is not much left—"

I glanced over at Devlin to find him still perusing the room service menu. I looked back at the screen. As the newscaster had said, there wasn't much left. The house was leveled, the few remains gutted by fire, still smoldering in places. Firefighters were there on the scene, picking through the outlying rubble.

"No one will trace this back to us," Devlin said, not looking up. "Al was brokering a deal with some Eastern terrorists for some guns he had for sale. It was not going well. They will be blamed for this attack, for his death." He looked at me, then back down. "My people are good at what they do. Very good."

I knew well what circles he traveled in. For once, that was a good thing. "Good."

He got up suddenly, turned off the TV, then he went to the door. He was back in a moment, handing me the tray of food. "Please eat," he said, acquiescent. "You were right, Sar. I need more blood and soon. I'm starting to feel weak."

I was starving, so the eating went pretty quickly. I savored my cake though. It was wonderful, moist and gooey. When I was done, he took my tray from me and set it outside the door. I went into the bathroom and brushed my teeth, telling myself I could do this.

Now that it was time, I was regretting saying I'd do this. I was nervous, thinking about him slipping his fangs into me. Did I trust him enough?

If he wanted to hurt me, he could've let me die tonight. It would have been easy to not help me. For that matter, why had he helped me, watched out for me? Holding Brian's wife to ensure his constancy was extreme. It hadn't been a few days; it had been months.

"Sar?" Devlin said from outside the door. "Are you coming out, or did you change your mind?"

I took a breath, opened the door and went out hesitantly. He was lounging on the bed, smiling seductively. I stood before him, unsure of what to do.

"Lie down," he said, patting the bed beside him.

I lay down, my heart hammering.

"Close your eyes," he said, moving close to me.

I closed them. The moment I couldn't see, my fear ratcheted up a notch.

"Don't be afraid, Sar," he said softly, his breath sliding over my skin. I heard his voice and remembered him telling me how much he loved the taste of my fear. Chills went through me, as my fear climbed another three notches.

Devlin sighed. It was the sigh of someone who hadn't wanted to do something but was resigned to having to do it now. "Pretend I am Danial."

"I can't," I said, opening my eyes. "You don't sound like him."

"Close your eyes and think of him," Devlin said. "It's worth a try."

I closed my eyes again.

"I won't hurt you, Sar," Devlin said in Danial's voice. "Trust me. I'll not hurt you, my darling." His voice had always been similar to Danial's, in pattern and inflection. Now he sounded exactly like him. "Kiss me."

His cool lips brushed mine gently, then lingering, as Danial had always liked to do. But I remained tense, my heart hammering.

"Please, Sar," he whispered into my ear. "I love you. And I need you badly, my darling. Please help me."

"Kiss me," I said hesitantly, willing myself to relax.

His cool lips brushed mine again gently. I tried to help him, focusing on my memories of Danial. I kissed Devlin back, my tongue sliding between his lips to open him to me. When he responded, I put my arms around him. He moved closer, his arms encircling me, rolling slightly atop me. Danial/Devlin kissed down my throat, ran the edge of one fang down my neck. I let out a moan, feeling him suck lightly at my throat.

"Danial, please—" I cried.

Abruptly, his fangs pierced me, their sharpness sliding through my scar tissue easily. There was pain, but it seemed faint, unimportant. He held me fast, drinking me down, making those sounds of pleasure and gratification I'd always loved to hear. I clasped him to me, feeling him swallowing in time to my heartbeat, moaning softly.

Devlin gently withdrew his fangs and pushed up from me. "How do you feel?" he said, concerned.

"I'm okay," I said, letting out a breath. "I'm not lightheaded or anything."

"Because it's been a long time since you did this, Sar," Devlin said, purring almost. "I didn't take much, either."

In the way he said it, he'd wanted to take more and was hoping for an invitation. I didn't reply.

He stretched back out beside me, licking and kissing my neck intermittently. "You are the only one, Sar, who tastes of summer," he said longingly. "The only one."

"How does summer taste?" I said. "I've never understood what you meant by that."

"Like warmth, fresh air and green grass, if such things had a taste. Contentment. Happiness."

Wow. "What do others taste of?" I said, not really wanting to know, but wanting a basis for comparison.

"Emotions and feelings often come through the blood. Most taste of lust or sexual excitement," he said, licking me in long strokes between words. "Others taste of their emotions. Al tasted of fear and anger tonight. Some rarer ones are love or naivety or peace."

"I am not a popsicle," I said, turning to him with a slight glare.

"Forgive me," he said, licking me again. "I can't help it. The taste of you is addictive."

I was beginning to think I'd made a big mistake, giving him my blood. "I need to sleep," I said pointedly.

"So sleep," Devlin said, not moving his body at all. He leaned in to kiss my neck again and began sucking slightly.

"Ouch!" I said, pushing him away and glaring at him.

"That couldn't have hurt," he said with a grin. "Just one more taste?"

"No. The time for tasting is over," I said, getting beneath the covers.

Devlin gave me an exultant look. "Are you offering to—?"

"No!" I shouted at him, giving him a shove. "I'm not!"

Devlin laughed richly and then pulled me back to him, his mouth immediately at my neck, again sucking slightly.

"Stop it," I said annoyed. "You've had enough."

"Not nearly enough," he murmured. "God, you taste good, Sarelle."

I was creeped out by his raw desire, but also secretly flattered that I could incite so much passion in him. He always seemed so immovable when he'd been teaching me, when he'd visited with Danial or guarded me. So I let him lick me, closing my eyes as he intermittently kissed and sucked at my neck. In another minute, the bite had closed.

Devlin gave the healed wound one last kiss. "You're all set."

I turned to give him a smart remark and caught sight of his eyes. If I'd ever thought they were molten before, I'd been wrong. Now they were hot as a forge, almost glowing in the dim room. I tensed immediately.

Devlin bent quickly and kissed me chastely on the forehead. Then he moved off to sit in the love seat, putting his feet up on the opposite end and flipping the TV back on.

Relaxing in relief, I lay down and closed my eyes. I said a quick prayer to God for getting me through safely, that Brian would be okay, and thanks that Theoron and Elle were safe with Terian, then fell asleep.

Of course, all my relief brought on a nightmare of epic proportions. I dreamed that I was walking down a road. All had been lost. Vampires ruled the night, and I was never safe. I was desperately trying to leave the town I was in and go out to a more secluded area where there were no buildings for them to hide in the day. I journeyed by day in sunlight, but to go under a river, I had to use a tunnel. In it, I found a man and a woman survivor. They teamed up with me. They had no weapons, and I had a gun. Safety in numbers.

We lost the man the first time we were attacked. He gave himself to save the woman.

She and I made it out of the town, but her will was broken. I knew looking at her that I'd lose her the next night. I did, though that day, more survivors that were also leaving the city found us: another woman and two young men. We all made it to a hotel that night. We bedded down and slept. I knew if we could make it a few more days, maybe then we'd be safe.

I slept alone, apart from them, with my gun. I needed to get away if we were attacked. My sleep was uneasy; I would always hear footsteps and hissing in the quiet of the night. I trusted another to be my ears. My last living pet, a striped tiger cat who was scarred from one attack, lay on me. I'd lost my other animals to attack months ago. I was in a constantly numb state where survival mattered at all costs. That was all I could do; all I was.

Earlier, that day, I found some bowls for us in the hotel kitchen. We were thrilled. We'd been sharing one cracked one, and now we each had our own. It was amazing the things we had taken for granted before our world had become this apocalypse. I was dreaming of how things used to be when I thought I heard something. I held my breath and listened.

Someone was here.

I waited, gun in hand, safety off. There was a cry suddenly cut off and then rattling, something closing or shutting.

My companions were most likely dead, taken by another bloodsucker. The door opened, and the cat's head swiveled, instantly hissing as it sank in its claws to warn me. An Asian woman vampire dressed in red who resembled Suri came in. She said nothing. I took aim at her, knowing I'd kill her; I'd be able to save myself. But I knew that my companions were dead. Drained. I was alone again, all alone…

I woke screaming loudly, flailing.

Devlin was beside me. He rolled over immediately and gathered me into his arms.

I was soaked with sweat and utterly terrified in the grip of my dream. I took a shuddering breath and let out another scream.

"You're safe," Devlin whispered soothingly. "I've got you, Sar. You're safe."

I began crying, sobbing in his arms. He stroked my hair, holding me tightly, murmuring again that I was safe. Finally, I slept again in his arms.

Again, I dreamed. I was tied to a chair, and Aspen was telling me again about having Theo every night in graphic details. I began screaming at her to shut up, and suddenly the dream switched to Theo and me lying naked next to one another in the hotel bed, not speaking.

"You don't love me," he said, tears in his blue eyes. "Not really."

"You know I love you," I said, burrowing into his chest. "Make love to me."

He kissed me softly, his mouth exploring mine. I kissed him back hard, and he groaned, slipping his tongue inside my mouth. I touched his with mine, and he pulled me on top of him, pushing my hips against his so I could feel him hard against me.

"Tell me you want me, Sar," he said softly in my ear. "Tell me you want me inside you."

"I always want you, Theo," I said, kissing his neck. "Take me."

He rolled over on me, kissing me hard. I put my hands on his face and ran them up into his hair. He reached down to caress my breasts possessively as I arched my back for him, the movement bringing our hips together. I felt his erect penis throbbing as he rubbed himself against me. He felt huge, and I couldn't wait for him to enter me.

"Please," I moaned, rubbing him with my hips. "Please."

Theo began shaking, his breaths coming fast, so he was almost panting. I opened my mouth to ask him what was the matter, and then my words became sighs as I felt the edge of delicate fangs run up my throat, pressing lightly, but not breaking the skin. A rush of cool breath caressed on my throat, as lips kissed my scars.

Delicate fangs?

I awoke with a start, my eyes opening to look into eyes of molten gold above me. Devlin was on top of me, his naked body pressed to mine as he shifted his hips, rubbing his erection against me.

"Get off me!" I screamed, writhing.

Devlin laughed, holding me to the bed with ease. "Come on, Sar," he said, the lust in his voice thick as tar. "I'll let you call me Theo."

He kissed me hungrily, and I bit him. He drew back, bleeding, the small tear closing immediately.

"Let me up," I said hatefully.

"No." Devlin pressed his body down against mine, rubbing on me again.

Tears from helplessness clouded my vision. "Get off me."

"You know I can have you right now if I want to," Devlin purred.

As I opened my mouth to curse him, he bent down and suckled my breast. I cried out in shock at the feel of his mouth and tried to move away, but he held me fast and sucked harder. My nipple tightened under his kiss, and I let out another cry, this one of pleasure.

Immediately, I felt shame. The dream of Theo had aroused me. But it hadn't been Theo. It had been Devlin all along...

"You like that, don't you?" Devlin said, moving to my other breast. He sucked gently.

I jerked hard, trying to dislodge him. "Danial will kill you for this," I said angrily. "Theo would kill you for even thinking it—"

"But that would be after I had you, Sar," he said, looking down at me arrogantly. "And I'd have you more than once, every inch of you." He ran his fangs up my neck and bit gently. "Every last drop."

My breath caught in my throat. I would heal from whatever else he did to me, but once I was vampire, there would be no going back. "Don't."

"I know how close you are to becoming vampire, Sar," he said slowly, deliberately pronouncing the words. "I could taste it in your blood. If I take enough blood from you tonight, you'll turn. Do you want that, to be vampire and never again see the sun?"

"No," I said desperately. "Please—"

"Let me in then, Sar. Let me have my way."

Tears slid down my cheeks. He kissed them away, waiting for my answer.

"You'll hurt me anyway," I said, afraid. "You'll turn me."

"I give you my word that I won't," Devlin said earnestly. "If you tell me yes right now."

"Why do this to me now, after so much time has passed? I trusted you to keep me safe. I believed what you said. That you'd changed."

"I want you, Sar and for me, that's enough," he said simply. He kissed my neck again, shuddering. He looked down at me beneath him, breathing deeply as he looked at me. "I will never have another chance as good as this one." He paused. "Delay in love's a lingering pain that never can be cured; Unless that love have love again 'tis not to be endured."

"You don't love me," I accused. "Don't quote me poetry like those words mean anything to you."

"Ah, but they do, Sar," Devlin said, kissing my throat. "They mean I want you, and I'm going to have you, because I've had enough of waiting. That is the point of Rowley's poem."

I didn't reply.

"Sar, answer me now," Devlin said determinedly. "I will be inside you one way or another in a few seconds. Choose, or I will choose for you."

I'd heard those words before from him, years ago. But this time there would be no last minute save, no reprieve. "Use protection," I whispered, closing my eyes.

"Sar, you know I can't—"

"I don't want you leaving anything of yourself behind," I said bitterly. "Not anything."

"Do you have any protection?" Devlin asked gently. "I do not carry any, I'm afraid."

"In my purse, on the dresser," I said, disbelieving he was actually going to do as I asked.

"Very well. I'll do as you request. But know that if you try to run, I'll be on you in a few seconds. I won't hurt you or turn you, as I've promised not to. But I'll have you as many times as I want then, understand? It won't just be once. And I won't wear anything. Now lie there, and don't move until I tell you to."

I shuddered and nodded, keeping my eyes closed.

Devlin got up from me, then came the sound of him rummaging around in my purse. I trembled at the soft rip of tearing plastic. A few seconds later, he lay down again on me again.

"I've done as you asked," Devlin whispered in my ear. "Now spread your legs for me, beautiful Sarelle, and lie still."

I did, tears rolling down my face, keeping my eyes closed.

Devlin moved into position, then bore down with his hips. Slowly, I felt him began to push inside me. He was enormous. The lubrication of the condom helped some. True to his word, he didn't hurt me, taking as long as he did to move inside inch by inch.

As I felt him enter me, hopelessness swept through me. It didn't matter if Theo somehow got here in a few minutes and stopped him. It was already too late.

Devlin kept pushing until he filled me completely. Then, with a groan, he began to move. He was gentle in his movements, trying not to hurt me. Instinctively, my body responded, betraying me, easing the tightness of my body's grip on him. Devlin felt it happen, and he let out a cry of delight, working himself in and out of me faster.

I begin to tremble as feelings of primal pleasure engulfed me in waves. I pushed them away, immediate guilt flooding me.

Devlin reached down with one hand and held my hips hard against his, thrusting deeply into me. There was pain, and I cried out, fresh tears trickling down my face.

Devlin stopped at once. "I'm sorry," he whispered. Then he started again, thrusting more shallowly into me. "Look at me, Sarelle," he said softly. "I want to see your eyes."

I opened my eyes and found myself looking into his. They were melting gold now, filled with heat and fire. Devlin let out a groan and quickened his movements, thrusting faster.

I tried to turn away, but he stopped me, holding my face with one hand and my hands above my head with the other. His eyes held mine as he began to groan over and over, pumping wildly, his actions more and more frantic.

A tremor went through him. He abruptly let go of my arms and grasped my hips, thrusting as deep as he could. There was pain again, sharp this time, and I cried out. I pushed back from him with all my strength, trying to get away, trying to get him out of me. But he held me fast by my hips, shuddering as he threw his head back and yelled my name.

"Sar! Ahh! Ahh! Ahhh!"

Devlin clutched me to him, his body giving a few last jerks. At once, he rolled off me onto his back, panting. I moved away from him to the edge of the bed and curled myself into a ball.

I heard him remove the condom and throw it in the wastebasket, his breathing slowing.

"You were wonderful," Devlin said languidly. "Go and shower if you'd like. You'll feel better if you do."

I got up and went into the bathroom on unsteady feet, glancing at myself in the mirror. The sight of my red face and spring green eyes made me start crying again. I turned on the shower and got in, not caring it wasn't warm yet.

I stayed in the shower for a half an hour, washing myself over and over. Then I got out, dried myself off and wrapped a towel around me. I didn't want to go out into the room, but I had to. I opened the door to see Devlin sleeping in the bed where he'd had me, his back to me. I looked at him lying there and thought about killing him as he slept. There was a explosive bullets gun right there on the dresser; it would be easy. Yet I was filled with fear just looking at him, remembering his body jerking on me and the way he'd screamed my name.

He'd used my body to bring himself pleasure. But the worst was I'd felt him there inside me, and some part of me had wanted him there, had responded to him. If it had lasted longer…

I bit my lip to keep from screaming, brushing away fresh tears. The bastard had broken something in me. I was too afraid of him to risk shooting him. What if he woke up before I got to the gun? Before I had a chance to shoot him?

No, I had to get away. I had to get away now before he decided he wanted me again. What was to stop him from offering me the same deal when he woke up? Nothing.

I picked up the discarded pajamas I'd been wearing and put them on. They were better than being naked. My clothes had already been sent to be cleaned.

I grabbed the key for the room and bolted for the door. I had to get outside, into the daylight where Devlin couldn't follow.

I opened the door, took one step and was jerked backward by my hair.

"I thought I told you what would happen if you ran?" Devlin said, holding me by my hair. He jerked me backwards, shut the door and wrapped his arms around me. "You smell fresh and clean, Sar," he breathed on my neck. "But soon you'll smell of my lovemaking again—"

I fought him hard, kicking, slapping and screaming.

He quickly put his hand over my mouth. "No screaming, unless it's pleasure."

I bit him again, drawing blood.

"No biting," he said, putting his fangs to my neck and pressing hard to make his point. "Or I'll bite you back next time. And mine will be deeper."

I went still, my chest heaving. "Please no," I whispered, fresh tears on my face.

"Sarelle, I told you what would happen if you ran," Devlin said seductively yet sinisterly.

He pushed me up against the wall, leaning his body up against my back possessively as his hand fastened on the back of my neck. The other hand grabbed the waistband of the pajama bottoms and jerked them down, so they pooled at my ankles. He slid his erect penis to the cleft of my buttocks. I shuddered.

"Remember that night?" he said, kissing my scarred throat. "I wanted you so much back then. But your demon half-breed robbed me of my power and ruined everything." He drew back, angry. "The worst night of my life—almost. To add insult to injury, you were off limits to me, untouchable, under pain of death." He leaned closer to whisper to me. "But your blood tonight made me remember how good you tasted, Sar. How good your body felt against mine."

I struggled frantically.

"When I felt you moving against me in your sleep, dreaming of Theo, I decided I'd had enough of playing the hero and being good." Devlin turned and threw me on bed. "Take off your clothes, my love." He stalked toward me, his fangs bared in a wide smile.

I backed away from him. "Please don't hurt me."

He stopped. "Do it, Sar, or I'll do it for you. You remember your first lesson? Do it, and I won't hurt you."

I did as he asked and took the rest of my pajamas off.

He climbed onto the bed. "Come to me."

I ran for the door. He caught me within a step. I struggled, crying, but he brought me back to the bed, holding my body to the bed with his.

"Sarelle, I'm going to have you all day long until we leave tonight," he said casually. "You can submit and enjoy it, or you can fight me. But it's going to happen."

I began to sob, waiting for him to begin. Instead, he got off me, grabbed some tissues from the box on the nightstand and wiped my eyes.

"Stop crying," he said softly. "The only one coming to save you was me. Don't fight me. I would much rather make this good for you, if you'll cooperate—"

"Devlin, I can't. I'm married," I said pleadingly.

"I said you have no choice, Sarelle. Put your guilt to rest. It has no place in this room."

He could've had me again by now, but he kept backing off. I focused on that, trying to get control. Maybe I could talk him out of this.

"Devlin, you don't really want to have normal sex with me. You want to see my fear. How could I possibly enjoy being with you?"

"The first is certainly true. Who wants to have 'normal' sex, ever?" He rolled his eyes at me. "But I don't want you to fear me," Devlin added gently. He handed me another tissue. "I know I felt good to you, just as you felt to me," he whispered seductively. "Lie back for me. I'll give you the kind of pleasure you've only dreamed of."

Fear swept me, that he'd felt my desire, weak as it had been. If he touched me again...

I bolted for the door. Devlin grabbed me instantly.

"I can't do this!" I said hysterically. "Please don't make me do this. Not again!"

Devlin grabbed a handful of my hair, pulling it back so I looked him full in the face. "Sarelle, either kiss me right now, or I'll find another use for your mouth." He lowered his head slightly, raised his eyebrows in a quick movement and then stared at me, making sure I got his point.

Fear flooded me again, as I looked at him in shock. He would do it, if just to prove to me he could.

Chapter Fifteen

I kissed him hard, and he groaned, pushing me back to the nearest wall. He pressed his body to mine, rubbing himself against me. I braced myself, waiting for him to act.

"Shh," he whispered softly. "This is not a B movie, despite our surroundings. I haven't waited this long to be either crude or quick."

I drew a hitching breath.

"Sorry if I squeezed too tightly." He loosened his grip on me, holding me gently. "I'm going to discover all of you tonight, Sarelle," he whispered. "Prepare yourself to be loved."

I drew a long shuddering breath.

"You haven't known intimacy. Not really. But I'm going to take you there tonight with me. Relax for me, and don't forget to breathe."

Devlin held me there against the wall and kissed me slowly. He kissed me over and over, until I was pliable in his arms. Then he took me to the bed and settled me down on it. He kissed me everywhere, from my neck to my ankles, running his fangs over all of my body's curves. He stroked my body with his hands, every inch of flesh, until despite my best intentions I was breathing fast, and my body was trying hard to convince me that this wasn't wrong. That he wasn't wrong to make me feel this way. Next, he kissed my breasts, taking each one in his mouth carefully, so as not to cut me on his fangs. I was writhing now, hating myself for responding to him.

"There's a sigh for yes and a sigh for no and a sigh for I can't bear it,'" he whispered to me. "Let me hear you sigh for me, to tell me you can't bear not to feel me inside you again."

He suckled me gently again, then moved up, kissing the spot he'd bitten tonight. Then he switched sides, kissing the scar he'd made years ago.

I went rigid, remembering him biting me, telling me I was a bitch. I held onto that memory, using it to push away the desires of my body.

"I'm sorry," he said softly, drawing back from me. "I'm sorry for that."

He began again, kissing me again, softly, gently. Touching me, caressing me, taking all the time in the world to move from my ankles to my neck. And as he kissed me he whispered to me softly:

"I draw you close to me, you woman,
I cannot let you go, I would do you good
I am for you and you are for me, not only for our own sake, but for others sakes,
Enveloped in you sleep greater heroes and bards,
They refuse to awaken at the touch of any man but me."
It is I, you woman, I make my way,
I am stern, acrid, large, un-dissuadable but I love you.
I do not hurt you any more than is necessary for you.
I press with slow rude muscle.
I brace myself effectually.
I listen to no entreaties.
I dare not withdraw until I give to you what has for so long accumulated in me."

"Who—?" I said softly.

"Whitman," he said, kissing me still. "The poet, not the chocolatier."

Slowly I relaxed again, his soft caress and kiss soothing me, melting my resistance.

Finally, he again kissed my throat. When I didn't tense this time, he moved his body onto mine carefully. His erection nudged me gently, pressed against my lower belly.

I tensed up in fear, holding my breath.

"I won't hurt you. Let me love you," he whispered, kissing my lips gently. Then he slid down and pushed up from me with one hand, his head near my chest. He began suckling me gently. I felt the tip of his penis press against my opening. Slowly, he rubbed it against me.

I took a sharp intake of breath, then began to breathe faster, as I felt the head of him become slippery. Involuntarily, my body relaxed, my hip flexing upwards slightly as I let out a soft moan.

Devlin rubbed again slightly, easing the tip inside, then gave a thrust, burying himself in me with a loud groan.

All at once, I realized he didn't have a condom on. "You'll turn me," I said desperately, trying to pull my body out from under his. "Please stop. Please don't—!"

Devlin sighed and withdrew completely. "Sarelle, much as it pains me to say it, I am not what I used to be. When Danial took my blood, he took too much." He leaned closer, his golden eyes inches from mine. "My seed can't turn you," he said softly. "Trust me. Our making love won't turn you."

I gave him a look of complete disbelief.

That irritated him. "Sarelle, have I hurt you yet today, or bitten you after I said I wouldn't?"

"You forced me to agree to have sex with you," I said flatly. "That counts as hurting in my book."

"Then we differ there," Devlin replied flatly.

He lowered his body as he had before and began suckling my breasts gently, rubbing the tip of himself on my opening. As before, within a few moments my body lubricated him. But this time, he waited until I was writhing before he filled me with a soft contented moan.

"God, you feel good, Sarelle," he sighed. "You're so warm."

Devlin pulled out slowly and then slowly thrust in again. I was surprised at his control. I could feel how much he wanted to thrust himself into me hard and fast. Instead, he moved slowly, his engorged penis stroking me pleasurably in a gentle, unhurried motion.

My body responded to his almost instantly with desire. Soon I was slick, and he moved in me easily.

"Sar, I can feel that you want me," he whispered to me lustfully. "Your body is helping me love you as it did before."

I didn't answer, trying hard to stop my body's response to his, hating my weakness.

Devlin still didn't thrust fast or hard, just that slow stroking over and over. Despite my efforts not to, I was soon panting with desire, my body betraying me with eager cries as I approached orgasm.

"Your eyes, Sarelle, they're so dark, like emeralds, but filled with so much wanting." He kissed me softly, sensuously. "I know what it is you are wanting," he whispered, stroking me slowly, his golden eyes gleaming. "I want it, too, desperately—"

I began to shake. "Please—stop," I said raggedly. "Please."

"I want to hear you, Sarelle. I want to see your face as you climax and for you to know it was me, my body, that made you feel this way." His voice was strained and heavy with need.

"No," I said weakly, as I tried to shift under him. "Don't make me."

"Yes," he said, moving his hands gently to stop me as he slowly moved in rhythm within me. He shifted slightly as he thrust in, the extra stimulation bringing an explosion of sudden pleasure. A needful cry burst from my lips as my hips instinctively pressed to his.

He brought his lips to mine, kissing them gently. "Yes," he murmured, drawing back slightly before he kissed me softly again. "Cry out for me."

I struggled one last time to get away from him. Devlin held me firmly, still stroking me unhurriedly over and over. Suddenly, my orgasm burst within me, breaking me into a million pieces. I screamed loudly, spasming around him. In that split second, Devlin began driving into me deeply, as hard and as fast as he could. He held my face as before and looked into my eyes as the orgasm washed though me. In the space of a second, he came too, screaming wordlessly as he clutched me, his hips pumping rhythmically on mine.

As the last pleasure of our orgasms faded, I expected him to roll off me as before, but he stayed there inside me, holding me. We were both breathing hard. His heart was racing as mine was. He kissed my throat and grinned down at me.

"I love the sight of your eyes filled with desire for me, Sarelle. I don't ever want to see fear in them again. Not for me," he said softly, kissing me. He leaned in close. "I loved your body's need for me, too, how easily you let me in, despite my size."

I had desired him, badly. I started crying again.

Devlin drew back. "Did I hurt you?" he said softly, his eyes concerned. "Did I go too deep?"

It was in his voice that he cared that he might have hurt me. It was too much.

"No," I said faintly, closing my eyes, sniffling, not wanting to see him.

"Tell me then why you're crying," he said, troubled.

"Because I...because you..." I cried, trying to push him away.

"Because it felt good?" he whispered to me. "Because I feel good to you?"

I shuddered at his words and didn't reply.

He held me tightly and kissed me softly again. "That's as it should be, Sarelle. I want to feel good to you. I want you to enjoy my body the way I'm enjoying yours." There was a deep contentment in his words or what was maybe happiness. "Great loves come with tears."

I looked at him angrily through my tears. "We are not great loves!"

"Ah, but we are, Sweet Sar," he said with a faint smile. "And for me, that will never change."

Devlin pulled out of me in one long movement and took me into his arms. He spoke to me in his beautiful voice and as he did, he touched me intimately.

"A hundred years should go to praise thine eyes and on thy forehead gaze.
Two hundred to adore each breast, but thirty thousand for the rest.
An age at least to every part and the last age should show your heart
For, Lady, you deserve this state, nor would I love at lower rate."

I looked at him in surprise. He gave me a long slow kiss, then began speaking to me again, gently.

"Now let us sport us while we may,
and now like amorous birds of prey,
Rather at once our time devour,
than languish in his slow chapped power.
Let us roll all our strength and all
our sweetness up into one ball,
And tear our pleasures with rough strife
through the iron gates of life.
Thus though we cannot make our sun
stand still, yet we will make him run."

I listened to him speaking, his words like music, breathing in the sweet scent of him, the scent of us. My eyes lingered over his perfect body and his beautiful features, all of them. I'd wondered how Devlin had seduced Danial's loves away from him over the years. Now I knew.

Devlin rolled me on top of him and looked up at me. "Tell me your fantasies, Sar," he said softly, stroking my arms with his fingers.

I rolled my eyes at him. "You have to be joking."

Devlin looked irritated, and then he smiled at me, really smiled at me as I thought he never could. He began tickling me with his hands. In two seconds, I was flat on my back, shrieking with laughter, trying to get away from him.

"Stop! Stop! Aaahhh! Stop, Devlin! Stop, please!"

"You little minx," he said devilishly "Tell me! Tell me, or I won't stop."

"I'll tell you," I gasped. "Please, I can't breathe!"

He abruptly stopped, gave me another smile and then grabbed me, covering my mouth with his in a tender kiss. He rolled onto his back, moving me to straddle him. His hands clasped my hips lightly and then with a grin, he pushed up lightly with his hips. I felt his hard penis flex against me, nudging me insistently again, seeking entrance.

"Tell me, Sar," he said softly. "I'll do anything you like, except let you go or stop touching you like this."

"Anything?" I asked him hesitantly.

"Anything you ask for, within reason and physical limitations," he amended with a smile.

I blushed and swallowed, suddenly very shy. I bit my lip, looking down at him.

"Tell me," Devlin said with an amused and intrigued look. "You have nothing to hide from me, Sar. I'll not judge you strange or think it odd, no matter what you ask."

"Sing for me," I blurted, blushing harder.

He blinked his eyes in shock. "Sing what?" he said curiously, looking at me attentively.

"Something appropriate," I said shyly. "Something that isn't a dirge or about happiness turned to ashes."

"I can't sing during lovemaking, but after, yes," Devlin said, grinning. "Anything else?"

I closed my eyes. If I could say the other, I could say this. "Pretend you care about me … really care about me, just for today."

I hoped he wouldn't joke or make fun. I kept my eyes averted, unwilling to face him.

"Do not be embarrassed," he said softly. "I'm not anything but flattered and surprised. Please give me a moment."

"Why do you need a moment?" I retorted, upset for some reason. I moved to get off him quickly, but he stopped me with his hands.

"Please stay," he said, bringing me down to enfold me in his arms. "If this is your fantasy, I'm more than willing to give it to you. But this is not the fantasy of different forms of physical love I meant by my words. What you are asking for is a dream of emotional love. I need to know that you accept that it will be only a dream, Sar, and that it will last only this day no matter the words I'll utter."

"Never mind," I said tearfully, pushing violently away from him. "I don't know why I even asked—"

Devlin grabbed me with supernatural speed and brought me back into his arms. "I'm sorry. Please forgive me, my love." He kissed my hand gently. "Please don't cry."

"You're hateful," I sobbed. "You do all this to seduce me, and then when I open myself to you, you tell me I mean nothing to you—"

"I love you," Devlin said tenderly. "I'm sorry I hurt you. You do mean a great deal to me." He kissed my tears away gently. "Please don't cry. I only want you to be happy."

"Then why don't you let me go home?" I said, sniffling.

"Because I can't stand knowing that we'll never be like this ever again," Devlin said despondently, clutching me tightly. "I've wanted you for years, Sar.

Do you know how many nights I dreamed of this happening? Dreamed of making love with you?" He kissed me tenderly. "I was maddened that anyone else should see your hair unbound or feel your flesh part beneath their fangs. Do you know how much I longed to hear you tell me you wanted me?" He kissed my cheek gently. "That you want me to care for you means you must care for me." He let out a gentle sigh. "And that is best of all."

"I don't believe you," I whispered, uncertain.

"I've wanted you to want me ever since I laid eyes on you," Devlin said seriously, cradling me in his arms. "Now you do. Believe me when I tell you this moment is one of the best of my long life."

I opened my mouth to speak, but Devlin put his finger to them.

"Shh," he said gently. "There is much I'd love to hear you say. But there is far more that has waited within me, hoping for a moment like this. Please, let me finally share it with you."

"Yes," I said softly. "Tell me."

Devlin pulled me down beside him, then turned toward me. He took my warm hand in his cool one, kissing the back gently. His lips suddenly parted as if to bite, his top fangs carefully pricking without breaking the skin. Then he stopped still, languidly raising his head to look up at me with eyes of molten fire through his blond curls. "I have not felt this way for someone for centuries." He flipped my hand over to show the palm, then brought it to his face, gently rubbing his cheek as he closed his eyes. "You have haunted my dreams for these last years."

With every word, I desired him more. I reached out to run my hands over him, delighting in the soft down of his chest.

"Touch me," he whispered, desire and command equal in his tone. "I want your hands on me."

I ran my hands over his pale skin, loving the hungry way he watched me discover all of him. The groan he uttered when my lips first met his throat emboldened me. I kissed down his chest, my mouth opening on his skin to bite and tease.

His arms went around me, then grasped my hair, making me meet his hot gaze. "Being unable to touch you like this has been sweet torture these years." He kissed me ardently, then drew back. "I knew we could have this." He began kissing down my throat. "Your hair is the most beautiful I've seen, like a golden river. I want to drown in it. I want to drown in you."

I clasped him to me, burying my fingers in his golden hair, losing myself in his caress.

Devlin took my silence for dissent. "I have been so cold and unfeeling to hide my feelings for you," he whispered between kisses.

His loving words eased my heart somewhat, even though I knew they weren't true. His voice was sweet to me, and he was a good actor. And I wanted to believe his words, because if he'd done this out of love for me, then at least his actions made sense.

"Make love with me," he said when he'd finished, moving me to straddle him again. "I am dying to be within you again, my love."

"Yes," I said softly. "Will you sit there on the edge of the love seat and let me—?"

"Of course," Devlin said, moving into position. "You have only to instruct me. I want to please you." He helped me straddle him, his lips parting in a loud moan as I pushed him inside me and settled my hips on his.

"Stroke me as you did before," I said huskily, running my hands over his chest.

"Anything you want," Devlin said heatedly, as he began to move under me. "You have only to ask."

"Kiss me," I moaned. "Please kiss me—"

Devlin brought his lips to mine in a ravishing kiss, his arms going around me, his hands tangling in my hair. I kissed him back passionately, then let out a loud groan, already feeling the first stirrings of orgasm. Devlin began kissing my throat and neck, murmuring to me how beautiful I was, how much he wanted me. I let my head loll backward, closed my eyes and gave myself up to bliss with soft eager cries.

My cries and his repeated throughout the day. When we rested, he caressed me and whispered poetry, describing my body or how I made him feel. He sang to me several times, holding me in his arms on the love seat, or standing, walking around me or cradling my body against his. He sang different types of songs, some newer that I recognized and others much older. In his voice was everything I wanted, and I was motionless as he sang, rapt as the notes fell with crystal clarity in the air to break over me.

I was deeply ashamed that I enjoyed him so much, that I could behave this way while I was married to another man. I didn't love Devlin. Yet I gave him credit for being one of the best lovers I'd ever had, if not the best.

I slept briefly around noon, but Devlin awakened me with kisses. "The day will be over too soon for me as it is, Sarelle. You can sleep tomorrow. Be with me."

About noon, I told him I had to eat something. He handed me the room service menu again, and I ordered a bottle of wine, some more hamburgers and French fries and two pieces of cake. I needed the wine. I was feeling guiltier by the minute, being with him. Who cared if it was barely noon?

We made love once more before I slept briefly again. This time he let me, seeing that I was too exhausted to continue unless he did. He awakened me when the food came. I dug in eagerly. Surprisingly, Devlin joined me in having some wine.

"How can this be?" I said in amazement, watching him sip. "Won't you get sick?"

"I built up a tolerance for it over a decade, though it was a very unpleasant undertaking," Devlin said, rolling his empty glass in his hand. "I found that no one would be suspicious if I didn't eat, as long as I drank. There were too many times that I needed to be unnoticed, Sarelle. Now it doesn't bother me, though I can only drink a glass or two at most."

"Do you want another?" I said, filling my glass to the brim.

"Yes, Love," he said, handing it to me. "And then a toast. Forgive me that I forgot the first time."

I poured him a glass, handed it to him, and raised mine.

"To us," he said, clinking my glass with his. "To great loves and stolen breaths, soft sighs and dreams fulfilled."

"Yes," I said, taking a large sip. I wanted to add some poetry I knew to the toast, but was too shy to utter the words.

We finished the bottle together. Soon after he was kissing me and asking me to lie back for him, so that he might bring me pleasure again.

There was no position, no sexual act he didn't ask to try with me. Most I said "no" to, out of fear or squeamishness. He was large enough that some positions that weren't possible with the men I had been with before could be done with him. And some others were too scary to try.

He spooned me and had me that way, holding my hips hard against his as he thrust into me, his other arm turning and holding my upper body so he could kiss me as he moved in me. We also spent some time in the Jacuzzi, letting the hot water soothe our sore muscles. I was getting tired. Devlin showed no signs of getting tired at all. When he made a move in the Jacuzzi for me, I led him back to the bed.

Later, perhaps the twentieth time, Devlin again sat on the bed edge and I rode him, his one hand on the small of my back and the other in my hair, holding my head back, so he could kiss and nibble my neck as he moved his hips under me. I knew how much he wanted to bite me then, as he kissed the healed scars and trembled slightly. Yet he didn't ask, and I didn't offer. We rested afterwards, lying in each other's arms.

I cast a look at the clock. It was close to six p.m.

"I cannot sing more," Devlin said awkwardly. "My throat is sore, despite my healing power. It has been a very long time since I sang this much in such a short time."

"Why has it been so long?" I asked dreamily. "Your voice is beautiful."

"I have not sung to a lover in many long years," he said sadly. He hugged me gently. "I haven't wanted to. In any case, I'm sorry to disappoint you."

"I'm not disappointed. You don't need to do anything but be yourself," I said softly. "That was only who you ever had to be."

Devlin didn't reply, but his arms tightened around me.

When he turned to me for what I knew would be the last time, just before dark, I evaded his grasp and got out of bed. He was surprised, then quickly moved to block the door. I shook my head with a smile, then leaned back against the wall, raising my arms over my head, so they were together. I gazed at him and moved my body gently, sliding up the wall a few inches and down again.

"Tell me we've just begun," I said seductively. "I'm yours for the taking."

His expression was instant and pure desire. He was there in front of me rapidly, pushing me hard against the wall. I made to turn around for him, so he could have me as he had wanted to those years ago, but he stopped me.

"No, Sar. I want to see your face," he groaned, kissing me.

He bent his legs, pushing inside as he raised me up in his hands to steady me. In a flash, he had me against the wall, my legs on his thighs. One hand he kept at my hips to steady me. The other he ran up my body to hold my arms above my head as he thrust himself into me, kissing me hard, his tongue entwining with mine as he loved me.

Devlin began thrusting hard almost at once, gasping as the breath tore out of him. Before long he was close, his muscles starting to lose their rhythm as he lost himself in pursuit of the sensations he was feeling, his body wanting release.

"Take it," I said softly.

He almost dropped me in his shock. I slid down the wall a little, then he moved quickly to hold me up again.

"No," he said, resuming his thrusting, sucking gently on my neck. "I promised not to."

"I know you want to, Dev," I said, drawing back from him, slipping my hands to his face to make him look into my eyes. "I can feel it, how much you want to sink your fangs into me. But it's not nearly as much as I want to feel you slide them in."

His stunned eyes were as hot as flame as he drew back from me. "You're never called me Dev before."

I was just as shocked as he was at the words I was saying. But when would we ever be like this again? The truth was I had a fantasy of him just like this, where my making love to him rocked his world, changing it forever. And that fantasy included his fangs.

"I shouldn't," he whispered. But he began running his fangs over my neck and pressing gently between kisses.

"Take just a little," I whispered seductively. "I want you to, Dev, please."

Devlin groaned. He was trembling hard now as he watched me, his fangs slightly bared. But he was keeping himself in check.

"Sar, are you sure? This is what you want?"

I trailed kisses down his throat, then bit him gently. A shudder went through him.

"I know it will feel a hundred times better to you, if you taste me as you have me," I whispered huskily in his ear. "Do it, Dev. I want to hear you scream for me and know it was my blood, my body that made you feel that good, mine and no one else's—"

Devlin cut me off with a rough deep kiss, his mouth moving on mine. He drew back and then darted in beneath my chin, twisting his head. With a swift movement of his fangs, he nicked me, opening a small but deep cut on the front of my throat. Strangely, there was no pain. He leaned in under my chin, tilting his head sideways and pressed his mouth to the wound, simultaneously thrusting himself fully inside with a powerful push of his hips

The moment he tasted my blood, he convulsed. He began sucking insistently on the cut, sighing repeatedly as he fed from me, his hips now pumping frantically. I held him to me, my hands in his hair, gripping his head of golden curls in my hand, loving the feel of him stroking me, touching me, taking so much joy in me.

I began to moan, the pressure within me cresting. Devlin drew back from me to watch my face, his lips parted, his liquid eyes hot as forges, as he stroked me.

"Please, Dev. Please, take me," I moaned desperately. "Please, I'm so close—"

Devlin trapped my body between the wall and himself, grinding me against him, and my pleading moans became loud gratified screams. Seeing me come and hearing me say his name like that was enough to push him over. He began to jerk, his eyes burning pools of fire, his face tight with pleasure. I held him to me fiercely as he came screaming my name with enough volume and passion to shake the room.

"Saaaaaaaarrrrrrrrrrrrrrrrrr!"

Devlin and I slid down to the floor, holding one another, For a while we stayed there, gripping each other and saying nothing, our bodies still shaking.

In time, Devlin helped me to my feet as he got to his. We almost didn't make it over to the bed, but he steadied me with his hands, helping me get under the covers. He got under them too and nestled himself near me with a sigh. We lay then for a long time, in each other's arms, not speaking.

Why had I done that? Given myself to him? Said those things? What had come over me? Was it because I was so close to turning? That must be it. Devlin had been as surprised as me though...I fell asleep beside him before I could finish the thought.

I awoke to find Devlin kissing me softly on my throat. He drew back from me, and I slid one hand up to touch where the wound had been and discovered I was again healed.

He began whispering to me again softly, as he had all through the day. The poems had differed, but the heat in his voice had never diminished. Nor was it diminished now.

"All women are beautiful as they rise
Exultant from the ruins they make of us
And this woman, who lies back informing the sheets
Has slain me all day with love and now
Keeps vigil at the tomb of my desire."

I looked at him expectantly.

"Robert Kelly," he said softly, looking at me with consideration.

My body wasn't sore as it usually was after this much sex, but Theo was usually rougher. There wasn't one bruise on me anywhere. Yet I ached gently all through my body from what Dev had done to me, and it was a delicious feeling. Delicious enough that I drowned again in guilt the moment I admitted how good I felt.

"Go and shower," he said, kissing me a final time. "You smell of our lovemaking. As much as that pleases me, we will need to leave within the hour. Night is nearly here. "

"Devlin, I am going to have to tell Theo about what happened here," I said, biting my lip.

"Go ahead," he said, grinning. "Tell him every detail if you want."

"He'll kill you," I said softly.

"Would you cry for me, Sarelle?" he said inquiringly. "Would you mourn me?"

"I'd cry for the man you could've been," I replied. "There is a gentleness in you that you cover even better than Danial covers his."

His hand caressed my cheek. "I do not understand."

"I would never have thought you could touch me this way, make me feel this way. It's completely at odds with how you've acted the whole time we've known one another."

"I have never wanted to be other than what we were today," Devlin corrected. "If you believed otherwise, you were wrong."

"It may have been all your talk of lessons," I said icily. "You've been distant and cold or sarcastic to me for the last few years, even when you saved me from harm. And now you've forced me to have sex with you all day long."

"It started being consensual hours ago," Devlin said confidently.

"Really?" I said sarcastically. "Consent implies choice. If I had asked to leave at any time today, to stop having sex with you, you would have let me go? Give me a break."

"We both know you ceased to be unwilling the moment you first came," Devlin said patronizingly. "But you call it whatever you want to. What matters is that you enjoyed being with me, having me, at least after the first time." He let out a satisfied sigh. "You are quite the seductress, Sar. That last time was inspired. I lost complete control."

"But that's my point," I said persistently. "If you hadn't scared me when I first met you, not threatened me from the first, there might have come a time when I'd have come to you willingly. I'd have yearned for your touch. You wouldn't have had to force me at all."

"Sarelle, I'm not a boy whose hope springs eternal," Devlin said bitterly. "I was Ruler of The States for almost two hundred years. Do you know how cold you have to be to hold onto that kind of power? Do you know how ruthless you have to be? You have to be the worst, the most ruthless. The one capable of doing anything, no matter how terrible, to keep that power. Because once you claim it, you can't relinquish it. Someone has to take it from you."

"What are you saying?"

"This wasn't what I wanted. I wanted a normal life, maybe a child or two. Instead, I became vampire. In the world I had joined, however unwillingly, you either have power, or you are under someone else's power. It was an easy choice. When I found out I had the power to be the one in charge in The States, I took it quickly. I embraced freely the cruelty I needed to keep that power. I enjoyed wielding it, like Danial does to a lesser extent now. I reveled in it."

I'd have to ask Danial what exactly Devlin had meant by that. "And?"

Devlin looked at me, his eyes sad. "If I had it to do over, I'd do it again. I'm not sorry for the choices I made since I became vampire, and I'm damned because of it. I knew long ago there wasn't a happy ending written for me." He kissed me, softly, lingeringly. "But there is for you, my dear. Forget what happened here today. No one knows but you and me."

"I can't lie to Theo," I said tiredly.

"What will you gain by telling him?" Devlin said, his eyes searching mine. "Nothing except my death and possibly his wrath."

"Do you want me to protect you, Dev?" I said incredulously. "You just said you're not sorry at all for any of what you've done. How can I empathize with you?"

"Will he look at you the same way, knowing you enjoyed being with me?" Devlin said, swiftly changing tactics. "You are not a good actress, not nearly good enough to make him believe you didn't." His tone turned darker. "If Theo kills me, he's killed his best friend Danial's only brother. How do you think that will affect their being best friends?"

Danial might not mind when he found out what Devlin had done to me. But I'd killed Monica, his lover. That would have some emotional fallout. Not to mention that in the past, so far as I knew, once Devlin had been with a woman of Danial's, then Danial had blamed the woman for being weak. Maybe he would blame me, too.

Devlin saw me wavering and pushed harder. "You can spin this only one way if you tell Theo—that I raped you. To make him believe that, you'll have to create some very terrible scenarios, as he knows my reputation. Given that, how will you explain you're being unscathed? Worse, how will he feel when he learns he has failed again to save you?"

Doubt descended on me. I was unmarked; even my whip marks had completely healed. Worse, admitting to Theo what had happened would likely be the killing blow to our relationship. Devlin was manipulative, but he was right. "What are you suggesting?"

He looked at me and quoted:

"Tis no sin love's fruit to steal, but the sweet theft to reveal
To be taken, to be seen, these are crimes accounted been."

I gave him an exasperated look. "Just say it in plain English, please."

"A Roman, Catullus, said that it was the revelation of what had happened that caused problems, not the actual event." Devlin looked down at me, propping himself up on one arm. "Say nothing, to anyone. I will say the same. I saved you, then we slept the day away. We drive home tonight and then go our separate ways."

"I can't act like this day didn't happen, not when I see you so often—"

"You will not be seeing me again," Devlin interrupted, pushing a stray lock of hair out of my eyes. "I am leaving the States after I drop you off tonight and moving my base of operations permanently. I can't trust you. Even if you tell me you'll keep this day a secret, guilt might eventually change your mind. I know all too well what Theo will do to me should he find out about us, to say nothing of Danial."

Distance wouldn't stop Theo from looking for Devlin if he found out about today. Nothing would. Not oceans. Not guards. Not Danial. Yet Devlin was right; nothing would be gained. And what if Theo died somehow, pursuing Devlin? He wasn't immortal.

"Why did you do this?" I said, frustrated, shoving Devlin so he rolled over on his back. "I'd begun to like you. I trusted you. You betrayed that trust."

"I told you why, Sarelle. I wanted you," he replied, folding his arms under his head. "And I have to say, you were worth it—"

"That's a surprise to me, Dev," I shot back. "You told me when you met me I was nothing special. You called me a bitch on several occasions. Given that, what we've done can't have been that exceptional for you." Self-loathing filled me as realization dawned. "Because you don't feel anything for me. Not really. I'm likely just one more conquest in a long line of women who don't matter to you at all, except in that they were Danial's lovers once."

"You don't understand," he said curtly, looking away.

"Damn straight I don't!" I shouted back. "What is your obsession with having Danial's lovers? Just because of some woman years ago that Danial took from you?"

"Go shower, Sarelle. Right now," Devlin growled. "I've had enough of your prying."

"Or what?"

"Or I'll take you again. But this time I won't be gentle, as I have been."

"I thought you didn't want me to fear you?" I said spitefully.

"If fear is the only thing that shuts your mouth—" he said, reaching for me angrily.

I jumped out of bed and ran to the shower. I turned it on quickly, then locked the door. As soon as the water warmed up, I climbed in, scrubbing myself and washing my hair.

What had happened didn't matter. Today was over, and I'd be home soon...

The shower curtain was pulled back suddenly. Devlin stood there naked, his eyes roaming me.

"Get out!" I said angrily.

He stepped in, pulled the curtain forward and then gathered me into his arms under the spray. I began struggling immediately.

"Stop flailing and listen," he said seriously. "I'll tell you why."

I stopped struggling, waiting expectantly.

"I did it because I wanted to be happy," he said.

"You forced me to have sex with you because you thought it would make you happy?" I said, incredulous.

"Danial has been miserable for the last fifty years," Devlin said, upset. "He's had women on and off, but none that have lasted more than a few months. He lived for his business mainly. Then you came, and everything changed. Danial was happy, like he hadn't been in a long, long time. When you had Theoron, he was like he had been when we were alive centuries ago. He was himself again, the man he'd been."

Devlin looked into my eyes, wistful. Astonishingly, what I'd taken for water was actually tears.

"I wanted to change like he did, Sar. I want to be like I used to be, the man I used to be, before I became vampire and lost myself in bloodletting and cruelty."

"I can't change you," I said slowly. "Only you can change you."

"You can, but you won't," Devlin said bitterly. "I knew you hated and feared me. That I'd blown whatever chance I had to win your affections because of my actions years ago. Even after I saved your life, I still saw distrust sometimes in your eyes."

"How did you think that making me accept you today would make me trust you more?" I said skeptically. "You betrayed me."

"I didn't know what else to do," Devlin said angrily, leaving the shower. "I tried everything else. I saved your life, guarded you, spent time helping you improve your singing, comforted you and kissed your tears away, healed you and killed people for you. I did some of those repeatedly. Yet you treated me exactly the same, as if I was someone who couldn't be trusted."

"That's not true," I said, grabbing a towel and drying off.

"It is," Devlin said sadly, even as he handed me another towel for my hair. "I've tried everything to make you treat me as a friend and not a hated enemy. But nothing worked. Patience has never been one of my virtues. When I saw the chance to be with you, I took it, figuring there was no point in trying to make nice anymore."

"I always treated you as a friend—" I began coolly.

"I wanted to be more than your friend," Devlin said seductively. "I wanted to be your lover."

I opened my mouth to speak, but he put his finger to my lips. "Know this—my actions have not been rooted in revenge on Danial, not since that day I tried to seduce you at his house," Devlin said tenderly. "My longing for you has never been because of some other woman. I genuinely care for you."

"Since when?" I scoffed. "Since you tried to kill me?"

"We made love today," Devlin said, heat creeping back into his words. "That wasn't an accident. It was on purpose. I didn't want to rape you. I wanted to love you—"

"You forced me," I said accusingly. "Nothing would've happened if you hadn't threatened me. You threatened to turn me!"

"I'm sorry," Devlin said quickly. "I'm sorry that the first time was so fast. That it wasn't better for you." He swallowed quickly. "I know I hurt you when I had you that time. I'm sorry."

"You aren't!" I shouted suddenly. "You just told me that you weren't, back in bed!"

Devlin grabbed hold of me, forcing me to look at him. "Are you sorry, Sar? Tell me right now. Honestly—are you sorry about today?"

I looked at him, enraged and then dissolved into tears. "No," I said shamefully.

"Neither am I," Devlin said, hugging me close. "You had fantasies about me just as I had about you, didn't you?"

"Yes," I admitted. "I feel so much guilt I'm drowning in it."

"Don't feel regret," Devlin said, rubbing my hair dry. "We took joy in one another, something that happens too seldom."

"I broke my promise to Theo," I said shamefully.

"Promises get broken sometimes," Devlin said with a shrug.

"Not mine," I said resolutely, pushing past him.

He followed me into the other room, where we began dressing. I was uncomfortable, wanting him to say something, but not sure what. I blushed, realizing part of me wanted him to tell me that this hadn't been just a fling for him, that it had meant something. But he wasn't going to say that, because for him it had been exactly that. Self-pity swept me, and I blinked back tears. I was not going to cry, not until I got home.

"Are you ready?" Devlin said curiously.

"Yes," I said coolly, pushing past him out the door.

We walked down to the front desk and checked out.

"Glad you guys had a good time today," the bellhop said, grinning at us.

Devlin grinned back at him, as I flushed scarlet, knowing our passionate cries had been overheard.

We went out to the black Hummer, and Devlin checked it over to make sure that it hadn't been tampered with. It was on the tip of my tongue to ask him where our lone guard had gone, but I didn't, not wanting to talk to him.

Devlin started the SUV and drove us to the highway. I sat in silence, looking out the window, wondering what I was going to do.

Chapter Sixteen

I thought about what to do for hours as we traveled, but didn't know what was best. If I told Danial, he would blame Devlin and probably me, too. Theo would want to kill Devlin and wouldn't rest until he had. I was so mixed up, thinking about what had happened to me and what I'd done willingly that I couldn't figure out what was best to do.

"You've been quiet the whole trip back," Devlin said, glancing over at me. "Are you okay?"

I gave him a look to let him know that was one of the dumbest questions ever. "I'm thinking what to say," I said with a sigh, leaning back in the seat. "I'm thinking of all the things that could go wrong and trying to decide what's the best thing for me to do."

"I'm telling you now. Don't say anything. You of all people deserve to be happy, especially after all you've gone through. Pretend it was a dream and nothing more."

"I can't," I said softly.

"Sarelle—"

"Call me Sar," I said softly, looking out into the night.

Devlin narrowly missed an oncoming truck. "Why now?" he asked, when he had control of the Hummer again. "After all the times you've made a point—"

"Because there isn't any point. Not anymore. I wanted you to call me by my full name because it put some distance between us. I wanted to keep you at arm's length. But it's too late for that now. You've been inside me, Devlin, even if I didn't want you there." I looked over at him, then away. "And the truth is that today, part of me did. That's why I can't pretend it didn't happen." I let out a sniffle, blinking back sudden tears.

Devlin sighed. "Sar, I—"

His phone suddenly rang in the quiet. He clicked it on with one hand. "Yes, Theo, she's right here." He handed me the phone, his eyes watchful on mine before they returned to the road.

I took it. "Hello?"

"Sar, is that you?" Theo said.

"Yes," I said softly.

"What's wrong? You sound funny?" he said, worried.

"I'm okay," I said, trying hard to sound normal. "It's been a rough couple days."

"I have good news. Brian is alive."

"Good," I said with relief.

"He told us how Monica had shot him and was planning to get you out of the way."

I didn't reply, though I wanted to ask him why he'd doubted me.

"Danial doesn't blame you for killing her. He said to tell you if you hadn't, he was going to ask Devlin for help in draining her."

I didn't reply, remembering my own bad memories of that "punishment". I wouldn't wish it on my worst enemy, even Monica.

"He wants to talk to you when I hang up, but he's on another call right now."

It was better if I didn't talk to him. Danial knew me better than anyone. He would know something was wrong "Tell him to call me when he gets home. I'll be home by then."

"Okay, I'll tell him. Danial and I are landing soon. I'll be home in a few hours, give or take." Theo's voice became husky. "Everyone is back at Danial's, Sar. We'll have the house to ourselves."

"I'll be waiting for you," I said quickly, wanting desperately to get off the phone.

"I can't wait to see you," he said softly. "I've missed you."

"I love you," I said quickly, wanting badly to say something, anything, to assuage the guilt I was feeling.

"I love you, too," he replied. "I'll show you how much when I see you."

"Good-bye," I said and quickly hung up. I handed the phone back to Devlin, who took it without a word.

The last miles passed, and soon enough, he was pulling off at my exit. He drove to my door and stopped the truck. I went to get out, and he pulled me into his arms.

"Sar, don't go back to your old life," he said seductively. "Come with me. We can be in Rio tonight. You can start a new life with me."

"Devlin, are you insane?" I said, trying to get free of him. "I just told Theo I'd be here. I'm not going with you to Rio."

"Well, it was worth a try," Devlin said, smiling down at me.

"That's just it," I said, suddenly fighting tears again. "This is a game to you. It always has been. I'm done playing."

"This is not a game," Devlin said dangerously, grabbing my hair in his fist. "It is you who have treated my words as nonsense and my feelings like floor tiles."

I looked up at him, disbelieving. "What are you saying?"

He let go of my hair and embraced me suddenly. "Sar, don't go back to Theo. Stay with me. Be with me," he whispered into my ear, his voice breaking. "Be mine."

"I'm not going to be your whore," I said icily, struggling to escape him.

He grimaced in distaste. "Where do you get whore from? I've wanted you from the first time I saw you, when you were standing there on the dance floor with Danial. I wanted you for my own then, to be with you as we were today. I knew that it wasn't going to happen, not unless I made it happen." He paused then, looking at me. "I fell in love with you today, Sar."

I froze. There was nothing he could have said that would have shocked me more. I opened my mouth to speak, then stopped, my words forgotten in my amazement.

"Yes, I'm crying again," Devlin said, tears shining in his eyes. "Likely you'll say they are crocodile tears."

"Why are you crying?" I asked softly.

"It's been a long, long time, but I remember how it feels, to be in love," he said in a raw voice. "And I know you don't love me. I thought you cared for me, when you told me your fantasy today. But it's obvious now that you don't."

"What are you saying?" I said incredulously.

"Did you ever consider that your fantasy was mine as well?" Devlin said softly. "To tell you I wanted you and love you and have you relish the words? I told you that I didn't savor who I was, that I wanted to change." He took my hand and kissed it. "I want to be a man you want to touch you, not one you shrink from."

I pulled it back. "You told me I had to accept that my fantasy would only last a day. I did. Why are you saying these things now? Are you trying to hurt me?"

"I'm sorry for sounding cold then," Devlin said regretfully. "I just never expected you to care for me. I knew you desired me. That was obvious. I thought you were trying to trick me, that you'd somehow seen through my façade. I thought you were trying to hurt me."

"I don't understand."

"You told me what I most wanted to hear," he whispered. "I had to know if it was a trick. When you got so upset so fast, I knew it wasn't." He hugged me tighter, kissing my forehead. "I'm sorry for what I said. And I'm telling you now this isn't a fantasy. This is real. I'm in love with you. I want you to come with me tonight. Say yes, and we'll be gone."

"I do care about you," I said guiltily. "I wanted you to touch me and everything that happened between us. But this can't work."

"It could, but you won't give me a chance," Devlin said, sighing. "None of that changes what I feel, unfortunately for me." He kissed me once more. "You won't see me again, Sar. I'm not planning to return in your lifetime. But if you ever need me, call me, and I'll come back to you. I'll send you a number where you can reach me."

I held him close, not saying anything. There was nothing to say that was going to ease the upset we were both feeling. Because wrong as it was, I did care about him, and part of me wanted to go with him. When he drove away tonight, I was going to regret not going with him.

"Devlin, I—"

"From now on, call me Dev," he said affectionately.

"You said I won't see you again," I said, confused.

"You likely won't, unless you reconsider," Devlin said, kissing me again on the cheek. "But I'm making the request just the same."

The thought of never seeing him again suddenly terrified me, and I hugged him close. He went still, then hugged me back hard.

"Come with me," he said persistently, taking a deep breath. "I'm immersed in the heady aroma of your desire. Beneath is the faint scent of my semen within you. The mix of the two is driving me crazy with wanting you." He pressed my hand to his jeans, where the long hard length of him was flexing gently.

"I can't," I said regretfully, reaching to open the SUV door.

"You'll never have another day like the one we just shared if you don't," Devlin whispered. Surprisingly, his words were not tempting, but filled with sadness. "Come with me, and we'll make many days like the one we just had." He kissed my hand gently. "I've had graves instead of love for many years, Sar. Many, many years. Come and replant my Garden of Love." He pressed my hand to his cheek. "Under your care it will blossom forth anew."

"I can't," I said, wiping away sudden tears. "I have responsibilities here."

"Then stay for now," Devlin said sadly, releasing my hand. "I can only hope you'll reconsider in time."

His despair broke something in me, propelling me into reckless action. "I have reconsidered," I said huskily. I kicked off my shoes, slipped off my jeans and then reached down and unbuttoned his pants, jerking the zipper down as I moved to straddle him.

Devlin's lips parted, his head lolling, as I slipped him inside me. "Yes, please, Sar. Oh...Ahh..."

"No holding back this time," I commanded, beginning to rock on him. "When I come, bite me. I want to feel your fangs, Dev. I want all of you buried in me."

Devlin bared his fangs, moved his hands to my breasts and ripped my shirt down the front. He snapped the bra with a swift tug and filled his mouth with my breast, cupping the other in his hand. I threw my head back with a loud cry, rocking faster. Devlin moved to the other breast, sucking insistently.

I let out a scream as the orgasm burst over me. "Dev!"

Devlin pulled me down and sank his fangs into my throat. I clutched him to me, my loud cries frantic and frenzied. Again oddly, there was no pain, only sheer pleasure.

Devlin gave a muffled shout, then jerked hard under me. He shoved up with his hips a few more times, then eased back into the seat, his mouth still at my neck, sucking hard. I leaned into him, feeling drunk on pleasure, as my last tremors faded.

Devlin gave my throat a last long kiss, then sank back limp to the seat, his head again lolling. "God, I'm utterly spent. You are incredible, Sar."

"Thank you," I said contentedly.

"I love you," Devlin said ardently, clutching me close, his hand pushing my head into his shoulder. "I love you, I love you, I love you. Please come with me. Please, Sar."

I drew back from him reluctantly. "You asked me once if I liked your eyes."

"And?" he said, a faint smile on his lips.

"I don't like them. I love them," I said passionately.

He stared at me, stunned. "You love them?" he said in disbelief. "Why? Most women think them disquieting, if not downright odd."

"I always have," I said softly, caressing his cheek with my hand. "Even when I was scared of you, when I hated you, when you hurt me, I loved them. It seemed horribly unfair to me that someone who could hurt me so casually could have such beautiful eyes. They're like gold," I said heatedly, looking into them intently. "Like molten gold that is rich and beautiful and hot to the touch." I cleared my throat, blushing a little. "More beautiful than your eyes is my love for your eyes. And when you sing, all beings sing."

He blinked, then his beautiful eyes widened. "That was Sa'id 'Aql."

I smiled, glad he'd recognized the poem. "You are not the only one who knows poetry, thought I admit I'm not in your league—"

He kissed me deeply, wrapping me in his arms, the tears on his cheeks making my face wet. Then he thrust up lightly, and I cried out, his organ hard again within me. He held my hips, pushing me down to receive him as he thrust up repeatedly, his eyes gleaming wickedly.

"You said you were spent," I groaned, blissful sensations washing over me.

"I thought I was," Devlin murmured, kissing my throat. "But your words hardened me." He kissed me passionately. "Your words and the tight warmth of your body around mine. I love being within you, Sar. I love that you want me there. And your cries as you climax are delicious."

"Make love to me again," I whispered, kissing his neck and his face. "Please, Dev."

"Come with me, and I will," he murmured, in between kisses. "There is not enough room here to properly cherish you." He hugged me close. "And there is not enough time."

"Quickly then," I said, moving on him rhythmically. "Please."

Devlin kissed my throat. "Do you want my fangs again?"

"Do you want to bite?" I whispered.

"You, always," he whispered hungrily. "Scream for me, Sar. Scream as loud as you can."

He began to stoke me gently, his hands rubbing my breasts, his lips worshipping me. Minutes later, my orgasm hit me, and I let out a loud scream. Devlin bit into me again, his hips pumping frenziedly beneath me. Again he gave a muffled groan as he climaxed, this time his hands holding my hips tight to his as he finished.

"I love you," he whispered. "But if I don't leave you now I won't be able to at all. Forgive me, my love." He lifted me off him, his soft penis slipping easily out of me and sat me beside him. Then he zipped and buttoned his jeans.

He kissed me a final time. "Please come with me, Sar. Or else please go beyond my reach quickly, I beg you."

I kissed him back once and then opened the door and got out quickly before I reconsidered Rio.

"Good-bye, Devlin," I said, then remembered what he'd said. "Good-bye, Dev," I amended softly, drinking in the last sight of him. "Take care of yourself."

"Fare thee well, my only love," he said smiling down at me. "Fare thee well awhile. Watch your back."

"You, too," I replied.

He backed up his Hummer, and a moment later, he was driving off.

The moment he was gone, reality came crashing back. Theo would be home soon.

I ran into the house, and the dogs jumped all over me, sniffing interestedly. I hurriedly made a fire in the wood stove. When it was roaring hot, I took off my soaked underwear and threw it in. Next, I took off all my clothes and put them into the wash along with special scent removing detergent. I'd gotten it for the dog beds, but it was going to be put to better use tonight. Then I took a shower, trying to get every last trace of Devlin out of my body. I washed my hair again, then hopped out and dried off. The phone rang while I was conditioning my hair, likely Danial. That meant Theo would be here in a half hour or so, the way he drove.

The problem was what to do now. I wanted to think about Devlin and remember how he'd been with me. Instead, I somehow had to get ready for sex with someone else.

I burst into tears again. Theo wasn't just someone else. I'd loved him for years now and done so much to be with him. I'd spent one day in bed with another man, and now I was going to throw my marriage away? Bad enough I'd done what I had, I didn't have to sit dwelling on it. I sank to the bed, grabbing the tissue box. What the hell was wrong with me?

The phone rang again. I didn't answer it, instead getting a cold washcloth for my face.

Suddenly, my cell phone rang. Worried that the calls I'd ignored were about some attack, I answered. "Hello?"

"It's me, Love," Devlin whispered.

The moment I heard his voice, desire washed through me. I bit my lip hard, using the pain to push it down. "We just said goodbye—"

"I love you," he said gently. "Which means I'm not inclined to abandon you to your own schemes of deception. Have you destroyed your clothes and bathed?"

"Yes," I answered.

"He'll still smell me in you," Devlin said, raw satisfaction in his words. "Do you have perfume, or a strongly scented lotion?"

I ran to my bathroom and rummaged. "Yes, both."

"Put both on liberally all over. By the time it fades, my scent will also. And don't worry about how you seem. You were kidnapped, tortured and almost gang raped. There is no normal behavior after something like that."

"Theo knows?"

"I told Danial of how I found you. He told Theo, I'm sure."

Not likely, with how ardor-filled Theo had been on the phone.

"I have your pajamas," Devlin said happily. "I love how they smell of our lovemaking—"

Headlights shone in the darkness of the road, then slowed to turn into the driveway.

"Shit, he's here—"

"Go quickly," Devlin said curtly. "And if you need me tonight, just call."

I hung up and raced for the bathroom. Quickly I slathered on the lotion and sprayed the perfume, almost choking on the strong floral scent. Hurrying into a long white nightgown, I climbed into bed and waited.

Theo called from the next room, "Sar, I'm home."

"I'm in here," I called back.

Theo came in a minute later. "Hi, sweetheart," he said tenderly.

The sight of him made me ache: his feathered back blonde hair, his blue eyes, his smile that said how happy he was to see me. Guilt hit me so hard that I wanted to throw up. I forced it down, swallowing the bitterness.

He scented the air, looking confused. "It smells like a florist's in here. Is that some new lotion?"

"Do you hate it?" I whispered.

"No, it's just strong," he said, trying not to grimace. "You could use a little less next time maybe." He shed his clothes and climbed into bed. "Come here."

As I went into his arms, I kept waiting for him to accuse me, to ask me who's scent was on my body, to ask me if I'd liked it. But he said none of those things.

"Sar, tell me what happened," Theo said.

"You know already, don't you?"

"I'd rather you told me, if you don't mind."

It would be suspicious not to want to if I was innocent. I related the story of my capture and Devlin saving me, telling the lie he'd suggested, that we'd slept the day away. "I just got home about an hour ago."

"I owe him two now," Theo said gratefully.

"You don't owe him anything," I retorted. "He was doing a favor for Danial. He had his own agenda."

"Still, he saved you, Sar. It's too bad that he's already left. Danial said that he would be leaving soon. That Devlin had decided to relocate his base of operations."

"When did he decide to do that?" I choked out.

"About a month ago or so?" Theo said. "I'm not sure."

"I'll be right back," I said and ran to the bathroom. I sat on the toilet, trembling hard.

Devlin had planned this. I remembered the pajamas he'd happened to have that fit me, the bag of his clothes he'd had with him. He had known the men who attacked me, who had taken me. He'd worked all this out to get me alone, when he knew that I wouldn't be able to call out to Terian or Danial or especially Theo to come to my rescue. Then he had conveniently been there to save my ass. But worse of all was that all his talk of love and devotion had been lies.

"Sar, what is it?" Theo asked from the doorway.

I sighed.

"There's a sigh for yes and a sigh for no and a sigh for I can't bear it."

I shut my eyes tight, wanting to block out the sound of Devlin's voice and the images flooding through my brain.

Theo came and crouched down in front of me. "What's wrong? Tell me."

"I'm okay," I lied. "I'm just getting my period."

"Sar, are you happy? Here with me?"

I looked at him in surprise. "Of course I'm happy with you. Why wouldn't I be?"

"I just mean that you're apart from Theoron. I know how much you love him."

"What are you saying?"

"I'm saying that if you wanted to, we could move closer to Danial's home. Maybe even build a small home on his property. You wouldn't have to be so far from Theoron or from Elle."

I relaxed instantly. "No, it's okay. I see Theoron every day I work, and on weekends too sometimes. He lacks for nothing."

"Except seeing his mother every day," Theo said softly.

That stung. "Theo, leave it," I replied stiffly, in no mood to have this conversation with him.

"Then what's wrong, Sar?" he said worriedly. "Your body language is telling me that you're not okay, that something's bothering you. What is it?"

"Nothing," I said quickly. "I'm just tired. Can we please just go to bed?"

"Sar, did one of those men who took you, did they … hurt you?" he said.

I looked up at him, and all the blood drained out of my face. "Why did you ask me that?"

"I—" Theo began and faltered. He cleared his throat. "I know you. You never wear perfume, especially not to bed. It's almost as if you're using it to cover something—"

I dissolved into tears.

His eyes went yellow. "Why didn't you tell me?" he shouted at me. "How could you not tell me immediately?"

I tried to break away from him, but he held me fast.

"We need to get you to a doctor. Camlyn's got an emergency number—"

I had enough suddenly. I turned to him, enraged at him for pushing so hard and at Devlin for putting me in this position. "No, I'm not going anywhere! Get your hands off me!"

"I'm taking you to Camlyn right now," Theo said and lunged for me.

What if Dr. Camlyn found traces of Devlin inside me? What if he could tell it had been a vampire who'd had me? "No!" I screamed at him. "I'm not hurt! I'll be okay! I just want to forget it ever happened! Please don't—"

"Sar, how could you lie to me?" he roared, louder than ever before. His eyes were yellow slits, his hands claws.

"Because I came!" I shouted back.

His face registered utter shock, then disgust.

"That's why," I said weakly, tears streaming down my face. "Because I never wanted to see that look on your face." I turned from him, grabbing my long overcoat and getting my keys. I was almost out the door when he grabbed me.

"Let me go!" I shouted at him. "Let me go!"

"Where are you going?" he shouted.

"I'm going to Danial."

"Why?" he said jealously.

"Because he'll understand," I said, pushing him away. "He would never judge me as you just did. Nothing I could ever do would make him look at me with disgust, not after what he put up with under The Lust—"

Theo grabbed hold of me. "Sar, I'm sorry. Please don't leave—"

I dissolved into tears again, beating at him half-heartedly.

"This wasn't your fault," he said roughly. "This is my fault. I should have been there—"

"No," I said vehemently, sudden hatred of Devlin filling me. "There is only one person to blame for this—the man who did this to me."

Theo pulled me close, stroking my hair as his eyes changed back to their storm cloud blue. "He's lucky he's roasting in hell now. I know how to break someone piece by piece into jagged shards of themselves. And I would do worse to him."

I shivered hearing that and did not correct him.

He kissed my forehead. "Get some sleep, Sar. I'll be right here."

I swallowed hard, blinked back tears and didn't reply.

* * * *

The next morning I was awakened by sun streaming in the windows. Theo was beside me, his arm thrown over me, his chest rising and falling in his sleep. Everything was peaceful. Then I remembered Devlin and everything we'd done.

I grabbed the tissue box and wiped my filling eyes. If only I hadn't wanted him. If only I hadn't fed him. If I hadn't tasted of summer. If we'd had double beds and not one bed. If he hadn't held me when I was dreaming of Theo. If only, if only…

Theo stirred then, and I got up, leaving the room. I wasn't ready to talk anymore this morning. As I was feeding the dogs and cats, I hit the play button on the answering machine.

"Sar?" Danial's voice said questioningly. "Are you there?" Then he paused, and the machine hung up on him.

The next call was from him, too. "Sar, it's me. Call me when you get this, even if it's day."

I paused, debating whether to call or not. As soon as he heard my voice, he'd know I was upset. Yet that was suddenly oddly comforting. I resolutely picked up the phone and dialed Danial's cell.

It rang for a long time, and then a woman picked up. "Hello?"

This was a surprise. "Is Danial there?" I said awkwardly.

"Sar, it's Janice. Sorry, I didn't recognize your voice."

"It's okay, Janice, I didn't recognize yours either," I said, relieved.

"Danial left this upstairs with me, to field calls. But he wants to talk to you. Hold on just a minute." There were sounds of her opening the basement door and descending. "It's Sar."

Danial grumbled something to her, then said, "Why didn't you call back last night—?"

"I'm here," I said carefully, in as normal a voice as was possible.

"There is something in your voice," Danial said, alert. "What's wrong?"

I ignored his question. "I'm sorry about Monica."

"You know as well as I that is not what I'm talking about. What is wrong? Did you and Theo fight?"

I pretended I hadn't heard and kept talking. "I know how you felt about her, Danial. I'm sorry—"

"Sar," he interrupted. "Come with Theo to work tonight. I need your help with a few new clients. The house is a mess, but we can get some work done."

"Now who is lying?" I said to him.

"Both of us," Danial said flatly. "But you either show up with him, or I'm coming to see you tonight. Something is badly wrong, and if it wasn't day I'd be heading to you now. As it is, I want to ask someone to go get you and bring you here to me now. The only reason I don't is that Theo would throw a fit. But make sure both of you are here by sundown, if not before."

"Okay," I acquiesced.

"Put him on," Danial ordered.

I took the phone into Theo, who was just getting dressed. "Danial for you."

He took it with irritation. "Yes? Fine, Danial, I was going to be there anyway. But I think Sar should stay here." Pause. "Fine, okay, I'll bring her. I'm sure she wants to see Elle and Theoron, too." He hung up and handed me back the phone.

"Do you mind going?" Theo said, rubbing his eyes. "Both of the kids want to see you, to make sure you're okay."

"No," I replied, resigned. "I want to see them, too."

Chapter Seventeen

I busied myself that day cleaning the house, moving on to autumn chores as Theo slept. This year the weather was turning cold faster than ever. It would be an early winter. I tried not to think as I worked, which was an exercise in futility. But I did succeed in ignoring all thoughts of Devlin.

After finishing my gardening, I took Ghost and Darkness for a long walk. The leaves were changing early, and already the huge red maple was red as blood, its leaves brilliant on this cloudless day, its branches swaying in the wind. I walked slowly, thinking about what to tell Danial and what not to. Finally, I decided not to make any preparation. The plan I'd tried last night with Theo had been a disaster.

The dogs and I got back to the house just in time to see Theo coming out. "We have to get going," he said. "It's almost five now."

"Okay," I said. "Let me put the dogs inside."

I put them in, grabbed my purse, and then the phone rang. I looked at the caller ID and didn't recognize the number. The call was from out of state, but it wasn't a telemarketer.

I stopped still, looking at the phone as if it might bite me. What if it was Devlin again? I didn't want to talk to him, not after the mess he'd made of my life. But did I dare let the answering machine get it?

The machine picked up, and Theo's voice came on, saying that the caller had reached Theo and Sarelle, to leave a message. I held my breath, waiting.

"Sar, it's your mother-in-law, well, former mother-in-law—"

I had to sit down I was so relieved.

"—How is married life? I hope you and your new husband are happy. I mean that—"

"Sar, we have to go!" Theo yelled from outside.

Startled into movement, I grabbed my keys, locked the door after me and ran to his truck. He'd already backed it out of the garage, and as soon as I got in, he floored it, getting to thirty just in the driveway.

"Did you get enough sleep?" I asked him, as he spun the wheel.

"Enough," he said, giving me a smile. Then his smile faded. "Sar, I know you want to forget what happened. Probably like I do, with what I went through." He paused. "When and if you want to tell me, I want you to know that you can. That I'll listen. If that takes a while, it's okay. I'm still not ready to tell you what happened to me in Europe, though I'm working toward a point where I will be."

I expected him to say more, but he stopped there. I kept silent for a few minutes, thinking. Finally, I said, "Theo, give me some time. Please understand—there are some parts I don't know if I can talk about—ever."

"I feel the same about my own ordeal," Theo replied. "I understand."

He reached out and grabbed my hand. I squeezed his, and we rode in silence the rest of the way. It was a comfortable silence, one we didn't need to fill with words.

Theo pulled up to Danial's a good ten minutes before sundown. He parked the truck, and we got out, walking to the front door. Janice was there to meet us.

"Theo, Danial wants to see you inside," she said.

Theo nodded, then ran up the stairs and in the front door.

Janice turned to me. "Sar, Theoron and Elle are with Terian at the compound. They are walking over and should be here shortly."

"Good," I said, relieved.

"Are you okay?" Janice said, concerned.

"I'm still shaken up," I admitted. "But I'll be okay."

She gave me a reassuring smile, and I gave her one back.

"Mom!"

I turned as Elle launched herself in the air at me. I caught her, but my muscles were sore, and I gasped.

"Mom? Are you okay?" she said worriedly, alarm on her face.

"I'm okay, Elle," I hugged her tightly to me. "I'm glad to see you."

"I'm glad you're safe," Terian said as he walked up to us. "I should have tried to take you with me when I took the kids." There was a large amount of guilt on his face.

"Frankly, I'm just grateful to you for getting them out of here that night. I'm surprised you were able to take both Elle and Theoron at the same time."

"It was hard," he said grudgingly. "That spell is meant to teleport one person, not for taking people along with you. There are ways to widen it, but you have to work up to that slowly. I'm still a novice—"

"You did wonderfully then," I said, hugging him.

As I did, I noticed Theoron strapped to Terian's back in his baby harness. He was reaching for me eagerly. I got him out with a little difficulty and held him.

Two more people walked up that I didn't recognize. I turned to Terian questioningly.

"Sarelle, this is Hans and Warren," Terian said, gesturing to them to come over.

Warren was older, maybe about thirty-five or so. He had brown hair and brown eyes. His smile was friendly, and he had a Western accent as he said, "Good to meet you, Sarelle."

Hans was almost Nordic looking. His skin was as pale as Danial's, and his eyes were pale blue. His hair was platinum blond and cut so short it was almost buzzed. "Nice to meet you, Sarelle," he said with no accent.

"It's good to meet you both," I said, smiling at them uncertainly.

Theo came down the stairs, all business. "Okay, guys, Danial wants me to take you out to the range and see what you know. Follow me." He headed off toward the fox compound, walking fast, and they strode after him.

Janice turned to me and said hesitantly, "I'm sorry, but I need to feed Theoron."

I handed him back to her reluctantly, and she took him inside.

I'd wanted to start feeding him myself, but Danial was worried Theoron would associate me again with food. I conceded he had a point and comforted myself with the fact that at the very least, in a few months, I could start making him cookies, soup, pies and maybe even homemade ice cream. I'd never made the last, but for him, I was willing to try it. How hard could it be?

Then Elle had my attention again, squeezing me so tightly I couldn't breathe. "And how about you, Elle?" I asked. "What are you up to?"

"Tears is taking me to the movies," Elle said happily. "We are going to see the newest *Saw*."

"She started calling me that last week." Terian explained, smiling. "As far as the movie, I voted for that animated one, but I couldn't change her mind, Sar."

"Did your father say that was okay?" I asked her.

"He said it was fine and to keep track of the traps to let him know about them later."

I made a mental note to talk to Theo. He was going to warp Elle, teaching her this stuff.

Yet was her life any less scary? People attacking her home, having to shoot them to survive? Well, I could do something about her entertainment, even if I couldn't do anything about real life. I made another mental note to get her some "G" rated DVDs.

"Bye, Mom!"

"Have a good time!" I called as they drove off, waving.

I stood there for a moment, knowing I had to go in. Still, I couldn't make myself do it. "Coward," I muttered and put my foot on the first step, looking up to meet Danial's eyes.

He slowly descended the stairs. "Come with me," he said, walking toward the garage.

I walked with him. "Where are we going?"

"We need more office supplies," he said, getting into one of the black Expeditions and opening the door for me from the inside. "We're going to Staples."

"Danial—"

"Sar, get in the truck. Now."

He wasn't angry, but he clearly expected me to obey him. I shrugged and got in. It was his money. I didn't mind a road trip for work now and again, and this wasn't a surprise. We had been low on manila folders and stamps, staples and printer ink since last week.

He drove in silence, his eyes on the road. That was fine with me as I let my mind drift, trying to determine how to handle him. But to my horror, instead of Staples, we pulled up in front of Dr. Camlyn's office.

I turned to him in horror. "Theo—"

"Yes, he told me," Danial said, turning to me. "You are getting checked out. Right now."

No. Way. I threw open the door and jumped out of the SUV. Danial was faster, already in front of me.

I struggled with him. "Please, Danial, don't make me do this!"

"You are going in there if I have to drag you in," he said, a red glint in his eyes.

"No, I'm not."

"Yes, you are." Danial tossed me over his shoulder easily and carried me in still thrashing. He nodded to the stunned secretary and took me through the door, setting me down in one of the exam rooms. "Stephen, we're here!"

Stephen came in. "Sar, please get undressed. My examination will only take a few minutes."

Danial walked to the door and stood in front of it, his arms crossed over his chest.

"I don't want to do this," I said, pulling my legs under me, making myself as small as possible.

"Sarelle," Stephen said. "What happened to you is not your fault. You know that. I just need to see if you're hurt."

"I'm not hurt," I said softly, not looking at either of them.

"You can't know that," Stephen said gently. "Just let me—"

"Yes, I can," I said steely. "Don't tell me what I know. It's my body."

"At the very least," Stephen said neutrally, "I have to check you for diseases. It's normal protocol for this situation."

"He didn't have any."

"You can't know that," Stephen said patiently. "He—"

"I know it," I asserted.

Stephen said slowly, "Sarelle, please, just get undressed. It will only take a minute to examine you. Then you can go home."

"Please step outside," Danial interrupted. "Come back in a few moments, and Sar will be ready to cooperate."

Dr. Camlyn nodded, then walked out and closed the door behind him.

I gave in, knowing it was hopeless to fight anymore. What was I hoping to gain by resisting anyway? Better to get this over with. Without speaking to Danial, I got undressed. Soon, I was being examined, Dr. Camlyn poking me and prodding me. Now that I was cooperating, Danial leaned against the wall, no longer blocking the door. I didn't look at him, though I felt his eyes on me.

"Sarelle, were you with Theo last night?"

"No," I said, flushing.

Dr. Camlyn put my legs back together and stripped off his gloves. "Sarelle, you have slight bruising, but nothing outside the norm for you. Everything is well within normal limits."

"I figured," I said haltingly, my eyes filling with tears. "He promised not to hurt me if I let him have his way."

"Sarelle, you aren't pregnant because of the pill and your own physiology. I also verified that just now when I examined you. Physically you're just fine. I'll run the screening today and let you know in a few days—"

"Fine," I interrupted. "Can I leave now?"

"Shortly. As you're here, I want to take some of your blood to see how present the vampire virus is in your system. I'll be right back to collect a sample."

Oh, shit. "Okay," I replied.

Stephen came back, drew a little of my blood and then left again. Danial and I waited in silence.

Stephen came back in about ten minutes and shut the door behind him. "Sar, your blood is unchanged."

"I'm still partly turned?" I said flatly.

"Yes," he said with a nod. "This is good, as you'll most likely heal the scars you have on your uterus. In another four months, you might be able to bear children again."

While I was not pleased to hear that, Danial was overjoyed. "Are you sure?" he asked Stephen excitedly.

"I believe so," Stephen replied. "But only time will tell for sure, Danial." He turned back to me. "But I am concerned about one thing, Sar. You are slightly anemic. Were you hurt or injured when you were taken? Beyond the rape?"

Danial's grin faded hearing those words, then his head turned slowly toward me.

"I let Devlin feed from me," I said, my eyes downcast. "He took five explosive rounds to the chest saving me. I was also….they…a man whipped me. Devlin healed them that night."

Stephen didn't reply, and the silence stretched. Finally, I looked up to meet his eyes.

"Was Devlin the man that raped you?" Stephen asked, his anger barely held in check.

"No," I said immediately, drawing my legs up tight to my body.

Stephen came over to me and put his hand on my shoulder. "If he did, you have recourse—"

"Stephen, leave us for a moment," Danial interrupted.

Stephen ignored him. "—I know of his reputation. You have rights—"

"I do not make idle threats," Danial said menacingly, moving between Stephen and me. "If what you say happened, it is I that Sar would seek recourse from, not you. Now get out of this room."

Stephen left abruptly, closing the door behind him with a hard snap. Danial turned to me.

"The anemia will go away on its own. I need to know if he gave you any of his blood."

"Not that I know of," I answered. "He healed the cuts he made and the…the others with kisses—"

"Do you want vengeance?" he asked seriously.

I didn't reply.

"I'll ask again—do you want vengeance for what he did to you?"

"No," I whispered. "What I want is for no one else to know."

"No one else will," Danial assured me. "I'll make sure of it." He went to the door.

"What are you going to do?" I said shrilly.

Danial stopped and turned back to me. "What you really want to know is what I'm not going to do. I'm not going to put out a bounty on my brother. Nor am I going to tell Theo about this. Stephen cannot violate patient privilege and tell him without your permission, so your secret is safe."

"I'm sorry."

"I'm the one who is sorry," Danial said, coming back quickly and hugging me. "Get dressed. I will deal with Stephen." He strode out.

I got dressed, then paid my co-pay. Danial was waiting for me in his SUV when I left the office. It was with effort that I made myself get in. "We still need the office supplies," he said as I put on my seatbelt. "Would you mind the trip?"

I'd braced myself for accusations, or at least for Danial being angry or upset. Instead, he was detached. "No," I answered, relieved. "Is there a lot of emails or filing?"

"Not really," Danial answered. "In a few weeks there will be, as I'm close to closing a slew of cases and have word of more than a few new ones pending." He began to go over some of the new business.

Throughout the rest of that day, we didn't speak of Devlin or my secret.

* * * *

Weeks passed. Danial was as distant and polite as he'd been when Monica was alive, though I saw him much more frequently. What I found harder to handle was that Theo had adopted the same attitude Danial had. Physical proximity with no closeness at all.

Three weeks passed this way. Finally, on a Thursday night, I walked into the living room where Theo was lounging on the couch. With no warning, I straddled him and gave him a big kiss. He started back from me, and I stopped still, then moved off him.

"Sorry," he said tentatively. "I was into the movie."

I sat beside him. "Maybe you could get into me?" I said meaningfully.

Theo blushed beet red. "I can't believe you said that."

I wasn't going to play games. "We haven't even hugged in weeks. Don't you want me anymore?"

"I do," he said seriously, turning the movie off. "But I wanted to talk to you first before we're intimate. I've been putting that off because I'm worried what I'm going to say may make you not want me."

"There's only one way to know for sure," I replied. "Tell me."

"Some of this you know. I was angry that night that we went to get Peterson. You and Elle had almost been killed, and I wanted revenge at all costs. Finding Will there waiting for me was a bonus. He wanted me dead for screwing Tawny all those years, for making Elle with her. He was shot from behind before I could shoot him. As he died, he got off a round, hitting me in the shoulder. The men that shot him took my cell and my jacket to make it look like he was me."

"They could tell I was wereanimal from how fast my wound was healing. A man named Gene had been told to send his men to that place and time to capture a werelion. He was pleased when they brought back a cougar. He'd never sold one before, he said."

"I know," I added softly. "Nineva told us about that bastard who bought you. Van and Eric killed him and Gene."

Theo nodded, then continued. "It was Erickson that crippled me. He broke some of my bones over and over. If a broken bone isn't quickly set right on a were, it can heal badly. By the time I got away from him, I couldn't walk on four legs anymore as cougar and as human. My hands were useless."

I held his hand tightly, then motioned for him to go on.

"I escaped in winter. I walked for days, finally taking refuge deep in a forest in Turkey. Crippled and starving, I ate whatever was available. I spent that winter in an abandoned cabin, waiting for my hands to heal. I couldn't run as a cougar, but as a man, I froze. I couldn't break and set my bones, but as they reformed with each change of my form they healed some. There was some dried food stored in the cabin that I made last as long as possible. Still, I was hungry most of the time. When it ran out, I knew I had to eat or die."

"I ventured out of the forest and was able to kill a sheep of a neighboring farmer. With careful rationing, it sustained me for the rest of that year. By then, I was healed enough to hunt as a cougar, though putting weight on my forelegs hurt. But the meat I caught came with the price of being seen."

He paused and then continued. "A man saw me kill a deer as a cougar. He tracked me to the cabin and saw me change. He called me a devil, then tried to shoot me. I tore him apart, then took his gun and all of his supplies."

"I understand not being able to contact me during that winter," I said tentatively. "But why didn't you try later?"

"I had no money and nothing to identify myself. I couldn't go to the American Embassy in any case. I'm wanted in Europe, Sar. There were several jobs over there that got messy years back. My name would have sent me to the nearest detention center, and it would be a matter of time until they found out what I was."

"Couldn't you find a phone, even a private one and call?" I said persistently.

"I tried several times, but I couldn't get through. Phone reception over there in rural areas is spotty at best, especially in the countries I was in. And most times, there was no phone I could get my hands on that worked."

Theo had to be lying to me about that, though for my life I had no idea why. "Go on."

"I got on a ship, but it took me to Egypt instead of Europe. I tried to sell myself as a mercenary there, in exchange for a fake passport. That night I was captured again, as I slept in cougar form in a deserted warehouse. This time, I was to be sent to a sheik as a present—"

"That was you?" I said tearfully. "We heard you escaped."

"I did, but by then, I was already in Isfahan, Iran. As I made my way north, I had the bad luck to be noticed by a sorcerer in Iraq. He froze me in my cougar form and sold me to a group of insurgents. They had a great interest in weres. That is where the explosive bullet scarring comes from. They shot me over and over, to research how fast a were could heal and how many shots it took before the healing stopped."

I wanted to tell Theo to stop, that the horror his words made me imagine was too much. Instead, I wiped my eyes and then squeezed his hand.

"My spirit was broken by then, Sar. I was in a lot of pain and wanted nothing more than to die. It had been a year since I'd first been sold into slavery, and I felt in my bones that I was never going to see either of you again. Seeing I was finished, the army sold me to a distant Russian who wanted a pet werecougar. He sent me to his country home, where I stayed for weeks and slowly recovered until I could walk again."

"The set-up was the same as the other times I'd been held prisoner: a strong yet tiny cage and meat served in a bowl twice a day. There I finally caught some luck. The Russian's daughter was there, and she befriended me as a cougar. She nursed me back to health until I could run again." He looked at me. "Her name was Natasha," he said softly. "She was sixteen."

It was all there in the way he said her name. "You loved her."

"She was kind to me," Theo said, swallowing hard. "I followed her around like a tame puppy, figuring to heal completely, then escape. Everything was going according to plan until she saw me change one night. When she saw I was a man and not a cougar, she brought me clothes, then took me into her house in human form, telling everyone she had hired me to be her bodyguard. I lived for the first time in a year in peace and comfort."

"I'm glad she helped you," I ventured, trying hard not to sound judgmental. "Go on."

"Two weeks afterwards, she came to my room at night. I hadn't been with anyone since you, Sar. Had not felt the touch of another person in kindness since then. She and I became lovers." Theo paused again and took a deep breath. "She was a virgin."

I said nothing, too much in shock that he'd had sex with a girl that young.

"Soon after, we gave up the pretense of bodyguard, and I moved into her room."

"Were you in love with her?"

"Yes. I loved her as much as I had loved you."

I was hurt deeply by this, but said only, "Go on."

"She asked me to stay with her, to marry her. She had plenty of money. When I confessed about Tawny dying after having Elle, Tasha said she had siblings to carry on the family name, so we didn't have to have children."

Why the hell hadn't he told her he had a child to get back to, a fiancée he had left hanging years before? "Did you tell her about me?" I asked.

"Yes," he said softly. "She said she understood if I had to go back to you and Elle."

Good for her. "Go on."

"She arranged passage to get me out of the country. The night I was to leave, I told her I would come back to her. I told her that I would end things with you and come back to her. Maybe bring Elle with me, if I could—"

I took a deep, deep breath and said nothing. It was everything I could do to keep being, keep breathing. Theo had betrayed me. I'd been so worried about him and his feelings for Aspen, and here he'd had a way more serious romance I'd not even known about. "How did you end up in Casper then?"

"Her father arrived finally to look over his new pet and caught us together in bed. He shot at me. I was still not fast in human form, still crippled because of the gunshot wounds that were taking so long to heal so I was hit. Still I escaped and got to the ship heading for California. When I was aboard, I called Tasha. But she wasn't there. I spoke to a maid I'd come to know well, one that was happy for the two of us. She said that Tasha had left in tears that night with her father. That he'd arranged a marriage for her the next morning. She said Tasha had told her to tell me to forget her, that our plan to be together could never happen now, even though she wanted it more than anything."

Theo was crying hard now. Though I held his hand, I couldn't muster any words of sympathy or comfort. I was too angry.

"I headed back here to New York after accessing one of my hidden accounts. I got here in February." He wiped his eyes, then said curtly, "I can tell how angry you are that I loved someone else. But how do you think I felt to come back here to find you not only with Danial, but pregnant?"

I didn't answer his question. It was hard enough to talk and not think about the hurricane of emotions I was feeling inside. "Terian told me how he found you, that you'd seen us and decided to leave."

"I saw that your Oathing scars were back and the ring on your finger, and I knew I'd lost you. And watching Elle and Danial, I knew I had lost her to him, too."

"Why did you choose to go west?" I asked. "Why Casper?"

"I wanted to be by myself," Theo said. "I thought there might be some natural mountain lions there that would be companions. I wasn't looking for love. I was looking for solace."

He'd found that and more in Aspen. "Thank you for telling me," I said politely. "I know it wasn't easy, and I appreciate your honesty."

"Does it change what you feel for me? To know that?"

Yes. A resounding yes. I'd been an absolute idiot to stay faithful in my heart to a man who could have called me up at any time in the last year he'd been gone and told me he was alive but had moved on. He'd have freed me to have a complete life with Danial—freed me of so much guilt. But he hadn't, out of either jealousness or sheer thoughtlessness.

"Sar?"

"I worried for so long you were alive and hurt," I said tonelessly. "I'm floored that you could have picked up the phone and called me so many times, and you didn't. And don't blame spotty reception."

"How could I have known you were thinking about me at all?" Theo countered. "I figured that you'd moved on, either with Danial or someone else. There was nothing I saw that night in February that made me think you had any feelings left for me at all."

My hackles rose, the resentment and bitterness welling up within me. Oddly, as it had before, my feelings of betrayal vanished as I considered his words. Theo had loved someone else, but so had I. And I hadn't waited a year to have sex, move in, or even try for a baby. The only real difference was that I'd rejected Danial's offer of commitment, and Theo had embraced Tasha's…

"I can tell you're upset," Theo said, squeezing my hand. "I'm not saying you don't have a right to be. We both went through an ordeal with me disappearing for almost two years. But we do love each other, and we can work through it together, if you'll work with me."

I squeezed his hand gently, searching for something besides "okay" to say.

"We're committed to each other," Theo said, hugging me. "Whatever I felt for Tasha, I'm married to you. I pledged to be faithful, and I'm going to stick to that vow."

Guilt flooded me, Devlin springing immediately to mind. "I know."

"Talk to me," Theo said. "Tell me you think we can work this out. Tell me you still want me."

"I think we can work it out," I said distantly.

"You can tell me anything," he said tenderly. "Don't hold back what you're feeling."

I looked at him, so earnest, and knew that was a lie. I couldn't tell him I'd had sex with Devlin and enjoyed it, or that I was still devastated he'd admitted to loving another woman and wanting her over me. Admitting just those together to myself made me feel like a world-class hypocrite. I knew only one thing with crystal clarity: I would be apologizing to Danial first thing tomorrow on my knees for how I'd treated him. I'd put Theo and our love up on a pedestal and treated Danial's love for me like the floor tiles Devlin had alluded to. He deserved an apology for all he'd done for me and put up with.

Theo wasn't a perfect man, but he was a good and decent one. We did love each other, and we could be happy together—once we worked through our baggage.

As for Devlin, whatever he'd been after—a good lay or a psychological screwing—he was gone, and he wasn't coming back. The best thing to do would be what he advised: forget him and pretend like our day of making love never happened...

Theo began kissing up my neck. "I want you, too," he whispered. "I'm so glad we talked. I was so worried—"

He'd picked up on my arousal. Hastily, I turned to him and kissed him back. "I want you."

He picked me up and carried me into the bedroom, kissing me feverishly. He quickly helped me off with my clothes, then pulled off his own.

"Tell me you love me," Theo said desperately, pulling me on top of him.

"I love you, Theo," I murmured, kissing down his chest.

"Tell me you still want me," he said, his hesitancy mixed with fear.

"I will always want you, always need you, always love you," I said, running my hands over his strong body, the now barely visible scars and especially the patches of white scar tissue by his hips that were unchanged. "Now take me, Husband. I'm yours."

Theo kissed me back tenderly. He held me still, gently slipping into me with none of his usual franticness. Every caress of his body and mine was filled with emotion that slowly built to a panic, our orgasms leaving us shaken, clutching one another. Afterward we lay in bed, holding each other as if we'd never let go.

* * * *

The next morning, Theo and I talked as we drove into work, the tension that had been between us so long replaced with easy familiarity.

"Will you be target practicing today with the newer foxes, or does Danial have conference meetings? You've said Hans can't hit the broad side of a barn."

"Neither. Brian and I are going to take both Hans and Warren into Syracuse to get fitted for a type of armor to repel those explosive bullets. We'll be gone all day, but I'll be back to pick you up around four or so. Terian will be watching over you and the kids today."

Well, a promise was a promise. "Theo, do both you and Danial have that same armor? Devlin had a form of it, but not much was left once he'd been shot. The damage he had to heal was extreme. If you don't have some, can you

212

please get some while you're gone?" I squeezed his hand "I don't want anything to happen to either of you."

"Don't worry. Danial has a full vest. He's safe from everything except maybe a missile."

"What about you?" I said worriedly.

"I have a set of full body armor now," he said, giving my hand a hard squeeze. "I'm coming back to you in one piece, Sar, no matter what might happen."

"Good," I said with relief. "Since you'll be back in time, do you want to go out tonight and have dinner?"

"Sure," he said, almost purring. "It's a date."

He parked the truck and then got into one of the black Expeditions as I walked up the steps of Danial's porch.

As he started the engine I called after him, "Don't forget, this weekend is the one we're all going to go get pumpkins!"

"I didn't forget," Theo shouted back. "Remind Danial though!" Then he was gone in a cloud of dust, headed to the werefox compound.

I went inside, locking the door behind me, then went to check on Theoron. He was sleeping. Janice wouldn't be in to feed him until noon or so. Leaving his room, I stopped and paused before Danial's door, knowing I should make good on my idea of an apology. Then, like the coward I was, I went upstairs instead and checked on e-mail first. There were a few new clients, a new hate mail to stick in the possible suspects file and one client thanking Danial for a job well done. I printed that one out and left it on his desk, drawing a big happy face near the bottom. Danial kept a bulging file of good notes to remind himself on bad days that he did a great job with a lot of clients, even if they all didn't praise him.

Now that e-mail was done, I could put it off no longer. I went downstairs and knocked on Danial's bedroom door. A strange man threw it open to my surprise.

"Sorry!" he said, extending his hand. "I'm Paul. Me and my guys are fixing the hole someone made in the wall here." He pointed backward. Looking in, his men were visible in the back room putting finishing touches on the repaired wall Brian had smashed through.

"Looks good!" I said, giving him a smile. "Sorry to disturb you."

"No problem," he said, giving me an appreciative glance. "We'll be leaving in a few minutes anyway. Which is good as we were late completing this job."

Danial hadn't been happy about that, Theo had said. The basement wasn't as secure, obviously. "Thank you."

I moved into the great room, then stopped, considering if I should wait until the workmen left to knock on the basement door. I didn't want to, but neither did I want to draw attention to Danial below. We were still low on guards with Hans and Warren not up to speed yet, even with Brian's wife having arrived a few weeks ago, after Devlin had released her. Terian had agreed to stay until spring, according to Theo, but that was only six months away…

My cell phone rang. "Hello?"

"I hear you walking around up there," Danial said sleepily. "Come down, please, before you wear a hole in the floor."

"Okay." I hung up, opened the door and walked downstairs. Danial was waiting for me in jeans, buttoning his shirt.

"Are the workers keeping you up or just me?"

"They were. I'm glad they're leaving soon." He led me over to the bed, and we sat at the edge of it. "Sar, we need to talk. I have something to ask you."

"I have something to ask you, too," I said, my voice cracking with emotion.

"What is it?" he said anxiously and made to get up.

"Please sit down."

He eased back down, looking at me in trepidation.

I got up, went over to stand before him and then got on my knees.

"Sar, what are you doing?" Danial asked, confused and apprehensive. "I was just teasing about your walking around—"

"Danial," I said, looking up at him through tears. "I'm so sorry for everything I did to you and for how you must have felt when I left." My voice was all over the place, cracking and breaking and warbling so much that I hoped Danial could understand my words.

"Sar, get up. This is—"

"Theo told me about Tasha."

Danial gave a sigh and sank back down, looking at me sadly. "I'm sorry-"

"I feel now how you felt. How you must still feel. He is only with me because she's with someone else, and he can't be with her. The anger and jealousy eats at me inside like poison."

"Sar, please—" he started again.

I cut him off again. "It was easy for me to act like you should be happy taking what I could give. I was callous and stupid and unfeeling. I want you to know that there's not a day that's passed that I didn't love you. I was wrong to leave you the way I did, both times. I'm sorry that I thought too much of myself and what I wanted and not enough of you. I'm grateful that we had Theoron together, that we had that time together raising Elle. I'm sorry I wasn't more grateful for all you did for Elle and me. I'm sorry I was too selfish to see any of this until now."

Danial came off the bed and sat beside me on the floor. He pulled me into his lap and held me close. "I forgive you," he said softly. "Be at peace, Sar. Don't go over the past. It can't be changed. You and I both made mistakes and suffered for them. None of it matters now. I love you, regardless of what you did or didn't do, and that's never going to change."

I shut my eyes, relaxing in the comforting familiarity of his cool body close to mine, the slow beat of his heart, the rise and fall of his chest as he breathed and the strength of his arms around me. We said nothing for some time. It was enough that we were together, that he'd forgiven me.

Finally he spoke. "There were times I wanted you to say some of what you just said, terrible times when I wondered if you had ever loved me. Still I'm sorry you're as hurt as you are."

"I'm not hurt. I'm wrecked."

"Theo's confession of loving another woman and his plan to not come back unsettled me, too, the night he told me. It sounded like the reflections of an infatuated teenager. There was no logical reason for not contacting us when he had the opportunity," Danial reflected.

"I thought that, too. What do you think was the real reason he didn't call?"

"He's obviously ashamed of his scarring and likely was worried about returning to find you repelled by how he'd changed. Knowing you as I do, I don't understand his fear over that. But then, I'm not the one who's carrying the scars. It's also obvious when he found you with me and pregnant, his worst expectations were confirmed. I believe he didn't call because he didn't want me to tell him that I'd reclaimed you. What we were to each other obviously still makes him jealous, even though we've ended our relationship."

That made a skewed kind of sense, in the way that most men's actions usually did. "But what about Elle? How could he not come back to her?"

"I mean no insult by this," Danial said slowly. "But Theo's fatherly instincts do not run as strong as mine do. He doesn't protest her living here with me and not the two of you where I would if I were him. I think it's enough for him to know she's well taken care of. He knew I'd do that if something happened to him."

"You're making me feel like a bad mother," I sighed. "I'm acting the same as him."

"You could not have done anything differently with Theoron than you did," Danial countered. "Dr. Camlyn himself advised it, even for you to separate from me. It was I who acted badly, trying to convince you to stay in spite of the evidence you were turning."

"And I'm still at the same point now," I said dejectedly.

"That is what I wanted to talk to you about," Danial said tentatively. "Tell me what happened with Devlin. All of it."

"Why?" I answered. "It will hurt you to hear it. I know how you felt about him being intimate with your past loves."

"It will hurt you more to not tell someone," he countered. "You didn't tell Theo. He believes the man who forced you is dead." He paused. "I need to know if it was force or just seduction."

"For what?" I said, exasperated. "I don't want Devlin dead or to lose Theo for weeks or months while he pursues a vendetta. I forgave Devlin for what he did."

Danial sighed. "Did you go to him willingly?"

"No," I said defensively. "He threatened to turn me if I didn't submit, so I did."

"How did he go from savior to defiler? What prompted his attack?"

"A taste of my blood. He was weak from blood loss, so I gave him my blood willingly. He said I tasted of summer, that I was the only one who tasted like that." I turned to look up at him. "Is that true?"

"It's true," Danial replied. "I have never known why, but your blood does taste unusual. It is almost addictive in its sweetness. It was hard to be with you sometimes when we were intimate, knowing I couldn't take any from you but that it was there just beneath your skin."

"Why did you never say anything?" I said accusingly.

"Because I thought you might be worried that I'd lose control and take too much or that I wanted you only for how you tasted," Danial answered. "It was important to me that you knew that your blood was not the reason I loved you."

Pride swelled within me that I was so special and unique. Yet there was more than a little fear there, too. If both Danial and Devlin could taste the difference in my blood, likely any vampire could. What if another vampire tasted me, one who didn't care if I lived or died? I'd be dead when they decided they couldn't get enough of me. "Danial, I've been wearing the choker," I said quickly. "I'm going to continue to wear it. Manir is still unaccounted for—"

"Please do. It gives me happiness to see you wear it," he said, kissing me on my cheek. "But you were telling me of what happened with Devlin."

"What exactly do you want to know?" I said, flushing. "How many times the both of us reached orgasm?"

"You misunderstand me. I know what he did to you in the hours of that day," Danial said finally.

I looked at him in shock and horror. "He didn't *tell* you about it, did he?"

"He refused to talk about it," Danial said, annoyed. "Even when I told him that I knew he was lying, that something happened, he denied it."

"Then how can you know what he did to me?"

"Sar, I've known Devlin my whole life. Hundreds of years. You think that in all that time we never shared a woman?"

"I never thought about it…" I trailed off, as images rose unbidden in my mind of Danial and Devlin together, light and dark at the same time loving me as one.

"Ahh," Danial said huskily. "I see you are thinking about what it would have been like with the two of us in bed with you."

I flushed red to my toes. Danial chuckled, seeing my embarrassment.

"Did he ever ask you to—?" I began hesitantly.

"Of course he asked," Danial said, looking down at me like that was so obvious he couldn't believe that I needed to ask the question. "He asked that first night he met you, right after he tasted you for the first time and Tatiana had gotten you away from him. I refused, Sar. I didn't want to share you." He sighed. "I knew what letting you be like that with him would do to us. Even if you were afraid of him at first, I knew he would work at you, until he got you to trust him enough to let him touch you without fear. Then I'd lose you to him, as I lost the other women I'd shared with him over the years. I know well what he can do to a woman, both with his body and his voice."

A tremor went through me at his words, remembering Devlin's lovemaking. Unsettled, I said, "Why did you ask about this? It was more than just lending an ear, Danial."

"I needed to talk to you about this for two reasons. The first was to hear the truth from you, so you can stop holding it inside. The second reason was because I have something to give you."

Danial got up and went to the edge of the basement, returning with a large box. He put it on the bed. "This came yesterday for you."

"What is it?" I asked.

"I don't know," he said, gazing at me with serious eyes. "It's not my present to you."

Curious to see what Devlin had sent me, I opened the box. Inside was a pair of women's boots made of polished supple black leather. They were long, to be worn up over the knee, with ties behind it to make the boots fit snugly. They were in the style of Danial's old-fashioned boots, the ones he and Devlin favored. Devlin had remembered my liking them years before and my comment that I wanted some of my own. "They're beautiful," I said passionately, stroking the smooth leather with my fingertips.

"Try them on," Danial said, putting the box aside.

I tried them on over my leggings. "They fit perfectly."

"He likely had them made for you," Danial said, handing me a note. "This was in the attached card to me, which is why it has no envelope."

"I know you too well to think you'd open my mail," I reassured, unfolding the note.

Danial, Give these to Sar with my apologies. I'll call you soon. Dev

I put the note in the box with my sneakers and closed it, leaving the boots on. "What should I do?" I asked, resting one hand on my knee. "Should I keep the boots?"

"Do you want them?" Danial answered pointedly.

"Yes," I said, barely audible. "Of course." That was an understatement. I didn't ever want to take them off. I loved the way they fit me, like a second skin stretching to conform to my shape.

"Then keep them," Danial said. "If you like, I can say that I gave them to you."

I met his eyes. "Why are you so eager to cover for me and him? Theo's your best friend. Why aren't you angry with me? I expected you to be, to denounce me, in fact."

"Because I love you," he replied gently. "And I love Devlin also, despite what he's done. He's my brother. I don't want him dead. You are protecting him by not telling Theo. Theo would kill him if he knew that Devlin had been with you, if not for revenge than out of sheer jealousy." He let out a sigh. "And there is nothing to be angry about or to get revenge for."

"You're taking this very well," I said in disbelief. "You carried me into Dr. Camlyn's on your shoulder."

"I believed you were hurt then. You haven't been. I can accept what happened, knowing you wanted it to happen."

"Please tell me you forgive me," I asked guiltily. "It eats at me that I wanted Devlin as much as he wanted me, that I desire him still."

"You think that you'd feel better if you had been raped?" Danial asked incredulously.

"I'd still have the dishonor, but none of the guilt. I could be angry. Instead I feel weak and immoral."

"You are not either weak or immoral. I told you, you are not the first to succumb to him. Dev has always been a great lover of women. He has a gift for it."

"I suspected as much," I muttered. "I was likely one in a long line. What he did and said was just to bed me."

"Does that matter?" Danial said dismissively, hugging me. "You both enjoyed yourselves."

"He said he wanted to change," I said disgustedly. "To be a better man. God, what a line. And I fell for it."

"Don't be so sure you had no affect on him," Danial cautioned. "Dev is without a moral compass as he ever was, yet something is different about him."

"What do you mean?" I said, disdainful. "Because he paid me with a pair of boots?"

He raised my chin so I looked up into his eyes. "You touch everyone around you, Sar. No one after remains as they were before you. Don't sell yourself short. I'm serious."

"I'm sorry. What do you mean?"

"Dev called me. He was somewhere in South America, he said." Danial's eyes were moist. "He asked me to forgive him for what he had done, for letting what happened to us both happen all those centuries ago. He apologized for keeping his blood from me, for not sharing his power with me. He has never mentioned any of this to me before. We have never talked about it, not in all the time we've been vampire." Danial paused. "I forgave him. We are brothers again, as we haven't been since we were mortal. That's all due to you. He didn't just wake up one morning after hundreds of years and decide it was time to say he was sorry. Something you did or said prompted this."

"You're saying my behavior is excusable. Yet what if I was yours, if I had oathed to you instead of marrying Theo? Would you still think it was fine that I'd been with another man?"

Danial took a sharp intake of breath and held it. A few moments passed.

"Depends on the man," Danial said finally, letting out the breath. "I trust you. You've never given me reason not to. But you're right in thinking I'd kill a human, vampire or any other being who'd entered your body in any way without my permission, especially against your will. If Devlin had turned you or hurt you in that hotel room, I'd have had him executed, brother or no."

"He did hurt me—" I began stubbornly.

"Sar, be honest with yourself. Devlin seduced you. You're feeling guilt, plain and simple."

"He said he would turn me—"

"Sar, if he turned you, you would never again want him or any other vampire to take your blood," Danial said chidingly in my ear. His arms tightened around me just perceptibly. "At the very least, once you were vampire, your blood would no longer taste of summer. Why would he destroy your mortality after he made such a point to tell you how wonderful you tasted?"

Devlin had drunk from me repeatedly, yet I wasn't any closer to turning that I'd been before. That meant he'd taken very little blood, despite all the bites. I didn't reply.

"Further, if you turned, you would lose your ability to have a child. Do you think he would risk that either? You are the only one who has given birth to a vampire's child in millennia. Stephen said you might be able to heal the damage you sustained birthing Theoron. I shared that with Devlin when Theo told me about it months ago. Dev knows that your being half turned is slowly healing you. Word is spreading about Theoron. All the Rulers already know. Your name is being whispered around the globe. No vampire who valued his own life would risk turning you or hurting you, including Devlin. You are far, far too valuable."

Devlin's words to Al came back to me. He had called me valuable, very valuable....

"And what of the hotel curtains?" Danial said softly. "You had only to rip them back and Devlin would have fled into the bathroom or at least beneath the bed, letting you escape. Did you not think of that?"

I hadn't, even though Devlin had made such a big point of them being a danger when we'd been in that hotel in Pennsylvania together. Guilt hit me like a fist, and I took a shaky breath.

"Sar, let go of your guilt. What's done is done. Devlin didn't leave a mark on you, though he seems to have left one on your heart."

"I—"

"Shh," Danial whispered, hugging me. "He saved your life when no one else could have. That matters most."

"I keep thinking about him," I whispered. "I tell myself not to, but I do—"

Danial shifted, then his lips grazed my neck, kissing lightly. "Why? He is an ocean away, Sar. If you want to fantasize about him, what's to stop you?" He kissed harder, moving upwards.

I stretched up under his caresses, leaning into him and letting my head loll back. "You're not going to tell me I'm weak and immoral?" I murmured.

"I'm just jealous you're not fantasizing of me," Danial whispered heatedly in my ear. "But perhaps you are. I can visualize you and him together, entwined and then joining you, loving you together with him—"

Images came of being with Devlin again, of losing myself in his lovemaking and Danial there watching us not with angry judgment, but with his own love and lust. Danial kissed me as Devlin made love to me, then Danial made love to me as Devlin sang to me. Having them both touch me together, our bodies meshing together in slippery need as we strained toward climax…

"Sar," Danial said hungrily, rubbing his cheek on mine. "You are radiating want and need like a cat in heat. Does the thought of having us both move you that much?"

"Yes," I said lustily, my face heating. "I'm sorry."

"Don't be," Danial said forcefully as he kissed me. After all I'd just imagined, his kiss was like lighting a case of firecrackers all at once. We both exploded with passion.

Chapter Eighteen

I pulled him to me, and he rolled on top of me in one motion, his tongue thrusting into me. I opened my mouth on his, trying to draw him in further. He ripped his shirt from his body with a sound of tearing cloth, and then he was on me, grinding his hard penis against me, his hands slipping beneath my sweater to touch my breasts. I arched my body off the bed, wanting him, the stretchy material of my leggings so thin it was like having nothing between us.

"I want you," Danial said roughly, kissing me on my neck and face. "Let me have you, Sar." There had never been so much need in his voice before, so much wanting. His eyes were wild, a frenzy to his movements.

"Yes," I said, shakily, "Please, Danial, please." If I didn't have him inside me in a few seconds, I was going to die. Nothing mattered to me but getting off my clothes and his. If I could only get him inside me, I could live through the next few moments.

He yanked off his jeans with a grunt as I pulled off my sweater and my bra. In a second, he was stripping off my boots and my leggings and underwear, throwing them aside. Then we were naked together, as we hadn't been for so long. I felt the brush of his fangs as he kissed me and the coolness of his skin against mine. We were half-mad with lust and love, with the desire we'd lived with for months and hadn't been able to satisfy. It poured out of us like a river, and like a river, we drowned in it together. He groaned when he slipped his fingers inside me, my body drenching him quickly in slick eagerness.

It was his penetration of me that shocked me back into myself. What was I doing? This was going to make everything ten times worse!

I gathered every bit of willpower left inside me and pushed him away from me. It was like trying to move a tree. Danial put his body over me and moved his hips, ready to thrust inside me. I took a breath to scream for him to stop and then felt Danial's fangs against my neck, gently pricking me.

All thoughts of stopping him vanished, swallowed in sheer unbridled desire. "Bite me," I said gutturally, pushing up my hips to rub against his. "Take me."

Danial hesitated a second, his body shaking with need above mine. And then he bit down deeply, sliding his erection into me completely. I let out a scream of pleasure and clasped him hard, bucking beneath him, trying to get him further inside. He sucked greedily at my throat, his movements on me frantic. I climaxed in seconds, letting out piercing, gratified screams. Danial suddenly arched his back, driving deep and let out a primal scream of utter release. He pumped his hips repeatedly, then slowed, pushing deeply into me one last time before his body sagged on mine. I lay beneath him, fighting to get my breath. My heart was beating wildly. Guilt flooded me, yet it couldn't dislodge the raw bliss engulfing me.

Danial pushed up from me slightly, smoothing back a lock of my hair. "I'm not sure what to say," he said tenderly. "I'm not sorry for what just happened, but I think you are."

I wriggled out from under him and walked over to the stairs where I sat, still breathing hard. He paused only to wrap the bed sheet around him before he followed me. He took my hand in his gently, sitting beside me. "Was this how it was with him?" he asked. "With Dev?"

"The last few times, yes," I said, wiping at sudden tears. "I knew I shouldn't do it, and yet I did. Hell, it was worse than that. I instigated it."

"I'm sorry you're upset," Danial said, slipping his arm around me. "Please know I only took a few swallows." He paused. "I'm sorry also for not wearing protection—"

"Forget it," I cried, borderline hysterical. I waved my hand. "Devlin didn't wear any either—"

"Shh," Danial said, picking me up and bringing me back to his bed. "Come, I'll help you dress."

"There's no fucking point!" I shouted, struggling. "I might as well just get back in bed with you—"

"No," Danial said coolly, gathering up my clothes with one hand and trying to keep me still. "If we're together I want you to want me, not act in thrall to my will." He handed my clothes to me. "Now get dressed, please. We need to figure this out."

We put our clothes on quickly, then sat back down on the bed. He didn't speak. Finally, I asked, "What just happened to us?"

"I don't know," Danial said, concerned. "I felt like I had to be inside you at all costs."

"I felt the same way," I said. "There was no pain when you bit me, just pleasure."

"Something has changed between us," Danial said with self-loathing. "I constantly desire you, but I always could control my lust before this. Worse, I knew I should resist. That you didn't really want to have sex. Instead, I gave in to my desire."

"The problem is I did want sex, though I knew I shouldn't. I've become a slut."

Danial pulled me close. "Don't say that," he said sternly. "You are no more a slut than I am. Whatever had hold of us was irresistible, and it caught the both of us completely off guard."

"It must be that I'm turning," I said finally. "It explains everything. The lack of pain when you bite and the desire for your fangs. It was when I felt them that all thoughts of stopping you disappeared."

"Maybe, but then why the desire for sex we both had?" Danial asked. "Sure, as Stephen said, enough sex with a male vampire might be able to turn a human female, though I've never heard of that actually happening. Sex has never been part of the turning process. It's accomplished through blood exchange. And if you're turning, why was it so easy for me to stop drinking? Though I desperately wanted to taste you, I didn't feel like that time I marked you, when I didn't want to stop. I stopped easily, and I had no desire to give you any of my blood."

I shrugged. "For my part, I didn't notice that you were turning me back when we were together. I've never before felt I had to have your fangs, or I would die. Letting you drink was just part of lovemaking with you, a shared intimacy. What I felt just now reminds me of that feeling of The Lust, but not exactly the same. I don't want to be hurt at all. And I don't want just anyone." Tears filled my eyes. "Theo and I had a lot of sex last night, Danial, and I didn't feel like this once." I swallowed. "My desire wasn't just wanting sex, it was wanting sex with a vampire. It has to be I'm turning because I'm sure as hell not pregnant again with a dhamphir."

"Come," Danial said, standing and offering me his hand. "We'll go talk to Terian. He can look up the signs of turning and tell us if this fits. I've got to say it makes the most sense to me, too."

"It's day," I said, following him upstairs.

"Terian can teleport here and bring us to his lab," Danial replied, dialing his cell. "He's worked up to two people he can carry with him. Or we can just talk in the great room, if he can tear himself away from his experiments."

A few moments later, Terian was standing before us, disapproval written all over his face. That changed to worry and resignation after Danial explained what had happened to us.

"Is this because of her turning?" Danial asked finally. "If it is, what do we do?"

Terian grimaced. "There's nothing you can do. Despite your love for Theo, Sar, Danial is your sire. It's unlikely you'll be able to stay away from him. He's going to be drawn to you as well. Blood calls to blood, and you've had a lot of his over the years."

I felt immensely better about my wanton behavior, though I chastened myself that it was no excuse. "Advice?"

Terian turned to Danial. "Danial, you have never been around someone who is partly turned, because your power to create vampires is so new. You probably could talk to Devlin about it. He could instruct you—"

"Tell us what you know," I said, cutting him off. Nobody here would be calling Devlin about this, not if I could help it. "We need facts, well-documented ones."

Terian shot me a look, then continued, facing Danial. "Sar is partly turned. The vampire virus in her came from your blood. What's within her isn't enough to turn her, now she's no longer getting your bodily fluids, Danial. Still, it *wants* to, despite its losing the battle. She's reverting to human with every day she goes without an infusion from you. Sar has always had a strong resistance to the virus you carry, and she hasn't been with you for months now—"

I hadn't been with Danial, but I had been with another vampire, one who had drunk my blood and spilled himself inside me many times in that day we'd spent together. Had Devlin somehow been the catalyst of this new problem? A tremor went through me.

"—so the virus is doing the only thing it can. It's telling her body and her mind to seek you out, Danial. To keep the change progressing."

"Why am I affected then?" Danial said angrily. "She's not the only one who lost control."

"Because your body and mind recognize that need in her, that she's close to turning. Your cells are hardwired to respond to that need now. It's part of having the power to make other vampires. The virus in you wants to replicate itself. You're drawn to her like a moth to a flame."

Maybe this was why I'd responded to Devlin as I had and even why he'd forced me to be with him. This sounded much more plausible to me than him secretly being in love with me. Still, he'd had no problem with self-control; he hadn't been in the grip of anything but his own desires. No, he'd just been an asshole who'd taken me on a whim as he had taken everything else he'd ever wanted in his long life...

"So what do we do?" Danial asked.

"You have three choices," Terian said slowly. "One, you can turn her here and now."

"No," I said.

"That isn't even a choice," Danial said wearily. "Next?"

"Two, Sar can leave with Theo. You stay away from her for months until she is completely back to normal and no longer a temptation."

I shut my eyes and shook my head. "No."

"That would be impossible," Danial said with anger. "I can't take Sar away from Theoron. Even with Al dead, Manir is still out there. Also," he added. "We have no idea that Sar wouldn't respond the same way to any vampire who was around. Just because Devlin took only what he needed from her doesn't mean she didn't want him to take more—"

"You let that bastard drink your blood!" Terian yelled at me incredulously.

"He needed it, Terian," Danial said quickly. "He'd taken serious damage saving her. Anyway, Sar may react to other male non-vampires. Remember that time she went after you."

"Sar, that you let him do that to you..." Terian trailed off as he closed his eyes and rubbed them. "I can see how affected you are," he finished dejectedly. "Though there's nothing I've ever read indicating that a turning female of any species would seek out strange men to have sex with—"

We didn't need to reopen that embarrassing subject. "Choice three, Tears," I said flatly.

Terian turned to me. "Three, you agree to let Danial take care of your needs. If he sates you like he did in your pregnancy, you'll be okay, even around other vampires. Eventually, you'll revert and stop craving the touch and bite of a vampire."

"That's your solution?" I yelled. "In what world do you think Theo's going to go for that?"

"He may not," Terian shot back. "But that's your only other option I know of."

"Thank you, Terian," Danial said coolly. "Leave us."

Terian gave me a reserved look, then disappeared.

Danial and I were silent for a long time, lost in our own thoughts. The longer the silence stretched, the guiltier I felt. Finally, I couldn't stand the silence anymore. "Can I ask you something?"

"Of course," Danial said, shaking himself slightly. "What is it?"

"I have a moral question for you. Say you're in a position where you have to kill a few innocent people to protect a lot more innocents. If you don't, the group of innocents will all be attacked and likely at least half killed. What do you do?"

Danial gave me a calculating look. "This is a moral riddle. Theo told me you asked him something similar. Before I answer, I need particulars."

"Such as?"

"Where is my family? Do I have children, parents, a wife, siblings? Are they safe somewhere else or among the innocents?"

I thought for a moment. "You have a woman among the group of innocents, but not among the ones you'd have to kill. Any other family you have is safe somewhere else."

"Does the group give me total power over it as leader?"

I shook my head. "As a possible war leader only, but they aren't sacrificial lambs who'll die for you mindlessly. The ones you'd have to kill will fight to live, and you'd have to kill at least a few personally."

Danial studied me. "What do I get out of this? Personally?" he asked.

"Nothing except saving the people," I replied. "You might say they'd make you king out of gratitude if you want to."

"Will I have to fight personally if I don't sacrifice the innocents? In either way, will my woman see battle herself?"

If we hadn't come so far, I would've been tempted to tell Danial to forget it. "You will unless you kill the innocents. Your woman would be in the larger battle, but not involved in sacrificing the innocents unless she wanted to be. So, will you kill them?"

"I can see you're wondering why I ask so many questions," Danial replied. "But remember, Sar, I've seen real battles. The blood is real, not stage makeup. The cruelty of men is a fearsome thing when its only rein is the zeal of their beliefs."

"What would you do?"

"Why do you ask, Sar?" Danial countered softly. "Why now of all times? What does this have to do with you and me and our feelings for each other?"

"I want to know if you'll kill a few to protect many."

"No," he said simply. "Maybe in years past, but not now."

"Then what would you do?"

He took my hand. "I would go to the woman I loved and ask her if she wanted me enough to leave with me. Power is fleeting. No matter how good it feels to have a kingdom, they are easily lost."

"You would abandon your people?"

"People always die in battle, Sar. That's cold, but it's the truth. If I am not the king, it's not my fight or my responsibility to protect them. And even then, there are conditions, such as did my fellow people bring this attack on themselves with some evil of their own. Say an unprovoked attack?"

"For arguments sake, your people didn't provoke the attack. Given that, what if your woman had asked you to stay and fight and then to rule with her?"

"Then I would have stayed and done so to the best of my ability," he said simply. "It's a burden to rule, but at least you have a say in how things are done and the authority to stop atrocities from happening. Having power means you can protect the ones you love from those that would hurt them. I understand that a lot more now that I am a Vampire Ruler." He kissed my hand tenderly. "Now why did you want to know this answer?"

I didn't reply.

"A better question is what are you going to do, given your choices?" Danial continued. "Are you going to leave with Theo or become my lover again?"

"Become your lover again," I whispered.

My words were soft, but Danial reacted as if I'd slapped him. "Come again?"

"I'm not leaving so some other vampire can stumble onto me in one of my moods and drain me dry of my summer-tasting blood," I said angrily. "The question is, can you hold on to enough of your self-control to make sure you don't give me any more of the virus while you're sating me?"

"It'll be difficult, but I'll do my best," Danial said, coming to sit next to me. He slipped his arm around me.

"I thought you'd take the idea well," I said with a ghost of a smile. "Do you have any ideas of how to break it to Theo?"

"First, are you certain this is what you want? Your quickly made decision to return to my bed may prompt a divorce, or at the least, a separation."

"I know I'm impulsive sometimes," I replied, irritated. "So is Theo. But you aren't, Danial. All of your decisions are thought out beforehand and then planned thoroughly. If there's a way to take me through this safely and sanely, you'll find it."

Danial hugged me. "Your confidence in me is very flattering, Sar, but it's also terrifying. I don't know what's happening to you. But I will do what I can to help you get through it—"

"Sure you will," Theo growled from the doorway. His eyes were yellow. "After all, she's the way she is because of you—"

"Don't fucking fight again!" I shouted, rounding on him. "He didn't do this on purpose."

"Theo, I do have to apologize—" Danial began.

"And what might you need to apologize for?" Theo snarled, rage building fast. "Fucking my wife?"

"Yes, we fucked," Danial said curtly, his eyes bleeding to red. "Now deal with it, because it wasn't a fling or a good time. It was scary for the both of us."

Theo blinked his eyes, his rage ebbing to confusion and skepticism. "How was it scary exactly?"

"I told you about The Lust," I said to him, wishing hard for my flush to recede. "I felt the same today as I did then. Danial felt something similar. Terian says it's because I'm close to turning. That Danial's being drawn to me to make me vampire—"

"Then how does getting naked with him again lead you back to human?" Theo said sarcastically. "Did I miss something?"

"This is not her fault," Danial interjected. "Stop acting jealous, and let her explain."

I explained to Theo what Terian had suggested in terms of options. "He said in enough time I'll go back to human, and this will stop," I finished.

"When will that be?" Theo asked pointedly.

"He's not sure," Danial supplied. "Camlyn tested her blood. Sar's blood is still at the virus levels it was last May."

"So you're saying months," Theo said, his resentment and anger again building. "Maybe even years. But you don't want me to consider taking her out of state to protect her—"

"There's no place you can go in my territory that's vampire free. Even the states out West have a steady population. It's her life at risk if she leaves with you—"

"It is her life, and she's my wife!" Theo shouted. "I don't need you telling me how to protect her from vampires or anyone else!"

"I'm not leaving," I said to Theo flatly. "It is my life, so it's my decision. I'm going to try Terian's suggestion with Danial."

Theo gave me a furious look, then stormed out, slamming the front door hard.

"I'm sorry that went so badly," Danial said, taking me in his arms again.

I pushed him away gently. "So am I. But there isn't another choice I'm comfortable with."

Danial kissed my cheek gently. "Me either. So how do you want to work this?"

"I don't know how much we can plan," I said, grimacing. "I was fine with you for three weeks after being with Devlin, but he and I were intimate many times. I'd guess we've probably got a week of normalness until I flip out again and bring you with me."

"Nice description," Danial said, rolling his eyes. "But we'll try that span to start with. As you get more and more human, we likely can increase the span of time between being intimate. I'm not sure how you want to work that part either. I propose you just stay over once a week on the weekend. We'll need to keep it from Elle, of course."

"Yes," I said, nodding once. "That sounds fine. Saturdays would be best." That would give us a week to prepare and me a week to try to convince Theo this was the best option.

"For me also," Danial said, then kissed my cheek. "Then I'll see you next Saturday. Bring a change of clothes and whatever else you'll need for the night. I'll arrange the rest."

I nodded and gave him a quick kiss on the cheek. "Thanks. I feel odd to be thanking you, but it's right to. What you're going to have to do with me isn't going to be the lovefest Theo's envisioning."

"I'll manage to sneak some in somewhere. Don't worry," Danial said seductively. "Now go after him and try to talk some sense into his thick head. You and he are done with work here until Monday."

I nodded and went to go, but he grabbed my arm. "Sar."

I turned back to him. "What?"

"If he won't come around, I'd like you to come back here to live," Danial said, biting one lip with the edge of his fang. "We got through The Lust together. We can get through this, too."

"I hope it won't come to that," I said slowly, looking into his eyes. "But if it does, I'm going to."

Danial's lips parted in relief, though his fangs grazed his lip, keeping his face serious. "I can live with that." He leaned down and kissed me lightly on the lips. "I'm going back to bed downstairs. You're welcome to use my bedroom shower if you want to. The workmen are long gone. Leave your clothes outside the door. Mary can wash them tomorrow."

Maybe that was best. Smelling sex on me wouldn't make Theo more receptive to my plan. "Thanks," I said, heading into the bedroom as Danial went to the basement.

The shower improved my mood. Oddly, I didn't look like any more of a harlot than usual in the bathroom mirror, even after putting on Monica's purple satin robe to venture outside the bedroom door to leave my clothes for Mary. There was a change of clothes waiting on Danial's bed. Everything was new. Relieved, I put on the clothes, threw out Monica's robe, left a note of thanks for Danial and then went looking for Theo.

He was not at the werefox compound or the firing ranges. No one had seen him since he'd returned with Hans and Warren from getting armor two hours earlier. Deciding he was working things out for himself in the forest, I went back to Danial's house to wait for him. Since I had no idea how long he'd be, I got some ice cream I'd made a few days before and went in to spend some time with Theoron.

He was awake when I came to his crib, reaching for me eagerly with a smile. "You look about two," I said, picking him up. "Must be all the good things you eat. Want some ice cream?"

I slowly fed it to him. He loved it, licking the spoon, trying to bite it with his fangs occasionally. He didn't understand yet that he didn't need to grow his fangs to eat this kind of food. When he was done, I put the empty dish and spoon aside and began to sing to him.

"Love is touch. Touch is Love.
Love is living, living love.
Love is needing to be loved.
Love is you, you and me
Love is wanting to be free
Love is knowing we will be."

I kissed him gently. "You like that? You're not going to tell me I need voice lessons, I hope."

Theoron watched me, rapt.

"We could put on one of Elle's new DVDs," I offered. "You like the one about the black horse. Or we could watch the one about the last unicorn. That has songs you like, too." I had told Theo no more *Saw* movies until Elle at least looked thirteen. She and I had sung often together, sometimes off key, all through her growing up. She liked to sing as much as I did. Maybe she would want voice lessons herself soon...

Drop that thought, Sar. "Want me to sing the Love song again, Theoron?"

Theoron looked at me and concentrated. "Luv?" he said softly.

He'd finally spoken! I stared at him in shock, afraid to move.

"Luv?" he said again, studying me.

"Love," I said, smiling encouragement. "Love."

"Luv!" he said loudly.

I kissed him excitedly. "Ah! You spoke! Ah!"

He laughed delightedly.

Maybe I could get him to say other words. "Mom," I said, then repeated it twice.

He looked at me. "Mum?" he said questioningly.

I shrieked in joy and triumph. He shrieked back at me, laughing again.

Danial came in, my dirty clothes in one hand. "What's wrong? Why are you—?"

Theoron looked at Danial. "Mum?" he said questioningly.

My clothes fell out of Danial's hands to the floor as he stared at us.

"Dad," I said to Theoron, holding him so he could see Danial. "Dad." Theoron looked at Danial, then at me. Danial came closer, and Theoron reached for him. "Dad," I said again. "Daddy."

"Day," Theoron said.

"Yes," said Danial with a sigh of happiness. He brought Theoron into his arms.

"Daddy," I said one more time.

Theoron looked at me, then back at Danial. "Day-dy," he said finally.

"Ah!" Danial cried, then a wide smile split his face, and he hugged Theoron tightly. Danial looked up at me. In his eyes was the most intense love I'd ever seen. It said without words that Theoron was his greatest joy, and I, the giver of his happiness, was his greatest love. He shifted Theoron to one arm and opened the other to me.

I went to him, put my arms around Theoron and him and then kissed them both. Danial trembled slightly as he held the two of us.

"Day-dy!" Theoron said, laughing and wriggling. "Day-dy! Mum! Luv! Day-dy!"

I laughed gleefully despite my eyes were wet. So did Danial, still hugging us fiercely.

EPILOGUE

It was more than an hour later when I emerged from Danial's house. Theo was waiting for me in the truck, the engine off. I went to the passenger side and climbed in.

"I was beginning to think you'd never come out," Theo said darkly. "I was going to wait another hour and then leave."

"Theoron said his first words," I said coolly. "You should have come in instead and seen him."

"I'd just have been in the way, wouldn't I?" Theo said bitterly. "I'm in the way now of you two. Just tell me go, and I'll go, Sar. You can have your vampire back. Hell, you can turn if you want. But I need to know right now where I stand with you."

"Did you see Terian?"

"Of course, I went there first. He told me just what you did. It's like a knife in the side."

"I have to try this," I said, taking his hand carefully. "You weren't here to see The Lust. Things with me might get bad. I need to know you can handle it. Because if you can't, as much as I do love you, it might be easier if you left."

"I'm not leaving," Theo growled low, squeezing my hand. "I'm not leaving you or Elle behind. Much as I hate it, Danial's right. There's no place I know of without at least a couple vampires living nearby. And I'm not a match for a sorcerer. We determined that years ago."

His old bitterness over Terian saving me when he hadn't been able to alone. "This isn't your fault. I told you I'm not leaving anyway. Now can you handle me going to Danial every week for all of Saturday night?"

"What exactly is going to happen?" Theo said, looking over with yellow eyes. "Tell me."

"Danial's going to have sex with me, protected sex," I said quietly, flushing. "He's not going to bite me or exchange blood. I'll likely do everything I can to provoke him into biting me and be a bitch in general when I don't get my way. He'll do this every time. Over time, I'll grow less and less wild as the urge to turn lessens. Then we'll stop getting together Saturday nights."

"How is this going to help you if he's not giving you what you want?"

"It's going to hopefully stop me from looking for other vampire company to finish my turning," I said angrily. "Even so, I'm going to have to be escorted by you everywhere when I'm not here. Really, I'm guessing until this passes, I shouldn't go out anywhere even with you as escort, except maybe in the daytime. It's going to suck."

"Actually, it isn't," Theo said with a sardonic smile.

Play this very careful. "Remember, too, I've given blood to Devlin recently, and he healed my wounds, both from the assassin's bullet months ago and from Al's whip man a month ago. That likely affected my blood. But there won't be any more of that, so the reversion may happen quickly."

"You aren't happy about this," Theo murmured. "You're scared."

"Of course I'm scared," I said exasperated. "I hate not being in control. I'm not looking forward to being with Danial. I'm not going to be me with him." I wiped away a tear. "I almost lost my mind when this happened before, Theo. That was for only three months. This might be longer."

Theo drew me into his arms. "I'm sorry I got angry. A lot of my anger is that I want to help you, and I can't. This isn't something I know how to fix. But Danial can, of course. That you're going to have sex again just makes it that much harder to take."

"I understand that," I sighed. "You have a right to be angry, just not at me or him."

Theo didn't reply for a few minutes. "I sent Ivan to our house to watch over it when it began to get dark. He said he'd walk the dogs and get the cats in for the night. Do you still want to go out?"

"Do you?"

"Yes," he said. "I want to be with you out where people can see us together. Put your seatbelt on."

Theo drove us to our favorite local restaurant. Today being Friday, a musician was singing sixties and seventies songs as he strummed his guitar. A lavish seafood buffet was spread across two long tables. The place was busy, many couples and families having a late dinner.

Theo had his usual four helpings, but I was strangely not very hungry. Even so, we stayed longer than usual, listening to the music and holding hands. I couldn't shake the thought that this was going to be one of our last times together, and I didn't want the night to end.

"Your hands, they are so cold, Sar," Theo said, worried. His were warm, like an oven as they rubbed mine. Then he began rubbing my wedding band and the diamond ring he'd given me with his fingers. His wedding band shone in the low light from the candle on our table.

Part of me wanted to say I was sorry again, but I was too worn out and exhausted. The wine I'd drunk had relaxed me, but it had made me sad again in the process. The musician was singing one of our favorite songs, "Fire and Rain." It was almost over.

Been walking my mind to an easy time, my back turned toward the sun
Lord knows when the cold wind blows it will turn your head around
There's hours of time on the telephone line, to talk about things to come,
Sweet dreams and flying machines in pieces on the ground.

I began crying again softly. Theo said nothing, just squeezed my hands in his and handed me a tissue from his pocket. I wiped my eyes.

"Let's go," he said when the song ended.

We said good-bye to everyone as we left. "Thanks for the great food and music!"

"Come back soon," said the manager, beaming at us.

I hesitated in replying, looking at Theo and then he said, "We will."

The musician began singing his next song, "Desperado," as we walked out into the night. I shivered, the words seeming somehow portentous of something bad to come.

"Sar, get in the truck," Theo said, unlocking the door. "I'll put on the heater for you."

Theo helped me in, his hands so warm against me that I didn't want to let him go to drive.

"You're so cold, Sar," he repeated, worriedly. He pushed back his seat, got out a polar fleece blanket and tucked it around me. He reached over and held my hand. "Better?"

I brought it to my face, trapping it between my neck and my shoulder and held it there with my hands. "Yes. Thanks."

As we drove home, Theo touched me gently with that hand, the touch of his fingers comforting and caressing me. Somehow during the journey, I fell asleep.

* * * *

Later, we sat before the fire and watched the flames dance.

"Sar," Theo said suddenly. "I know you want me to sign off on Danial, despite you're planning on doing it anyway. But I can't tell you my answer until I've thought it over."

There was pain in his voice, and I felt like shit knowing I'd put it there. "I understand. And I understand if you can't say it's okay, too."

Theo hugged me tighter. "Give me a week. I'll tell you at the end of this week."

"Okay," I replied, squeezing his hand. "Okay."

* * * *

The bees were buzzing wildly on the wild asters the next morning. Even with the unusual warm temperatures, I couldn't manage their level of enthusiasm. But I couldn't lie awake next to Theo, wondering what he might be deciding in his dreams. There was a job to be done, and I had to do it alone.

The problem was that the cut branches from trimming my shrubbery and dead branches that had come down in the last storm wouldn't light. I had spent the morning gathering them up. The wood was damp, the little flames I created with paper fizzling out each time.

I tried again. The flickering orange with an edge of red and yellow danced along a curling blackening scrap, flaring up and threatening to engulf the wood. Yet again, the flame winked out, leaving only a little smoke wafting up from the wood.

"Son of a bitch," I swore, then threw down the matches and went into the barn to get some gasoline. Returning, I carefully poured a few cups of gasoline on the wood. If there had been a fire, there would have been substantial danger. Instead, there was a sizzling sound and then dripping of the gas. Gasoline fumes clogged my nose, and I moved away, holding my breath.

Setting down the gas can a minimum safe distance of ten feet, I grabbed the book of matches and stepped upwind of the fire. What I was doing was dangerous. There was more danger in every minute that passed with no fire. Yet worse would be no fire to destroy what lay in the simple box at my feet.

I carefully lit the match and tossed it on the pile. My nervousness made my aim off. The match hit rain-wet ashes instead of gasoline-wet wood. I took a breath and waited a few seconds, just in case it was going to catch suddenly, but nothing happened.

"Son of a bitch." Time for try number two. I struck a match and tossed it in. With a loud "WHOOMP!" the gas ignited, and the pile of wood became a burning pyre. A wall of heat struck me and I moved back.

Now we were getting somewhere. I cast a glance at the house, praying Theo was still asleep. Then I dug out the book from the box. *Erotic Poetry* was the title. That was what was inside, cover to cover.

Yesterday, after showering, I'd taken off the boots and returned them to the box. When I'd put them back in the box, I'd discovered that the boots were not the only gift Dev had sent me. Nestled in a corner had been this book, a velvet box and inside that box a letter addressed to me in flowing script.

I sighed and looked at the book in my hands again. I had read through it this morning, noting that Dev had marked the page that had the poem I'd quoted to him, *Nothing is more beautiful than your eyes (except my love for your eyes,)* with the book ribbon. He hadn't inscribed it at all. What stimulated me most was that it smelled like he had when we'd been in bed. Just how he'd accomplished that, I wasn't sure. In any case, it was too dangerous to stay in my keeping.

I tossed the book in and watched it burn, the cover smoking and then catching, the pages curling. Then I took out Dev's last gift. It lay in my palm, the gold shining in the sun.

It was a choker, almost identical to the one I wore now. But the one in my hand had a bear's form dangling from it, a grizzly stalking something, its head turned and its teeth bared. The emeralds that were its eyes winked at me in the sunlight. Devlin's symbol.

I should toss it in, melt it down in the fire. Yet it was so beautiful I couldn't make myself do it. More evocative, he had put emeralds in the eyes to be symbolic of my eyes. I'd seen his crest once or twice through the years, enough to know that his bear usually had red eyes, not green.

Taking out Devlin's note, I read it again.

Sar,
Come live with me and be my love
And we will all the pleasures prove
Of peace and plenty, bed and board
That chance employment may afford.

This part of the poem, called only "Song," had been written by a man named C. Day Lewis. I had googled the first line on the Internet. Yet the rest written here was not in any poetry book, according to the Internet. Devlin had written it himself. For me.

Your silken kiss, your whispered sigh
Is what I long for as I lie
In bed alone these miles away
Alas, I wish you would come to stay.
Sar, come into my arms again
Say you'll love me even when
I tell you that the words I said
That fateful day we lay in bed.
Were not pretend, were not a lie.
They were instead a truthful cry
From my heart to yours so you would know
That I have loved you ever so.

Beneath was written:

Should you decide to come to me, call me at the number at the bottom of this note. I'll arrange a flight for you. Wear this for me, and I will welcome you with open arms.
Love,

Dev

I held his note in my hand, tears blurring my eyes. Part of me longed to go to him and was dying to hear him sing to me again and feel his caress. It was that part that made me put the choker and note back in my pocket and trudge slowly back to the house, the dogs following me.

Theo was still sleeping when I returned. Relieved, I sealed the choker and the note in a manila envelope and put it in my safe, writing "Brennan" on it in large bold letters. Locked in there and labeled with my first husband's name, Theo would not bother with it. Better still, I wouldn't be tempted to look at it, put it on, call Dev, or to read the poem for the seventeenth time.

I started some bacon and sausage for Theo as the phone rang. Without looking, I knew it was Danial.

"Good morning," I said warmly. "Did Theoron say anything else?"

"He did not, but we can get to that later. I want to know if Theo accepted your plan."

I sighed. "He said he wanted a week to think it over before he gave me his answer."

Danial was silent, almost surely frustrated.

"It's fair," I said, prompted by loyalty to defend Theo's decision. "I'd want that if I were him. And it won't impact what you and I discussed anyway. It'll be a week from today."

"Very well. Call me the moment he tells you his decision," Danial said commandingly. "I will be traveling this entire week, first with Terian and then with Brian. But I want to know immediately, Sar. Day, night, whatever I'm doing, wherever I am, call me on my cell. If he says no, I want you to agree—"

"I will," I said reassuringly. "Now go catch up on work. I'm sure you didn't get any sleep last night."

"Between worrying about you and being excited over Theoron's first words, it was possibly about an hour," Danial conceded. "You rest yourself, please. I love you."

"And I, you," I said. "Hug him for me. Bye."

As I was finishing preparing breakfast, Theo walked into the kitchen and came over to stand behind me. "Are you feeling okay?"

"I'm okay. Go sit," I said. "I'll bring it into you."

"I'll stay," he said, kissing my cheek. "Besides, I want to know if you still want to go do the pumpkin thing tonight."

Shit, I'd forgotten. "Can you be around Danial?"

"Yes, of course," Theo said confidently. "This isn't his fault. He didn't seduce you." He hugged me gently. "I want to go," he continued. "I want us to go together."

"Good," I said, kissing him tenderly, "because I want to go with you."

He was a good man, and I loved him. So why wasn't this easier?

Maybe it wasn't supposed to be easy.

"Do you want to go?" he asked.

"Very much. I can't wait to see Theoron's face when he sees his first pumpkin. Elle is really looking forward to it, too."

"So am I," Theo said. "We're going to have a good time."

Sudden worry settled on me. What would happen in a week when Theo had to make his decision? Would Danial be able to keep his control if I lost mine? Would The Lust go away, ever, now that it had returned? And what of Devlin? Would he be content to remain where he was, loving from afar? Or would he return to try and claim me again?

"I love you," Theo whispered.

Moved, I pushed my disturbing thoughts away. I could think about all of this later. For now, it was enough that I had this moment to share with Theo, that he loved me and that despite everything that had happened to us, we were still together.

The End

Coming soon

Immortal Confessions, Book 5 of the Promise Me Series